Poseidon's Spear

Poseidon's Spear

CHRISTIAN CAMERON

First published in Great Britain in 2012 by Orion Books,
an imprint of The Orion Publishing Group Ltd
Orion House, 5 Upper Saint Martin's Lane
London WC2H 9EA

An Hachette UK Company

1 3 5 7 9 10 8 6 4 2

A CIP catalogue record for this book
is available from the British Library.

ISBN (Hardback) 978 1 4091 1411 6
ISBN (Export Trade Paperback) 978 1 4091 1412 3
ISBN (Ebook) 978 1 4091 1413 0

Typeset by Deltatype Ltd, Birkenhead, Merseyside

Printed in Great Britain by CPI Group (UK) Ltd,
Croydon CR0 4YY

The Orion Publishing Group's policy is to use papers
that are natural, renewable and recyclable products and
made from wood grown in sustainable forests. The logging
and manufacturing processes are expected to conform to
the environmental regulations of the country of origin.

www.orionbooks.co.uk

For Sarah

Some say an army of horsemen, or infantry,
A fleet of ships is the fairest thing
On the face of the black earth, but I say
It's what one loves.

Sappho

Glossary

I am an *amateur* Greek scholar. My definitions are my own, but taken from the LSJ or Routeledge's *Handbook of Greek Mythology* or Smith's *Classical Dictionary*. On some military issues I have the temerity to disagree with the received wisdom on the subject. Also check my website at www.hippeis.com for more information and some helpful pictures.

Akinakes A Scythian short sword or long knife, also sometimes carried by Medes and Persians.

Andron The 'men's room' of a proper Greek house – where men have symposia. Recent research has cast real doubt as to the sexual exclusivity of the room, but the name sticks.

Apobatai The Chariot Warriors. In many towns, towns that hadn't used chariots in warfare for centuries, the *Apobatai* were the elite three hundred or so. In Athens, they competed in special events; in Thebes, they may have been the forerunners of the Sacred Band.

Archon A city's senior official or, in some cases, one of three or four. A magnate.

Aspis The Greek hoplite's shield (which is not called a hoplon!).

The *aspis* is about a yard in diameter, is deeply dished (up to six inches deep) and should weigh between eight and sixteen pounds.

Basileus An aristocratic title from a bygone era (at least in 500 BC) that means 'king' or 'lord'.

Bireme A warship rowed by two tiers of oars, as opposed to a *trireme*, which has three tiers.

Chiton The standard tunic for most men, made by taking a single continuous piece of cloth and folding it in half, pinning the shoulders and open side. Can be made quite fitted by means of pleating. Often made of very fine quality material – usually wool, sometimes linen, especially in the upper classes. A full *chiton* was ankle length for men and women.

Chitoniskos A small *chiton*, usually just longer than modesty demanded – or not as long as modern modesty would demand! Worn by warriors and farmers, often heavily bloused and very full by warriors to pad their armour. Usually wool.

Chlamys A short cloak made from a rectangle of cloth roughly 60 by 90 inches – could also be worn as a *chiton* if folded and pinned a different way. Or slept under as a blanket.

Corslet/Thorax In 500 BC, the best *corslets* were made of bronze, mostly of the so-called 'bell' *thorax* variety. A few muscle *corslets* appear at the end of this period, gaining popularity into the 450s. Another style is the 'white' *corslet*, seen to appear just as the Persian Wars begin – reenactors call this the 'Tube and Yoke' *corslet*, and some people call it (erroneously) the *linothorax*. Some of them may have been made of linen – we'll never know – but the likelier material is Athenian leather, which was often tanned and finished with alum, thus being bright white. Yet another style was a tube and yoke of scale, which you can see the author wearing on his website. A scale *corslet* would have been the most expensive of all, and probably provided the best protection.

Daidala Cithaeron, the mountain that towered over Plataea, was the site of a remarkable fire-festival, the *Daidala*, which was celebrated by the Plataeans on the summit of the mountain. In the usual ceremony, as mounted by the Plataeans in every seventh year, a wooden idol (*daidalon*) would be dressed in bridal robes and dragged on an ox-cart from Plataea to the top of the mountain, where it would be burned after appropriate rituals. Or, in the *Great Daidala*, which were celebrated every forty-nine years, fourteen *daidala* from different Boeotian towns would be burned on a large wooden pyre heaped with brushwood, together with a cow and a bull that were sacrificed to Zeus and Hera. This huge pyre on the mountain top must have provided a most impressive spectacle; Pausanias remarks that he knew of no other flame that rose as high or could be seen from so far.

The cultic legend that was offered to account for the festival ran as follows. When Hera had once quarrelled with Zeus, as she often did, she had withdrawn to her childhood home of Euboea and had refused every attempt at reconciliation. So Zeus sought the advice of the wisest man on earth, Cithaeron (the eponym of the mountain), who ruled at Plataea in the earliest times. Cithaeron advised him to make a wooden image of a woman, to veil it in the manner of a bride, and then to have it drawn along in an ox-cart after spreading the rumour that he was planning to marry the nymph Plataea, a daughter of the river god Asopus. When Hera rushed to the scene and tore away the veils, she was so relieved to find a wooden effigy rather than the expected bride that she at last consented to be reconciled with Zeus. (Routledge *Handbook of Greek Mythology*, pp. 137–8)

Daimon Literally a spirit, the *daimon* of combat might be adrenaline, and the *daimon* of philosophy might simply be native intelligence. Suffice it to say that very intelligent men – like Socrates – believed that god-sent spirits could infuse a man and influence his actions.

Daktyloi Literally digits or fingers, in common talk 'inches' in the system of measurement. Systems differed from city to city. I have taken the liberty of using just the Athenian units.

Despoina Lady. A term of formal address.

Diekplous A complex naval tactic about which some debate remains. In this book, the *Diekplous*, or through stroke, is commenced with an attack by the ramming ship's bow (picture the two ships approaching bow to bow or head on) and cathead on the enemy oars. Oars were the most vulnerable part of a fighting ship, something very difficult to imagine unless you've rowed in a big boat and

understand how lethal your own oars can be – to you! After the attacker crushes the enemy's oars, he passes, flank to flank, and then turns when astern, coming up easily (the defender is almost dead in the water) and ramming the enemy under the stern or counter as desired.

Doru A spear, about ten feet long, with a bronze butt-spike.

Eleutheria Freedom.

Ephebe A young, free man of property. A young man in training to be a *hoplite*. Usually performing service to his city and, in ancient terms, at one of the two peaks of male beauty.

Eromenos The 'beloved' in a same-sex pair in ancient Greece. Usually younger, about seventeen. This is a complex, almost dangerous subject in the modern world – were these pair-bonds about sex, or chivalric love, or just a 'brotherhood' of warriors? I suspect there were elements of all three. And to write about this period without discussing the *eromenos/erastes* bond would, I fear, be like putting all the warriors in steel armour instead of bronze ...

Erastes The 'lover' in a same-sex pair bond – the older man, a tried warrior, twenty-five to thirty years old.

Eudaimonia Literally 'well-spirited'. A feeling of extreme joy.

Exhedra The porch of the women's quarters – in some

cases, any porch over a farm's central courtyard.

Helots The 'race of slaves' of Ancient Sparta – the conquered peoples who lived with the Spartiates and did all of their work so that they could concentrate entirely on making war and more Spartans.

Hetaira Literally a 'female companion'. In ancient Athens, a *hetaira* was a courtesan, a highly skilled woman who provided sexual companionship as well as fashion, political advice and music.

Himation A very large piece of rich, often embroidered wool, worn as an outer garment by wealthy citizen women or as a sole garment by older men, especially those in authority.

Hoplite A Greek upper-class warrior. Possession of a heavy spear, a helmet and an *aspis* (see above) and income above the marginal lowest free class were all required to serve as a *hoplite*. Although much is made of the 'citizen soldier' of ancient Greece, it would be fairer to compare *hoplites* to medieval knights than to Roman legionnaires or modern National Guardsmen. Poorer citizens did serve, and sometimes as *hoplites* or marines, but in general, the front ranks were the preserve of upper-class men who could afford the best training and the essential armour.

Hoplitodromos The *hoplite* race, or race in armour. Two *stades* with an *aspis* on your shoulder, a helmet and greaves in the early runs. I've run this race in armour. It is no picnic.

Hoplomachia A *hoplite* contest, or sparring match. Again, there is enormous debate as to when *hoplomachia* came into existence and how much training Greek *hoplites* received. One thing that they didn't do is drill like modern soldiers – there's no mention of it in all of Greek literature. However, they had highly evolved martial arts (see *pankration*) and it is almost certain that *hoplomachia* was a term that referred to 'the martial art of fighting when fully equipped as a *hoplite*'.

Hoplomachos A participant in *hoplomachia*.

Hypaspist Literally 'under the shield'. A squire or military servant – by the time of Arimnestos, the *hypaspist* was usually a younger man of the same class as the *hoplite*.

Kithara A stringed instrument of some complexity, with a hollow body as a soundboard.

Kline A couch.

Kopis The heavy, back-curved sabre of the Greeks. Like a longer, heavier modern kukri or Gurkha knife.

Kore A maiden or daughter.

Kylix A wide, shallow, handled bowl for drinking wine.

Logos Literally 'word'. In pre-Socratic Greek philosophy the word is everything – the power beyond the gods.

Longche A six to seven foot throwing spear, also used for hunting. A *hoplite* might carry a pair of *longchai*, or a single, longer and heavier *doru*.

Machaira A heavy sword or long knife.

Maenads The 'raving ones' – ecstatic female followers of Dionysus.

Mastos A woman's breast. A *mastos* cup is shaped like a woman's breast with a rattle in the nipple – so when you drink, you lick the nipple and the rattle shows that you emptied the cup. I'll leave the rest to imagination . . .

Medimnos A grain measure. Very roughly – 35 to 100 pounds of grain.

Megaron A style of building with a roofed porch.

Navarch An admiral.

Oikia The household – all the family and all the slaves, and sometimes the animals and the farmland itself.

Opson Whatever spread, dip or accompaniment an ancient Greek had with bread.

Pais A child.

Palaestra The exercise sands of the gymnasium.

Pankration The military martial art of the ancient Greeks – an unarmed combat system that bears more than a passing resemblance to modern MMA techniques, with a series of carefully structured blows and domination holds that is, by modern standards, very advanced. Also the basis of the Greek sword and spear-based martial arts. Kicking, punching, wrestling, grappling, on the ground and standing, were all permitted.

Peplos A short over-fold of cloth that women could wear as a hood or to cover the breasts.

Phalanx The full military potential of a town; the actual, formed body of men before a battle (all of the smaller groups formed together made a *phalanx*). In this period, it would be a mistake to imagine a carefully drilled military machine.

Phylarch A file-leader – an officer commanding the four to sixteen men standing behind him in the *phalanx*.

Polemarch The war leader.

Polis The city. The basis of all Greek political thought and expression, the government that was held to be more important – a higher god – than any individual or even family. To this day, when we talk about politics, we're talking about the 'things of our city'.

Porne A prostitute.

Porpax The bronze or leather band that encloses the forearm on a Greek *aspis*.

Psiloi Light infantrymen – usually slaves or adolescent freemen who, in this period, were not organised and seldom had any weapon beyond some rocks to throw.

Pyrrhiche The 'War Dance'. A line dance in armour done by all of the warriors, often very complex. There's reason to believe that the *Pyrrhiche* was the method by which the young were trained in basic martial arts and by which 'drill' was inculcated.

Pyxis A box, often circular, turned from wood or made of metal.

Rhapsode A master-poet, often a performer who told epic works like the *Iliad* from memory.

Satrap A Persian ruler of a province of the Persian Empire.

Skeuophoros Literally a 'shield carrier', unlike the *hypaspist*, this is a slave or freed man who does camp work and carries the armour and baggage.

Sparabara The large wicker shield of the Persian and Mede elite infantry. Also the name of those soldiers.

Spolas Another name for a leather *corslet*, often used for the lion skin of Heracles.

Stade A measure of distance. An Athenian *stade* is about 185 metres.

Strategos In Athens, the commander of one of the ten military tribes. Elsewhere, any senior Greek officer – sometimes the commanding general.

Synaspismos The closest order that *hoplites* could form – so close that the shields overlap, hence 'shield on shield'.

Taxis Any group but, in military terms, a company; I use it for 60 to 300 men.

Thetes The lowest free class – citizens with limited rights.

Thorax See *corslet*.

Thugater Daughter. Look at the word carefully and you'll see the 'daughter' in it ...

Triakonter A small rowed galley of thirty oars.

Trierarch The captain of a ship – sometimes just the owner or builder, sometimes the fighting captain.

Zone A belt, often just rope or finely wrought cord, but could be a heavy bronze kidney belt for war.

General Note on Names and Personages

This series is set in the very dawn of the so-called Classical Era, often measured from the Battle of Marathon (490 BC). Some, if not most, of the famous names of this era are characters in this series – and that's not happenstance. Athens of this period is as magical, in many ways, as Tolkien's Gondor, and even the quickest list of artists, poets, and soldiers of this era reads like a 'who's who' of western civilization. Nor is the author tossing them together by happenstance – these people were almost all aristocrats, men (and women) who knew each other well – and might be adversaries or friends in need. Names in bold are historical characters – yes, even Arimnestos – and you can get a glimpse into their lives by looking at Wikipedia or Britannia online. For more in-depth information, I recommend Plutarch and Herodotus, to whom I owe a great deal.

Arimnestos of Plataea may – just may – have been Herodotus's source for the events of the Persian Wars. The careful reader will note that Herodotus himself – a scribe from Halicarnassus – appears several times ...

Archilogos – Ephesian, son of Hipponax the poet; a typical Ionian aristocrat, who loves Persian culture and Greek culture too, who serves his city, not some cause of 'Greece' or 'Hellas', and who finds the rule of the Great King fairer and more 'democratic' than the rule of a Greek tyrant.

Arimnestos – Child of Chalkeotechnes and Euthalia.

Aristagoras – Son of Molpagoras, nephew of Histiaeus. Aristagoras led Miletus while Histiaeus was a virtual prisoner of the Great King Darius at Susa. Aristagoras seems to have initiated the Ionian Revolt – and later to have regretted it.

Aristides – Son of Lysimachus, lived roughly 525–468 BC, known later in life as 'The Just'. Perhaps best known as one of the commanders at

Marathon. Usually sided with the Aristocratic party.

Artaphernes – Brother of Darius, Great King of Persia, and Satrap of Sardis. A senior Persian with powerful connections.

Behon – A Kelt from Alba; a fisherman and former slave.

Bion – A slave name, meaning 'life'. The most loyal family retainer of the Corvaxae.

Briseis – Daughter of Hipponax, sister of Archilogos.

Calchus – A former warrior, now the keeper of the shrine of the Plataean Hero of Troy, Leitus.

Chalkeotechnes – The Smith of Plataea; head of the family Corvaxae, who claim descent from Herakles.

Chalkidis – Brother of Arimnestos, son of Chalkeotechnes.

Cimon – Son of Miltiades, a professional soldier, sometime pirate, and Athenian aristocrat.

Cleisthenes – was a noble Athenian of the Alcmaeonid family. He is credited with reforming the constitution of ancient Athens and setting it on a democratic footing in 508/7 BC.

Collam – A Gallic lord in the Central Massif at the headwaters of the Seine.

Dano of Croton – Daughter of the philosopher and mathematician Pythagoras.

Darius – King of Kings, the lord of the Persian Empire, brother to Artaphernes.

Doola – Numidian ex-slave.

Draco – Wheelwright and wagon builder of Plataea, a leading man of the town.

Empedocles – A priest of Hephaestus, the Smith God.

Epaphroditos – A warrior, an aristocrat of Lesbos.

Eualcides – A Hero. Eualcidas is typical of a class of aristocratic men – professional warriors, adventurers, occasionally pirates or merchants by turns. From Euboeoa.

Heraclitus – c.535–475 BC. One of the ancient world's most famous philosophers. Born to an aristocratic family, he chose philosophy over political power. Perhaps most famous for his statement about time: 'You cannot step twice into the same river'. His belief that 'strife is justice' and other similar sayings which you'll find scattered through these pages made him a favourite with Nietzsche. His works, mostly now lost, probably established the later philosophy of Stoicism.

Herakleides – An Aeolian, a Greek of Asia Minor. With his brothers Nestor and Orestes, he becomes a retainer – a warrior – in service to Arimnestos. It is easy, when looking at the birth of Greek democracy, to see the whole form of modern government firmly established

– but at the time of this book, democracy was less than skin deep and most armies were formed of semi-feudal war bands following an aristocrat.

Heraklides – Aristides' helmsman, a lower-class Athenian who has made a name for himself in war.

Hermogenes – Son of Bion, Arimnestos's slave.

Hesiod – A great poet (or a great tradition of poetry) from Boeotia in Greece, Hesiod's 'Works and Days' and 'Theogony' were widely read in the sixth century and remain fresh today – they are the chief source we have on Greek farming, and this book owes an enormous debt to them.

Hippias – Last tyrant of Athens, overthrown around 510 BC (that is, just around the beginning of this series), Hippias escaped into exile and became a pensioner of Darius of Persia.

Hipponax – 540–c.498 BC. A Greek poet and satirist, considered the inventor of parody. He is supposed to have said 'There are two days when a woman is a pleasure: the day one marries her and the day one buries her'.

Histiaeus – Tyrant of Miletus and ally of Darius of Persia, possible originator of the plan for the Ionian Revolt.

Homer – Another great poet, roughly Hesiod's contemporary (give or take fifty years!) and again, possibly more a poetic tradition than an individual man. Homer is reputed as the author of the *Iliad* and the *Odyssey*, two great epic poems which, between them, largely defined what heroism and aristocratic good behaviour should be in Greek society – and, you might say, to this very day.

Idomeneus – Cretan warrior, priest of Leitus.

Kylix – A boy, slave of Hipponax.

Leukas – Alban sailor, later deck master on *Lydia*. Kelt of the Dumnones of Briton.

Miltiades – Tyrant of the Thracian Chersonese. His son, Cimon or Kimon, rose to be a great man in Athenian politics. Probably the author of the Athenian victory of Marathon, Miltiades was a complex man, a pirate, a warlord, and a supporter of Athenian democracy.

Penelope – Daughter of Chalkeotechnes, sister of Arimnestos.

Polymarchos – ex-slave swordmaster of Syracusa.

Phrynicus – Ancient Athenian playwright and warrior.

Sappho – A Greek poetess from the island of Lesbos, born sometime around 630 BC and died between 570 and 550 BC. Her father was probably Lord of Eressos. Widely considered the greatest lyric poet of Ancient Greece.

Seckla – Numidian ex-slave.

Simonalkes – Head of the collateral branch of the Plataean Corvaxae, cousin to Arimnestos.

Simonides – Another great lyric poet, he lived c.556–468 BC, and his nephew, Bacchylides, was as famous as he. Perhaps best known for his epigrams, one of which is:

> Ὦ ξεῖν’, ἀγγέλλειν Λακεδαιμονίοις ὅτι τῇδε
> κείμεθα, τοῖς κείνων ῥήμασι πειθόμενοι.
> *Go tell the Spartans, thou who passest by,*
> *That here, obedient to their laws, we lie.*

Thales – c.624–c.546 BC The first philosopher of the Greek tradition, whose writings were still current in Arimnestos's time. Thales used geometry to solve problems such as calculating the height of the pyramids in Aegypt and the distance of ships from the shore. He made at least one trip to Aegypt. He is widely accepted as the founder of western mathematics.

Themistocles – Leader of the demos party in Athens, father of the Athenian Fleet. Political enemy of Aristides.

Theognis – Theognis of Megara was almost certainly not one man but a whole canon of aristocratic poetry under that name, much of it practical. There are maxims, many very wise, laments on the decline of man and the age, and the woes of old age and poverty, songs for symposia, etc. In later sections there are songs and poems about homosexual love and laments for failed romances. Despite widespread attributions, there was, at some point, a real Theognis who may have lived in the mid-6th century BC, or just before the events of this series. His poetry would have been central to the world of Arimnestos's mother.

Vasileos – master shipwright and helmsman.

ALBA

VECTI

LOLVMA

SEQVANA·R.

GALLIA

OLARIO

LVDVNCA

RHODANVS·R.

OIASSO

ARIA

MASSAL

CENTRONA

IBERIA

PILLARS OF
HERACLES

Prologue

So – here we are again.

Last night, I told you of Marathon – truly the greatest of days for a warrior, the day that every man who was present, great or small, remembers as his finest. But even Marathon – the great victory of Athens and Plataea against the might of Persia – did not end the Long War.

In fact, *thugater*, an honest man might say that the Battle of Marathon *started* the Long War. Until Marathon, there was the failed revolt of the Ionians, and any sane man would have said they had lost. That the Greeks had lost. In far-off Sardis – in Persepolis, capital of the Persian Empire – they barely knew that Athens existed, or Sparta, and I will wager not a one of the gold-wearing bastards had heard of Plataea.

I was born in Plataea, of course, and my father raised me to be a smith – but my tutor Calchus saw the man of blood inside me, and made me a warrior, as well. And even that isn't really fair – my pater was a fine warrior, the polemarch of our city, and he led us out to war with Sparta and Corinth in the week of three battles, and fought like a lion, and died – murdered, stabbed in the back while he fought, by his own cousin Simon, and may the vultures tear his liver in eternal torment!

Simon sold me as a slave. I had fallen wounded across my pater's corpse, and Simon took me from the battlefield and sold me. Why didn't he kill me? It might have helped him, but often, evil men beget their own destruction with their own acts – that is how the gods behave in the world of men.

I grew to full manhood as a slave in Ionia, the slave of Hipponax and his son Archilogos, and to be honest, I loved them, and seldom resented being a slave. But Archilogos had a sister, Briseis, and she is Helen reborn, so that even at thirteen and fourteen, men competed for her favours – grown men.

I loved her, and still do.

Not that that love brought me much joy.

And I received the education of an aristocrat, by attending lessons with my young master – so that I was taught the wisdom of Heraclitus, whom many worship as a god to this very day.

When I was seventeen or so, events shattered our household – betrayal, adultery and civil war. I've already told that story. But in the end, the Ionians – all the Greeks of Asia and the Islands – left the allegiance of Persia and went to war. In my own house, I was freed, and became Archilogos's friend and war-companion. But in my hubris I lay with Briseis, and was banned from the house and sent to wander the world.

A world suddenly at war.

I marched and fought through the first campaign, from the victory at Sardis to black defeat on the plains by Ephesus, the city of my slavery, and then I fled with the Athenians. I served as a mercenary on Crete, and found myself with my own black ship at Amathus, the first naval battle in the Ionian Revolt. We won at sea. But we lost on land, and again, I was on the run in a captured ship with a bad crew.

Eventually, I found a new home with the Athenian lord, Miltiades. As a pirate. Let's not mince words, friends! We killed men and took their ships, and that made us pirates, whatever we may now claim.

But Miltiades was instrumental in keeping the Ionian Revolt alive, as I've told on other nights. We fought and fought, and eventually we drove the Medes from the parts of the Xhersonese they'd seized, and used it as a base to wreck them – until they sent armies to clear us from the peninsula.

I did as Miltiades bade me: killed, stole, and my name gained renown.

After a year of fighting, we were losing. But we caught a Persian squadron far from its base, in Thrace, and we destroyed them – and in the fighting, I murdered Briseis' useless husband. Again, I've told this story already – ask someone who was here.

I thought that, now Briseis was free to marry me, she would.

I was wrong. She went back east to marry someone older, wiser and more powerful.

So I went back to Plataea.

I worked my father's farm, and tried to be a bronze-smith.

But a man died at the shrine on the hill – and his death sent me to Athens, and before long I was back at sea, killing men and taking their goods. Hard to explain in a sentence or two, my daughter. But that's what I did. And so, I was back to fighting the Persians. I served Miltiades – I ran cargoes into Miletus, the greatest city of Ionia, besieged by the Persians, and we saved them. And then the East Greeks formed a mighty fleet, and we went to save Miletus.

And we *failed*.

We fought the battle of Lade, and the Samians betrayed us, and most of my friends died. Miletus fell, and in the wake of that defeat, Ionia was conquered and the East Greeks ceased to be free men. The men of some islands were all killed, and the women sold into slavery.

It's odd, thugater, because I loved the Persians, their truth-telling and their brilliant society. They were good men, and honourable, and yet war brought the worst of them to the fore and they behaved like animals – like men inevitably do, in war.

They raped Ionia and Aetolia, and we – the survivors – scuttled into exile. I ran home, after Briseis spurned me again.

So I went back to the smithy in Plataea. I began, in fact, to learn to be a fine smith.

But I had famous friends and a famous name. I had occasion to save Miltiades of Athens from a treason charge – heh, I'll tell that story again for an obol – and as a consequence, my sister got me a beautiful wife. Listen, do you doubt me? She was beautiful, and had I not saved Miltiades ...

At any rate, I married Euphoria.

And a summer later, when she was full of my seed, I led the Plataean phalanx over the mountains to Attica, to help save Athens. This time, when the Persians forced us to battle, we had no traitors in our ranks and we were not found wanting. This time, the gods stood by us. This time Apollo and Zeus and Ares and Athena lent us aid, and we beat the Persians at Marathon.

But I told that story last night.

And when I came home, my beautiful Euphoria was dead in childbirth. Her newborn child – I never saw it – lay in swaddling with a slave. I assumed it dead. My sister still blames herself for that error, but I have never blamed her. Yet, to understand my tale, you must understand – I thought my child had died ...

So I picked my beloved wife up, took her to my farm and burned it, and her, with every piece of jewellery and every scrap of cloth she'd ever worn or woven.

And then I took a horse and rode away.

That ought to have been the end. But it was, of course, another beginning, because that's how the gods make men.

You need to understand this. After Marathon, nothing was the same. No one was the same. Life did not taste sweet. Indeed, most of us felt that our greatest deed, and days, were behind us, and there was not much left for us to do. And I had lost wife and child. I had nothing to live for, and no life to which to return.

Part I
Sicily

Σιληνός

ὁρῶ πρὸς ἀκταῖς ναὸς Ἑλλάδος σκάφος
κώπης τ᾽ ἄνακτας σὺν στρατηλάτῃ τινὶ
στείχοντας ἐς τόδ᾽ ἄντρον: ἀμφὶ δ᾽ αὐχέσιν
τεύχη φέρονται κενά, βορᾶς κεχρημένοι,
κρωσσούς θ᾽ ὑδρηλούς. ὦ ταλαίπωροι ξένοι:
90 τίνες ποτ᾽ εἰσίν; οὐκ ἴσασι δεσπότην
Πολύφημον οἷός ἐστιν ἄξενόν τε γῆν
τήνδ᾽ ἐμβεβῶτες καὶ Κυκλωπίαν γνάθον
τὴν ἀνδροβρῶτα δυστυχῶς ἀφιγμένοι.
ἀλλ᾽ ἥσυχοι γίγνεσθ᾽, ἵν᾽ ἐκπυθώμεθα
πόθεν πάρεισι Σικελὸν Αἰτναῖον πάγον.

I see a Greek ship on the beach, and sailors who ply the oar coming
to this cave with one who must be their commander. About their
necks they carry empty vessels, since it is food they need, and pails
for water. O unlucky strangers! [90] Who can they be? They know
not what our master Polyphemus is like, nor that this ground they
stand on is no friend to guests, and that they have arrived with
wretched bad luck at the man-eating jaws of the Cyclops. But hold
your peace so that we may learn [95] where they have come from
to Sicilian Aetna's crag.

Euripides Cyclops 85

I

I was off my head.

I rode south past the shrine in a thunder of hooves, so that Idomeneus came out with a spear in his hand. But I did not want his blood-mad comfort. I rode past him, up the mountain.

Up the Cithaeron, to the altar of my family. The old altar of ash and ancient stone where the Corvaxae have worshipped the mountain since Leitos left for Troy, and before.

I had nothing to sacrifice, and it had begun to rain. The rain fell and fell, and I stood at the ash altar watching the rains wash it, watching the water rush down the hillside. And my life was like those ashes – so useless it was fit only to be washed away. Lightning flashed in the sky, the thunderbolts of Zeus struck the earth and I stood by the altar and prayed that Zeus would take me – what a grand way to go! I stood straight, and with every crash I expected—

But the lightning passed me by. It is odd – I decided to slay myself, and only then realized that I had neither sword nor spear. Looking back, it is almost comic. I was exhausted – I had fought at Marathon only a week before, and I hadn't recovered, and the cold rain soaked me. My sword and spear were back on the plains below me – at my sister's house, where even now they would be looking for me, and looking for Euphoria to bury her.

I wasn't going back.

Cithaeron is not a mountain with a crag from which a man can easily hurl himself. The whole thing has an aura of dark comedy – Arimnestos, the great hero, seeks to slay himself like Ajax, but he's too damned tired.

Before darkness fell, I started down the mountain, headed west over the seaward shoulder, intending – nothing. Intending, I think, to jump from the very first promontory that I came to.

Or perhaps intending nothing at all. May you never be so tired and so utterly god-cursed that you seek only oblivion, my daughter. May your days be filled with light, and never see that darkness, where all you want is an end to pain. But that was me.

I walked and walked, and it grew dark.

And I fell, and then I slept, or rather, I passed out of this world.

I woke in the morning to the cold, the rain, deep mist – and to the knowledge that there was nothing awaiting me. It came to me immediately – my first thought on waking was of her death. And I rose and wandered the woods, and I remember calling her name aloud, more a groan than a greeting.

On and on I walked, always down and east and south.

I slept again, and rose the third day, with no food, no water, endless rain and cold. I wept, and the rain carried my tears to the earth. I prayed, and the skies answered me. I thought of how, on the eve of Marathon, I had dreamed of Briseis and not of Euphoria, and I *knew* in my heart that I had killed her with my betrayal.

I was an animal, fit only to kill other animals, and I was not a worthy man: death was what I deserved.

It may seem impossible, my friends, that one of the victors of Marathon should feel this way a week after the greatest victory in all the annals of men, but if you know any warriors, you know the revulsion and the fatigue that comes with killing. Truly we were greater than human at Marathon. But the cost was high.

I could see the faces of the men I'd killed, back and back and back to the first helot I'd put down with a spear cast at Oinoe.

I thought of the slave girl I'd sworn to protect, and then abandoned.

I thought of the beautiful boy I'd killed on the battlefield by Ephesus, while he lay screaming in pain.

And of the woman I had left, pregnant, on Crete.

And of Euphoria, with whom I had often fought, and seldom enough praised.

I went down the mountain, looking for a cliff face.

Eventually I found one.

The rain stopped when I reached the top of the cliff. I couldn't see the base – it was hidden in fog. But the sun was about to burst through the clouds. And even as I stood there, it did – a single arm of Helios's might reached through a tiny gap to shine on the ground before my feet and dispel the cloud of fog below the cliff.

Well.

Apollo pointed the way. He has never been my friend, that god, and I might have ignored his summons, but I wanted only extinction.

I said a prayer. I said her name out loud.

I jumped.

I hit water.

How the gods must laugh at men!

I had jumped into the ocean. It was a long fall, and I struck badly. It knocked the wind out of me, and then I became the butt of the laughter of the gods because instead of letting the cold water close over my head and drowning – I had, after all, intended to die – I began to fight to live. My arms moved, my legs kicked and my lungs starved for precious air until my head burst from under the waves and my mouth drank air like precious wine.

Against my own desire, I began to swim.

I was just a few horse-lengths off a rocky coast – it was deep water, or I'd have been dead – but with nowhere to land.

Oh, how the gods laughed.

Because now, suddenly, I was filled with a desire to live, and my arms swam powerfully, and yet there was nowhere to go but onto rocks. The sea struck the rocks sharply – three days of rain had raised a swell.

I turned my head out to sea in the fog and began to swim.

The change from suicide to struggle for life was so swift that I never questioned it. I merely moved my arms – as strong as any man's arms, and yet weak from four days of no food, and from the incredible effort that was Marathon. I was not going to last long. But I swam, drank mouthfuls of air and swam more, and eventually – long after I think I should have been dead – I turned the headland and saw a beach at the base of the next cove, a beach with a small fire on it. The smell of the burning spruce came to me like a message from the gods, and I swam like a porpoise – twenty strokes, fifty strokes.

My toes brushed sand.

I was swimming in an arm's-span of water.

I dragged myself up the beach.

I lay with my legs in the water and my elbows in the sea wrack and kelp, and strong arms came and lifted me clear. They dragged me up the beach. I didn't know their language, but they rolled me over and they had serious, hairy faces – skin the colour of old wood, and black beards.

I stammered my thanks. And went down into the darkness.

That was probably for the best.

Because when I awoke, we were at sea, and I was chained to an oar bench.

Remember, I had been a slave before.

This was worse. Far, far worse, but having been a slave before saved me. I knew all the petty degradations, I knew the perils and I knew the penalties.

I was chained in the very depths of a trireme – as a thranite, the very lowest tier of oarsmen. Air came to me through my oar-port, which was mostly covered in leather and leaked air and water in equal profusion.

When the men above me relieved themselves, the piss and shit fell on me. Oh, yes. That's the way in the lower decks of a slave-driven trireme.

I lay quietly for as long as I possibly could, because I knew that as soon as they noticed me, I would be made to row. But a man can only stand so much piss in his hair and beard. I moved my arm, and the oar-master was on me. He struck me several times with a stick, grinning with delight, and put an oar in my hands. It took time for him to bring it from amidships.

He seemed to speak a little Greek, and I barely understood him, but the man above me in the second deck leaned down.

'He's a killer, mate,' he said. 'Obey, or he'll gut you.'

For a moment I thought he was talking *about* me, rather than to me. I thought perhaps he was telling the oar-master that I was a killer.

Hah!

Pride goes first, when you are a slave.

The oar-master grinned at me, took a knife from under his arm and poked it into my groin. Smiled more broadly.

'Tell him I know how to pull an oar!' I shouted. Instant surrender.

The oar-master laughed. And hit me.

I'm sure you are waiting to hear, my friends, how I recovered my wits, rose from my bench and slaughtered my enemies.

Well, you haven't been a slave, have you? Any of you.

In a week, I was used to it. I was strong enough, and there was food – badly cooked fish, barley bread, sour beer.

I ate. I no longer wanted to die. Or rather, I only wanted to live to kill the oar-master, whom I hated. And I hated him with a pure, searing hate. But I was a slave, and he laughed at my hate. He was big, and very strong – fully muscled like a Pankrationist. He enjoyed inflicting pain – on us, the slaves, but he even enjoyed inflicting petty, verbal hurst on his subordinates and the helmsmen and the deck crew.

I was ridden like a horse. For the first week I rowed in the depths of the ship, with water and shit over my ankles, the smell enough to stop a man from work. But even exhausted and injured, I was strong compared to other men, and that crew had seen better days. After a long pull – I have no idea when, or where we landed – I was 'promoted' to the top deck of rowers, the 'elite'. I, who had commanded my own ship, who could steer and make sail. And fight.

The top deck was not an improvement, except for the clean ocean air. Here I was constantly under the eye of the oar-master and his minions, the six men he used to impose his authority. The ship carried no marines – or, just possibly, these men were the marines – a surly, churlish lot. They proved their manhood by tormenting the rowers.

It is a thing I have often noted, how the stamp of a leader imprints itself on his followers. Hasdrubal – the captain – was a beak-nosed Phoenician from far-off Carthage. He was tall, he was strong and he was a vicious bully. He never gave a direct order – rather, he wheedled and manipulated when strength would have done better, and then turned into a right tyrant when some persuasion might have served the trick.

He was handsome, in a burly way, and had the pointiest, heaviest, most perfumed beard I'd ever seen on a man. Well, a man at sea, anyway. I'd seen such things on Thebans.

But his bad command skills transmitted themselves to this captain's officers as effectively as Miltiades' were transmitted to his. The oar-master was a torturing tyrant, the sailing-master was a weak man with a drink problem who knuckled under to the oar-master in every situation and hated him for it and the helmsmen – a pair of them, both Carthaginians learning the trade – were young, silent, morose and bitter. My guess, from the yawning chasm that separated us – you can't imagine I ever talked to these bastards – was that the two helmsmen were better men, just trying to survive under the regime of a bully and a madman.

For Dagon, the oar-master, was mad. Mad with power, mad with rage, mad with the cunning, plotting madness of a long-time drunkard, or a man who enjoys the pain of others.

It was days before I truly felt his displeasure. I know now that we were somewhere on the coast of Dalmatia, rowing north. I had gathered from talk on deck – slaves were forbidden to speak unless spoken to – that we had a cargo of Athenian hides and pottery and some Cyprian copper, and that we were going to bump our way up the coast until we found someone to sell us iron and tin.

I was rowing. When you are in peak physical condition, it is possible to row for a long time while your mind is elsewhere. Despite despair and wounds and struggle, I was sound enough to row – all day – without pain. But my head was in a dark place, considering my life. My life with Briseis. My life with Euphoria. My life as a hero, and my life as a smith. I wasn't despairing – it takes longer than three days to drive me to despair. But I had started pretty far down, and being enslaved certainly hadn't helped.

The stick hit me a glancing blow on the left shoulder. 'Off the beat,' the oar-master roared, his spittle raining on my left ear.

'Like fuck!' I said, before I'd thought about it. In fact, I was dead on the beat – my stroke was perfect.

The next blow hit my head, and I gave a half-scream and sort of fell across my oar, and then he hit me again, five or six blows to the head and neck. My nose broke, and blood showered across me.

'Silence, scum,' he roared at me. 'Do not even scream!'

I grunted.

He hit me again. It was an oak stick.

I must have made some noise. Or maybe not.

'Silence!' he said in the kind of voice a man uses to a lover, and hit me again.

My oar caught in the backwash of another man's oar, jumped and slammed into my chest, cracking ribs. I grunted.

He hit me again. 'Silence, slave!'

I tried to gain control of the oar. Tears were pouring down my face, and blood.

He laughed. 'You need to learn what you are. You are a sack full of pain, and I will let it out when I want to. For anything. Until you

12

die, cursing me.' He moved around until he was in my sight line. 'I am Dagon, Lord of Pain.' He laughed.

Just then, the trierarch came up. I knew his voice already. That needs to be said, because I could barely see. And you have to imagine, I was trying to manage an eighteen-foot oar while he hit me in the back.

'You are off the stroke,' he said teasingly, and hit me on my left shoulder. He was expert. He hit me so hard I could barely manage the pain – but he didn't break a bone.

I guess I whimpered.

Dagon laughed again. 'Silence!' he said, and hit me again.

The trierarch laughed. 'New slaves are useless, aren't they?' he said.

The oar-master tapped his stick on the deck. 'He can't get the rhythm,' the oar-master said. A lie.

'You lie,' I spat.

The blow that struck me put me out.

When I awoke, I was the stern oar of the thranites – the lowest of the low, and since most triremes row a little down by the stern, all of the piss and shit of the whole slave ship was around my ankles and calves. The moment I groaned and shook, one of the oar-master's minions threw seawater over me and put an oar in my hands, feeding it through the oar-port – it was, of course, a short and difficult oar because of the curve of the ship. Rowing here was always a punishment, even on my ships.

I threw up.

On myself, of course.

And started rowing.

Time lost meaning. I rowed, and hurt, and rowed, and hurt. Men came and hit me with sticks and I rowed, and hurt. We landed for a night, somewhere north of Corcyra, and I was left chained to my bench while other men went ashore. Kritias, a Greek, one of the oar-master's bully-boys, came to me with stale bread, dipped it in the stinking brown water by my ankles and put it in my lap. 'I have five obols on this,' he said. 'That you'll eat it.'

He got his five obols.

Then I was sick – sick with one of Apollo's arrows in me, and shit poured from me into the water at my feet and I vomited, over and over.

And I rowed.

The sun beat down, and men above me died. I was hardly the only victim – indeed, so ill was that ship that men died every second or third day. So that after some more time – I have no idea how much time, but we were somewhere on the coast of Illyria – we landed, and even I was allowed ashore. We ate pig – the slaves got crap, but it was delicious, and we ate *everything*.

That was the night I realized we were in Illyria. A party of nobles came down to the ship, and I had the energy to pay attention. There were two men and two women on horseback, and they rode straight down the beach.

They gave Hasdrubal the signs of peace, and dismounted warily. He offered them bread and salt and wine.

The two women were young and pretty, tough the way all Illyrians are, as blond as the sun, tanned like old leather, in fine wool with gold bracelets. The men were taller and older, with beards and more gold jewellery. Their servants had tin. We could see it in ingots, brought by donkey from somewhere even farther north.

Illyrians are a strange lot – they have nothing but lords and slaves, and the lords are at war with each other all the time. They look Greek, they sometimes speak Greek – worship our gods, too. Many of them know the *Iliad* and the *Odyssey*. But they are not Greek. Or rather, sometimes I think that they are Hellenes who never found the rule of law.

But I was not thinking such rational and philosophical thoughts that night.

I was too far away to hear any of the conversation, but the style of their pins and their clothes, their horse-furniture and a thousand other little details, all made it plain where we were.

Well, while there's life, there's hope, or so it is said. Illyrians are the worst pirates in the Middle Sea, and suddenly, it occurred to me that if Hasdrubal would just keep sailing up the coast, an Illyrian coaster was bound to attack us. And the gods knew that we wouldn't have lasted a moment in a sea fight – a two-thirds crew of sick slaves and bully-boys as marines.

It has to say something for my state that being taken by Illyrians, who enslaved all captives regardless of social status, was my *hope*.

We were tied together with rope while ashore and put in a stock-ade, more like a pen, with two armed men as guards. When we were ashore – this was my first time ashore since my first day on board – it was impossible to keep us from talking. Yet, to my utter puzzlement, none of the other oar-slaves would speak.

Not even a word.

It was the lowest part of the whole experience. I had never seen slaves who would not mutter – who would not rebel in a thousand little ways, even if they were too cowed to rebel in the ways that mattered.

The slaves sat silent, every one of them with their eyes closed.

I moved from man to man, whispering, until a guard came into the pen. I froze, but he'd seen me, and he struck me with his spear shaft – heavy ash. He almost broke my arm. He hit me so hard – I'll just say this as an aside – that he raised a black bruise on the side of the arm *opposite* to the blow, and it covered the arm. It made a nice counterpoint to the ache in my ribs.

I didn't even whimper. I'd learned better.

He laughed. 'Beg me not to hit you again, *pais*. Beg me. Offer to suck my dick.'

Sometimes, having been a slave before saved my life. This was one of those times. A man who'd always been free might have had to knuckle under and been broken – or might have had to resist, and been killed.

I held my head and looked dumb.

He hit me lightly. 'You know what I said!' he grunted.

I held my head, met his eye and then cocked my head to one side.

He sneered. 'Not even your wits left, eh?'

Outside, there were shouts – rage – a scream.

He ran out of the pen and slammed the rickety gate closed.

The palisade was hastily built – badly cut palings rammed into the sand and held together with a heavy rope woven in and out of the palings. I could see. My arm hurt, but I got myself to an edge.

Two other slaves came to look.

The rest just lay still with their eyes closed.

Our guards were running full tilt for the central fire of the camp. One of the Illyrian servants was making for the wood line; another was face down, and experience told me he wasn't ever getting up.

'You're an idiot,' said the Thracian at my elbow. 'Make trouble.'

'Uh,' said the other, a Greek. 'Never fucking talk when they can hear.'

'Sorry,' I muttered.

'Skethes,' said the Thracian.

'Arimnestos,' I said.

'Nestor,' said the Greek. He looked to be fifty years old, and as hard as an old oak tree.

Something was happening at the fire. A woman was screaming.

We couldn't see anything because it was too dark. But we didn't have to.

There was the unmistakable sound of a man being beaten with spear shafts – blows falling like hail on a tent, the hollow sound of a man's head and chest taking them.

And the women, screaming. They were being raped.

One by one, many of the slaves went to sleep.

I couldn't. I lay there and hated.

Towards morning, two more guards opened the pen and threw in the body. It was a man, and he was alive. I didn't have to be a philosopher to figure out that he was one of the Illyrian men, although his face was a swollen pulp and he was covered in weals and blood and shit – his own.

All the slaves woke when he was tossed into the pen. He lay there, bleeding, for a long time. Too damned long.

Finally, I couldn't stand it. I guess I wasn't broken. Again, my experience as a slave helped me because I wasn't shocked and I was learning the 'rules', sick as they were. So I stripped my loincloth off my groin, dipped it in our drinking water – well might you flinch, young woman – and started to wash the man.

I gave him some water when his eyes opened – they were just slits.

He punched me as hard as he could in the nose – my recently broken nose.

He roared some sort of war cry, and Skethes pinned his shoulders and Nestor rammed my loincloth into his mouth.

The guards, watching through the palisade, laughed.

Fuck them, I thought. I had found a way to rebel. I went back to washing the brutalized man.

The three of us got him cleaner, and we dripped some water into him, and when the sun rose above the rim of the world, we fed bread to him, too. By then, he knew where he was. He didn't speak. He was, in fact, in shock.

As soon as the light was strong, we could see the bodies. Six of them. The two girls, the other Illyrian nobleman, two Illyrian

16

servants or slaves and one of the oar-master's bully-boys, all dead in the sand, with a lot of blood around them.

The oar-master woke the slaves with cold water, and ordered us to bury the bodies.

'You useless fucks,' he went on to his guards, 'can watch them, and you can think about how I'm going to take the price of two blond slave girls out of your pay.' He hit a guard.

The guard flinched.

'Useless coward,' the oar-master said. 'And one of them escaped. So we won't get all their tin, and their war party will come. Your fault!' he screamed. He looked at Kritias. 'If my contact here is killed, I'll sell the lot of you as slaves.'

Really, you have to wonder that someone didn't kill him. But I caught that. I'm still proud I did – neither hate nor shock nor the will of the Gods plugged my ears. Dagon had a contact among the Illyrians.

I must have seemed to be listening too closely.

He struck out with his stick and hit me.

I didn't make a sound.

The guards stood over us and prodded us with their spear points while we dug in the sand. Planting corpses in sand is useless – an offence to gods and men, an invitation to scavengers. But he didn't care, and the trierarch was silent and withdrawn.

We were down into the gravel layer under the sand, and making heavy work of it – we were digging with bare hands and no shovels – when the trierarch came up, stroking his beard.

'A little hasty, attacking guests,' he said. His voice trembled. He was speaking to the oar-master, but since no one on the beach was making a noise, his voice carried. He spoke in Greek, accented, but clear enough.

'You think so?' said the oar-master. He sneered. 'Don't be weak. We need slaves. That's what we are here for. And now we don't have to pay for the tin.' He looked at the wood line. 'Besides, you know as well as I, *my lord*, that his uncle offered us—'

The trierarch spat. 'We are here for iron,' he said primly. 'Not tribal feuds.'

'Bullshit, I'm here for slaves and tin.' The oar-master smiled. 'And we'll get more. The same way. Epidavros has promised.'

'We let them approach as guests,' the trierarch said.

'Don't be weak,' the oar-master said. 'We need Epidavros.'

There was a long pause. I had to assume that Epidavros was the oar-master's contact.

'Why were the women killed?' Hasdrubal asked.

The oar-master shrugged. 'My people got carried away,' he said. 'It won't happen again.'

'See that it doesn't. Now I want out of here.' Hasdrubal gestured at the ship. 'They're too weak to dig gravel with their hands. Leave the bodies. Let's be gone.' He paused, his fear showing even in the way his right foot moved on the sand. 'One escaped. They will attack us.'

The oar-master shrugged his infuriating shrug. I could tell that he, not the trierarch, was actually in command. And the name *Epidavros* stuck in my head. There's a town of that name on Lesbos. I met Briseis there, once. At any rate, he smiled insolently. 'Epidavros won't attack us,' he said. 'Even if he wanted to – it'll be days before he's finished off their relatives.'

The Carthaginian trierarch turned and looked at those of us digging. 'I want the men who killed those women to pay,' he said. 'Those women were worth the value of the rest of our cargo.'

The guard next to me kicked me. 'Work faster, motherfucker,' he spat. He knew his turn was coming, so like a good flunky, he passed his anxiety straight on to a slave.

Hasdrubal pushed us back onto the ship. He switched any slave who was slow getting aboard, and he ordered the oar-master, in a voice suddenly as strong as bronze, to flog the last man on his bench, and when that order was given, we went like a tide up the side and almost swamped the ship.

The Illyrian man could barely walk.

The oar-master ordered me to carry him, thus guaranteeing I would be the last man up the side. And I was. I was naked, my loincloth lost in the night, and he shoved me over a bench and caned me, his stick making that dry, meaty sound as he struck me.

Then he put his head close to mine. 'I can read your thoughts, pais. You take good care of the Illyrian slave. Show me what you are made of. The more you care for him, the longer he'll live for me.' He smiled and let me up. 'He called me a coward, do you know that, pais? So I'll keep him alive a long time, and show him what a man is.'

Somehow, I got the Illyrian onto a bench – the starboard-stern thranite's bench, that had been mine. Lekythos, the biggest guard, pointed at it, and then put me in the bench above.

18

Now I noticed that a third of the benches were empty. The mad fucks were killing oarsmen and not replacing them.

All we needed was an Illyrian pirate. At worst, he'd kill the lot of us. I really didn't care.

Time passed.

I cared for the Illyrian a little – not really that much. I had to survive myself. I'd like to say the Thracians and the Greek helped, but I never heard a word from them. They were somewhere else – funny that, in a hull only as long as a dozen horses end to end, I had no idea where they were. They weren't among the twenty men I could see when I rowed, and the others around me were silent and utterly broken. In fact, one died. He just expired, and his oar came up and slammed his head and he didn't cry out because he was dead.

I managed to get to the Illyrian in the evening, when the oarsmen were rested, and in the morning, before we began to row. We were off the coast of Illyria now, and we stayed at sea, and every islet on that coast – seen out of the oar-port of the man in front of me – seemed like a potential ship. But our pace never varied, and we rowed on and on. We never raised our boatsail, the small sail in the bow, and we seemed perpetually in motion.

And we never landed.

After a week, the food failed. Suddenly, there was no more barley, much less pig or thin wine. The guards complained and hit us more often.

My Illyrian awoke from whatever torpor had seized him and was given an oar.

We continued north. I assumed it was north – I could seldom see the waves.

The Illyrian didn't know a word of Greek. I tried to teach him, in grunts and whispered bits, but he wasn't listening: he didn't care, and, after a while, I gave up.

The oar-master came to him every day. Stood over him and laughed, and called him a boy and a coward, and told him that he would be sold in Athens to a brothel. But the Illyrian was too far gone, and spoke no Greek, so he endured the abuse.

Another day, he was told he was rowing out of time and beaten, and then beaten for crying out.

You know that feeling you get in the gut, when another man gets what should be yours? That feeling you have when you hear a good man abused? The feeling between your shoulders when a woman screams for help?

When you are a slave, all that happens. For a while. But by taking away from you your ability to respond to these, they take your honour. After a while, a man can be beaten to death an arm's-length away and you don't even clench your stomach muscles.

On and on.

We rowed.

We rowed all the way up the coast of Illyria and Dalmatia, and men continued to die, and we rowed without food for a while, as I say. It's hard to tell this, not just because it's all so low and disgusting, but because there's nothing on which to seize. Abuse was routine. Pain was routine. Men hit us, and we rowed. Our muscles ached, and we rowed. Sometimes we slept, and that was as good as our lives ever were.

We came to an archipelago of islets, and they had small villages on them. Finally, we landed. None of us was allowed ashore, and all I can say is that after a time, a dozen slaves and some food came onto the ship and some copper was unloaded.

And then it all happened again.

My Illyrian was moved out of the stern-post rowing station, and I was moved back to the upper deck, and we rowed. There was food. That seemed good.

We rowed.

We made another landfall, and were beached again. This place had a ready-built palisade for slaves, and we could see it was full from our benches, with forty or fifty male slaves waiting to be sold.

Our Illyrian looked at the beach and wept.

We were pushed ashore, roped together and put in the palisade. By luck, I was roped to the Greek, Nestor.

After darkness fell, and the guards went off to fuck the female slaves in another pen – I call these things by their proper names, children, and may you never know what slavery is! – we lay side by side, and whispered very quietly.

'Still alive, brother?' he said.

'Yes,' I said.

He nodded in the dark, so close I could feel it more than see it. 'Good,' he said. 'I was thinking,' he went on. 'Arimnestos is an odd name. Where you from?'

Where was I from? May I tell you the truth, friends? I hadn't thought of home, of *anything*, for weeks.

'Plataea,' I said, and it was as if a dam opened in my head and thoughts poured in. My forge, my wife, the night she died, the fire.

The *Pyrrhiche* and how we danced it. The feel of a spear in my hand.

'You are Arimnestos of Plataea?' he asked. 'By the gods!' he muttered. 'I'm a man who's been a slave his whole life, but you! A gent!'

'I've been a slave before,' I said.

'Ahh,' he said, and nodded again. 'Ahh . . . that's why you are alive.'

We ate better after that port. We were also a lighter ship by the weight of our Cyprian copper, and we had forty more rowers, fresher men who hadn't been abused. Indeed, there were too many for the oar-master to ruin them all at once, and we had easier lives for a week.

We rowed.

Not one man died that week. That's all I can say.

We made one more port call. None of us was allowed on the beach, and we picked up women – twenty women, all Keltoi with tattoos. They were filthy, hollow-eyed, and the first night at sea the oar-master discovered one was pregnant, and he killed her on the deck and threw her corpse over the side. I don't know why, even now.

The bully-boys forced the slave women every night. Sometimes these acts happened a few feet over my head. The despair, the sheer horror that those women experienced was somehow worse than any of the blows I had received because it was all so casual. They were used like . . . like old cloaks to keep off rain.

And none of us could do a thing.

Or perhaps what is worse is that we *could have* done something, if we had been willing to die. Die without revenge – die nameless, achieving nothing, our bodies dumped in the sea. That would have taken a special courage I didn't have. But it took yet more of my honour. I was a *slave*.

Then we turned south. I was moved to a stern oar on the top deck, and I, who feared no man in war, was terrified to be so close to the oar-master. Indeed, I was just a few steps from him at all times.

Luckily, he was mad. So mad, he'd forgotten me and the Illyrian both. He hated women – all women – far more than he hated us. So while I had to witness his brutal degradation of the slave women, I was merely beaten occasionally, as an afterthought. Tapped with his heavy stick when he was bored.

After some time – by Zeus the Saviour, I have no idea how far south we'd come – the oar-master cut the throats of a pair of the women in a sacrifice. He did it in the bow, and I never knew exactly what happened. But after that, the other women stopped being alive. That is to say, they were still warm and breathing, but they were dead inside. A few days later they started to die.

The trierarch simply let it happen.

Sometimes he reacted in anger and hit a slave, but mostly he just fingered his beard and watched the heavens. His two helmsmen said little.

From their stilted conversations, I gathered that we were on our way home, and that home was Carthage.

And I began to learn other things.

I was a good navigator – my best helmsman and friends had taught me well enough – but the Phoenicians have secrets about navigation, and they hold them close. They use stars and the sun. All of us do, but they do it with far more accuracy than we Greeks. Now, since Marathon, we've taken enough of their ships to enslave a generation of their navigators, and we have all their secrets, but back then there were still tricks we didn't know: the aiming stick for taking the height of a star, or the secrets of the Pleiades and the Little Bear. Ah – I see that the lad from Halicarnassus knows whereof I speak!

But the helmsmen and the trierarch were careless. They took their sun sights and their star sights a few feet from my silent back, and they discussed their sightings. Hamilcar, the younger helmsman, was obviously under instruction and very slow. I think – I will never know – that he was so deeply unhappy with the life he was living that his brain had shut down.

And Hasdrubal, the trierarch, used him as his scapegoat. Every wrong answer was punished with a blow. His every thought and opinion was ridiculed.

Another week at sea, and the new slaves began to be broken. Our rations were cut – I can't even remember why, just the satisfied voice of the oar-master telling us that we deserved it.

We rowed.

Another week.

But the navigational lessons at my back had begun to keep

me alive. They gave my brain something on which to seize. And Hamilcar's obstinate ignorance became my closest friend, because my understanding of the Phoenician tongue – bad to start with – became more proficient, and because Hamilcar needed everything repeated two or three times, three days in a row. Bless him.

One night, the sea grew rougher and the wind came from all directions, and after a while, rowing grew dangerous. A new slave below me lost the stroke, got his oar-handle in the teeth and died. His oar went mad, and other men were injured. None of us was very strong, and the sea was against us – and suddenly the bully-boys were afraid, and they showed their fear by beating us with sticks and spear butts.

The wind steadied down from the north, but it grew stronger and stronger.

We got our stern into the wind by more luck than skill, and suddenly, we had to row or die.

'Do you want to die, you scum!' roared the oar-master. He laughed and laughed. 'If you die, I die too!' he shouted. 'Here's your chance! Rebel, and we all go down to Hades together – you as slaves, and me as your master!'

The trierarch and the two helmsmen had three shouted conferences on the spray-blown deck that convinced me we were close to the coast of Africa – too damned close to be running before a north wind. But the oarsmen were badly trained and brutalized, and the officers were shit – pardon me, ladies – and the trierarch didn't have the balls to try anything. So on we rushed, the oars just touching the water to keep our stern into the wind.

After some time – it was dark, cold and wet and all I knew was the fire in my arms – one of the Keltoi women stepped over me and jumped over the side. I saw her face in a flash of lightning – she was Medea come to life. To me, that face is printed for ever on my thoughts the way a man writes on papyrus, or carves in stone. It was set with purpose – hate, determination, agony and even a tiny element of joy. She was gone before my heart beat again, sucked under by Poseidon. To a kinder place, I hope.

But something passed from her to me. Her courage, I think.

Right there, in the storm, I swore an oath to the gods.

And we rowed.

We took a lot of water, but we weren't lucky enough to sink. About a third of our oarsmen drowned or died under their oars, and yet somehow we made it. The bully-boys threw the corpses over the side, and cut the oars free, too. And on we went.

The morning dawned blue and gold, and we were alive.

After that, there was no food and only about eighty whole men to row, and we were on the deep blue. We rowed, and we rowed, and we rowed.

I should have been dead, or nearly dead. But the Keltoi slave woman had told me something with her eyes – I can hardly put this into words. That resistance was worthy. Perhaps, that I could always restore my dignity with death. Either way, I was coming to my senses.

And of course, my brain was engaged, too. I had taken to listening to the men at the steering oars, and now I was interested. Hasdrubal talked about the trade – about how the tin was no longer coming in from northern Illyria in the old amounts, and how the Greeks were trying to cut into the trade from Alba, and that interested me. He talked about new sources of copper down the coast of Africa and up the coast of Iberia, outside the Gates of Herakles, and I discovered, from listening to him, that Africa was much bigger than I had imagined.

I had no cross-staff with which to try calculations, but I used my fingers. Star lessons happened at night, just a horse-length at my back. I was careful, but I tried their sightings as I got the hang of their method.

It worked.

Mind you, it wasn't that I'd ever needed to do such esoteric navigation, and if Hasdrubal hadn't been such a poor sailor, neither would he! He was a fine navigator, but a dreadful sailor. We always knew where we were, but we never seemed to be able to move from where we were to where we needed to be. And a big trireme – even a twenty-oared boat – can't hold enough food to feed its oarsmen for even a few days and nights. This is why all ships coast – they go from beach to beach, buying food from locals, whether they are a tubby merchantman with four oarsmen and a dozen sailors to a fleet of warships with two hundred oarsmen apiece – the ironclad rules of *logistika* are the same either way.

But I digress.

After some more time – I have no idea how long – we came to Carthage. I'll tell you about Carthage in good time, but when I first rowed that ship in between the fortress and the mole, I saw nothing.

I was not really alive. I was a human machine that pulled an oar, silent, unthinking, at least by day.

The hull bumped the wharf.

The trierarch had the gangplank rigged, and then he, his two helmsmen and the oar-master walked off the ship. An hour later, after we'd grilled in the African sun, twenty soldiers – *Poieni*, which is their word for citizen infantry, like our hoplites – came to the ship and ordered us off. Many of us could not walk.

The phylarch shook his head. 'Useless fuck. These men are ruined.' He spat. Came and looked at me. He pointed at my legs.

My once-mighty legs were like sticks.

'Look at this one,' he said. 'Good-size man. Filthy, lice, and hasn't been allowed exercise.' He shook his head. 'Hasdrubal is a useless fool. Sell this lot to anyone who will take them.'

And with that, he took the surviving women and marched them away. That left another man in charge, and he averted his eyes and his nose and ordered those of us who could walk to carry the rest. I ended up carrying the Illyrian. I have been back to that spot – we only walked about fifty horse-lengths. Less than a stade.

I remember it as being more like fifty stades. It went on for ever. Oddly, they never struck us, and one of the Poieni asked us why we were so silent.

No one spoke.

We were put in stone slave pens with a roof and shade. There was water in which to bathe, drinking water and a shit-hole. I saw men break there – men who had been free and were now slaves.

But for us, fresh from Hasdrubal's grim trireme, it was like the Elysian Fields. We had barley porridge for dinner and again at breakfast, and red wine so thin it was like water. It made me drunk, so I laughed and sang the Paean of Apollo. I was the first to give way to sound. After a second helping of that awful wine, a dozen men were grunting at my song. Or my attempt at song.

We passed out. But in the morning, I found that the Illyrian was curled tight against me, and the Greek, Nestor, was lying against the wall with the Thracian.

Nestor looked me in the eye. 'We lived,' he said quietly.

The Thracian grunted.

'Now,' I said, 'we need to get free.'

Both men nodded.

And the Illyrian stiffened. *'Eleuthera,'* he said. Freedom.
Free. That's what we thought.

2

My Illyrian's name was Neoptolymos. He considered himself a direct descendant of Achilles, and he was willing to kill every man who had even *seen* him enslaved. His humiliation had *almost* broken him. But after two days in Carthage, he joined me for my morning prayer to Apollo – in awful Greek – and we began to talk.

We were allowed to talk, in Carthage. Talk, and eat. They fattened us up for about a week. We got cheap pork sausage with bread in it and green stuff – I still hate cheap pork sausage. They gave it to us three times a day, and took us out in a tiny yard for exercise, where we had to leap and jump and do foolish antics – stupid stuff that any gymnasium would have frowned on.

I knew how to condition myself, so I did proper exercises whenever I could, and taught them to my companions. The guards didn't care.

A little at a time, I put some of the moves of *pankration* into my callisthenics. They gave me weights. I boxed with my shadow. The guards took an interest, but not much of one, and it was a small rebellion – the kind that means a great deal to the morale of a slave.

And that was a good thing, because eight days after we landed, Dagon came into our exercise yard and ordered us to be marched to a ship.

It still seems incredible to me that we could have gotten him again. Perhaps his deep – well, I'll call it a sickness for lack of a better word, though I think he was cursed by the gods for something – at any rate, his sickness drove him to want to torment us. Again. It's the only rational explanation why he, an officer, wanted the same broken men he'd just brought in.

We were marched through the streets, surrounded by guards.

Dagon took all eighty of the survivors, and we were added to a hundred fresh slaves – Sikels, recently taken in war, who spoke little Greek and had never pulled an oar.

As we walked through the darkened streets of Carthage, Dagon walked by me. He didn't say anything at all. He just smiled at me, and rubbed the butt of his thonged whip against my thighs and arse like a caress. Still makes me shudder.

And then he hit me with the whip – the butt, not the thongs – across the temple.

And when I kept pace and didn't scream, he laughed.

I think the Sikels saved my life. Because they were so bloody awful that Dagon never had a chance at me those first two weeks at sea. He beat them raw, and they still couldn't – and wouldn't – row. He killed a pair who he said were fomenting mutiny, and they killed one of his bully-boys in the dark.

We were ten days out, somewhere on the deep blue north of Africa and south of Sicily, and the sun was a relentless foe, an *aspis* of fire slamming into our heads and backs. The ship stank of excrement and sweat and fear. The masts were stowed, there wasn't a breath of wind and sweat ran straight down my chest and into my groin to drip onto the man below – I say below, because after eight days at sea, I was a top-deck oar.

We all knew that Kritias was dead and over the side, slain in the dark, and the Sikels were waiting to see what Dagon would do.

As luck would have it, I was across the bench from Neoptolymos, who was on the port side while I was on the starboard. Skethes and Nestor – both, by the standards of our new ship, the *Baal Shamra*, expert oarsmen – sat several benches behind us, but together. I'd managed to exchange a long look with Skethes. Slaves can communicate a great deal in a look. And we'd learned to tap on the wood of our benches. We had a few rhythms – nothing like communication, but it could convey simple messages. My look said: 'I'm alert and ready'. His said: 'Me too'. My taps said: 'Be ready'.

Watch your slaves sometime, honey. They have many ways to communicate.

We pulled. The rowers were tired, but not exhausted, and we hadn't been fed. I had a feeling that the bullies were arming in the stern behind me, although I couldn't see them.

And then Dagon was standing beside me. He was in bronze – a

good breastplate, a heavy helmet. He put the point of a spear at my back. It was very sharp.

'I don't want you to die easily, lover,' he said with his usual smile. 'But if you move, I kill you.'

Suddenly, there were screams.

The Sikels rose off their benches.

And died.

Seven men in armour were more than a match for seventy naked, tired men without even the shafts of their oars. I know. I've done it myself.

The Sikels fought hard for a few minutes, while we, on the upper tier, sat silently. Dagon was behind me and above me on the catwalk – there was no combination of moves that would allow me to rise off my bench and trip him. I considered it, anyway.

If the Sikels failed, I knew my life would become much, much worse, because Dagon would have no distraction from me. And because eighty of us – his 'survivors' – would have to row the pig of the ship, laden with African iron ore.

About the time the Sikels began to give way to despair, I decided that my life wasn't worth an obol. I thought of the Keltoi woman. There just comes a point where either you submit and become an object, not a person, or you break and go mad. Or you fight.

Or die. Or both.

I gave a great shout. Sometimes, sound can throw a man off. And I turned, trying to get an arm behind me to block his thrust.

Warned by my shout, Neoptolymos came off his bench and went for Dagon's ankles.

As slave attacks went, it was a fine attempt. But Dagon foiled it by the simple expedient of stepping back. Then he whirled, ignoring us, and stabbed Skethes, his point in and out of the Thracian's eye socket in a heartbeat. The Thracian fell forward, dead, his blood running out of his eye in a steady stream like wine from a wineskin.

Nestor didn't rise off his bench. Instead, he kicked. It was a remarkable kick – I was around by then, fouled by the two useless slaves behind me who were cowering instead of helping. But the kick caught Dagon in the arse and he stumbled, and I was on him.

I was in bad shape – tired, arms weak, far from my conditioning as a smith or a warrior. And he was in armour.

And as soon as I had one of his arms, I found out just how skilled he was. He broke my armlock and countered it: in three beats of my heart, he had my left arm in a lock and had begun to dislocate my left shoulder.

The *daimon* of combat flew to my aid. I put the crown of my head into his jutting jaw – he had a helmet on, but the cheek plates didn't break the force of my blow. Where a man's head moves his body follows, and I moved him off his feet and Nestor sank his teeth into the hated man's thigh.

But he wriggled like a worm, caught me a blow to my head with his right elbow, slammed the shaft of his spear into Nestor and he was away from us – back three steps. If even one oarsman had aided us—

But none did.

He grinned. 'I knew you'd try, lover,' he said, in Phoenician. 'I'd have thought less of you, if you hadn't.'

And then – only then – did we all notice that another ship was coming alongside, up from our stern. She was a beautiful low trireme, her hull black with new pitch, with a long line of woad-blue painted down her side along the upper-deck oar-ports and eyes over her ram. Her oars were beautifully handled.

The oars came in, all together, even as we watched. I backed up two steps, looking for *anything* to use as a weapon. A boarding pike, a staff for poling off another ship, a stick—

What I got was a bucket.

A wooden bucket.

And the other ship was boarding us.

Her marines came at us – ten men in bronze, with aspides and fighting spears and greaves. They leaped onto our catwalk and our stern like experts, and I retreated to the bow, looking for a place to hide – I didn't want to die at the hands of Greeks. I didn't know what they intended, but I assumed they were Greek pirates – men of my own kind – who would at least take me as a slave.

Their lord – it was obvious, from the rope of lapis and gold beads at his throat to the solid-gold hilt on his sword – shouted at Dagon.

And Dagon nodded and grinned. 'My slaves,' he shouted. 'They rose against me. Thank the gods, lord, for your rescue!'

The Greek lord – I now knew he was Greek by the long hair emerging from under his helmet to the shape of his feet – laughed. 'I hate you Phoenicians like I hate poverty and fear,' he said. 'But we are at peace.' He grinned wolfishly, turned to his marines and pointed his spear.

'Clear away the riff-raff,' he said.

Nestor grabbed his knees. 'We're Greek!' he said. 'Master, this man—'

The Greek put his sword into Nestor. 'Tell them in Carthage of the service I do for you,' he said, and his men set about killing the Sikels.

Two men chased me into the bows, where I turned at bay.

I put the bucket into the helmet of the first to reach me, swinging it at the end of its rope handle, and he fell without a sound.

The other man stepped back and yelled for help.

Just for a moment, I felt as if I were Arimnestos. I stepped forward, and he stepped back.

And then Dagon came up. He had an aspis on his shoulder, and his spear licked out and caught me in the meat of the thigh, quick as thought. Ares, that wound hurt, and I stumbled.

He stepped back, laughed and spiked my other thigh.

I fell to my knees.

As fast as I can tell it, he put his fine spear point through both of my hands, so that I dropped the bucket and waited for death.

He laughed.

'You think I'm going to kill you?' he asked.

He didn't kill me, obviously. What he did do was to help the Greeks kill all of the Sikels on board. Then he bartered half his cargo of iron ore for twenty of the Greeks' rowers – men of a race I didn't know at all.

I wasn't paying very close attention by then, because he had me crucified on the foremast and spar, my arms and legs lashed far apart. The pain of my wounds was enough to make me puke.

Unfortunately, it was still early morning and the sun rose, higher and higher, as the slaves rowed us towards the shore. From my new vantage point I could see the land – a low smudge to the north. Sicily.

We rowed. Or rather, I bled and burned, naked in the sun, and the men beneath me rowed, and the corpses of the Sikels stank. Dagon wouldn't let the slaves throw them over the side. He insisted on leaving the dead men at their benches. He trod the catwalk, muttering and laughing, and from time to time he would come up behind me – remember, I was crucified and couldn't see him – and he'd strike me with his staff. Or place the butt of it against my back or my stomach and just rub it up and down.

'We will have such fun,' he said. He used a pleasant tone, as a man might talk to his wife, and it made my skin crawl. Even in exhausted despair – his tone made me afraid.

But the sun was worse than the mad oar-master. The sun scorched me. I had never been exposed without water to the sun all day, and it stripped me of everything except the desire for water.

And that was only the first day.

Night fell, and I awoke. I hadn't been aware that I had passed out – who is? But I came to hanging from my wrists, and the pressure on my abdomen and lungs was uncomfortable, and the sunburn on my stomach and groin was painful, and the wounds in my thighs and hands. Ares, it all hurt.

We were riding at anchor in a great bay under a vast mountain – Aetna, I know now. Even in the state I was in, I looked long at Aetna in the full moon and it was beautiful. And I prayed to the gods that someone would avenge me. I managed to pray for Nestor and Skethes, good companions who had died trying to be free. I had no idea what had happened to Neoptolymos.

The Greek ship was ten horse-lengths astern of ours. I didn't see it for a long time, until the tide moved us at our anchor and I caught a glimpse of her.

I began to pass in and out of life. I cannot describe it any other way. My life unrolled before me as if I were facing a jury of gods, except that there were no voices, no figures, but merely the strongest feeling, every time I surfaced to pain and the real world, that I had been judged.

And then it was morning.

Dagon came and stood in the bows, and another voice called orders as the rowers awoke to the stink of the corpses. Seabirds came and tried the corpses – a great gull ripping at a dead man's face can interfere with anyone's rowing.

The bully-boys used their canes freely.

The ship moved, and we went inshore.

There was a breakwater, well to the west along the great bay, and we pointed our bow at it. The sun crested the horizon, and my torment began in earnest. Now the weight of my body was on my abdomen. My feet couldn't really support my weight any longer. And breathing started to become difficult. Not really difficult, but painful. There was another body pressing against mine, at my back – it took me hours to realize that Neoptolymos was crucified against me.

'They say that if you survive three days,' Dagon said, 'your chest and back are so ruined you can never be a man again.' Dagon raised his face and looked at me. 'And then I can sell you to a brothel. You won't even be able to fight a brutal client. Isn't that what you deserve, eh?'

I could feel it happening, that was the worst of it. I could feel my muscles dying. The strain was gradual, but the result was brutal.

And the sun—

By noon, we were up with the breakwater, and our charnel-house ship entered the harbour and very, very slowly docked at the pier – a well-built stone pier.

The Greek ship came and anchored close in, almost across our stern.

I could no longer speak. I may well have done some screaming, in there somewhere, but by this point I couldn't even thrash in my bonds, and from time to time I'd make an effort and raise myself on my ankle ropes, just to get the pressure off my wrists and my lungs, and for a few brief moments I would have some clarity and then, gradually, I would collapse again.

I assumed Neoptolymos was dead.

One time, Brassos, one of the bullies, watched me raise myself and then slammed his spear shaft into my groin. I collapsed onto my bonds and choked.

Dagon struck the man. 'He could die of your carelessness,' Dagon said.

When I had the ability to use my head, I prayed to Apollo, to Herakles my ancestor and to Poseidon for release.

Just after the sun reached his awful height, men came and began to unload the iron ore from the ship. Then the slaves were taken out of their benches, with twenty guards watching them, and they were put ashore, three at a time, and tied with heavy ropes inside a palisade.

After some time – I cannot remember any of it – I was cut down.

The relief was indescribable. The first moments off the great X of the mast and its yard were like water for a parched man. Like the release of sex.

They tied me to a log and left me in the shade of a linen sail and, after some time, Dagon came. He had Nestor.

Nestor was still alive.

Dagon had the wounded man's litter left under my awning. And he had slaves fill a bronze cauldron with water. They left it next to Nestor, who was in such pain from a mortal wound in the guts that all he did was writhe and scream.

'Enjoy your time together,' Dagon said, and giggled. He put a hand on my shoulder while Nestor gurgled.

'I would love to spend the evening with you,' he said, 'but I have some foolish Greeks to fleece. And then, when I have made a fortune from their idiocy, I will have time for you.' He giggled again, and his touch burned me.

And then he went away.

I would have slept, but Nestor was in pain, and dying. Horribly.

I'd like to say we talked, or resolved to die together, but he was already gone with pain, and he simply lay and moaned and screamed, and I watched him die. I even slept a little.

In the night, he breathed in hard, his throat closed, he coughed and he was dead.

Just before the sun rose, there were screams. The sound of them scarcely registered with me. Had I understood them, I would have despaired. Hah! As if I had not already despaired.

Dagon had invited the Greeks to dinner.

And murdered them.

That was the way he thanked them for saving him.

Dawn rose, and the bully-boys were carrying corpses down the beach, throwing them into the waves.

I recognized the Greek lord from his long blond hair. His throat was slit, his genitals cut away.

A while later, a pair of men came and dragged me down the wharf to the ship and tied me to the foremast again.

The sun began to rise as overseers drove the slaves back onto the ship – a hundred men to row a trireme. The Greek ship's oarsmen had spent the night aboard, and my first hint of what had happened was that Dagon and seven of his men were rowing a small boat out to the Greek ship – which was Greek no more.

Screams. Curses. Blows and spear-thrusts. The music of Dagon. How they must have cursed to find him their master. Many of the Greek rowers would have been free men – up until then.

We had Brassos as both trierarch and oar-master. He had most of the old deck crew as 'marines' in the looted armour of the dead Greeks, and he had a whip. In an hour, we were out of the harbour and our bow was pointed towards Carthage. The swift trireme ran ahead of us, out to the horizon, and stayed there, a notch on the edge of my world. My eyes grew sun-dazzled, and I lost the ability to see, or to make sense of the world around me.

The slaves who had tied me to the mast were lazy. They had left me a great deal more slack for my body, so that I could writhe and change positions in subtle ways. Had it been the first day of cruci-fixion, it might have saved me. As it was, it prolonged the agony. And they tied Neoptolymos behind me, but his bands were slack too.

By noon, I cannot pretend I was any longer an observer. I was there, but I was unaware of anything that happened.

And then, out of a clear, hot day, a storm struck us. It caught our ship utterly unprepared, so I'll assume it was what sailors call a white squall – a small, vicious burst of wind and rain, usually confined to a few stades, and often so pale in colour that on a hot day it's virtually invisible until it hits you.

I awoke to the rain, and I was moving – back and forth – through wild swings, because I was well up the foremast, and every pitch of the ship beneath me moved my body through fifty degrees of an arc. At the ends of the pitch, my bonds took enormous strain, but in the middle I got a rest, the odd pitching motion taking all the weight off my hands and feet.

It was a miracle. I swear that Poseidon sent it to me. Rain lashed me, as hard as I have ever known, and it flowed into my mouth so fast I might have drowned, and I drank it all. And the pitching ship delivered me from pain, here and there.

And then – hope.

The strain on my bonds was loosening the hastily tied ropes. They began to grow looser with every pitch and roll of the ship beneath me.

I was going to fall into the sea.

And drown.

I realize that what I am about to say will strain your credulity, my friends, but I didn't fear drowning. Poseidon had so palpably sent the storm to save me, that I had to assume that falling into the sea was the very best thing for me.

And I confess that I thought of the Keltoi woman jumping into the storm, and I thought that it might not be the worst way to die. My body would, at any rate, be safe from insult.

The storm reached a pitch of frenzy like the dance of the Bacchae, and the wind screamed through the ship's standing rigging and the boatsail mast whipped through its arc. I could feel the ties on my ankles going, and to my horror, they went first, and suddenly I was hanging from my wrists. Pain flooded me.

Then the ropes gave way.

Not on my ankles.

But the cross of ropes that kept the yard on the mast.

The yard fell to the deck, but the deck was heeled well over, and while one end of the spar struck the bow, the other fell across the ram, and suddenly Neoptolymos and I were catapulted into the raging sea.

We went deep.

My arms were still tied to the spar, and I writhed in agony as the salt water hit my wounds, and that burst ripped one arm – my right – free of my bonds.

Then the yard shot to the surface, the light wood all but leaping clear of the water.

The water was deep and cold. The pain of my salt-washed wounds was almost pleasant. I fought the storm for dear life, using my wounded left arm to push myself above the spar and drink air out of the spume at the wave's top.

Even that fight became routine. It went on and on, and my left shoulder began to fail, and I assumed I would die.

But Neoptolymos had more left in him than I, and he pinned my shoulder to the spar in a clamp of iron. He saved me.

And then the storm abated, sailing by as quickly as it had overtaken us. The tone of the roar went down, the rhythm of the waves changed and the sky lightened. The thunder strokes came slower and slower.

I had time to think that it was like the end of a fight, or a battle, when men come apart, out of the rage of Ares, and the sound of spear on shield comes less and less frequently. I know it well.

Before I could think another thought, or pray to Poseidon, we were alone on the Great Blue, our hands linked to a wooden spar. The sun pounded us, and the sea calmed, and we were alone.

3

We were only a few stades from the coast – indeed, as soon as the clouds blew past, I could see Aetna, the beach and trees to the south. I think I might have swum to shore.

But it was not to be. A coaster – a small ship with one mast and a few oarsmen – came out of the storm, throwing a fine bow wave. She was well handled, cutting slantwise across the wind, tacking back and forth in the straits.

A lookout must have spotted us. I was facing the other way and missed all this. Neoptolymos grunted once or twice, but I don't think he was fully alive at that point, and both of us were parched.

Perhaps I baked for fifteen minutes in the sun, and then I was shocked to hear a hail, and the coaster was a stade away. It was as if a sea monster had surfaced by my side.

The boat dropped its scrap of sail – the breeze was still stiff – and four oarsmen pulled towards me, almost into the eye of the wind, moving the little ship. I paddled weakly towards them.

They pulled me aboard. They spoke Greek, in a way, more like trade lingo. I assumed they were Sikels, and I was right. The leader – trierarch seems too grand a term for a forty-five-foot trading boat – ran his hands over my injuries, gave me a hard smile and nodded to another, younger man who had to be his younger brother. Then he turned to Neoptolymos.

After the sort of examination a man gives to a ram he's buying in the agora, the two Sikels spoke to each other. The older man's name was Hektor. Even here, among barbarians, the poet's work lived. That gave me a ray of hope.

The ray of hope lasted until we found ourselves assigned to oars. The shackles were more figurative than real, but it was clear that I was rowing for my food, at least. Since I could barely speak with any of the men on board, I assumed I was a slave. Again. I was with two men with heavy, hooked noses and deep-set eyes, and two men who were as black as any men I'd ever seen, and Neoptolymos.

On a positive note, we were not forbidden to talk, and as soon as we'd rowed the ship around the headland, the work of an hour, the nearer African smiled at me. 'Doola,' he said. I took it for his name.

'Arimnestos,' I said. I tapped my chest.

'Ari?' Doola asked.

Close enough.

I nodded.

The younger African tapped his chest. 'Seckla!' he said sharply.

'Ari,' I said again.

You get the picture.

The other two men were not Phoenicians, although they looked the part, nor were they Sikels or Hebrews or anything I knew. They didn't speak much. But within a few hours, I knew that the ruddy-haired man was Gaius and the dark-haired one was Daud, and that they didn't really share a language, either. They just looked as if they did. In fact, I'll save time and say that Gaius was Etruscan and Daud was all Keltoi, from northern Gallia, and spoke a few words of Greek and a few more of Sikel and no other tongue but his own.

It is amazing how much information you can convey without many words. And it is perhaps a comment on my former servitude how happy I was on that boat. The food was good, mostly grilled fish. We had wine every night. The Sikels treated us as – well, more as employees than slaves, and I never was entirely sure as to my status. We moved from small port to small port – really, just a stone house and some wattle huts on a headland with a beach. We rowed past the Greek towns and their temples and familiar smells. We sailed past the Carthaginian towns and well out to sea, and it occurred to me that my new hosts feared the Carthaginians far more than they feared the Greeks, the Italiotes or the Etruscans.

Mostly, we loaded dry fish and sold metal. Every town had a small forge and a bronze-smith, and our ingots of copper and tin were their life's blood. I was shocked when I finally understood the price of tin. It was absurdly high, and I thought of my time as a smith on Crete – about as far from the tin mines of northern Illyria as a man can be, and still be in the world – and wondered. What had happened? Tin hadn't ever been that high.

You cannot make bronze without tin. And the tin has to be high quality. You don't need to add much tin to the copper to make bronze – a little more than one to twenty. But without tin, all you have is soft copper, whether you are making cook pots or helmets.

So an increase in the price of tin – affected everyone.

Neoptolymos was the only man to whom I could really talk. As I recovered a little, so did he, and I went back to work on his Greek. He was sullen, and it was only then that I began to understand the depth of his betrayal. The man I had heard mentioned on the beach – Epidavros – was his uncle. Neoptolymos didn't need me to tell him who had sold him to the Carthaginians. He already knew. He chewed on his desire for revenge every minute. Illyrians are good haters, and in this case, I think his need for revenge kept him alive.

Mind you, I thought of Dagon constantly. I hated him: I wanted to torture him to death, and I knew, in my heart, that I was afraid of him. This had not happened to me before, and the sensation was like the ache of a tooth. I had to probe it with my tongue.

A week passed, and another. We were not shackled or roped at night. I began to prowl the encampment when the boat was beached, testing the boundaries. We were well along the west coast of Sicily – I have no notion greater than that – in a town that had several stone houses with tile roofs, and I had been a rower for perhaps three weeks when I walked boldly down the beach away from the encampment and into the streets of the town. I made it to their very small agora just before dark, and there was the younger brother, sitting on a blanket, with various ingots of Cyprian copper and a few knucklebones of tin – clearly not Illyrian tin, let me add, because that comes in plainer ingots.

Hektor's brother rose from his blanket, walked over to me and put a hand on my arm. But there wasn't any threat.

I shrugged. 'I want to see the town,' I said in Greek.

He shrugged and let go my arm.

I walked about. In truth, they were subsistence farmers with no temple and very little to see – a pair of stone statues that were really just phallic pillars. A bronze brooch was the town's chief adornment for a woman, and only one man wore a sword, and it was more like a dagger.

In the days of my lordship, I'd have walked past them all like a king. As a semi-slave rower, I found the town fascinating. Or rather, a welcome break.

In a very few minutes, I was back in the small agora, and Hektor's brother met me, led me to the blanket and offered me a cup of wine. So I sat with him. Drank his wine. And, with a smile, got up and walked back down to the boat. I still didn't know his name, because his brother never used it.

It may seem odd to you, thugater, but I was not unhappy. My body was healing, and no one was unfriendly. Doola and I were becoming comrades. I learned some of his words – I still remember that *nitaka* means 'I want'. He learned more of mine. Enough words that when I came back from my wander – he had been sleeping – he rose, threw a *chiton* over his nudity and sat with me.

'Was it good?' he asked. Let me just say that there were grunts, gestures and incomprehensible words interspersed with our very small shared vocabulary. I'll leave that out.

'Not bad,' I said, and shrugged. 'Hektor's brother gave me wine.'

'He's not bad,' Doola agreed.

We sat in companionable silence until Hektor himself joined us. He lay down. He was a very big man – a head taller than me – and handsome. He had a small amphora and a *mastos* cup, and he poured a libation. Doola and I both raised our hands in the universal sign of prayer to the gods, and he grinned. He said some words. Then he drank from the cup and passed it. After a while a small boy, I think Hektor's son, came and brought small fish fried in olive oil. Neoptolymos joined us and ate the fish with the closest thing to a smile I'd seen from him. We ate them, got greasy, drank the wine. One by one the other rowers came, and then the rest of Hektor's deck crew – all relatives, I guess.

I still think they had made a profit. It was a good little party.

So the next morning, when the boat rowed away, I was at my bench. I was happy enough.

That's the best evening I remember. I can't say exactly how long I rowed for the Sikels. At least a month, and perhaps longer. But sometime after that, on a clear day, we saw a trireme hull up to the north, and the Sikels spoke in agitated tones, and we turned south and ran downwind. The two brothers argued, and I will assume that the younger was in favour of maintaining our course to the west and appearing unfazed, while the older was in favor of running immediately and gaining sea room.

We ran south across a darkening sea, and as the wind grew less and less, we went to the oars and pulled. Hektor began to cheat the helm more and more west of south.

But the black trireme was on us.

I rowed looking over my shoulder. I'd been the hunter a hundred times. I'd snapped up coasters just like this one – sometimes three and four at a time. I knew in an hour that the trireme had us.

So did Hektor.

He gathered his family in the stern. I couldn't hear them, or understand them. But they didn't shout, and they took weapons. They had a look about them that I know too well. They weren't planning to resist because they believed they could win. They were resisting so they would die with honour.

The youngest boy smiled and kissed his father and uncles and brothers and then jumped into the sea just before the trireme came alongside, and drowned. Just like that.

Hektor was a giant, a fine figure of a man, but he was no fighter, and the marines from the black hull knew their business. He inflicted no wounds. They spitted him on a spear. He screamed a few times, until one of the marines hit him with the hilt of his *kopis* the way a fisherman whacks a fish to kill it. Hektor died.

The other Sikels fought, but they didn't fight well. Two were wounded. But Hektor's brother and the rest were taken.

They looted the boat, and then they took us aboard. In less time than it takes to tell it, I was a slave rower. Again. On a Carthaginian military trireme.

I know you think I should have risen from my bench with Doola and perhaps Seckla and killed all the marines. But my body was far from healed – healed for fighting, I mean – and I had neither weapon nor armour, and they had everything. I considered fighting. I wondered, almost idly, if I had learned cowardice at last. Doola and I certainly exchanged a look, in the last few moments before the marines came aboard. Neoptolymos grunted once, in real agitation. He wanted to fight, but he looked for my lead.

Well, I'd led once before, and failed.

If Hektor had armed us—

I'd be dead. So there. Poseidon frowned, and smiled too. I went to a bench, and I had Doola and Seckla at arm's length, and Hektor's brother below me, Neoptolymos a dozen benches ahead of us.

The trireme was called the *Sea Sister* in Phoenician. I didn't know a man aboard, but in an hour I knew that the trierarch was a capable man with an expert set of officers. Nor were the rowers slaves. This was a military ship, run for a profit by means of piracy. We preyed on the Sikels and the Etruscans, too, as well as the Greeks of Magna Greca. In my first week aboard we took six ships – none much larger than the coaster on which I'd served. Ours was the only one that resisted, and for several weeks they treated us with care, keeping us at arm's length when we were fed. Wine was rare, and meant we were in for a fight. But at the end of the fifth week, we pulled into Laroussa, a Carthaginian port on Sicily, and the rowers were marched down the wharf from the ship to a barracks – and paid.

I almost expired from shock. I had assumed I was a slave. The *Sea Sister* was run in Phoenician, of course, and I spoke a little and understood more; and most of the officers spoke enough Greek to be understood. None had bothered to suggest to me that I was *not* a slave. But in the barracks, I was shown a bed and handed a little less than sixty drachmas.

Doola and I had managed to expand our shared vocabulary, although, to be honest, we spoke neither Greek nor Numidian, but our own language. Now that we were in barracks, though, I found that there were a dozen more Greeks in our crew and they knew the town and the drill.

'We're not slaves,' said an Athenian guttersnipe named Aristocles. 'But we have very limited rights. You can go to the whorehouses or the agora or the wine shops. You cannot leave town. You cannot refuse to row.' He shrugged. 'It is like being a slave with some privileges.' He grinned, showing me all ten of his teeth. 'You look like a gent,' he said. 'Want to share a ride?'

He meant share a *porne* at the brothel, and I didn't really fancy that, but I bought a pitcher of wine and fruit juice on ice – extravagant aristocrat that I was – and a dozen of us drank it in a taverna that smelled like old octopus. Then we ate a huge meal.

The whores came around when the serious drinking started. They didn't want sex – the ideal customer paid and passed out. But I hadn't even talked to a woman in months, and my body felt better – the soreness in my side and my shoulders was a little less every morning, and the wounds from Dagon's spear were healed. I wanted one of them. So I talked, chatted, flirted.

For my pains, I ended up riding one of the older women – she seemed quite old to me – a near-hag of thirty. She had beautiful hair and some teeth and a deep tan and a ready laugh, and she was the only one of the porne who had much of a smile. We drank wine afterwards, and she sat with me, a hand on my arm, for the rest of the evening, and we had another ride after dark. Of course I paid. Porne don't ride for free, and men who say so lie. But she liked me well enough, and I her. Her name was Lin, or enough. She was a Sikel.

I went from mourning Euphoria to riding an old prostitute. Yes. I was alive.

We were on shore a little less than a week. The *Sea Sister* was provisioned for sea again, and an officer came and fetched us. We each got a few coins for signing on – not that we had any choice – and in an hour the shore was a dream and Lin's body was a mirage, and I was rowing.

This time, we went north along the coast of Sardinia, and the sea was empty. The officers were cautious about our landing beaches. Then we turned east into the setting sun and sailed on the ocean's wind. On the second day, we picked up a small coaster. The crew fought. Two of our marines were killed and the crew of the coaster all suicided, the survivors diving in armour into the sea.

Carthage had a terrible reputation, in those days. A lot of what happened came from the way they treated slaves. The *Sea Sister* was an exception, but our victims had no way of knowing that. Most Carthaginians, sea officers or lubbers, treated slaves as an expendable resource. Always more where this one came from, whether this one was a skilled rower or a fine mosaicist or an ignorant yokel.

But I digress.

Later that afternoon, we found out why the coaster had fought so hard. Out of the afternoon haze came her consort, a heavy Etruscan trireme. She was ready to fight, and so were we, and our trierarch turned into the wind, dropped his boatsail and we took the oars in our hands.

The trierarchs gave us a short speech. My Phoenician was up to it, so I could tell that he promised all the rowers a share if we won. I passed that on to Seckla and Doola and Neoptolymos and Hektor's brother.

I was on the top deck, and I knew the business. We went for a straight head-to-head ram, the helmsman watching the enemy ship like a cat watches a mouse's hole.

'Oars in!' he shouted, when we were half a stadion from our enemy, the two ships hurtling together with the speed of two galloping horses.

All our oars came in. On the top deck it was easy, but the lower decks needed time to get the oars across – at the bow and stern, the rowers had to cooperate, putting the blades out through the opposite oar-port. But we were a good crew.

So were the Etruscans.

We hit, not ram to ram but cathead to cathead, and our forward-row gallery took the blow of theirs and both splintered, and men screamed as their bodies were ground to bloody pulp between the uncaring masses of the two ships. All the momentum came off both ships, and we coasted to a near stop, broadside to broadside, the height of a tall man apart.

Our archers began to shoot into their command deck, and their archers did the same, and then the grapnels flew. Indeed, both sides had decided to fight it out.

Men are foolish animals. No one needed to die. I don't think there was a man on either ship who stood to gain much from victory. This wasn't a struggle for freedom or domination, except at the lowest level. This wasn't Lade or Marathon. This was more like two travellers wrestling at a crossroads, with no spectators.

But there was no less ferocity for all that.

Their marines came at us first. They wore full panoply and they were men who knew their business, and I thought, as a spectator, that they were better men than ours. And we were short by two men of our complement, and when each side has only a dozen armoured warriors, the loss of two is sufficient to swing a contest.

It was odd to sit and watch a deadly fight. One Etruscan went down immediately. A lucky shot from a boarding pike sent him over the side, where he sank without a trace. But our captain took his death wound in the very next fight – a moment's inattention, a mistake by the man at his side and he was spouting blood. They dragged his bleeding body clear of the fight and dropped him near the stern, and then the melee grew desperate – the Carthaginians knew that they were losing, and the Etruscans knew they were close to winning.

The Etruscans pushed our marines relentlessly down the central gangway – a catwalk that was at the height of our heads and open to the weather. Our ship wasn't covered with a solid deck, as some of the newest ships are today, so we could watch the whole fight.

The helmsman led a counter-attack from the stern, and his spear put down an Etruscan marine who fell across the catwalk about even with Doola's bench, one forward from mine. His spear snapped, and he plucked an axe from behind his shield and spiked a second Etruscan in the temple. One of the Carthaginians at his side took a spear in the thigh at the same moment, and the two men fell in a tangle, right onto my bench. And the fight locked up – the catwalk could just fit two men wide, and there they were, like two teams pushing against each other at an athletic contest.

The dying Etruscan was in my lap, bleeding on me. And shitting on me, as well. His sword clattered at my feet out of his dead hand, and lay in a pool of his own blood on the boards where I rested my feet to row.

I had the strangest thoughts. And a great deal of time seemed to pass while I had them, all between one drip of blood from the corpse and another. Just for a few beats of my heart, I think that I saw the world as Heraclitus saw it. It seemed to me, and it still does, as one of the pivotal moments of my life.

The sword lay at my feet, beckoning me. Indeed, it all but called out to me.

I looked at it. But I didn't take it, because I had a thousand conflicting thoughts in an instant.

It seemed to me that I was four feet lower than any opponent, and that after I cut the ankles of one or two men, I'd be skewered, shieldless, like a dog in a pit.

It seemed to me that I owed Carthage nothing.

I looked at the Carthaginian marines fighting – literally at my head – and I felt no kinship. No brotherhood. They paid, and I rowed, and I was not free to leave. Had Hektor been captain, had the crew been Sikels, I might have felt a bond.

And the man lying across my lap *looked* Greek. He smelled of coriander, his skin was brown and tanned and his eyes were like my eyes, and his armour – a handsome bronze thorax, a beautiful Corinthian helmet with plumes and a crest of red horsehair – was Greek armour. I didn't feel the least inclination to risk my skin to help the barbarian Carthaginians fight – and win – against the barbarian Etruscans who at least looked Greek.

And yet another voice urged me to take up the sword.

Because with it in my hand, I was a different man. A free man. The master of my own destiny.

And then came a moment of superb, crystalline clarity. It was absurd.

I – a slave, or near enough – held the key to the fight. If I rose from my bench, sword in hand, the side I backed would triumph. I saw this as if it were written in carved letters on stone.

I, an unarmed slave, held the fate of twenty armoured men and four hundred rowers in my sword hand. Not because I was a great fighter. Not because I was Arimnestos of Plataea. But because I was in the right place, at the right moment of time, and a sword had fallen at my feet.

And I thought, this is how all the world is, in every minute, in every heartbeat in which every human makes any decision. This is the river into which Heraclitus said we could not twice dip our toes. This was the moment, and from this moment every other moment would flow.

I picked up the sword.

The river flowed on. Or rather, a dozen rivers flowed away from that moment. Alive, dead, slave, free – all flowed away from that moment.

The helmsman swung over an Etruscan marine's shield and cut the fingers off the man's sword hand.

I caught Doola's eye. He, too, had a knife in his hand.

So did Hektor's brother.

I had never spoken a word to him since he poured me wine in the market of some tiny town in Sicily. But now he watched me.

I decided. I swear that in that moment, I saw the future – that the stream came together in a mighty river, and time flowed. I once joked to Doola that we won the Battle of Mycale in that moment, he and I. Fifteen years before the Persians beached there, and we landed our marines, and fought it out for the supremacy of the world.

Every stream flowed from there.

I rose on my bench, dumping the dead Etruscan into the benches below me but wrestling the corpse for his aspis, the round shield on his left arm. It was a perfect fit, and that meant it would not come off cleanly. My moment was passing.

I gave up on the shield. The kopis whirled up over my head, and I cut—

—and severed the helmsman's foot at the ankle. He screamed and fell to the deck, and I cut his throat.

Doola was off his bench and onto mine, crawling aft, with Hektor's brother and Seckla right behind him. Seckla stripped the helmsman of his dagger and sword as he passed, and Hektor's brother had his spear – all as smoothly as if we'd planned this a hundred times. Perhaps we had. In truth, I think that the fates were there – immanent. At our shoulders.

And then the four of us burst off the benches into the rear files of the Carthaginians. I got my hands on one man's shoulders and pulled him down, and Seckla cut a man's hamstrings and Hektor's brother rammed his spear deep into the side of a third marine under his fine bronze corselet.

In three heartbeats, every top-deck rower was up. The last marines and officers died in a paroxysm of blood.

And then I had time to get the aspis on my arm.

And face the Etruscans.

The lead Etruscan stepped back and raised his helmet. Grinned.

The two ships rose and fell on the swell.

'Speak Greek?' I asked.

He looked at the man behind him.

He had a magnificent octopus on his shield and his helmet. He had ruddy blond hair, and didn't look a bit like a Greek. He was as handsome as Paris. He raised his helmet and nodded.

'A little,' he said.

'I don't know about the rest of these men,' I said slowly and carefully, 'but I've had enough of being a rower and a slave. If you'll give your word to the gods that you'll free us ashore and give us a share of the value of this ship, why, we'll row her to port for you. Otherwise—' I tapped my sword against my shield rim.

The other oarsmen made a lot of noise.

Ten marines can cow two hundred oarsmen – but not under these conditions. Not when we were already up off our benches, with many of us armed.

The Greek-speaker nodded to me and called to the other ship. I didn't understand a word.

But Gaius appeared at my hip – he was a lower-deck rower. He shouted with joy and clambered past me. Then looked back at me. He embraced an Etruscan, and they spoke, quickly, and then he came back and took my hand.

Message received.

'That's his cousin,' said the Greek-speaker. He gave me a grin. 'We'll see you right. I swear by the *daimon* of hospitality and the God of the Sea.'

We shook, and men cheered.

And the river flowed on.

It took me months to learn enough Etruscan to get a cup of wine. It sounds like the language petty kingdoms of northern Syria speak, and while I recognized the sounds, I didn't understand a word. Gaius left us immediately, and many of the rowers – like men of their kind – were rowing Etruscan hulls for pay before the week was out, collecting small wages, tupping different porne and drinking better wine, but living the same life.

I collected what I thought of as 'my people', and Gaius got us a fair price for our share of the trireme *Sea Sister*.

A year had passed since I found Euphoria dead – or more. I was drinking wine with strangers, in a place so foreign they'd never heard of the fight at Marathon, where Keltoi were thicker on the ground than Hellenes. I had no urge to go home, but I was sick of being a chattel, and whatever had been broken was healing. I wanted to live, and I wanted to be a lord and not a slave. I thought often of the Keltoi woman, stepping over the side. I thought often of the moment when the sword fell at my feet. From the gods.

I thought of Dagon.

Neoptolymos wanted to go to Illyria and kill his uncle, but his plans were adolescent.

We didn't have enough money to buy a ship. But the Etruscan cities in the north were fighting a war with the Keltoi, and I thought that my little *oikia* might earn money there.

One evening, as the money was running short, it came to a head in a taverna.

I threw a few obols on the table for wine. 'I say we go north and see what we can pick up,' I said. I looked at Doola, who shrugged.

'Wrong way for me,' he said. He grinned his huge grin. 'Home is that way.' He pointed a thumb over his shoulder.

'So's Carthage,' Demetrios said. He was Hektor's brother. By then, I knew his name. But he shrugged. 'And Sicily.'

Seckla looked interested in going north to fight. Not Daud. He shrugged. 'My home,' he said, pointing north. Even though he and Gaius looked like brothers, he was a Kelt.

'Come to Sicily,' Demetrios said suddenly. 'We can work the passage and save our money. Keep our arms.' We had all kept the weapons of the Carthaginians – what we were allowed to keep. I had the dead Etruscan's sword. 'Listen, my people are always fighting the Greeks – no offence, brother – or the Carthaginians.' He spat. 'We'll earn some money, buy a ship, be partners.'

Daud hugged us all. 'I'll go home,' he said.

'Where is home?' Demetrios asked him. 'My brother always wanted to ask you.'

Daud nodded. 'North and north and north. Over the mountains and up the great river; over a range of hills by the big forts, and then down the River of Fish to the Northern Sea.' He smiled. 'I was a great fool to leave home, but I'm grown-up now.'

'Where the tin comes from?' Demetrios asked suddenly – eagerly. Greedily, perhaps.

Daud shook his head. 'Yes and no. It comes through our town, but it's from across the Sea-River, on Alba. Or so the traders say.' He shrugged. 'I'm not of the Veneti. They know all about the tin. And they don't tell.'

'Hektor dreamed of taking a ship to Alba,' Demetrios said. 'We were going to take on a cargo of tin, and die rich men.'

Why does insane adventure appeal to me? That's the way I'm made. I remember leaning forward, like that young man who has just become interested in my tale – eh? Slavery is dull, but Alba is exotic, eh?

Just so.

'How far is Alba?' I asked.

Demetrios shrugged. 'No one knows. The Phoenicians have an absolute monopoly outside the Pillars of Heracles. Greek merchants used to go overland from Massalia – but those were gentler times.'

Doola shook his head. 'A dream,' he said, 'is an important thing, but a cup of wine is better. The tin of Alba is legendary. But with a little luck we could buy a small ship, and have a good life.'

'Don't you want to go home?' I asked.

Doola and Seckla exchanged a look.

'No,' Doola said. Sometimes he sounded like a Spartan.

I waved at the wine slave for more wine. 'I, for one, would like to go to Alba.'

Daud leaned over. 'If you are going to Alba, I'll stay,' he said.

Doola grinned. 'Insane,' he said.

'We don't even have a ship,' Seckla complained.

Doola looked at me. 'You can navigate?'

I nodded.

Demetrios looked offended. 'I can navigate.'

Doola grinned his big grin. 'This one has been a trierarch. I can see it. On a big ship – yes?'

I nodded.

Doola and Seckla exchanged a long look.

'Let's swear,' Doola said suddenly.

So we swore out a pact. It took some time to argue the details, but we swore to be brothers, to split shares evenly: to save and buy a ship, sail her to Alba, take on a cargo of tin and bring it home. We were as drunk as lords by the time we put our right fists together and swore by Zeus and four other gods.

With other men, it would have been a drunkard's oath. Something we talked about while we traded for bits of amber and salt fish.

But I was not the only man there under the hand of the fates. And when the seven of us were together, it seemed that there was nothing we could not do.

So we swore, and in the morning, we took ship for Sicily.

Now, I had been to Sicily several times by then, but never as a free man with a few obols and a sword, and it tasted better. This time, we landed on the beach by Syracusa, the greatest Greek city on the richest island in the ocean, and we gaped like country hicks. Syracusa is a magnificent city, the rival of Athens.

By all rights, we ought to have squandered our hard-earned drachma in brothels and gone back to sea as oarsmen, or at best, marines. But that's not how it fell out because, as I say, the gods were close. On landing, we went together up to the big Temple of Poseidon on the headland and spent good money on a ram. I sacrificed him myself, and his blood poured across the altar, and even as a junior priest collected his blood, a senior priest was dividing the meat. It was everyday work for both of them, but a few routine questions – they were courteous men, those priests – established that we were sailors looking for a boat, and that the junior priest's brother had a small boat to sell.

Twenty days of day-labour, and that boat was ours. It was scarcely forty feet long and just about wide enough to walk the length when the mast was down, but it could carry cargo. I guarded temples and carried sacks on the waterfront for a week, and then I found skilled work at a forge – and suddenly we had the silver to buy the boat. It was odd, and perhaps sad, that I made more in a day as an underpaid journeyman bronze-smith than all five of us earned doing the sort of day-jobs slaves usually did. But access to the shop allowed me to repair our war gear and to make us all some small things: cloak pins, clothes' pins, buckles. My new master liked my work a great deal – he was mostly a caster, not a forger – and he paid me well enough.

So the other four went to sea with a cargo of salt fish for the cities of Magna Greca, and I stayed in Syracusa making cheap cloak clasps in bulk because, truth to tell, I was making more cash than the boat.

It may seem funny, after a life as a pirate and a lord, that I took pride in keeping a tiny tenement apartment in Syracusa clean and neat, in earning a good wage smithing bronze. Nor did I ever think they'd sail away and leave me. In some way that I still cannot define, we were bonded, as deeply as I was bonded with Aristides and— Well, now that I think of it, most of the friends of my boyhood died at Lades, and I had never really replaced them. Hermogenes, Idomeneus – both were fine men, but more followers than friends. Too many men saw me as a hero, as distinct, as *above*.

Those six – Doola, Seckla, Daud, Gaius, Demetrios and Neopto-lymos – it was a different thing. And I find I've been a bad poet; I haven't sung you what they were like.

Doola was big without being tall, and always at the edge of fat without being fat. He had no hair on top of his head, and once we were free he grew a thick beard. He had heavy slabs of muscle, but a sensitive, intelligent face. He was quick to anger and quick to forgive.

Seckla was tall and thin, almost feminine in his face and hands, anything but feminine in his temperament – eager to resent a slight, eager for revenge. He never forgave. His dark skin was stretched tight over fine features, and his hands were long and thin. Despite his combative nature, he was really a craftsman, and his hands were never still, making nets, wrapping rope ends, making thole pins fit their holes better – he never stopped moving about the boat, and on land, he never stopped fussing with food.

Daud was all Keltoi – tall, heavily built, a fearsome sight in armour. He drank too much, and was quick to anger and as quick to weep. He tried so hard to hide his emotions, and failed so badly – here's to him, thugater. He had red-blond hair that was just starting to darken, eyes the colour of a new morning and skin so pale that it never tanned properly, and he often wore a chiton when the rest of us were naked, just to save himself from burning. I'm pale, and my paleness was nothing next to his. We used to mock him about it, and he would join in, agreeing that there was no sun where he came from. He could ride anything, and he was a trained warrior, where Seckla and Doola were really not very good when I met them.

Demetrios was a Sikel – small, swarthy, dour. He laughed easily but seldom showed his thoughts – unlike Daud, who sought to hide his thoughts but inevitably failed, at least back then. His skin was dark, his nose was prominent and he hated to fight, not from cowardice but from genuine aversion. He was slow to trust and quick to worry. He was, in many ways, a countryman among cosmopolitans. But he was a sure hand at sea and on land; he knew how to fish in any waters, and his boat-handling and seamanship were infinitely better than my own. Indeed, working with him quickly showed me how little a pirate chief actually knows about handling a boat. His navigation was weak; he preferred to coast everywhere, even in dangerous waters. He worried constantly, and he often reminded me of a pet rat I had as a boy – snout quivering, hands rubbing together. Yet he would have died for any one of us, if he'd had to.

Neoptolymos was, as I have said, Illyrian. He had muddy-blond hair and watery blue eyes and he drank – constantly. He was easily angered and, to be honest, never a very pleasant companion. He felt that he had forfeited his honour when his sister was raped to death. He seldom smiled. He was harsh with others and himself. Yet buried under the broken unhappiness of youth was a man who had the manners of a gentleman and the easy habits of a rich man. His purse was always open to his friends. His knife was always ready to defend us. His code was barbarous – but noble. He could also play any musical instrument he was given after a few hours of mucking about.

And finally, there was Gaius. He left us for a while, but he was one of us nonetheless. He was Etruscan; but that is like saying 'he is Greek', because every Etruscan city is at odds with every other, and they rarely unite. He, too, had red-blond hair and pale skin – when I first met the two of them, I thought he and Daud were brothers, when in fact they weren't even from the same people, and both were a little annoyed at my assumption.

We had divisions. Four of us were warriors, and three were not; three of us were at least nominally aristocratic, and three were working men. Slavery can erase arrogance, but it cannot erase habits of mind and body; so Daud, Neoptolymos, Gaius and I would work on our bodies and practise with weapons, which the other three looked on as an affectation or a foolish waste of money. We tended to spend freely. Daud especially could empty his purse for a beggar, even if the gesture meant that he was instantly a beggar himself. I would buy the best wine, and the best cloak, I could afford, and the three men born to labour would roll their eyes and pray to Hermes for deliverance from the spendthrift. I remember this happening in the Agora of Syracusa, and I laughed and told them that they reminded me of my aristocratic wife – and then I suddenly burst into tears.

I tell this now because, truth to tell, what they looked like and how they acted was – well, to put it bluntly, it was muted, unimportant while we rowed for our lives as slaves. Slavery made the bond, but once we had survived, we had to know each other.

My daughter is smiling. I have digressed too long. But those were good times.

The boat returned from its first voyage, and we had just about broken even. A small boat carries a limited cargo, and even if the skipper picks his cargo well, he has to sell all of it at a good price, over and over, to cover the cost of four men eating, drinking wine, their clothes ruined at sea, their oars broken on rocks. The overheads of a sea voyage are, to be blunt, enormous for poor men. Our little tub had four oars, a big central mast that could be unshipped and room for about two tons of cargo – which is nothing, in wine or grain. Less than nothing for metal.

On the positive side, we were not in debt to the vicious money-lenders of Sicily. They were notorious, and for good reason, and they had amazing networks of informants. So that by the second afternoon after our little boat was pulled up on the back, a pair of men came down to her. One sat on her gunwale and the other stood with his arms crossed. They were quite large men.

'You need more money to make a profit off a boat this size,' said the man sitting on our gunwale. We were all there, scrubbing black slime out of the bilge and weed and crap off the hull. Demetrios had brought in a cargo of Italian wine, and made what should have been a handsome profit, but about a third of the amphorae had either broken or slipped some seawater, so that his profits just about covered losses with a little left over.

Before this gets monotonous, let me add that had we not been ambitious to buy bigger ships and go farther, this would have been a good life. The boat covered expenses and then some, and I was starting, even after six weeks, to make a steady wage. It was only the scope of our ambition that rendered the pace slow.

I'm digressing again.

'I don't feel that I have your attention, gents,' said the man on the gunwale. His partner picked up a large piece of wood and came over to the boat. He struck the hull, hard, just where the strake met the bow.

None of the oak pins came loose, but no one likes to see a stranger hit his boat.

'I see I have your attention now,' said the man on our gunwale.

Daud and I walked down either side of the boat, and we must have looked like trouble. The man on the bow stood up, dusting his hands.

'I don't think you know me, gents. But if you touch me, you are all dead men.' He laughed. 'I'm a little surprised you don't know me. Hurt, even. But you're all strangers – foreigners. So I will let it go this time. Especially as I've come to offer you money.'

Demetrios shrugged. 'We don't need money,' he said.

'Really?' said the man by the bow. 'Let me introduce myself. I'm Anarchos, and if I wish to loan you money, then you need to take it. Please understand this, gents – I own you as surely as your former owner owned you. Your slavery is written in the sky. Don't pretend you are free men – I know escaped slaves when I see them. And I can sell you into slavery, or kill you – and no one in this city will even shrug. You aren't citizens. You aren't even registered metics. You are poor men, and you have no friends.' He smiled, and the hardness left his voice. 'But I am a reasonable man, and an easy master. You split your profits with me, and I loan you money when you fail. I am your patron, and you are my workers, and all is well. I will help you in the courts, and in the assembly, if it comes to that.' He looked around. 'No one in Syracusa will say Anarchos is a bad patron.'

Daud was ready to fight. I could see it in his posture.

I was calculating.

This was new to me, even though I prided myself in being more like Odysseus than Achilles.

If the man spoke the truth – even a wicked, cocked-up version of the truth – attacking him would serve little purpose. Nor did we plan to stay in Syracusa. No local crime lord could possibly imagine what we had in mind.

I put a hand on Daud's shoulder. 'My friend is a Gaul,' I said. 'And prone to violence.' I smiled at the hired muscle – the man was big. 'I know a little about violence myself,' I added. 'But we don't want any trouble.'

Anarchos nodded. 'You're the smart boy, then.'

I resented his tone and his use of the word *boy*. But I was not a great lord with fifty hoplites at my back. I was an ex-slave with six friends. I think my hands trembled.

But I smiled. 'We had a good voyage.' I had another knucklebone to roll, and I cast it slyly. 'And of course, I make a fair wage as a bronze-smith.'

He nodded, pursed his lips. I had scored a hit. Not a hit that would win the fight, but a real score, nonetheless. Bronze-smiths were a close-knit clan with their own rules and laws and status, and men like Anarchos, however powerful, didn't cross the smiths.

'I'll check on that,' he said. 'The bronze-smiths wouldn't like an ex-slave making a claim that wasn't true.'

I reached into the boat and took out my leather satchel – made by Seckla. From it, holding it up so that the hired muscle could see me, I took a bronze eating-knife with a pretty bone handle, the bone dyed green with verdigris; there were fine silver tacks in the handle for decoration. It was in a sheath of Seckla's make with a long bronze pick.

'My work,' I said, handing it to the moneylender.

He nodded.

'Keep it,' I said. 'A token of my esteem.'

His head shot up. 'Fuck you, slave,' he said. 'No one talks to me like that.'

I crossed my arms. 'You're off your mark here. I'm a craftsman. These men are my friends. I have other friends. We don't want trouble.'

He got up. Rubbed his chin, and then his face changed. 'I'll keep this,' he said, holding my eating-knife. 'And I'll make some enquiries. And I'll be back.' He looked around. 'I expect you'll need my money. And I'll expect you to be civil. Understand?'

By civil, he meant subservient.

Again, you might expect that I'd just kill him and be a local hero.

But it doesn't really work like that.

Some time much later, Daud told me that we could have saved a year of our lives by killing him then and there. And maybe we could have.

But Heraclitus was reaching me across the years. I had to learn other ways of solving my problems.

So I bowed my head. 'Of course, *Patron*.'

He nodded seriously. And strode off, full of self-importance, his sell-sword by his side.

Daud turned on me. 'Are you a *coward*?' he asked, and stomped off. I didn't see him for a day.

I must have turned red, because Doola came and put his arm around my shoulders. 'Well done,' he said.

'I don't feel that it was well done,' I admitted. Now that the man had walked away, I felt craven.

'We didn't fight, and we didn't take his money,' Demetrios said. 'Nice job. My brother was good with these vultures, but I – I fear them.'

So we went back to scraping the boat clean, and afterwards we returned to our two rooms under the thatch, where we counted our money. The taverna on our corner had taken all the wine that wasn't tinged with seawater at a good price, and all the tinged wine at one half that price. After Demetrios paid off our debts – mostly food, rope and wood – we had about sixty drachma. I had made another twenty-four drachma profit, after my own food, wine and clothes.

Eighty-four drachma, for six men.

Daud shook his head. 'We'll *never* get a twenty-oared ship at this rate.'

We had decided that if we were going to try the tin run to Alba, we needed *at least* a twenty-oared galley with a good mast. It was a common enough type of boat in the trade. And we needed a dozen slaves. We couldn't afford to pay rowers and sailors and build the boat.

We estimated that building the boat would cost us three hundred drachmas.

But Demetrios was altogether more sanguine. He put the money in a sack, and put the sack into the thatch. 'Not bad,' he said. He shrugged. 'Not bad. Ari is pulling more than his fair share. And without him, we'll never get it done.'

I didn't really want to hear that, because while I liked working in the shop, I wanted to be at sea. And my status – if you could call it that – as leader was suffering. All of them looked to Demetrios, not to me. He had become the skipper. I wasn't there, at sea. They told me stories of the storm that hit them in the straits off Sybarus, and how Demetrios stayed at the helm all day and all night—

You get the idea.

I might have been bitter. But I wasn't. Sometimes a dream was bigger than any reality. Sailing to Alba was a big dream – an heroic deed, a worthy thing. I was willing to sacrifice. We all were.

We were brothers.

'What about Illyria?' I asked. Neoptolymos raised his head and smiled. And then frowned and drank more wine.

'I will never go back until my sister is avenged,' he said.

I looked at them. 'There's still tin coming through Illyria,' I pointed out. 'And Neoptolymos knows where to get it.'

He shook his head. 'My cousins will have the keep now, and the river. I would be killed. I will return with a hundred warriors – with my friends.' He smiled at me, and for a moment we were brothers. He knew I would back him. I knew that, if we lived, someday we would go there. After we put Dagon down. We never talked about it, but Neoptolymos and I knew.

Many debts.

The money went into the thatch, and the boat went back to sea. They tried fishing for a few weeks, and made about six drachma over expenses. They accepted a cargo of artworks for the Etruscan coast and sailed off, leaving me to worry about the consequences of failure.

But I didn't worry much. I'm not much of a worrier, in that way. I went to work each morning as the sun rose. At the height of the sun in the sky, I would walk out of my master, Nikephorus's shop, and go two streets to a waterfront wine shop where I'd buy a skewer of somewhat questionable meat. After that meal, I'd walk back to Nikephorus's shop and work until late afternoon, when I'd go to the gymnasium, pay my foreigner's fee and exercise with much richer men. I'd lift weights, throw the discus and run on the track.

After some weeks, other men spoke to me. I was clearly a foreigner: despite its size, Syracusa had only about six thousand citizen males, and they all knew each other. They were like any Greek gentlemen – well spoken, talkative, friendly – but only with each other.

But hospitality overcame diffidence after some time, and eventually one of the richer men – I knew who he was, even if he had no idea who I was – came and asked me if I liked to box. His name was Theodorus, and his family owned stone quarries.

We exchanged blows for some time. He wasn't very good, and it wasn't my best sport, but a few minutes of contest taught each of us that the other was a solid opponent.

He laughed. 'So, you are a gentleman. The gatekeeper has … hmm … questioned your right to exercise here.'

I nodded. 'I'm a bronze-smith,' I said. 'From Plataea, in Boeotia.'
His face hardened. 'I fought in the front rank at Marathon,' I added.
I didn't like the way it sounded – a plain brag.

'Ahh!' he said, and took my hand. 'Things are a little different here.
I doubt there's another bronze-smith in our gymnasium.' He led
me over to a group of men just emerging from the dressing rooms.
They were in their thirties and forties, and they all wore the *chlamys*
the way much younger men would wear them, in Athens. But their
bodies were hard, and they all seemed to smile at the same time.

'Ari fought at Marathon,' he said, by way of introduction.

'By Nike!' said one man, with greying black hair and a thick beard.
'That's something!'

They all gathered around me, and one slapped my back.

'Tell us what it was like,' said Theodorus.

I started to tell the story – just as I have told you – and the tall
bearded man grinned and plucked my arm. 'Let the poor man get
dressed, and we'll buy him some wine. Talking is thirsty work.'

They were clearly surprised to see my plain chlamys and short
linen *chitoniskos*. I looked like a servant with them, and I resolved to
buy a better chlamys to wear to the gymnasium.

We sat in a wine shop, where a cup of wine cost an afternoon's
wage for a skilled bronze-smith, and where women, not men, waited
at the tables. Lovely women. Slaves, I assumed.

I told my story, and the men with me responded well.

Theodorus nodded at the end. 'I've been in a ship fight, and some
cattle raids,' he admitted, 'but nothing like that.'

'If Carthage keeps preying on our shipping, we'll see it here,'
another added. 'What do you think, Ari?'

I shrugged. 'I know nothing of the politics here, gentlemen. I have
no love for the Carthaginians, however.'

They all looked at me.

'They enslaved me,' I said.

From their looks, I might as well have said 'and sold me in a
brothel'. Every face closed.

'You are a *slave*?' Theodorus asked.

I shook my head, but I already knew we were done. I had seen this
attitude in Athens.

'I am not a slave, was not born a slave and was only made a slave
by force,' I said.

Theodorus got up. His hip had been against mine, sitting for wine,

58

and he moved away as one would from a leper. 'No slave can take exercise in our gymnasium,' he said.

They all looked at me with marked distaste.

I got up. 'I'm sorry to have intruded, gentlemen,' I said. I drained my cup – the wine was excellent. 'I appreciate your hospitality, even if you do not desire my company. May the gods be kind to you.' I collected my chlamys, and made what exit I could.

I could feel their stares until I got to the door of the wine shop, where one of the serving girls suddenly went up on tiptoe and brushed a kiss on my beard. 'I hate them,' she said.

Aphrodite, that little brush of a kiss went to the very roots of my being. And took much of the sting out of my humiliation.

The next morning I told my master, Nikephorus, the entire story.

We were polishing – a nasty job, and one usually done by slaves, but Nikephorus liked to see things gleam. Every day. So we often started the days polishing. I'd polished all day for my first week, until he had time to test me. And of course, I knew the grips and handshakes of a master. They were different for Syracusa, but not so different.

At any rate, we polished for a while and then he sat back on the bench and admired our work. 'I don't exercise as much as I should,' he said. 'But the crafts have a gymnasium with a bath. You should have asked.' He smiled his slow smile, and his eyes twinkled. He was grey without seeming old – bent, and strong, like Hephaestos himself. His wife, let me add, was much younger, and they fought often, and made up in the traditional way, and were equally loud in both pastimes. I liked his wife, too, Julia. She was, and she had a neat, orderly mind that catalogued everything that came her way – the heroes of the *Iliad*, the ships in the harbour, the wares in the shop – which was odd, as her house was the messiest I've ever seen. She never put anything away, and her slaves were just like her. But she was kind to apprentices and journeymen: she gave us food from her larder and juice from her store, wine was always free and she had a great store of scrolls to read – like a rich woman, which I think she was. I first read a good copy of *Pythagoras on Mathematics* at her house.

My daughter is making that face that means I'm rattling on.

So Nikephorus said, 'I'd have loved to see those rich fucks when they found out you had been a slave. Like you'd poured shit on them.' He laughed aloud. 'Well, well. After work today, we'll go and exercise.' He groaned. 'But it may kill me.'

We went through the streets at twilight, through parts of the city I hadn't yet seen. I discovered that the textiles I'd bought down by the harbour were a pale shadow of what was available in the weavers' street, where women hung recently completed items in the doors of their shops. Weaving is a woman's craft, and the women of Syracusa were at least as dexterous as those of Athens or Plataea.

I saw wine shops better than the ones I frequented, and a street of iron-smiths where we stopped to drop off a whole leather-wrapped bundle of bronze fittings. I saw good swords and bad, fine spears and cheap spears, good eating-knives and dull eating-knives.

The craftsmen's gymnasium was small, but quite pleasant. It didn't have its own track, but it did host three professional trainers, paid by the guilds, and it had good equipment – a matched set of lifting stones with handles, for instance. I was introduced around, and men watched me lift, and other men watched me box.

And there was a curious device I hadn't seen elsewhere – a room with a bright lamp with a lens focused on a whitewashed wall. On the bench was a single, heavy wooden sword.

'Shadow-fighting, friend,' said one of the trainers. He lit the lamp and shone it on the wall, and then fought his shadow for a few blows. It was good training and self-explanatory, and I set to.

The trainer, a freedman names Polimarchos, grinned at me. 'Had a sword in your hand before, I take it.'

I smiled.

'Care to have a try with padded swords?' he asked.

This was different from Boeotia, where we used wooden swords and hurt each other. The swords were padded with wool and leather, and he had small shields with central grips. I'd never used such a shield, and I pursed my lips.

'Not much like an aspis, is it?' I asked.

'Teaches the same lessons, though,' Polimarchos said. 'The small shield teaches the larger. Punch with your hand – deflect your opponent's blade before his blow is fully developed. Right? You're a fighter. We call it the shield bash, here, but I've heard it called a dozen names. And try keeping your sword inside the shield. Let the shield cover your sword hand.'

I had been fighting most of my life – I'd had a good teacher as a boy. But I hadn't ever given much thought to the theory of sword-play until that moment.

We picked up the padded weapons. The padded sword was badly balanced, and felt like a dead thing in my hand. The shield was odd.

But I set myself in my fighting position, with my sword high behind me and my left leg forward, and Polimarchos looked at me for a moment and shook his head.

He stepped forward, and we began to circle.

He managed our distance expertly, keeping me a little farther away than I would have liked. So I pushed him, and he struck, his right leg shooting forward across his left, and his padded blade slamming down towards my shield. I raised the shield slightly, and he rolled the blade off my little shield and cut into my thigh.

'Don't rely on the shield,' he said. 'Act with it.'

The third time he cut down at my thigh, I cut at his wrist and scored. He winced. 'Too hard, Ari,' he said. 'I have hit you twice, and not left a mark – eh?'

His point was a fair one.

But pain didn't make him flinch, and we went back at it. He could not hit me at will, but he could hit me often. I could hit him occasionally. He was twenty years older than I, and a freedman.

After an hour, I could scarcely breathe, and darkness was falling. 'Train me?' I asked him.

He nodded. 'You are a good fighter – a trained man, I can tell. But the Etruscans and the Latins and the Syracusans train in these things. Techniques that you don't know, I can tell. The way you stand – your legs are too far apart. You crouch forward slightly – surely your first trainer told you to keep your back straight? And there's other moves – cuts – worth knowing. I get a drachma for an hour of my time.'

I nodded. 'And spear-fighting?' I asked.

Polimarchos had a pleasant face. He was shorter, a little heavy at the waist like many trainers, and his arms and legs had the defined muscles of the professional athlete. He was bald on top, and his surviving hair was no colour at all, and neither were his eyes. He smiled a lot, especially when he hit me. He grinned. 'I know some things about spear-fighting,' he said.

We walked out of the gymnasium. I paid my fee – a month there cost the same for a smith as a day at the City Gymnasium for a foreigner, but a drachma to the trainer was painful.

Nonetheless, I took him out for a cup of wine. We came to an agreement – he was eager to teach a swordsman, I could tell, rather than pushing tradesmen to do a little exercise, which was his day-to-day fare.

The craft gymnasium added to my social life, as I met other men of my own age, and received some invitations, which reminded me that men my age with incomes assured were married. I had been married. I forgot for days, even weeks, at a time. I forgot I was married, and forgot she was dead.

I never forgot Briseis, though.

After seven or eight weeks, this life became my life. Plataea was far away, and the pirate lord was dead and buried. I made my first helmet, and my master clapped his hands to see it done, and sold it for a handsome price. He gave me almost half of the profit – by the standards of the day, this was very generous. A journeyman like me could be kept on for wages and food.

My share was twenty drachmas. That covered lessons at the gymnasium, where I had begun to question how I'd ever killed a single man in combat, so much of my posture and technique was being restructured by Polimarchos. I paid my teacher, and he was truly grateful.

A week later I produced another helmet, this one with repoussé work at the brow. It had been ordered, and I had fretted about the fit. Indeed, it was a fraction too small, and I was embarrassed to have to open the brow slightly in front of the client, alternately dishing and raising a few points to expand the metal, all the while hoping that I would not have to re-planish the whole shape.

But my customer, an Etruscan trierarch on business, loved my work. I think he loved more than just my work – he smiled a lot, and seemed to hang on my every word – but this time I received twenty-five drachmas.

A small thing happened at that time, one of many incidents. A boy came to our shop – really a young man, a gifted apprentice called Anaxsikles son of Dionysus. Dionysus was the master smith of the street. He himself was, I gather, a very gifted man, but I never saw anything he made. Rather, he managed a smithing empire – he had twenty-four sheds, with both slave and free smiths working iron and bronze. He was chief of the guild, and his voice was the voice that decided most things on the street, and yet, in as much as I knew him, he seemed fair and very intelligent. He was the sort of *tekne* every city values – prosperous, rich even, and yet not above his origins.

At any rate, he sent us his son. This sort of temporary fosterage binds the guilds together, and is good for all. It is the chief reason why cities and not workshops develop a style – fosterage creates an equality of knowledge.

But I digress. Don't look at me like that, honey, I know you want the story. Teaching Anaxsikles was a joy. He had a kind of aptitude for the work that transcends jealousy and competition. He was a god-sent talent. He never needed to be shown anything more than once. If I have a skill in working bronze that is better than other men's, it is in the construction of armour, and I think it is simply that I have used so much of it that I understand it from the inside in a way that other smiths don't. But Anaxsikles would drink in my views – on how to fabricate a Corinthian helmet, for instance; where to move the metal to stiffen the brow ridge, or, the way I made them, to leave a heavy plate over the brow – he took it all in. He seemed to *feel* it in his bones.

So Anaxsikles worked with me on the helmets. He was delighted with the result, and my work improved again.

I only worked with him for two months, but he made me a better smith. He – my student.

At any rate, Nikephorus had a small party in celebration of the final sale. The priest of Hephaestos came and gave me the seal of Syracusa, as a master smith. And Nikephorus's daughter Lydia came and sang. She was a pretty girl, fourteen years old, all legs and hips and small breasts and shyness, and I liked her. I didn't get to see many women, and she was lovely.

But I was a fool, so after dinner, when I'd had too much wine and was enjoying the sight of Lydia dancing, Nikephorus leaned over. 'She'll make you fine babies,' he said. 'Julia never lost a one. How about it? None of us cares you were a slave. Marry Lydia, and you'll have the shop when I'm a little older.'

This struck me from a clear blue sky although in retrospect, I was, as I say, a fool not to have seen it coming. Lydia was beautiful in her transparent Ionian chiton of Aegyptian linen – probably her best garment – with a flowing light *himation* falling in folds from her shoulders; very fashionable, and most likely her own work. I'd proven my work; I'd made the master some serious money and he had no son. How had I failed to be prepared?

Did I say he was a fine man? When I looked stunned, he laughed. 'Well, every man thinks his own daughter the most beautiful since

Helen. Perhaps the idea sticks in your craw. Will you think on it?' he asked.

I nodded.

He leaned over. 'I'm going to leave the two of you alone a little,' he said. 'If you ... touch her—' he shrugged.

I nodded. It is a funny thing, a human thing – I could have killed him any time, he was no fighter – but I feared him far more than he feared me. He was the master smith. He was a master, too; for all I'd just been raised to his 'level', he seemed, every day, to know a thousand things I didn't know.

Within an hour, Lydia was seated on the *kline* beside mine – to sit on mine would have led to other pastimes – with her arms around her knees. She asked me questions, slow questions, about my past.

So I answered them.

After an hour, Julia came in and sat on Lydia's couch. 'Time for bed, sweet,' she said. She smiled easily at me. 'Have you bragged and bragged, young man?'

I nodded sheepishly. I didn't want to marry Lydia and be a bronze-smith. I wanted to go to Alba, kill Dagon and then go back and—

And what?

In that heartbeat, it occurred to me that marrying Lydia and being the best smith in mighty Syracusa might be a golden future. The shop offered me a challenge – every day. I could see a life where I made things with Anaxsikles, or competed against him to be the best. There is as much arête in craft as in war. Standing in the haze of Ares was ... like another life. Making marvellous things under Nikephorus's guiding hand—

Sleeping with Lydia, who even now gave me a look that made both of us blush—

I blushed and stammered, Julia laughed and I found myself in the darkness with my cheap chlamys around my shoulders and the first kiss of autumn weather in the air, so that the city smell of cat piss and coriander was mixed with burning pine. The night seemed a marvellous place.

I went and had a cup of wine at my new favourite wine shop and went back to my two rooms.

And there they all were, faces beaming. Even Neoptolymos was beaming.

They'd made almost two hundred drachmas. They'd taken their cargo swiftly and safely, earned a bonus and come home laden to the gunwales with Etruscan olive oil and a small cargo of perfumes that had sold at a stiff profit before they'd even unloaded.

I added in forty-five drachmas on my own account.

We all looked at each other, and then we whooped like men giving the war cry, so that our upstairs neighbours thumped their floor and our downstairs neighbour, a prosperous whore, thumped her ceiling.

'Now we need three hundred and fifty more,' said Demetrios, who could calculate on an abacus and write slowly with a stylus on a wax tablet. I wrote better, so I took over the scribe's job.

'Slaves?' I asked.

'Cargo,' Demetrios said. 'And slaves, and ropes, and pitch for the hull – even at that, we really need five hundred more.'

'And we don't actually have three hundred drachmas,' Daud said morosely.

I glared at him. 'Count it again, then.'

'It's about to be winter,' he said. 'No sailing. We have to eat.'

'Even if we live off your smithing,' Doola said, 'we will only stay even. And we'll all feel like kept men.' He laughed.

Demetrios nodded. 'It's worse than that,' he said. 'Anarchos will know tomorrow what we made, and he'll be here for a cut.'

'I'll cut him,' said Daud.

'I'm with you,' said Neoptolymos. 'We're not bending over for him this time.'

I fingered my beard. It was odd for me to side with Demetrios. But I could see he was prepared to hand over something, some face-saving amount of our profits.

And I agreed. By the gods, I agreed.

'Twenty drachma,' I said. 'And another twenty to the Temple of Poseidon, as first fruits.'

'We saw Gaius,' Daud said, out of nowhere. He grinned. 'He wants to come to Alba with us. He's as poor as we are, and he has to pretend to be rich.'

'His family weren't altogether pleased when he came back,' Doola said. 'We're sending him a letter to come down with another load of perfumes.'

I nodded. 'Can we get one more load in before winter?'

Demetrios fingered his chin. 'Chancy.'

But we knew we had to try.

The next morning, I took ten drachma of my own money and went and bought myself a fine chlamys. It wasn't as fine as some men wore, but it was a beautiful red-brown, with a fine black-purple stripe and a field of embroidered stars. I had admired it for two weeks, and it gave me real pleasure to buy it from the maker for her full price. I didn't haggle. She grinned at me.

'You're the new smith,' she said, as she took my money. 'Going to marry our Lydia, are you, boy?'

News travels fast.

Then I went to the silversmith's ghetto, and traded six of my good bronze pins for one heavy silver cloak pin. The smith came out and dealt with me in person. I knew him from the gymnasium. He fingered the chlamys. 'I know that work,' he said. 'It's good to see a young man do well. See that you stay among us.'

Dressed in my finery, I went to the great Temple of Poseidon by the harbour, and there I counted twenty drachma into the bronze urn by the entrance, watched at a distance by one of Anarchos's runners. I knew most of them by now, as I was in the city all the time. A day-priest – one of the citizens – came and clasped my hand.

'First fruits of a trading voyage,' I said.

He nodded. 'But you are surely the new smith – the one who fought at Marathon?' he asked.

I shrugged. 'I am also sometimes a trader – a sailor.'

He laughed. 'Any Hellene serves the sea. The god thanks you. We do too. We need a new roof.'

From the temple, with my cloak on, pinned with fine silver, I walked down to the waterfront where Anarchos sat with his 'friends'. He had two big 'friends' who stood behind him. I stood at the edge of the terrace until a slave deigned to notice me, and then one of the big men came and led me to the great man's presence.

He looked me up and down slowly, and then gestured with his stick at the stool closest to him. 'Sit!' he said.

Wine was brought.

'You have something for me? And you have brought it with a proper humility?' he said, loudly, because this being a patron of the lower orders was a performance art.

I nodded. Took a purse from a fold of my cloak and put it in his hands.

'We put our first fruits in the temple,' I said. 'So you have our second fruits.'

He glanced in the bag, and if he was disappointed, he hid it well. 'Very proper,' he said with a firm nod. He leaned forward. 'Nice cloak,' he said.

'I may be courting,' I said.

He nodded. 'So I hear. Although other things come to my ears. You tried to mix with the citizens. That was foolish.'

I shrugged. And smiled.

Just for a moment, I threw back my cloak and looked him in the eye. Lydia, in a similar flash of the eye, could convey *I am a virgin, and yet I burn with a fire so hot that you would flinch from it.*

I could learn from a fourteen-year-old girl.

In one flash of the eye, I said *I fought in the front rank at Marathon, and I've buried more enemies than you'll ever have. You may have the upper hand here, but you do not want a fight.*

Then I dropped my eyes, smiled and went back to my wine, which was good wine.

He nodded, leaned forward, and put a hand on my shoulder. He was not afraid of me. That, by itself, was interesting.

'I wish you luck, smith. Your friends – they are lucky to have you. I think we understand each other.'

'I will continue to value your ... friendship, when I own a shop,' I said.

He took a breath.

I let one go.

We both smiled.

I rose, shook his hand as lesser man to greater, and walked away.

A few paces on, he called out: 'Are you really Arimnestos of Plataea?'

I turned back. 'Yes,' I called.

He nodded.

When I got home, Doola was sitting by the door with a cudgel, and Neoptolymos and Daud were in their leather armour. I shook my head.

'I told you so,' Daud said to Doola. He fingered my cloak. 'There goes all our profits.'

Demetrios raised an eyebrow.

'It is done,' I said.

Daud looked at me. 'You are the brains here, but I swear, Ari, you'll wish we'd killed the bastard.'

Neoptolymos agreed. 'We can take his whole gang.'

'And the citizens of the city? And the courts?' Demetrios nodded to me. 'How much?'

'I bought the cloak from my own money,' I said, a little defensively. 'Twenty for Anarchos, and twenty for Poseidon.'

Daud shrugged and Neoptolymos stared at the floor, but Doola clapped me on the back.

'And now, brothers, I have a plan.' I looked around. 'Are we still going to Alba?'

A chorus of cheers erupted. Damn, it makes me want to weep, even now. We had the dream – the best dream men ever dreamed. We were going to be heroes. That dream bound us as thoroughly as iron manacles, but better by far.

'Listen, then,' I said. 'Anarchos wants to own us. He *wants* to loan us money. When we can't pay it, he'll own our boat and our lives and get his claws into a smith.' I shrugged. 'I've been offered the bronze-smith's daughter, friends.'

You can imagine what response met this. I'll leave you to picture it, friends, because many of you are too young to hear the expressions that men use to each other.

Heh, heh.

'Listen, you sex-starved oarsmen! Anarchos has every reason to want a piece of us.' I smiled. 'So we risk it all – we make another voyage to Italy for perfume. If we make it, we make a good profit, and *then we go to Anarchos to borrow money for a larger ship.*' I looked around at them. 'He won't loan us enough for us to succeed. But he won't know how much we already have.'

Demetrios got it immediately. 'We could never come back here again,' he said. Just thinking about it made him breathe heavily.

Doola got it, too. 'So we take the great man's money, and we just sail away. Apparently to Etrusca, for perfumes.' He laughed his great laugh.

Daud joined the laughter, and Seckla, and finally, so did Neoptolymos.

One of my better plans.

The next morning I realized that my plan had two painful flaws.

One was that I had to pretend that I was going to marry Lydia, or at least, that I hadn't decided.

Herein lies the complexity of the human heart, my young friends. When I was in Nikephorus's shop, I wanted to marry her. I wanted that life.

When I was in my two rooms, staring at the place amid the thatch where the money rested, all I wanted was Alba. I was both men. Both men lied, both told the truth.

And so, though I had intended to make the dangerous winter crossing to Italy with the boat, I couldn't go. If I had, Anarchos would have seen in a moment that I wasn't staying.

So I had to sit at home, while they took the risks.

Or sit in the *andron* of Nikephorus's house, with Lydia playing the lyre, or singing. We were left together more and more.

Lydia was quite sure we were to wed. And she was quite prepared to move on. Quite aggressively prepared, really. She was perfectly modest. She didn't grab my shoulders and push her tongue down my throat – pardon me, ladies, but I've known it done. But autumn turned to winter, it grew colder and wetter outside, and Lydia wore less and less to our chaperoned evenings. Her mother either took no notice or cooperated actively. Things were said.

I remember one evening she finished a song and said, in a matter of fact voice: 'My best friend kissed her husband for months before they were wed.' She smiled, and went back to playing the lyre.

When she danced, her hips took on a life of their own. When she handed me wine, her fingers brushed mine.

Listen, my young friends. A woman has natural defences against the assault of a man. A woman is like a citadel – I'm hardly the first to draw this analogy. Women are trained from birth to walk a fine line between desirability and availability. Whether a woman is a queen or a whore, she knows how to draw that line.

Men know nothing. We only want. It is not our place to refuse. When a man is hunted by a woman, he has no weapons, no city wall, no place of refuge. Refusal appears very like cowardice.

Oh, I'm just saying.

I taught Anaxsikles in the shop, and then we worked together. I was learning from my master, and teaching my apprentice. I had very little to teach him, but I recall we were making a pair of greaves, and like all Sicilian smiths, he put a pair of intertwined snakes onto the front – fancy, and very beautiful. His repoussé was better than mine already.

Perhaps his superiority made me petulant, but his snakes had come to dominate the whole front of the greave, and when he brought them to me for my approval, I looked at them for a long time, formulating my criticism.

It is hard to be an honest critic. I was a little jealous of his skill. The snakes themselves were beautiful. Yet, in my heart, I knew that I wouldn't have worn them. Why? And was I just jealous?

So many grown-up thoughts.

Finally, I put them down. 'Your repoussé is superb,' I said.

He beamed.

'Better than mine,' I said.

He made noises of negation, but I could see that he, too, thought his work was better. And yet he wanted my admiration and my approval.

'But with the snakes so deep, look, a spear point can catch here, and punch right through into a man's leg.' The snakes stood so high out of the metal that their sinuous lines made a continuous catchment. If I were fighting a man wearing them ... Odd thought, as I hadn't fought anyone in a long time.

He shrugged, obviously uninterested in my criticism.

'You don't believe me,' I said.

He shrugged with all the easy arrogance of the very young. His shrug said *You are a little jealous and thus liable to lie. I know my repoussé is without compare.* He didn't quite smile.

'You don't believe me.'

'There's no spearman in the world who can place his point into so small a target,' he said.

I wanted to vanquish his youth's ignorant arrogance.

'Put them on,' I said.

He was close enough to his customer's size to clip them on his legs.

I fetched the master's spear from over the door. Effortlessly, I flicked it at him, and caught the in-curve of the snake each time – nicking the greave and making marks that would have to be polished out.

He shrugged. 'I don't have a spear or an aspis,' he said.

I found both for him.

We squared off in the street. I realized as we came on guard that Lydia was watching out of her window on the exedra. Well.

'Ready?' I said. My voice must have carried something. Anaxsikles paused, and lowered his aspis. 'You really can do it, can't you?' he said.

'Yes.' I said grimly.

But he changed his mind, settled his shield and laughed. 'Show me!' he said, and his spear lashed out at my face.

I nudged his spear aside and put the point of my spear into the snake's curves. Anaxsikles screamed and fell.

My spear had gone right through a flaw, and an inch into his shin.

No real ill came of it. I helped him inside, bandaged him and spent the next two weeks making a new greave to replace the one I'd ruined. He put snakes on it, less than one half the height of the last pair. We drank a cup of wine together most nights, and the little fight became quite famous in the smith's quarte – not as a feat of arms, but as an example of how seriously we took our business. I might have been punished, but instead, like most things in those days, it rebounded to make both of us appear serious in our work.

And Lydia told me that I looked like a god.

Well.

My friends had been gone eight weeks – double their last trip.

I was walking home one evening from my gymnasium, and a big man appeared at a corner. I knew him immediately; he was one of Anarchos's men. He jutted his chin at me.

I smiled and kept walking.

He ran after me, his heavy footfalls loud on the street. People turned to look, and then studiously looked away. The street was only twice the width of a man's shoulders, but grown men managed to make it wider to avoid Anarchos's men.

'Hey! You!' he shouted.

I turned.

He stopped. 'You heard me!' he shouted, spittle flying. He wanted a fight.

I didn't. So I nodded. 'I didn't understand,' I said.

'Anarchos wants you,' he said. 'Come.'

So I followed him. As it happened, I had been training with Polimarchos, and I had my beautiful Etruscan kopis under my arm, but I felt no need to use it. I had, indeed, changed. I thought of the two thugs in Athens I'd killed.

We walked in a light rain down to the waterfront. The taverna was closed up tight, and inside, fifty lamp wicks gave the place the light of a temple – and too much heat. A central hearth fire burned and fishermen, slave and free, jostled for wine.

But around Anarchos's table, there was a clear space as wide as a man's hips.

He bade me sit as if we were old friends. He got me a fine cup of wine.

'You must be worried about your friends,' he said.

I nodded.

He looked concerned. 'I could sell you information about them,' he said. 'But I would be a poor patron if I did. So here it is for free: they are well. They made the coast of Etrusca well enough, and bought their cargo. But then they were plagued with trouble, lost the boat, bought another and have been penned in Sybarus by adverse winds.' He shrugged. 'They will make a little off this voyage, but not enough to give Poseidon twenty drachmas. Or me,' he said. He shrugged again.

'Thanks!' I said, with genuine feeling.

He looked at me again. 'You are an odd fellow,' he said. 'You truly value these men.'

I stood. 'Yes. Like brothers.'

He clasped my hand. 'Very well. Be at ease.'

Damn him. He was so much easier to hate when he was being a money-grubbing bastard. And since I was going to swindle him, I wanted to hate him.

The world, it turns out, is a very complicated place. No man is the villain in his own tale. Every man has his reasons, no matter how selfish or evil.

I went home.

More weeks passed. I went with Nikephorus and Anaxsikles to the great winter religious festival they have in Syracusa. Lydia carried a garland in the craftsmen's part of the procession. Men commented on her. Two young aristocrats wrote her poems.

I was jealous.

So I wrote a poem for her myself.

Oh, the foolishness of men.

I am a fair poet. Better than my poetry is Sappho's, which I knew by heart, and Alcaeus's and Anacreon's and Hipponax's. It is easy to write a good love poem when you know all the classics by heart.

I went home from the Feast of the Kore with rage and jealousy in my heart, and I took wax and stylus and wrote a poem. Naming the parts of her body, I adored each in turn, adorned them with verse and crowned my technical achievement by starting each verse with a letter of her name.

I wrote it fair.

The next time I was served dinner by my master, I put it in her hand.

She didn't react at all. She scarcely noticed me, in fact. She made lovely small talk, asked after my friends and then went on to talk of her new friends since the festival – young women of the upper classes who had condescended to her before, but now sought her out.

Indeed, Nikephorus confessed to me that he'd had new clients the last few days – a gang of rich boys who wanted armour.

'My daughter is the talk of the town,' he said happily.

And Julia gave me a look – as expressive, in her way, as any of Lydia's.

I took the bait and swallowed it whole.

Several days passed. I worked very hard, and I exercised even harder. But her eyes seemed to be everywhere. For the first time in many years, I didn't imagine Briseis. I didn't pine for my dead Euphoria. I didn't ever stop thinking about Euphoria, precisely, but it was not her body I pictured in my arms.

The young sprigs came to be fitted for armour. I fitted them, and they were young, empty-headed and rich, so they were easy to hate. I guess they assumed I was a slave.

They wagered on which among them would have her first. Anaxsikles looked at me as if he expected me to kill one on the spot. Since our very short duel, he saw me as Achilles come to life. Funny, if you think about it.

She appeared from time to time, dressed to please in a carefully pleated chiton and blue himation, and served wine.

'I've never thought of bronze this way before,' said one sprig.

'So ruddy,' said the second.

'So ... hard,' said the third. They thought they were the wits of the world. They sailed out of the shop like triremes in a stiff breeze.

In that moment, seeing her watch them with something like adoration, I hated those three boys more than Dagon and Anarchos and my cousin Simon all put together in one awful husk.

But they were gone.

I kept working, and she went back to her rooms. Her father came in, looked at the three roughed-out helmets I'd done and the pairs of greaves Anaxsikles had nearly finished, and gave my arm a gentle squeeze. 'We'll all weather this,' he said. 'And be the richer and better for it.'

He straightened up and admired a nearly complete sword hilt I had on the table. I'd made a trade with a cutler so that I could have new swords for my friends. 'I'm going out to meet friends,' he said. 'Lock up.'

One by one, the slaves and apprentices looked to me for permission to withdraw. Already, in most minds, I was the young master. I remember Anaxsikles kept polishing at a greave until he put it down in disgust.

'I made a planishing error,' he said. 'I can't polish that out.'

'Go home,' I said. 'Look at it again in the morning.'

He laughed, grabbed his chiton and vanished.

Then Julia appeared in the shop with a cup of lukewarm wine – housekeeping was never her strong point. 'I need you to watch the house,' she said. 'My mother needs me for an hour.'

I went back to my work. It was getting dark too fast for anything but general work, and finally I missed a simple blow, shook my head in disgust and frowned at the apprentice boy. 'Go home,' I said. 'You're a good lad, but I can't see to work.'

He flushed at the praise, and was out of the door before I'd washed my hands.

I went and drank Julia's warmed wine. It was warm in the shop, but cold outside, and I'd left the wine far longer than I should have. It was cold, and had a fine layer of shop dust on the surface – a bronze smithy is never clean. I drank it off anyway. I remember that taste so well.

I took the cup – a fine piece of bronzework, of course – up the steps to Julia's kitchen. I gave the cup to a kitchen slave, a Sikel. She grinned.

'You staying for dinner, master?' she asked.

I shook my head. 'Not invited, lass,' I said.

'Oh!' said the serving girl. 'Cook! He ain't staying!'

Cook, a big Italiote woman who never seemed to understand that she was a slave, came out of the kitchen. 'Missy says you are staying to dinner, young master. And the mistress said so, too. Said she'd be home by now,' added the cook with a significant sniff.

Well.

'I'll give you a nice bowl of hot water and a towel, eh?' said Cook.

'Is it true you was a slave?' said the girl.

I nodded. 'Twice.'

She sighed. 'I'd like to be free.'

I washed my hands and face. I had a lesson. I was going to miss it, and I wasn't sure why.

No, that's a lie. I knew exactly why I was missing it. I was letting down my teacher, I was distracting myself from my exercise, and I was quite possibly about to betray my master's trust while deflowering his daughter.

That's why I stayed to dinner.

Men's reasons are complex animals, my young friends. I told myself many things, but here, with you, in the firelight of my own hearth, I know – *I know* – that I wanted her. And despite guest oaths, and friendship and trust and even love, I was willing to have her body, not even for the sweet desirability of it, but because other men wanted it, and I could not stop myself from this contest.

Bah! Fill my cup. I disgust myself. And I do not want to tell this part of the story.

Lydia came down to dinner dressed like a goddess in a play: like Artemis as the patron of young women, or Athena as Parthenos, the virgin. She had on a chiton of Syrian linen dyed the colour of a stormy sea that must have cost as much as five of my helmets. My critical eye saw that her pins had already ripped a line of very small holes in the cloth along the contrasting linen-tape edges of pure white. Over the chiton, which fell to the floor, she wore a himation of wool that was almost transparent, and fell in frilly folds to the floor – just off white, with a stripe of pure Tyrian purple. In her hair was a fillet of white linen tape, and on her feet—

Lydia had the most beautiful feet.

On her feet she wore sandals of gold. In fact, they were leather, with gold leaf laid carefully over the sandals, and again, I could see where she had now worn them enough that the gold had come away from the very top of the arch of leather over her foot.

Noticing these things is not the same as caring. She was as beautiful as a goddess. Her face was radiant, and her carriage was proud and erect. Every line of her body showed through the fabric. She had muscles on her legs and arms that enhanced her posture.

'The girl with the golden sandals has shot me with the dart of love,' I said. I knew my poets.

A man of twenty-six has every advantage with a girl of fifteen. Compared to any other possible suitor, I was better. I *was* better.

And I should have known better, as well.

I led her to the table. I clapped my hands for the slaves, and when they came, I pointed at Lydia.

'Does she not look like a goddess?' I asked.

Cook gave her a hug, and the two girl slaves curtsied.

And we sat to dine.

If we had been aristocrats, I'd have reclined, I suppose – I've honestly only eaten by myself about a dozen times in my life. She'd have sat in a chair, or even fed herself in the kitchen. But this had developed a sense of occasion, and so I sat in a chair – men did, you know, back then – and Cook served us herself. We had chicken with a lovely herb sauce thickened with barley, and thick bread with olive tapenade, and some other *opson* that was made with tuna and highly spiced. At every remove, we expected Julia home.

One of the slaves brought us honeyed almonds, which were a special treat, as we knew Cook didn't really like the mess. The slave girl had obviously sticky fingers and a lot of honey around her mouth, and Lydia and I both saw it: our eyes met, and we laughed aloud.

And her foot rubbed up along the length of the inside of my leg.

And she looked at me, an openly curious look. It said, *I surprised myself, there, but now that I've done it, what do we think?*

We drank wine. It wasn't great wine – Nikephorus didn't drink great wine. He bought good, dark-red local stuff and he liked it. But it was good wine, and we had two cups each, and then we shared a cup.

This is where I went over the edge.

When I went to the cupboard and took down the kantharos cup with two handles, I knew exactly what I was doing. But I had crossed over.

Her eyes were huge as she drank, and our hands touched a great deal.

We sat for a long time, just looking at each other, our now bare feet busy.

In my head, I was screaming at myself to get up and walk away.

I was going to sail to Alba.

Lydia was not coming.

I eventually got up to wash my hands – almonds in honey are sticky. As I rose, I saw that Lydia's chiton had come a long way above her knee – the sight inflamed me.

I have so many excuses.

I walked to the kitchen. Cook was smiling as I washed my hands.

'If I didn't know you was pledged to each other,' she said. She frowned, then grinned lasciviously. 'But I do. Never a word will be spoken, eh?'

I gave her a silver drachma.

There was a knock at the slave door, and a willowy boy stuck his head in and was instantly abashed, since he had to assume I was the master.

'What do you want, boy?' I asked.

'Just?' he said witlessly.

Cook made a cooing noise. 'He's the Mater's boy,' she said. 'What do you want, Petrio?'

He made a sort of sketchy bow. 'Only, my mistress says ... she is sick, and could you send fennel? And Mistress Julia says she'll be another hour at least, and please do not tell the young people.' He looked at me. 'And that's all she said.'

I smiled.

Cook frowned. 'You ain't supposed to have heard that,' she said.

Petrio ran for it.

I shrugged. And went back to the andron.

Lydia was standing by the door to the portico. Her back was to the steps to the exedra, and I assumed she was about to go. I stepped up to her—

I have no idea. We kissed. Who started it? Who stopped? Why?

No idea.

We were in a patch of absolute shadow, and we were fools, and my hands roved her body and hers began, hesitantly, and then with increasing knowledge, to roam mine.

Cook walked right up behind us and dropped a plate.

The crack of the plate was like a dose of cold salt water.

Cook glared at me.

I had Lydia's chiton around her hips, a hand deeply inside her himation and all the pins off her right shoulder.

She blushed, shook her clothes into place and bolted up into the exedra.

I had very little to repair. So I was left with Cook, who stood with her arms crossed, glaring at me.

'Don't tell the young people,' Cook said. 'That means she didn't want you necking in the portico. That's what I heard.'

I nodded and bowed.

'You had better marry her,' Cook said. She shook her head – the weary motion women make when men are involved.

You'll understand me better if you know that while I was repentant, all I could think of as I walked home was the perfect smoothness of her skin, the hard tip of her nipple under my hand, the softness . . .

Well, girls, you can giggle all you like. I'm helping you understand the enemy. Because men need only the touch of a breast to turn from lovers to predators. Sometimes less than that. And what do you get? A man gets an hour's pleasure, and a woman gets – if she's unlucky – pregnancy and death. But your bodies are built to tell you otherwise, and when a man's hand is on a woman's thigh, does she think of childbirth, of Artemis coming for her spirit as the baby wails?

No.

Nor does the man, I can tell you.

Even with a porne, the smart ones are careful, gathering seed in a sponge or using . . . other ways. I'm making you *all* blush: I'll stop. But listen, girls. The joy is the same for both. It's the *price* that's different.

The next day, I went to the shop and worked. At lunch, for the first time I can remember, Lydia came down into the shop with a chunk of bread and some excellent cheese and a cup of wine. When she put the wine into my hand, her whole hand wrapped around mine. She smiled up into my eyes. And then slipped away with grace.

I wanted her. All the time.

That afternoon, without any connivance, the two of us came together in the corridor behind the kitchen, and there wasn't another person in sight, slave or free. Before we could breathe, we were in each other's arms, drinking deep. Her hand was under my chiton, on my hip, and mine—

We had perhaps ten heartbeats, and we almost managed to make love. Luckily we heard movement, and we broke.

It was all just a matter of time.

And in between these trysts I cursed myself for a fool and a coward and a liar, leading her on, and I swore not to have her.

The problem is, you see, that it no longer mattered. Men make much of the act of sex, but it is the act of possession and love that makes the bond. I didn't need to ride her – she had given herself. We hadn't made a baby, but we had made a pact, and I knew I wasn't going to keep it.

Liar. Betrayer.

I thought that I could play her along until I was ready to leave. And 'let her down easily'.

But I never even tried.

I wanted her, body and soul. But not enough, you'll note, to change my plans, or take her with me.

The next day was the same. But I had begun to hedge my bets. I kissed her when I *knew* that Cook was close by and would end it.

See? There's no way to tell this to make myself good.

And I *still wanted her*, every minute. When I saw her, all my friends vanished, the boat was a chimera and I was willing to be a smith in Syracusa. For life.

And then, at the whim of the gods, our boat came back.

They had a better boat. As soon as she was pulled up on the shingle, I could see she had almost double the cargo space, and she was better built – the tongues of wood that held the planks together were tightly placed and beautifully pegged. The steering oars, rather than grey with age, were shining golden wood – new, and very handsome.

They had perfumes and some Etruscan tin. The Etruscan mines are small and stingy, and the Etruscans don't let much out of the country. But Gaius had arranged the sale, and the tin gave us an entry into the trade.

It was a step. Two steps.

As we drank that night in a wine shop, Doola pointed proudly at our new boat. 'We call her *Amphitrite*,' he said. 'She rides the waves like a girl riding a man. With passion.' He lifted his cup and we all drank, and Seckla put wine on the floor for luck.

'So—' Doola was hesitant, and they all looked at me.

'We want to change the plan a little,' Seckla said, all in a rush. His hands moved as he spoke. 'We want to get into the tin trade, first by selling the load we have down the coast, in the Sikel communities where Demetrios has friends. And then—'

Demetrios couldn't take it any more. '*Amphitrite* can take a longer voyage,' he said. 'We take her to Massalia, in Gaul. We load tin there, and we see if we can get someone to tell us about the north. Then, when we've sold some cargoes—'

'How long?' I asked.

Doola was the only one to meet my eyes. 'Two years,' he said. 'Maybe three, until we've got secure trade connections in Massalia and Etrusca and Latinium. Etrusca is rich, brother. There's no reason for us to be here. Sicily is not the hub. Etrusca is.'

I laughed. Shook my head. 'How's Gaius?' I asked.

'He's going to come back to us – with a small ship of his own,' Neoptolymos said. 'We visited his city.'

'It's a dung heap compared to Syracusa,' Daud said. He shrugged. 'And everything they have is taken from my people. But they are rich, and they buy tin – all ten cities. Eleven cities. However many; they pack more cities into the plains of Tusca than we have cities in all of Gaul.'

I shook my head. 'I've got myself into trouble,' I admitted. 'If I stay here two years, I'll be a married shop-owner with a pot belly and four kids. And no mistake.'

Their faces fell.

For the very first time, it occurred to me that we might part ways. Somewhere in another world, off to the east, I had a ship, a family, some wealth and the burned-out remains of a prosperous farm. I could always make a go of it there.

I could marry Lydia and take her to Plataea.

I could go and find Briseis. By Aphrodite, friends, I never, ever, forgot Briseis for more than ten heartbeats. Even then.

Heh.

'If we do as you suggest,' I said to Doola, 'we work our way up to the Alba run gradually. I see the value in it. But it is my observation – I hear the gossip here – that the Carthaginians have all but closed the Gates of Heracles. I don't know of any ship, Greek or Etruscan, that trades with Iberia or Alba. They carry it all, and they sink anyone who tries to run the gauntlet. Am I right?'

Neoptolymos took a swig of wine while keeping me in the corner of his eye, and he gave a hard grin. 'That sounds like a fight.'

Doola nodded, biting his lip. 'It's true.'

'Gaius is a trader, and he's filled your heads with trade. I'm a bronze-smith, but I'm also a warrior. If we go to Alba – even if we only go to the north coast of Iberia! – we will have to fight and sail and sneak, and fight again, if we must. And if we spend two or three years learning the trade, the bastards will see us coming. We need to take them by surprise – a crew of nobodies, a ship they don't know.'

'Two ships,' Demetrios said with a shrug. '*Amphitrite* goes too. We can fill her full of stores, and take a rowed ship for speed when we need it. Two ships double the profit, and make it more likely one gets home.'

I shrugged right back at him. 'Ten ships? A couple of triremes?'

Seckla punched me in the arm.

'When I touch our *patron* for money, he's not going to want to let us sail away,' I said. 'Not without security.' I shrugged again. 'If we do it, we can't ever come back here.' In fact, I knew I wasn't coming back anyway.

Oh, the gods must have laughed.

Well, I had their attention.

'Listen,' I said. 'We can build our second ship right now. We must have five hundred drachmas. I have more due to me at the shop. You have more in the tin. Let's get the hull under way. When it's finished, we hire rowers to get us to wherever slaves are cheap. And we buy them and train them ourselves.'

'Now?' Doola said.

I gave another shrug. 'Or we give up the whole enterprise. Look, it *is* insane. We're six former slaves, and we're going to take on the Carthaginian trade empire and sail across the Outer Sea to Alba? I agree. We can stay home, make money, take wives and be fat.'

Doola smiled bitterly. 'I knew my plan would founder on the rock of your desire for heroism.'

I shook my head. 'No. It doesn't have to be like that. If we all say so, we're absolved of our oaths and we can walk away.'

But they all shook their heads. That's how fate works. We knew we wanted something impossible, but we weren't willing to give it up.

The next day, Doola, Demetrios and I hired horses and rode along the coast to Marissilia, a little port full of fishing boats around the corner from Syracusa. It was sixty stades from the taverna where Anarchos sat and ruled the waterfront. I knew it wasn't far enough, but I had a master to serve and work to do, and my time and funds were limited.

We walked from boatbuilder to boatbuilder. The two largest were scarcely interested in our triakonter, and the smaller didn't have the labour to build her. The triakonter, or thirty-oared ship, was the backbone of most small military expeditions, and was also the most useful size for a rowed merchant ship.

The day was lost.

Lydia vanished into the women's quarters with her courses, and I was able to work without interruption, to meet my master's eye and to ask for another day off and receive it, as well as a purse with sixty drachma – my share of five helmets, all completed. The greaves and breastplates were now on my part of the shop floor.

I went and trained, boxed, sparred with the wooden swords and Polimarchos put bruises into my side. 'That's for standing me up, you ingrate whoreson,' he growled. 'I hope she was worth it.'

Your trainer always knows.

I was having trouble with my life. I kept different parts in different jars – I was a smith, I was an athlete, I was a sailor. I was looking for a shipbuilder, but I couldn't ask Nikephorus to help me, because that would lead very quickly to some shocking admissions. That meant I couldn't ask Polymarchos anything, either, or it would be known throughout the guild in a matter of days.

On one of those evenings, as the cold winter rain fell and the masseur worked my muscles, I remember two middle-aged men, both smiths, coming and sitting on my bench. They were good-natured, but firm.

'You're cutting into our business, you scamp,' one said. He was Diodorus, a master armourer who worked in a different street. I knew him well. The other I didn't know as well.

'Charge more for your damned helmets!' the younger man said. 'Or make them worse.'

They both laughed. But I took their point immediately, and when I went back to Nikephorus, he nodded.

'I've heard the same. We'll raise our price. And refuse a few commissions. I'm sorry, lad, but I don't want Diodorus to decide to go back to casting brooches. He used to, and he gave it up so that I could have that part of the business.' He tugged his beard and looked at me under his bushy eyebrows. 'Don't take it personally. But you have to work with people.'

That meant I was going to make a great deal less money.

On the other hand, I was lucky my master had shared the money with me from the start.

'I'm making some pieces for trade ... and the panoplies for Lydia's suitors,' I said with a smile that was false. 'After that, I'll stick to stock for a while.'

He ruffled my hair. I felt the traitor I was.

'Lydia misses you,' he said. And grinned. 'When's the wedding?'

I shook my head, put my eyes down and tried to hide. 'Not discussed. Yet.'

He nodded.

'Best discuss it,' he said, and rose to his feet. 'Soon.'

I left work and walked down to the port, where Neoptolymos and I watched a dancer while drinking decent wine. She was good. But I remember thinking at her every gyration that Lydia's hips were more expressive when she rose from her seat than this golden girl was as she moved.

Ah, lust. Eros.

We gave her the tips she expected from a couple of men and finished our amphora of wine, and then we wandered the waterfront, peering into boats.

'I'll need a trireme to get my place back,' Neoptolymos said, out of the darkness.

'I'll find us one, when it's time,' I said. 'This will sound foolish, but I *own* a trireme. If she still swims above the waves, I'll put her at your service.'

He was sitting on the dog's head that held the mooring lines for a pair of smugglers owned by Anarchos. Pretty little twenty-oared boats with lines like racehorses.

He laughed. 'You're an odd one. You *own* a trireme. You fought at Marathon. Yet you are living in a tenement in Syracusa with a pack of former slaves, trying to sail around the world.' He punched me. 'Why in Hades don't we take your Poseidon-forsaken trireme to Gades and Alba? Eh?'

I shook my head. It was hard to explain, and I didn't really want to, but—

'If I go back, I have to go back,' I said lamely. 'Political power, my farm, my family, war, Athens—' I realized that I sounded angry. I *was* angry.

What was I angry at?

'What happened?' Neoptolymos asked. He leaned forward and put a hand on my arm. 'It's none of my business. We all trust you. But you have things none of us has – none of us but bloody Gaius. It's funny that you're the one pressing us to move faster, as you are the one who has somewhere else to go. I'll never take back my little kingdom. Even if I do, I'll never ... make it right. My sister told me to be careful of pirates, and I left her to her death. A horrible death.' He stared at the stars, and wept.

I hugged him. 'Don't be an arse, brother. You did not rape your sister. You did not kill her. You are not responsible. Or rather—' I thought of Heraclitus. 'Rather, yes, you made an error, and you can atone for it by finding Dagon and putting a spear up his arse.'

At my crudity, he raised his face.

'You are a good hater,' he said.

'I have imagined killing him twenty thousand times,' I said.

'Killing who?' asked a gruff voice. Anarchos came out of the darkness with a half-dozen of his minions. He owned the boats. He wasn't the one out of place.

'A Phoenician named Dagon,' I said, with perfect honesty.

Anarchos frowned, whether in real interest or simulated, I could not tell. But then he shrugged. 'I hear you are looking to build a boat?' he asked. His flunkeys stood around him, trying to look tough, which is difficult in the dark. One of them had a torch, and it didn't throw enough light for anyone.

'Yes,' I said. 'A triakonter, big enough for the tin trade.' A little truth goes a long way.

'You have a regular source with the Etruscans?' Anarchos asked. He was really interested. We all knew this could lead to big money.

I shrugged.

Anarchos stepped up close to me, so I could smell the onion on his breath. 'You have a problem, my young friend. Everyone I know is waiting for you to marry the bronze-smith's daughter. Some say she's already baking your bread in her oven, eh? And yet, other people tell me you are looking to get a ship built.' He eyed me, his head a little to one side like a curious dog. 'And I say – to myself I say it – what if he's playing her for a fool?'

Shit. Anarchos was that smart. And that was going to make it nearly impossible to take him for money.

'And I wondered, does the old smith know his new young master is building a ship?' Anarchos was very close, and very quiet. 'Not that I'd tell him, unless I had reason. I am, after all, a reasonable man. And your patron.' He took a step back. 'I have six shipyards under my thumb, Arimnestos of Plataea. I think you know this, so I have to wonder why you don't come to me. And then I have to find you in the dark and ask you all this. And it seems to me that your slave friends have just made a fine profit on a voyage, but not an obol has found its way to me. I wonder if we don't need a little reminder of how this ought to work. Eh?'

It's hard to glare at a man by torchlight.

'I will apologize for our oversight,' I said slowly, 'and bring you our contribution in the morning. And you must understand, *patron*, that I might be a little shy about using your boatyards. I don't wish to say any more about it.'

'But I have two yards that need work – and can build your ship. By giving this work to either one, I am more important, and my patronage is secure. And you would deny me this?' He laughed, as a man will when explaining a sticky problem to an infant.

I shrugged in the darkness. 'We are not rich men,' I said. 'But I will try your yards.'

'Ah! You sound as if you are doing me a favour. And perhaps you are. You are an odd duck, Plataean. You demand to be treated differently from all the rest of my clients – and I *do* treat you differently. You think I'm a fool? I've held this waterfront for thirty years. I know what kind of man you are. Don't treat me as a fool, and we will continue as friends. Come and drink wine with me.'

'Tomorrow, *patron*.'

He laughed. 'You know what is funny, Plataean? You think you are a better man than I. You don't want to drink wine with a crime lord, eh? You have *aristocrat* embroidered on your forehead. And yet I like you, and I let you do things that I would kill other men for doing – like refusing to drink with me. And I'll go further. I'll bet that you've killed men and taken their gold without a qualm. Just like me. And you have friends and allies who depend on you – like I do. You keep your word. So do I.' He pointed at me, and the torchlight caught the grey in his hair and made it flare. 'I give you my word that if you come and drink with me, you will not regret it, and neither will your friends.'

He turned on his heel and walked up the wet stones to his house, leaving me with Neoptolymos and a body full of the daimon of combat. I had been so sure he was going to attack us.

The next evening I appeared at his house wearing a good Ionian chiton of my own, and over it a decent himation I'd bought second-hand. Of my friends, only Doola wanted to come, and I wasn't sure that an African, however dignified, was going to win Anarchos over.

Slaves took my stick and my himation, and I went into his andron, which was beautifully appointed – more like that of a very rich merchant than a street fixer. He had a pair of marble amphorae on columns – they must have been a thousand years old. His kline were all Ionian work, like the ones on which Briseis and I made love, with wicker mats on a fruitwood frame. I sank onto mine, a slave took my sandals and I was given a cup of red wine.

He was on the other kline, and he raised his head over the arm rest. 'So – you came,' he said. 'I'm surprised, after all my ranting last night. I'll have to kill a rival to convince my bullies I'm still tough.'

I laughed. I wanted to hate him, but in truth, I liked him for all the reasons he named. We had a great deal in common.

'Tell me about your boat,' he said.

'I have our contribution,' I said.

He shook his head. 'That's business. Bring it to me in public. This is private. No witnesses, no attribution. I'll take no revenge for what you say here. So speak the truth, or keep your breath in the fence of your teeth.'

The six of us had debated all day what we should do. Daud and Neoptolymos were for instant flight over the sea to Etrusca. Doola and Demetrios and I were for looking at what the crime lord had to offer.

'He can sell us to the Phoenicians!' Seckla said. He certainly had Anarchos sized up.

'Not if he's in love with Ari,' Doola said. He gave me a wicked smile.

Daud looked away. 'You two make me uncomfortable,' he said.

The Keltoi don't take the love of men for men with the ease that Greeks do. And Etruscans and Aegyptians and everyone else, for that matter. Barbarians.

'Not if he sees real profit,' Doola said. 'We represent a long shot at a lot of money, friends. Let's not undersell our own possibilities. I am not saying we should share the whole truth with the whoreson. Just that if he really can get our boat built, he might be an ally. An untrustworthy ally, but an ally.'

Doola. He put everything so well.

So I was allowed to bargain with Anarchos.

I leaned on the arm of my own kline and smiled.

'We want to enter the tin trade,' I admitted. 'We have the skills. We have the ability to do things few other men understand. I know what tin looks like at every stage. I can buy at the side of the stream, or at the mine head.

'We can navigate and sail. There's tin at Massalia in Gaul, and it comes from upcountry. There's tin in the mountains behind the Tuscan plain, and there's tin in Illyria. We have an Illyrian, a Gaul and an Etruscan.' I shrugged. 'I can't be plainer than that.'

Anarchos drank his wine, and his slaves bustled to refill the cup. Another oddity – he didn't have the terrified slaves of a bad master. He had the sort of slaves we all want to have. They were mostly silent, but when Anarchos made a witticism, they smiled or even laughed.

Interesting.

'And you can do all this with a triakonter?' he asked.

'Well ... yes. And the ship we have now.' I shrugged. 'And ten more, when we get into the trade.'

'And who protects you from the Phoenicians?' he asked. 'Their triremes are cruising for you, even now.' He shook his head. 'I made enquiries about this Dagon. He is – quite famous. Infamous. A slaver.' He fingered his beard. 'A typical fucking Carthaginian.' He looked at me. 'Seriously, Ari. May I call you that? Listen. In Syracusa, we all hate them. It's the unifying force that binds the commons and the lords together. And sooner or later, they will get their forces together and come for us. Iberians, Keltoi, their own Poieni infantry, their crack cavalry force. They'll load them on ships and try and finish us off. They mean to control all the trade in the Eastern Sea, and we are in the way.' He drank. 'Is this about revenge on this Dagon? I don't finance revenge. And when dealing with Carthage, anyone who sails from Syracusa does so under a death sentence. Why should I wager on you?'

'No reason at all,' I said. 'You invited me, and told me to speak my mind.'

'I've always wanted to fit out a couple of big privateers for cruising against Carthage,' he said.

I laughed. 'Listen, Anarchos. Last night you did me the honour of telling me a thing or two. And now I'll tell you straight back. I've been a pirate – with Miltiades. Know the name?'

'Of course.'

'So yes – I've killed men and taken their gold. Taken their ships and pushed them men into the sea. Taken the women and given them to my men.' I leaned over to him. 'I never meant to be that man, but that's the man I was, for a while. It's not a bad life, if you stay drunk and don't think too much.' I nodded. 'There's men who can live like that, all the time. I'm not one of them. Something tells me you aren't really, either. The captains you'd need to run a couple of corsairs – they wouldn't be men you could hope to control. And in a year – less, if they were successful – the assembly would have to have you executed. With five triremes, Miltiades virtually strangled the whole trade of Aegypt. D'you get me?'

He nodded.

I wasn't even lying.

'If we go for some tin, and succeed – well, it's no one's business but ours, eh? If we go to sea to take the ships of Carthage, it's only a matter of time.' I shrugged and lay back, and a slave refilled my cup.

'The odds against you ... ' he said.

'The odds are balanced by the pay-off if we succeed. What are a thousand talents of tin worth?' I remember waving my hands in the air.

He laughed.

'What is my silence with your jilted lover worth?' he asked.

I sat up.

'Relax, Ari. I really mean no harm, but it is clear to me that you are never going to be a settled bronze-smith, try as you will. You aren't going to marry that girl. You're going to go sailing off to Massalia ... or Alba.' He laughed. Damn him.

'Alba's too hard,' I said, knowing that he'd guessed it all.

'Hmm,' he said. 'Glad you know that. I know a dozen men who claim they've been there. You'll find more in Massalia, but no two of them tell the same tale, and I'm not sure that *Alba* isn't a myth that Carthage uses to hide the source of all that white tin.'

I shrugged. He might have been right, except that Daud knew where Alba was. It was an edge other rivals wouldn't have had.

'We're close to war with Carthage even now. That war is going to collapse our economy. How much money do I have to put in my bet with you, and what's my profit?' He sat up, too.

I drank almost a cup of wine, trying to find a path through all the lies, the subterfuge, the desires of my friends, the needs of the group.

Sticking men with a spear is much, much simpler.

'Your friend Miltiades is leading an expedition against Paros,' Anarchos added.

Well, that didn't tempt me. He was now the great man he'd always wanted to be.

I lay back. 'I'm done with all that,' I said.

He leaned in, and I realized this was what he wanted to talk about, more than the trade. 'Why? Tell me why, Plataean. You have a name, you survived slavery and now you are here – if you really are who you say you are. For a few months I told myself that the bronze-smith's daughter held you. Why not? She's a beauty. But now I see that you are using her. You really are a man like me, aren't you?' he leered. 'And yet, if you are, why not go back to Miltiades? He's living high, now. He'll be Tyrant of Athens if he takes Paros, or greater. He's building an empire in the east.'

I remember sighing. 'I said, I'm done with all that,' I remember responding. I sat up on my couch. 'Listen, I came as close to death as a man can come. I want a life. A real life.'

'But not a wife and a home,' he shot back.

'I am what I am,' I said.

He shook his head. We lay in silence – I remember listening to slaves in the kitchen, bickering about whether to serve the next course or not.

'What do you need?' he asked.

'We need to build our ship, and we need thirty good oarsmen. In a perfect world, they'd be slaves willing to work through to freedom for shares.' I shrugged. 'Slave oarsmen aren't what you want in a tight spot. I have reason to know.'

He chuckled. 'You have no doubt encountered the local attitude about slavery,' he said.

'Oh, yes,' I said.

He shook his head. 'In a year, war with Carthage may change everyone's tune,' he said. 'I'd want five to one for every silver mina I put in.'

'Three to one.'

'Five to one. Five to one, and I do you the justice that it's a straight business deal in which I'm a member – that is, I make sure the yard deals straight, I help find the oarsmen and I don't play the *patron* about control. In exchange, you give me your word, your absolute word, that you will bring your tin here and sell it through me, and give me my share first if you make it.'

I blinked. Five to one.

Of course, we could sail away and never come back.

'And another thing,' he said. 'You're going to spurn Despoina Lydia. So: how can I believe you'll come back?'

'My word? My oath to the gods?'

'Didn't you give her the same?' he said.

That stung, and like most comments that enrage you, it was true.

'So you marry her,' he said. 'And tell old Nikephorus the truth. Then I'll know you plan to come back.'

'Marry her and sail away?' I said.

'Isn't that better than *not* marrying her and sailing away?' he asked. 'Let me ask you, oh bold veteran of Marathon – when she kills herself, how will you feel?'

Something cold gripped the bottom of my stomach and my heart.

He laughed. 'You know, the hard men to touch are the dead ones who feel nothing. Men like you – you are easy. You care. I could make you do a great many things, simply by seizing on your own notions of right and wrong and twisting.' He put his wine cup down. 'But I won't. Here's my price: marry the girl, and give me five to one. I'll put up a couple of mina in silver, I'll coax the shipwrights and you'll start with a well-found ship. No one loses. In fact, I think I'm actually doing a good deed, and if you make it back, everyone will benefit.'

He raised his cup.

I raised mine.

We drank.

Let me say this. A local thug is a dangerous nuisance. A crime lord is often a much more complex animal. Anarchos was a man who, under other circumstances, would have ruled a city. I've seldom known anyone so intelligent, so attuned.

So terrifying.

It took me ten days to face Nikephorus.

I actually started several times, in a small voice – so small he walked past and called out to an apprentice, and the day moved on.

Finally, the day before the spring feast of Demeter, I caught him writing at his work table.

'We need to talk,' I said.

He looked at me. 'We certainly do,' he said. 'My daughter is very unhappy.'

I nodded. 'I want to marry her,' I said. 'But I have a problem, and I want to admit it to you.'

He nodded. 'You are already married.'

I shook my head. 'She died; I loved her very much. That is not what this is about.'

He nodded. I could tell he was gritting his teeth. I wasn't doing well.

'I want to take an expedition to Massalia to buy tin,' I said. 'It may be more than that.' I held up my hand, silencing his protest for a moment. 'I am not what you think, master. I am a smith – but I am also a warrior, and sometimes a sea captain.' I tried to read his expression. 'I wish to ask her to marry me, but I wish you to know that if I die at sea, I have nothing to leave her. I think you want a son to manage the shop, and I am not that man.'

He sat back and polished a bronze cup on his writing table absently – but thoroughly. He was angry – I could see the anger in the red blotches on his face, and in his posture. Finally, he got up.

'Leave this house,' he said. 'My curse on you. You have lied, and your lies have hurt us all. My daughter loves you. My wife loves you. I love you. And this is what you give us? That you wish to run away to sea?' He shook his head slowly. 'Have I treated you badly, that this is what you repay me with?'

I opened my mouth. I was shocked. I had expected – well, I had expected it would all be fine. I wanted Lydia – at this point, I was aware that Julia was keeping the girl from me for our mutual protection, so to speak. And in my worst nightmares, I hadn't imagined that Nikephorus would send me from the door.

I walked to the door in a haze.

'Don't go to the gymnasium. You will never work in this town again,' he said.

I stopped in the doorway, all youth and bluster. 'Why?' I asked. 'I love her – I mean—' I paused. 'I never meant to hurt any of you.'

'Really?' he asked, and closed the door.

I walked slowly towards our tenement. Before I'd gone a hundred steps, I heard a woman shriek. It was the sound men made when they knew a wound was mortal, the sound women made when childbirth became too much to be borne.

I prayed to Poseidon, to Heracles, to Apollo and to Aphrodite.

They ignored me, because I had done this myself. And, of course, to her.

★

Anarchos sent me word, by a thug, that our deal was off.

The thug said it in just that way.

'The *patron* says the deal is off. But he says, "No hard feelings". Eh?' The bruiser shrugged.

I shrugged too. We understood each other perfectly, the bruiser, the crime lord and I.

I drank too much, for the first time in my life. That is, I drank too much quite regularly for several days.

Doola found me drinking in the morning of the third day, and collected me and my bad temper and led me home.

'We're putting to sea,' he said.

'It's winter,' I answered.

None of them ever questioned me about the failure of my plan, or the loss of my work, or anything.

They stood by the hull of our boat, just about the same length as four horses, and together we pushed her down into the water on rollers. We warped her around to the pier that small merchants and smugglers used, and we loaded salt fish in bales. The bilge was already full of small amphorae.

Even in my mood of abject self-hatred, I was curious.

'What's in those, wine?' I asked Seckla. They didn't look like wine amphorae, unless it was a very fine vintage.

Seckla shrugged. 'Doola got a deal,' he said.

Doola grinned. 'Fish oil. From the Euxine.' He helped me hoist a bale of dried fish. 'The importer died, and I bid at his estate auction. It may be worthless, but I paid about the value of the jars.'

Well. Everyone else was pulling his weight, even if I had failed.

We got to sea with a favourable breeze. I hadn't sailed in months, I didn't know the boat and I was miserable and temperamental. I objected to everything, disliked the way the sails were stowed, disliked the placement of the helmsman's bench – on and on.

Everyone stayed out of my way.

And of course, I saw that I was not in command. Demetrios was in command.

Since my first slavery, I have always been a leader – often *the* leader. To see how well Demetrios commanded them ... in fact, he didn't command at all. He merely indicated what needed to be done, and it was done. He did it with smiles and shrugs.

It made perfect sense; he'd been running the boat for months without me. But it was another blow.

Luckily for me, we had a storm.

I don't remember the storm very well. It came up slowly, and I remember that we had time to tie everything down, to run cables to the masthead, to brail up the sail until it was just a scrap of heavy weather canvas; time for each man to prepare himself a nest against the gunwales where he could be warm and dry – well, that's a lie, but miserable in as much comfort as he could manage.

We were well north of Sicily, in the Etruscan Sea, and we had plenty of sea room, so we set the helm and sailed with the wind and waves under the windward quarter. Our boat climbed each wave, bobbing like a cork, and seemed to skid along the crest with an odd bumping motion until we slid down towards the next trough. It wasn't the biggest sea I'd ever seen, and the sky never took on the purple-black colour I associate with the worst weather. But it took me outside myself; focused me on survival and teamwork.

The storm took three days to blow itself out, and on the morning of the fourth, we were scudding along in a stiff winter breeze in bright sunshine. The sea was a deep blue, the whitecaps were a startling white and the mainland of Italy was visible on the horizon.

And I felt better.

We made landfall. None of us knew where we were, but after a day tacking north, we saw a cluster of rocks that Doola and Demetrios recognized, and then we were in the estuary of the Po, one of the larger rivers on the Etruscan plain. We entered the mouth of the river, got our mast down and landed in the mud and grassy fields of Italy. It had been a remarkable passage with a fine landing, and in midwinter, such a passage was worth a trip to the temple and the sacrifice of a young ram. We were the only foreign boat in the river mouth.

After a meal on the fruits of our sacrifice, we slept and headed upriver. The wind and current were against us, and we had to row all the way. Even a small boat is a heavy burden with four rowers, and we had to row near our peak effort to make any headway at all.

We rowed for about half a day, and gave it up, and spent another night in the estuary. Ostia, that's what the village is called. I remember that the wine was good.

We were windbound for four days, and despite the rain on the fifth, we were stir-crazy, and we set out again with rested muscles and a gentle breeze at our backs. We got the sail up, and between the fitful breeze and our new strength, we got upriver at a walking pace all day.

That night we slept on the boat, a tangle of arms and legs in a gentle but spray-filled wind. My cloak soaked through, and my spare.

On the third day out, we made Rome. Despite Daud's carping, Rome was, and is, a fine town with handsome buildings. The core town is not much bigger than Plataea, and I could see real similarities. They call Plataea 'Green Plataea' for the contrast between our tilled fields and the desert that is most of Greece. Italy is fertile, but Rome's surrounding plains are astonishingly fertile. The farms are larger than anything at home, with two-story houses, roofed in thatch, built around central courtyards.

There was a fine temple, visible from the water; it was painted in bright colours, with an impressive colonnade. We arrived on a sunny afternoon, and the red tile roof seemed like the welcoming hand of Zeus extended to us.

The town itself was unwalled, and seemed to have both planned and unplanned elements – hundreds of small houses built like peasant huts in Greece, shacks, really – and then a cluster of public buildings and larger houses. The waterfront and the ford over the river seemed the focal points, but perhaps that is merely a sailor's perspective.

We beached on mud below the ford. The bank had been so completely cleared of trees as to make it very difficult to moor our boat. After I had stood for what seemed like a long time, searching the bank for an old stump, a small boy appeared.

He spoke in a foreign tongue and held out his hand. I had no idea what he was saying – he wasn't speaking Etruscan. After several sallies, I understood that he wanted six coppers – the words were enough like Greek to make them out, especially when he ticked them off on his fingers.

Doola jumped ashore.

'It was the same last time. He'll find a place to moor us.' Doola laughed, and paid the boy in Sicilian obols. The boy looked at them, squinted at Doola and then nodded sharply. Two other boys came out with a heavy stake and a maul, drove the stake into the bank and moored us, bow and stern.

'Romans can make money out of anything,' Doola remarked.

Seckla ran off on his long legs to find Gaius, and we set to unloading the boat. There was a pier, but the charges were exorbitant, and the bank was firm enough to get our bales of dry fish over the side and onto our tarpaulins with relative ease. Before the tenth bale was ashore, a dozen men had appeared to sneer at our fish, and before the twentieth bale was ashore, Doola was bargaining furiously.

Gaius appeared in the midst of this, embraced every one of us, handed round a flask of wine and then issued a set of rapid-fire orders in the local tongue. He ordered four bales of fish set aside for his own use, he changed the bid price in the ongoing dickering, and he asked me to fetch him one of the jars of fish oil.

I had, in effect, been demoted to the level of holding mooring lines and fetching fish oil.

And I was fine with that. I wanted to work, to be useful.

He broke the seal on the first amphora and a smell hit us that was like raw human sewage. It was incredible.

He grinned, and dipped the tip of a finger into the stuff. Well, no one likes the smell – they say you can smell the factories in the Euxine from a hundred stades away.

He tasted it, and grinned. In Greek, he said: 'Four for me. The rest, I'll find a proper buyer for those.'

He had a donkey, which he left with us, and he walked away – he was wearing a good himation and carried a stick, like a gentleman, and he appeared unhurried, but when I got the next armload of the heavy little amphorae ashore, Gaius was gone.

He came back with a trio of slaves and a wagon. Doola and Demetrios had sold ten of the amphorae at a healthy two silver coins apiece – a wild profit – and we had covered the costs of the voyage on the salt fish. Sailing in winter is dangerous, but the profits are excellent, if you live. In the dead of winter, a spot of fish stew, a cup of good wine, a taste of fine fish sauce – these mean more.

In fact, by the time Gaius returned, Daud and Neoptolymos weren't unloading any more. They were standing guard with spears over the bales of fish. No one threatened violence and there was no out-and-out theft, but no one thought the two warriors were slacking, either.

We made a good profit. The fish oil was not all good – in fact, about one amphora in three was ruined or too old – but what was good was very good. Doola had performed his usual miracle, and we cleared almost fifty drachmas or their local, Latin equivalent. We climbed up the Capitoline Hill and made sacrifice at the Temple of Jupiter Optimus Maximus. They, like the Etruscans, had the same gods as Hellenes, but with different names, some interesting and some barbaric – Minerva for Athena, Jupiter for Zeus, and so on. Jupiter Optimus Maximus is 'Zeus Greatest and Best', and was worshipped in much the same way as our 'Zeus Sator'. Poseidon – Neptune in Rome – was not much worshipped, but we gave him our sheep, to the puzzlement of the two priests, both of whom were prominent local aristocrats, just as they are at home. Gaius introduced us to everyone as his companions in slavery, which didn't seem to have anything of the same stigma in Roma that it had in Syracusa.

The town was too small to hold our interest long, and had no shipbuilding. I saw some fine metalwork, most of it done by slaves, and I was very impressed by the Etruscan-style painting on plaster, which seemed to me much better than that which I had seen in Boeotia, and as good as the painting in Attica.

We picked up a cargo of tanned hides – rich, creamy leather from mature cattle. We got over two hundred hides at a good price – not a great price, but a good one – and a hundred big amphorae of local wine. And Gaius handed his share of the cash to his wife and came aboard.

None of us asked him about it, and he didn't say much, but he was happy to be at sea, and to be working. I'm guessing, but I think that the life of a penniless Etruscan aristocrat in Rome didn't agree with him. He had obligations he could barely fulfil, and he was a drain on his family. He never said so, but I saw how happy his wife was to receive ten good Athenian drachmas.

It can be hard, being an aristocrat. If you work, people make fun of you. You have to figure out a cunning way to make some money without appearing to get your hands dirty, unless you own a lot of land. Gaius didn't own a lot of land, but he wasn't afraid to work – once we were safely at sea.

And so, we did it again. Winter can be a cruel mistress, but we were blessed again, and we made Sardinia in two days and then did what Demetrios was best at – we coasted along until we found a town that wanted our hides. Some of the men of the town were Sikels, and Demetrios did most of the work, and we sold our hides at a profit, sold some of our wine, took on another cargo including copper and sailed for Marsala.

Marsala is a Greek town, for all that the Phoenicians established it. It is mostly Phocaeans, and when we made landfall it made me homesick, at least for Greece. Marsala *looks* like Greece.

The harbour is magnificent, and the two beaches are fine white sand. We beached, stern first, and ran the boat up above the tide line with the help of a dozen locals for a few coppers. Then we propped the hull to keep it sound and began unloading. Hawk-nosed Phoenicians came down to look at our wares, and tattooed Keltoi, tanned Greeks and even a couple of blond Iberians. Everyone expressed a unified contempt for our sour Roman wine and our ugly hides and our poor-quality Sardinian copper.

And then one of the Phoenicians offered us a handsome profit for a single sale – the whole cargo.

He was a big man, with a nose bigger than some men's faces, and he thumped his stick at Doola. 'Everything,' he said. 'One hundred and fifty drachma. Take it or leave it. And no shilly-shally.'

Other men began to shout.

Doola nodded. 'No,' he said.

The Phoenician shrugged, turned on his heel and walked off, attended by two slaves. A cold wind blew along the bay, and the islands off the coast were showing spray off their sandbars.

But as if his offer had changed the mood, the other potential buyers began to bid. They were like sharks on the corpse of a whale – as soon as one made a buy, two more would go after Doola as if he was the enemy. I'd never seen it like this; Rome, for example, had been much calmer. I went to his shoulder with some notion of supporting him, but Demetrios pulled me back.

'This is his element,' he said. 'Let him swim.'

The frenzy lasted less than an hour, but by the end of it, Doola's clay pot held more than two hundred drachma, and we had four damaged hides, a dozen amphorae of wine and one single ingot of copper.

Doola looked at the young Gaul standing there. 'I'll give you what's left for two silvers,' he said. 'The copper alone's worth twice that.'

The man beamed with gratitude, Doola took his cash and we had an empty hull. He gave me the clay pot full of silver. 'It doesn't pay to be too greedy,' he said. 'We were lucky – the only cargo on the beach.'

I shrugged under the weight of the pot. 'This is going to sound foolish,' I said, 'but why did you refuse the first offer? He met your price.'

Doola rocked back and laughed his laugh. 'Did he? I couldn't work it all out, so I assumed he was under my price.' He shook his head.

Demetrios laughed, too. 'You made almost twice that.'

Neoptolymos was carrying our belongings. There was nothing in the boat to guard but the oars, and we paid a local Gallic boy to handle that. 'Are we there yet?' he asked.

We sat in a very Greek taverna with two pretty slave girls, ten big wooden bench-tables and nets hanging from the rafters – we might have been in Piraeus. He poured the takings out on the table, and added the Sicilian money from a leather wallet he wore all the time.

We had a lot of money, so much money that the innkeeper came down from his perch and leaned into our group. 'Sorry to be the bearer of bad tidings, gents, but there's no watch here, and some hard men just sent runners for help. That's too much money to show in here.' He stepped back and raised his hands. 'I don't want trouble, and I don't want corpses.'

Doola shook his head in disgust. 'I should have known.'

Demetrios looked around. The taverna was empty.

I felt like a fool. I *was* a hard man, and I tended to watch these things for the rest of them. But after two months' black depression I was rising to the surface, and the money, and the feeling of victory, had excited me. Too much.

My eyes met those of Neoptolymos, and then we were arming. Gaius didn't have all his war gear, but he had a good sword and a heavy himation. Neoptolymos and I had all our gear. Daud had the gear I'd made him: a plain bronze Boeotian cap and the sword I'd traded for.

Seckla laced my leather *spola* while Doola did the same for Neoptolymos.

'I really don't want any trouble,' said the innkeeper.

Doola grinned at him. 'Then send a runner out there and tell them that it would be a mistake for them to attack us. Send another to the *archon* for the guard, and we'll be out of your hair in no time.'

The innkeeper spread his hands again. 'If only—'

Doola's grin took on a certain air. I got it.

'He's in on it,' I said.

Doola nodded. He had Neoptolymos in his harness and he fetched a bow.

I pointed at the gleaming pile of coins. 'Seckla, you stay right here, *no matter what*, and watch the money.' I handed him my long knife. It wasn't a fine weapon, but it would do the job. It cut twine well, and meat. And men.

The innkeeper backed across the room, but Gaius had him in a headlock before he could get out the door.

'By the gods! You've got this all wrong!' he whimpered.

Doola shook his head. 'He's probably not important enough to the gang to bargain with,' he said. He looked at Demetrios. 'I really fucked this up, brothers. Too much money.'

I won't surprise you if I say that, with armour on my back and an aspis leaning against the wall, I was a different man. I wanted the fight, and I could see that Neoptolymos did, too.

I hadn't fought in a year.

More than a year.

In fact, standing in a wretched waterfront tavern in Marsala, I realized I hadn't really fought since Marathon. I laughed aloud.

Daud looked at me. 'You aren't one of those madmen who love the fight, are you?' he asked.

I shook my head. 'No. Or maybe yes.' I laughed again; I sounded wild, even in my own ears. 'Listen, brothers. My last fight was at Marathon, for all the things men find worthy. And now I'm going to fight to the death for some coins in a tavern.'

Gaius was at the door. We had a simple building, a tavern with a portico full of tables outside, a single door and two windows facing the beach. I realized my brothers were readying themselves to die.

Suddenly, I was in charge.

'This is easy,' I insisted. 'They can only come at us a few at a time. Daud, make sure the kitchen is clear behind us and there's no back door.' I went to the entrance and looked out onto the seafront and the failing light. There were a dozen or more men.

They saw me.

I stood in the doorway. After a long minute, I made the universal sign that men make that means, *Give me your best shot.*

They hesitated.

Can I make you laugh? I seriously thought of charging them. *I wanted that fight.*

Doola loosed an arrow. It went over their heads, *just* over their heads, into the hull of an upturned boat.

And just like that, they folded and crept away.

I turned and glared at Doola, and he was unconcerned.

An hour later, we were drinking wine. Daud was on watch – our only fear was that they might set fire to our boat in sheer peevishness.

We let the innkeeper go. He served us himself, he was modestly obsequious, and by full dark it was obvious that no one was going to attack us.

About the same time, a dozen spearmen appeared out of the darkness, fully armed and carrying aspides. Daud whistled, we all took our places and Demetrios of Phocaea, of all men, came out of the darkness behind them. I'd last seen him sailing out of the wreck of the Ionian centre at Lades, waving his thanks. He'd been the navarch, or as close as; it made no matter.

He was the *archon basileus*, or something like that, and he had come with his guard to restore order. Householders had complained.

We embraced like old friends. We hadn't been close, as he'd thought I was an impudent young pup and I'd thought he was an arrogant old man.

But we slept that night around his hearth, and in the morning, everything was different.

He didn't ask any hard questions, but he was happy to show us to the shipyards, and when none of them wanted our work, he offered to pressure them. We shook our heads. Who wants a boat built unwillingly?

After another day or two, we rode north around the coast a full day to Tarsilla, a smaller port, not a city, but a prosperous town. Carthage burned it later, but it was a fine place, with a terraced town and a beautiful two-beach port. Even in winter, the trees were fresh and green. There were three shipyards, all two- and three-man operations, and Demetrios knew all the shipwrights. His own trading trireme had come from Tarsilla.

Vasileos was the lead shipwright of the town, and his yard had the best wood. He took our job immediately. He liked the size of the project for the time of year, because a larger ship needed more men to work on it and was usually built in spring or summer, right by the sea. But a smaller ship like a triakonter could be built well up the beach by just three men. He wasn't a tall man, and he had something of the Phoenician look about him – hawk-nosed, big-handed, with a thin frame and broad shoulders, and when he swung his adze, it cut with the accuracy that a trained spearman treasures.

After some negotiation, we bought a small house in Tarsilla and moved our sparse goods there. Doola, Seckla and Demetrios brought our little *Amphitrite* around the coast to the town, laden with bronze fittings for the ship.

Gaius, Neoptolymos and I went upcountry with Doola, looking for a crew.

That may sound foolish, but I had a notion – shared by Demetrios – that we'd have to fight, and that we wanted a free crew if we could get one – fighters rather than slaves, like the ancient men in Homer. And Daud thought that young men searching for adventure sounded like the cheapest labour.

There are mountains behind the coast; in places cliffs come right to the sea edge, and nowhere are the mountains far from the beach. We went up into the mountains, where the local folk live – more like Sikels than like Keltoi, for all that they speak Gallic and wear armbands and tattoos. They were hospitable, and we got a dozen potential oarsmen out of the little hill villages.

We got another dozen from among the fishermen themselves, though their parents resented us. But Doola, with his exotic looks, and Neoptolymos, with his lyre, made us sound like the Argonauts, and there was a tacit understanding – never quite spoken – that if we fought, we'd be going to fight Phoenicians. I'm not saying that they are bad men. I'm just saying that they seem to have a lot of enemies.

Demetrios of Phocaea provided the rest of my spear-carrying oars-men from his own tail.

I visited every time the business of building the boat took me to Marsala. We had to count every obol that winter and spring. The easiest way for the metalwork to get done was for me to rent shop space in Marsala, where charcoal and copper were available, and to smelt and forge the metal gear myself. So I did: I traded bronze-work for a pair of iron anchors – better than anything I'd used at home – but men said that beyond the Pillars of Heracles, the anchor stones didn't work so well. I forged bronze thole pins and I cast lead counterweights for the oars; I forged sixty bronze rings for the sail, while the women of Marsala wove and sewed the hemp for a full set of sails for each boat. I made some chain – chain's heavy and expensive, but it is better than rope – and I made war gear, caps for every oarsman and simple circular plates for their chest and back. I'd seen these in Etrusca and again in Rome, and they made sense to me: a disc of heavy bronze that covers a man's heart gives him confidence, and will protect him from many blows.

I bought or traded for knives – all Spanish blades that I hilted in bronze – and the last of our damaged hides went into making scab-bards and belts.

It was a little like arming Plataea. It made me happy enough.

Vasileos finished our ship before the spring feast of Demeter. We made a rich sacrifice to her and to Poseidon; I put a decent helmet on the altar of Heracles and a good bronze lamp on the altar of Hephaestos and another on the altar of Apollo. I confess that I felt my skills had diminished. I had betrayed Nikephorus and his daughter, and the smith-god withheld his hand from my shoulder. I marred my work often with stray blows; my helmets were not as neat as I expected them to be, and every one of them seemed to have its flaw. When I made Gaius a pair of greaves, I marred the work with a foolish error in the planishing that I could see every time he wore them.

I thought of Lydia a great deal. I wished, very hard, that she had suitors and another husband. And I wished other, conflicting things.

My friends stood by me. Doola would sit in the rented shop and pump the bellows silently for me. Seckla ran errands and bent metal. Demetrios sat with me when I was in the depths. Neoptolymos made me play the lyre, and I grew almost proficient. Gaius and I boxed.

Despite which, I lay every night and counted the people I'd betrayed, the way I'd done it, the reasons.

Listen; it may seem a small thing to you, trifling with a girl. I have mounted quite a few of them, and without regret.

When I was a pirate, I killed men, took their chattels and was accounted a hero. That is the life I led, then.

But when you are a pirate, you think like a pirate and you are judged – by other pirates. When you are a bronze-smith in a polis, you are judged by a different standard, and I'm enough of a pupil of Heraclitus to know that all of us are, to some extent, a reflection of the lives we lead and the men we trust and listen to. Lydia wouldn't even have been a bump on my road, the summer of Lades.

But I had become a different man. Or rather, I was striving to become a different man.

And failing.

I thought of standing at the door of the taverna in Marsala, longing for the clash. Knowing that I could probably take the whole pack of petty thieves. Eager for the spark.

And I'd sigh, and the whole thing would play again in the theatre of my mind. My last dinner with Lydia. Her foot on mine ... my hand on her hip. Her breasts.

Her father, and the look of bewildered anger.

And all the other men and women. Dead, abandoned. My son, somewhere on Crete.

Euphoria, dead in my arms.

Briseis.

It was a long winter, and a longer spring.

And then the ship was finished.

At thirty oars, she was probably the smallest ship I ever commanded. But no one ever questioned that I would command her. Demetrios was going to take *Amphitrite*, and he would have Doola, Seckla and Gaius, plus two of our fishermen, Giorgos (the oddest name for a fisherman) and Kosta. I had Neoptolymos and Daud; an older fisherman eager to make a fortune named Megakles, and the shipwright himself. Vasileos couldn't resist. He was a fine helmsman and a superb resource, the kind of man who could repair anything that nature or error destroyed.

He added a great deal to our crew. He was older, steady and had a knack – I have a bit of it, and Doola, too – of saying something and being obeyed without ever sounding as if an order had been given. With me, it is reputation – I'm the hero. With him, it was age and also reputation: he was perhaps the most renowned sailor on that coast, and the young men obeyed even the shift of his eyebrows.

I decided to emulate his extremely laconic manner.

As for my crew, I had, as I say, a dozen local lads, a dozen shepherds from the hills and six trained Greek oarsmen. They had been at Lades – they worshipped me, and every one of them felt he owed me his life, which is a secure foundation for leadership.

We spent a week building a set of oar benches on the beach, and then we practised every day while the farm boys and the shepherds ate us out of our wallets. The hill boys acted as if they'd never seen food before.

Or wine.

I expected fights, and there were fights, but the boys – all the locals – didn't quarrel with the men, Demetrios's oarsmen. I didn't break up the first fights, but after two evenings of it, I handed them all shields in the dawn of our third day together and made them run five stades. Most of them were puking by the third stade.

And so it went. I've trained crews before, and I've told you all about it. These were, in the main, better men than I usually had – eager, young and intelligent. The local fathers locked away their daughters, and we worked them hard, and in a week, we had something like a crew.

Our *Amphitrite* didn't waste the time. She ran up to Marsala and back twice, gathering cargo, and then down the Etruscan coast for hides, wine and all the Etruscan tin that Gaius could arrange, albeit in small quantities. I continued to train my oarsmen, now at sea. We pulled up and down the beach for two weeks, and my store of silver dwindled and the locals began to jack up their prices as my demands increased.

That's the way of the world.

Amphitrite came back from Veii and the Etruscan coast. She sold her cargo, loaded some Alban tin that had come over the passes from High Gaul, and sailed for Sardinia. The margin on tin was very small – the Phoenicians got most of the profit by sailing to Iberia, and their price made the price of the tin brought over the mountains on donkeys precious little. But Doola was finding buyers in Sardinia, Sicily and Etrusca from both ends of the trade, and he knew his business.

And besides, our dealings in Marsala netted us Sittonax. He was Daud's age, and spoke another dialect of Keltoi – they couldn't really understand each other, and mostly they spoke Greek, even though both of them could understand each other's poetry. He came over the mountains with the tin, as a guard. Someone gave him the 'mistaken' impression that we could sail him back to Alba.

He was the first Kelt I'd met who refused to adopt Greek dress, and wore trousers and all his barbaric finery all the time. Daud had been broken to our ways by years of slavery, but Sittonax made him wear trousers – and how we mocked him.

They got along like lovers, which is to say, they fought often, and made up swiftly – and they were brothers in all but name. And Sittonax knew a great deal about tin and where it came from.

He was my thirty-first oarsman. I don't think he ever pulled an oar in the whole voyage. He was the laziest man I've ever seen, and yet he seemed to get things done. He could tell lies without turning a hair, yet we all accepted him as an honourable man. My forge time went to trade goods, about which Sittonax and Daud advised me with conflicting and sometimes boastful advice, and my ram. I had decided to put a bronze sheath on the projection that, on small ships like a triakonter, was usually left bare. I wanted it light, but with enough punch to crack a hull. I had seen a number of rams, and I'd seen the flaws. Sharp rams cut the water nicely but got stuck in the prey; round rams made for uncertain steering.

I designed a different shape – a series of heavy plates held apart by spacers, like an empty packing crate with partitions for amphorae, but no amphorae. I asked around for weights and got a great many answers. Even alloying the metal myself, the tin and copper came to a great amount – almost fifty mina – and I wondered if I was up to the work, and if I was wasting money and bronze.

I had help from six other smiths when I cast the ram in sand in my rented shop yard. The neighbours complained I was going to burn the neighbourhood down.

My mould cracked and the molten metal ran all over the yard, and it was only by the will of Hephaestos that no one was injured.

I tried again. Fewer men came to help me, the second time. I had real trouble moving the gate, the piece of iron that kept the molten bronze out of the mould, and when it moved, it cracked, and the white bronze flowed awry.

I went to the shrine of Hephaestos and prayed. I spent a night on the mud floor in front of the terra cotta statue. I dedicated two rams and a good helmet.

Doola and Seckla and Neoptolymos came to help, the third time. They were already making coasting trips in *Amphitrite* by this time. But they were in, and they were friends. The local bronze-smiths were distant men.

I heated the bronze for longer. I'd made a huge wax model of the thing and built the mould carefully, with wood and iron strapping and sand.

Either the third time was the charm, or the god had forgiven me. I like to think it was the latter. But either way, the ram came shining from the mould. Vasileos shook his head and said the shape was all wrong. He wanted it to be sharp – and he said it would bite the water badly.

But a week later, we mounted it on the hull and it went on like a *porpax* on a man's arm. Perfectly.

Of course, in and out of all this, we were training our oarsmen. After four weeks of training, most of my shepherds were passable, and my fishermen were bored and threatening to go back to their fathers' boats, and it was time to take my ship to sea. So I paid for a priest to come from Marsala with my last funds, and we sacrificed a sheep and feasted. And in the morning, before their hangovers were clear, I had them all aboard, and we were running down the coast, headed east, to Italy.

Part II
Alba

ʿεξῆς δὲ τὸ πλάτος τῆς οἰκουμένης ἀφορίζων φησὶν ἀπὸ μὲν Μερόης ἐπὶ
τοῦ δι᾿ αὐτῆς μεσημβρινοῦ μέχρι Ἀλεξανδρείας εἶναι μυρίους, ἐνθένδε
εἰς τὸν Ἑλλήσποντον περὶ ὀκτακισχιλίους ἑκατόν, εἶτ᾿ εἰς Βορυσθένη
πεντακισχιλίους, εἶτ᾿ ἐπὶ τὸν κύκλον τὸν διὰ Θούλης ἥν φησι Πυθέας ἀπὸ
μὲν τῆς Βρεττανικῆς ἓξ ἡμερῶν πλοῦν ἀπέχειν πρὸς ἄρκτον, ἐγγὺς δ᾿ εἶναι
τῆς πεπηγυίας θαλάττης ἄλλους ὡς μυρίους χιλίους πεντακοσίους. ἐὰν οὖν ἔτι
προσθῶμεν ὑπὲρ τὴν Μερόην ἄλλους τρισχιλίους τετρακοσίους, ἵνα τὴν τῶν
Αἰγυπτίων νῆσον ἔχωμεν καὶ τὴν Κινναμωμοφόρον καὶ τὴν Ταπροβάνην,
ἔσεσθαι σταδίους τρισμυρίους ὀκτακισχιλίους.

After this he proceeds to determine the breadth of the habitable
earth: he tells us, that measuring from the meridian of Meroe to
Alexandria, there are 10,000 stadia. From thence to the Hellespont
about 8100. Again; from thence to the Dnieper, 5000; and thence
to the parallel of Thule, which Pytheas says is six days' sail north
from Britain, and near the Frozen Sea, other 11,500. To which if
we add 3400 stadia above Meroe in order to include the Island of
the Egyptians, the Cinnamon country, and Taprobane, there will
be in all 38,000 stadia.

Strabo, Geography 1.4

4

I'm a poor sailor and a mediocre bronze-smith, but I'm an expert pirate.

We coasted east and south, camping in sandy bays on the south coast of Gallia and eating deer and sheep. Stolen sheep.

Somewhere in the Etruscan Sea, we found a Phoenician coaster struggling against a west wind, headed for Sardinia. It was sheer luck – I had not intended to prey on anyone. But we pulled at her from the eye of the wind, and she ran – and there is something to the old saying that the bleating of the lamb excites the lion. I really didn't intend to take her until I saw her run.

And then—

She had a crew of five, four slaves and a Phoenician skipper from Carthage. I kept his slaves and enslaved him, took his ship and sold it still fully laden at Marsala. One of his countrymen ransomed him – he hadn't done much work, and the two mina in silver I charged for him seemed fair to everyone.

And the Phoenicians in Marsala marked me.

Demetrios came to visit me on the beach at Tarsilla.

'You can't do that again,' he said without preamble.

I laughed. 'I didn't intend to do it that time,' I said. 'They were just there.'

That quickly, I had made the change from merchant to pirate.

I put him on the kline of honour, fed him wine and sent him home in the morning with a hard head.

Two days later, before midsummer, *Amphitrite* swept in past the headland and unloaded her cargo.

This time, Doola had done his very best.

We had Roman helmets, Etruscan amphorae of wine, finished and dyed Aegyptian cloth, bags of local salt and even a small leather envelope of raw lapis from Persia. We had Cyprian copper and some dyes – Tyrian and Aegyptian.

Mostly, we had wine.

I had about thirty minas in worked bronze – brooches and scabbard fittings, because Sittonax said they would sell. And mirrors.

We had two bales of ostrich feathers I had taken off the coaster. No idea how he came to have them, but Carthage gets the best goods out of Africa.

Doola looked at them, heard the tale of the piracy and shook his head. 'I wish you hadn't done that, Ari,' he said. But then he shrugged, and went back to his lists.

And we had two great tusks of ivory, provided by Gaius.

We spent four days loading, working our boys to a frazzle. The triakonter was too stiff and had an odd lie under sail, and Demetrios, after watching us row, ordered the stern to be pushed down in the water. Ballast amphorae – we were literally ballasted in wine – were shifted, the stern went down a strake or two and the steering oars bit deeper.

I'm guessing, now that I'm a better shipwright and a better captain, that my ram – which bit the sea beautifully, although we hadn't tested it for its real purpose – had pulled the bow too deep and made her hard to steer. That ram bow could cut the waves, but if used badly or in heavy seas, could try to lead the ship to plunge too deep. I was lucky. And I had Vasileos, who supervised the reloading.

When it was all done, we ate a feast of fish and lobster on the beach. Men with partners bid them farewell. Men without made do, or didn't. I didn't. I had chosen celibacy.

Hah! I make myself laugh. I hadn't chosen it at all. I'd failed to find a partner, and done nothing much to find one. I was twenty-seven, by my own reckoning. Too old for the young girls, unless I wanted marriage.

Just right for paying prostitutes.

More wine, here.

It was two weeks to midsummer night, and the moon was waxing.

We slipped away in the dawn, two small ships against all the might of the ocean. It was a beautiful day, and we had a fair wind for the west, and all day we watched the water run down the sides of our heavily laden ship. Not a man touched an oar save the steersmen.

Three more days, and Poseidon gave us a west wind. At night, we sheltered on sandy beaches or heavy pebbles under cliffs, and we bartered for supplies or ate wild sheep and goats.

Those are the days when life at sea is a fine thing. We had new rigging, new sails and fresh hulls on both boats and we raced along, west and south.

On the fourth day, we saw the coast of Iberia rising before us and we put the helms over and started more south than west, and still we had the god's own wind in our sails.

By the end of the week, we had had some rowing. By the end of the second week, it was as if this was the only life we'd ever known. We sailed all day, rowing when the wind was calm or against us. *Amphitrite* could stay much closer to the wind, but couldn't row in anything like a breeze. *Lydia* – for so I called my new ship – could row in anything but a gale, so fine was her entry and her designs, and Vasileos beamed with pride as our oarsmen powered us into a heavy wind as if they were racing small boats on a beach.

But *Lydia* was never a good ship for sailing with the wind anywhere but her stern quarter, nor did I expect much more.

This resulted in a great many tortoise-and-hare days, where we'd crawl under oars, following a straight course across a bay, and *Amphitrite* would sail away – sometimes seemingly in the very opposite course to the one we were rowing – only to appear near close of day on the same beach.

We began to rotate our crews. Men on *Amphitrite* learned a great deal more about sailing than men on *Lydia*, and our shepherds were taken off their benches, three days at a time, and sent to make sail. So all my friends came to *Lydia*, from time to time, and I, too, took a trick on the sailing vessel and left command to Vasileos, who, I suspect, did it better than I.

Another week, and we came to the headland where Iberia juts the farthest into the Middle Sea. To port, we saw the Balearics. We could have traded there, for their famous wine and their fine wool, but we had wine, and we had wool, and we were under way on our great adventure.

That night, we had a talk at a great roaring fire on a pebble beach, with the sound of regular waves playing like a monotonous and low-tuned lyre in the background. The sky was full of stars, and our lads were singing the songs they'd sung to sheep and goats at home.

We lay on our cloaks, sipping wine. Every sip was that much less we had to deliver to our destination. We were getting thrifty, or perhaps greedy.

We fell silent, listening to the sea. And Demetrios picked up a stick from the fire and pointed south.

'Not a one of us has ever been through the Pillars of Heracles,' he said. He looked around. 'The rumours are that there is a heavy current, flowing out, and a brutal wind.'

Well, that shut us up.

Doola was picking his teeth, I remember that, because he spat, and then laughed his great laugh. 'We should quit and go home, then,' he said.

And we all laughed with him.

'Sounds as if it will be worse coming home than going out,' Neoptolymos said.

Demetrios shook his head. 'I really don't know,' he said. 'And that scares me. I want to run south with this fine wind and coast along Africa going west, rather than stay on the Iberian shore.'

'More chance of a Carthaginian,' I said.

Demetrios nodded. 'I know. But this coast gets rockier and rockier. Eventually we'll have no landing places. And ... there's Gades. I don't know its exact location, but it's a major port, according to men in Marsala, and it has a fleet. A Carthaginian fleet.' He looked around at all of us in the firelight. 'South is the coast of Libya, mostly desert down to the sea. I've never heard that it was thickly populated.'

None of the rest of us knew, either.

Really, we were shockingly unprepared. We had asked every sailor we could find about the route, but the Carthaginians wouldn't talk, or didn't know, and the Greeks were cagey. We knew that Africa had odd winds that could carry a lot of sand, and we knew that the coast of Iberia could be kind and could be harsh – we'd just experienced three weeks of pure sweet sailing, and we'd found her soft. But from here, the rest of the way was rumour and legend. I'd met five men who'd claimed to have sailed past the Pillars of Heracles.

None of them gave me the same description.

I assume that if I'd used my brief stay in Carthage better, I'd have learned more. Even as it was, I worked the calculations I'd learned while a slave, and I was none the wiser, because navigation by the heavens is relative, and I didn't have any fixed points from which to calculate. But I had a notion that Heracles wouldn't spurn me, and that the Pillars would be in his realm, not Poseidon's; and that if I took a precise bearing there on the heavens, I'd have something to go by. It's a little like a drunkard going out of his farmhouse for a piss in the middle of the night – he doesn't take his bearings in his bedroom or in the kitchen, but at the garden gate.

So none of us gainsaid Demetrios, and the next morning we left the land and ran due south, for Africa.

5

Africa was low, compared to Iberia. The coast rises slowly, and if it wasn't for the cloud banks and the wind, we might have run on her in the dark. The gods know that thousands of other sailors have drowned on that coast, but we were fortunate.

Having found the coast of Africa, we turned west, into the setting sun, and sailed. We had a good wind for it, and our only trouble was water. The coast of Africa didn't seem to have much of it, and what there was, someone owned. After passing three harbours, all obviously owned by the Carthaginians, we lay alongside one another and agreed that we had to go into the next small port.

They were Numidians, there. They weren't Doola's people, but they were black like him, and thin like Seckla, and while there were Phoenician merchants, we avoided them, filled with water from the stream and paid a small toll. We also bought bread and meat and grain: all outlay. We sold some wine. Before we left the beach, Doola had purchased two hundredweight of dates, dried dates. Who knew what ignorant barbarians might pay for delicious dates?

They couldn't get them into the hull of the *Amphitrite*, so we had to put them under tarpaulins between the benches of the *Lydia*.

We put to sea as soon as we could, and counted on our fingers. The prices were ruinous. And despite that, we knew we'd been absurdly lucky to find a port that wasn't dominated directly by Carthage.

But we were young and foolish, and we sailed on.

Two days farther west, and we had serious doubts. The land was rising on either hand – we could see the coast of Iberia. And the current was palpable – the sea was beginning to flow like a river. Out, into the Outer Sea.

If you have never been a sailor, this may not sound terrifying.

Worst of all was the wind. The wind was at our backs, and it grew stronger by the hour, a firm westerly that pushed our ships along at a breakneck pace. Turning back was no longer an option.

The current wasn't so very strong, but it denied us the opportunity to consider.

The wind rose, stronger and stronger.

The great rock of the Northern Pillar is much greater than the smaller rock at the southern side. And it is obvious, once you start to pass the straits, that this is not the hand of the gods – any more that everything else in the universe is. The wind is funnelled by the rising land – the sea wind – and what is merely a breeze elsewhere is virtually a gale between the Pillars. Add to that the current—

We were moving very fast indeed. And beyond, we could see the Great Sea – the Outer Sea. What some men call the Atlantic: the ocean on which Atlantis once lay.

Faster and faster.

Gades is a mighty port city in Iberia, sheltered behind the rock of the Northern Pillar. I prayed to Heracles, my ancestor – the port was visible now, and full of ships. The heavy construction of the big Phoenicians made more sense to me as I eyed the heavy rollers of the Outer Sea. The waves were twice as high.

We hit them in the rip – the confusing water between the oceans, just at the base of the Pillars – and before my crew had our sail down, we'd been turned all the way around and flung ten ship-lengths by a series of waves. Luck, the will of Poseidon and some expert ship-handling by Vasileos saved us, but it was terrifying in a rowed ship. Our fishermen's sons were the other vehicle of our salvation, for they saw the threat and, without orders, got to benches – any benches – and put oars in the water, and we managed not to swamp completely. But we took a great deal of water in those first few moments – and that was on a sunny day with a fine breeze.

The Phoenicians are fine sailors. And I had made a number of mistakes.

Demetrios did no better. The rip took him by surprise as well, and a flaw in the current took him away from us on the outflow, as a pair of boys may be swept apart when they attempt to swim in a strong river.

I couldn't watch. I was busy saving my own ship.

When all our rowers were rowing, we ought to have been safe, but we'd shipped too much water and the ship was a slug, and the big swells of the Atlantic threatened her low sides with every wave. I had to make ten decisions a minute, about who should row and who should bail. Sittonax bailed – one of the few times I watched him work like a working man. He bailed with his helmet until someone put a bucket in his hands.

Doola shipped the pump, a simple wooden contraption that fitted over gunwale, and he and I worked it as hard as we could, lifting a steady stream of water over the side. A dozen other men – all the shepherds – bailed as fast as they could.

But it wasn't a one-sided fight.

A wave a little higher than the others caught us – not quite broadside, thank the gods, but on our forward quarter, and suddenly we were taking water amidships. All our gains were lost, and more besides.

Men began to look around. And at me. The fishermen could swim. The herdsmen couldn't.

'Bail, friends,' I called. 'No one can swim in this.'

And we bailed.

Vasileos had the steering oars, and I could tell from his actions that he was not having a good time of it, that we didn't really have enough way on us. The obvious solution was to get the boatsail up.

That meant taking five good men off bailing.

I thought about it for as long as a man sings a prayer to the gods.

It still seemed incredible to me that, on a beautiful day, I was about to die at the mercy of the elements.

Nonetheless—

I made the decision. Without steerage way, we were doomed, and it was just a matter of time.

'Boatsail!' I called.

That took five of my best – very best – men off the benches and the bailing, too.

For a long minute, we were in the balance. The ship was, to all intents, sinking. We'd taken on a great deal of water. The wind wasn't going to save us.

But the wind gave a bite to the steering oars. And the steering oars allowed Vasileos to put the stern to the wind and the bow to the waves.

And then we were all bailing. And bailing. And bailing.

An hour became another hour, and the crisis seemed just as acute. Every rogue wave, every spill of wind that shipped a little water started the struggle again in earnest, and such is the nature of men that the deadly became routine. And still we bailed. There was no choice.

As the wind aided us, more and more men came off the rowing benches to bail.

That got us a little more.

At some point, the balance changed in the ship. We were lighter. The bilges still swirled with water, but we were afloat. And running before the wind, due west into the Atlantic.

Demetrios had made a different choice. Because of his rig, he'd had his sails up all along, and the vicious current had driven him inshore. The water closer in was calmer, and in fact (as any sailor who knows the Pillars learns), there was a countercurrent close in to the shore, just as there is in the Bosporus, if I'd only had the wit to think. Demetrios and *Amphitrite* had weathered the current and the rip better than we had, and now lay astern about two stades.

That might have been the end of our despair, except that for three hours we had had no lookout, because all hands were needed on the ship. When I sent Doola, who was grey with fatigue, to 'rest' in the bow, he turned.

'Warships!' he called.

How the bastard Carthaginians must have laughed. There we were, wallowing like pigs in a trough, because we didn't know the tide change for the Atlantic and we had chosen a stupid moment to pass the straits. Nor did we know where to lie to, where to wait. We knew *nothing*.

And they lay safe in Gades and watched, and when it became obvious that we were going to live, they came out like hawks on their prey. Like any predator, they liked us the better that we were tired.

Three heavy triremes came out of Gades, and all with just one thought – to take us.

Listen, thugater, and my lily-handed ladies. You are not sailors, and I imagine that to you, one body of water is much like another. I cannot express to you the fear – gut-churning and senseless – of the Atlantic. It is *not right*. The water *feels* different. It *tastes* different.

I swear to you that *Lydia* handled differently in the Outer Ocean.

Those three war-hawks leaped out of Gades in our wakes, and they were gaining on us before they had their lower oar-ports open. A hundred and eighty rowers will always beat thirty rowers, even if the thirty are all Argonauts and have Heracles himself at an oar.

I went aft, to where Vasileos was between the oars.

'Well?' he asked. He was tired.

I had the sense not to talk. I looked aft.

'I won't be a slave,' he said.

I had all the time in the world to see how this was, in the main, my fault. Of *course* we knew that the Carthaginians had a squadron in Gades.

I thought about it for fifty beats of my heart. The equation looked like this.

If we ran west on the wind, and raised the mainsail, and we were lucky, we would stay ahead of the big warships. They couldn't possibly have such heavy crews and still have supplies.

But we would have to go out of sight of land, and spend the night. A storm would kill us. A heavy west wind would kill us. And we had little water and no food beyond raw grain that we couldn't cook because we didn't have a beach.

If we cheated north, the triremes would have us.

And if we stood on under boatsail alone, the triremes would have us.

'Mainmast,' I said. I pretended to calm, unhurried command. Laconic, like Vasileos.

Men sprang to obey, and our mainmast went up and was belayed.

'Stays,' I said. 'Four.'

Four stays were the equivalent of preparing for a major storm.

The stays went up, too. Seckla raced aloft, his superb gymnastics acted out for our lives, and he slipped the noose of every stay over the masthead while the deck crew belayed.

The miracle is that the men didn't panic. I seemed calm, so they obeyed.

I was anything but calm. I wasn't even resigned. Inwardly, all I could do was curse my incredible hubris in thinking that we could pass the Pillars. And my lack of scouting, lack of preparation.

I seldom feel a complete fool, but I did then.

For the whole of these preparations, the warships gained, hand over fist. I know Vasileos thought the preventer-stays were a waste of time. But he said nothing, and I knew that if I didn't get them up immediately, they'd never go on later – in darkness, on a dirty night. And my sense of the weather was that it was getting worse.

As soon as the mainsail fell free, the ship's motion changed. The bow took far more punishment than in the Inner Sea, as the pace of the rollers was very different. But we were going faster – much faster.

Demetrios raised *Amphitrite's* mainsail and let the corners of the lateen go, and the little ship sprang forward.

For an hour, as the sun began to set, I thought we'd make it.

But *Amphitrite* was falling behind. It was slower at first, but we were not on her best point of sailing, so I put my helm up a few points and Demetrios matched our new course and then she seemed to hold her own. I went back to bailing.

She wasn't holding her own.

And the three Carthaginians weren't letting go.

At one remove, it didn't matter a damn whether they had the food and water to give chase, because I had done what could be done. I didn't have any other brilliant stratagems.

But when Vasileos summoned me to the steering platform and I saw how badly *Amphitrite* was sagging, I knew the triremes were going to catch us.

I swear, I just stood and watched for as long as it took the sun to go a finger's width across the sky.

'Armour,' I called.

The word tasted good in my mouth. I turned to Vasileos. 'I won't be a slave, either. But it's going to cost us.' I shrugged. 'And I won't let them die.' I pointed to *Amphitrite*.

Vasileos nodded.

All I could do was turn and dash back. If I went between two of the warships, anything might happen. I might lure them away. I might kill a helmsman with a lucky arrow shot. I might lure a foolish ship into an oar-rake – even my little triakonter could make trouble with the oars of a big line-of-battle ship.

I might. But these were the best sailors in the world, and I wasn't likely to surprise them. When I went about, they would have, at this rate, half an hour to see me coming.

That meant I needed to surprise them, which was nigh on impossible but worth an effort.

'Spill the wind,' I called to Seckla. He let fly the lower corners of the sail.

Our motion changed, and we slowed.

Men were standing about, staring at me.

'Into your armour!' I shouted.

We had just one advantage. Every man in our crew had a shield, a spear and a helmet – many had more. In effect, we had thirty marines. With luck – even a little luck – the Carthaginians would have their usual mixed crew of professionals and slaves, or, if not slaves, men with nothing to gain by victory.

I was an old hand at this. And I didn't think that was enough advantage to even consider turning and fighting.

But I confess that I found it appealing.

The wolf in me wanted to fight.

It was the tavern, all over again.

The sun sank towards the sea ahead of us, turning from yellow to red.

The land was gone behind us.

'Spill more wind,' I told Seckla.

We slowed more, and *Amphitrite* began to overtake us.

Everything depended on timing. I wanted *Amphitrite* to overtake us *exactly* as the lead of the three warships closed into archery range of *Amphitrite*.

As I considered my options, I imagined the Carthaginian skippers leaning over their bows and watching me. My twentieth mistake of the day had been showing all my speed and then slowing. If they were veterans, they would know that I was cheating the wind to lose seaway.

In fact, the northernmost warship began to put a little northing into his westerly helm – widening the gap between his ship and his next consort.

It might be coincidence, but my feeling was that he was on to my clever plan.

And still we raced west.

The three warships were confident and well handled, rowing two banks and using their boatsails to ease the rowers. It told me a great deal about them, and all of it bad for my friends.

Our sail crackled, and I looked up at it.

Vasileos nodded. 'Wind change,' he said, and shrugged, as if to say that he, a man of Marsala, could not be expected to predict these things on the Outer Ocean.

They were close to fetching our wakes – the entire chase had been with us sailing due west and they slanting down from the north-east. I could imagine that on the lead ship, the master archer was probably pulling his horn bow from its case.

Certainly Doola had his out, although he'd strung it and then wrapped the bow in a cloak to keep the spray off the string.

I pulled on my beard a dozen times, trying to find anything to do.

I had my spola on my shoulders, and someone had put my aspis against the bulkhead with two spears.

So I walked down the waist of *Lydia*, and clasped hands with all of them – shepherds and herdsmen, fishermen and coasters, and my friends last of all.

I gathered them in the waist. 'On my word, we lower the main-mast. We'll turn to port – on oars. Like lightning. Pass between the two southernmost ships and try for their oars.' I shrugged. 'After that, it's any man's game.'

I sounded sane enough, I suppose.

Men *smiled*.

The sails crackled again.

I walked aft, trying to appear calm.

'Want me to take the steering oars?' I asked.

Vasileos shook his head. 'I think the wind will veer north,' he said suddenly.

I looked at the sea and it told me ... *nothing*.

But a north wind—

Two of the warships were now to the south of us by several stades, closing off our escape, while the northernmost one caught us up.

They had made a mistake.

And further, it seemed to me that Vasileos had to be right, because otherwise we wouldn't be moving north at all.

So close.

I ran back along the waist, leaping benches.

'Listen!' I shouted. 'We will *not* take down the mast. Drop the sail – and be ready to put it up again. Ready!'

'It will tangle the oars,' shouted Vasileos.

An arrow leaped from a distant bow and fell into the water about a horse-length astern – too damned close.

Doola loosed. He arrow rose, and fell.

Three came at us in return, and he loosed again, his whole chest thrown into the curve of the bow.

One of the arrows struck the curved wood over the helmsman's bench.

'Ready at the oars!' I called. 'Mainsail down!'

The mainsail came down at a rush. The deck crew – all four of them – caught the great sheets as they came down, hauling them inboard in heaps of hemp. Again, Sittonax lent a hand.

Priceless time went by, heartbeat after heartbeat. There was no point in giving an order before the sail was clear of the oarsmen.

And then it was. Arrows were falling around us by then, a dozen every minute or more, and a single hit might have been the end of us – but suddenly the wind was failing, changing.

'Give way!' I roared. 'Hard to starboard!'

We had lots of speed, and the oars bit; the steering oars added their fulcrum and we heeled into the turn – heeled dangerously, but every spare man went to the outside rail.

Demetrios was ready. He turned with us, his sails already down.

'You fool!' I said. I wanted him to live, not to follow us.

We shot under his stern and continued our curve north, and then east.

An arrow struck my aspis and went a hand's breadth through it. I hadn't remembered putting it on my arm.

I put it up over Vasileos's head, and three more arrows struck it, the second passing right through the face and stopping only on the bronze arm guard inside the shield, punching deep into it so that my arm took a wound.

I dropped my arm. But the arrow was wedged in, pinning my arm to the porpax.

Doola loosed.

I followed his arrow and was stunned to find that we were going bow to bow with the northernmost warship, which would crush us like a water flea.

Astern, Demetrios had the *Amphitrite* around and under oars. Six oars didn't move her very fast, but he had his boatsail up, and it was full.

It was full.

That meant the wind had veered—

An arrow *whanged* off my helmet, putting a crease all along the brow ridge.

'Oars in!' I called.

Seckla took another in the hip and fell onto the sails.

The wind change staggered the bigger ship, who had his boatsail set, like the hand of Poseidon moving his bow off course by several points.

It caught our bare pole, too, and moved us.

We struck them just aft of their cathead, and glanced down the side. Their archers were unfazed by the collision, leaning out over the side to loose. I saw it happen – the oar loom taken by surprise, the glancing blow from our little ship, and an archer was caught in the broken oars and beaten down. Another leaped for his life and Doola shot him, like a hunter taking a bird on the rise.

And we were past.

Our mad rush had turned the big warship, but it was Demetrios with his cool hand at the helm and deep experience of the sea that really hurt them. He had his oars in – easy in a slab-sided tub with only six oar-ports. He was under sail alone, and his bluff bow struck the starboard rowers' stations *on the opposite side* from our very small strike, crushing a dozen oars and oarsmen and then poling off. His lightning strike took away momentum in him, and in a bigger fight he'd have been dead – but the enemy had no second line and the trireme carried forward, all his top-deck rowers in disarray.

We caught the new north wind, and sailed north.

We had barely stung our three mighty opponents. I doubt if we killed a dozen men, and crushed twenty oars.

But that northernmost trireme lost way, and wallowed in the swell in our wakes. Her consorts turned north and passed her, offering no assistance, bent on renewing the pursuit.

The sun in the west became a red ball on the horizon, and the sea-hawks weren't going to have us before darkness fell.

As soon as it was full dark, I passed *Amphitrite* and hailed her.

Demetrios came to the starboard side.

'We should turn west,' I said. 'As soon as we can, before moon-rise.'

Demetrios spat over the side. 'West,' he repeated. In his shouted tone, I heard it all. Doubt, and more doubt.

But he followed my lead. We turned west, slanting across the wind as it began to veer again, and by midnight we were again in a full westerly, and I was cursing because the wind change meant that the enemy would have every reason to follow in our wake.

I snatched sleep when I could, as did all of us. The oarsmen were fresh – so far – but Doola sent them to their benches to sleep. Still, any man who went to the ram to relieve himself was questioned when he went back to his bench.

The first grey light came, and we could see *Amphitrite* on the same tack, but well off to the north of us.

Men cheered.

The sky was increasingly red at our backs over Iberia, and I didn't like that. But the wind was steady, and in the wrong direction to turn, and we sailed along as the sun rose red as blood off the land and into the sky.

I saw three nicks, like the fins of sharks, on the eastern horizon, and my heart sank.

Vasileos went off to take breakfast, such as it was – unmilled barley and wine from our cargo. I took the oars and began to cheat the helm north. A triakonter doesn't sail many points off the wind – but it will sail a few, and I was going for all I could get.

An hour later, it was obvious that the triremes were gaining.

Doola and Vasileos came aft after Doola had looked at Seckla's wound. The young man was lucky – the arrow had struck the hip without severing the artery and glanced along the bone. Deeply painful, but one of the lightest wounds a man can take, if one must be wounded.

'Only a matter of time,' I said.

Doola looked at the sails on the horizon.

Vasileos smiled. 'Made it through yesterday,' he said. He looked at the sky.

I pointed at the red dawn over Iberia. 'If I were at sea in the Ionian,' I said, 'that would mean trouble.'

Vasileos took a deep breath and shook his head. 'Smells like lightning,' he said.

'Make all fast,' I ordered. I made my way aft, catching each man's eye. It wasn't an order for the sake of shouting. I wanted to make sure everyone understood. Heavy weather was not necessarily our friend but was, in many ways, a deadlier enemy.

As they put heavy linen tarpaulins across the standing cargo and rigged the big tarps that could cover the bilges, the wind began to veer, first north, then south, then all around.

We had the mainsail down in no time, and the boatsail up.

The wind veered again, and suddenly the sky began to cloud over.

'Feed them the dates,' I said. Dates were the only food we had aboard, by then. It was money lost. Or not – if we lived. And if we didn't live—

I laughed.

We ate twenty drachmas' worth of dates. We hadn't had a good meal in two days, and we *inhaled* the dates.

An hour later, I had to order the mainmast down, or cut it away. It was close.

And now the bigger ships were gaining. There's a belief among non-sailors that small ships are faster than big ships. This is far from true. Small ships are *nimbler* than large ships, and often shallower in draught and have other useful qualities, but the longer and heavier a ship is, the less it fights the motion of the sea. An old shipwright on Crete – my first son's grandfather, if you like – explained it to me when I was a complete lubber by saying that if a small boat rode the waves, she travelled *farther* with all the ups and downs than the bigger boat that cut the waves. I'm not altogether sure that's the answer, either. But bigger boats are faster, and in heavy weather, they are faster still.

Demetrios pulled alongside. 'I'm going to part company!' he shouted.

Let me add that I could barely hear him.

He waved west.

Of course, in this heavy wind, his tubby merchant hull could carry more sail, heel farther and manage a point or two closer to the wind than my triakonter – or our pursuers. It meant going due west, away from land.

In a storm.

'Go!' I shouted back.

We both waved.

Our deviation was slow at first, and then very rapid as his mainsail filled and he found his point of sailing.

My oarsmen were still eating dates. It was like something out of Aristophanes – thirty men pushing dates down their gullets as fast as they could. Sittonax looked like a drowned blond cat, sitting on someone else's bench with both hands full. Brasidas, the eldest of the herdsmen, was stripped naked despite the cold and rain – he'd just helped with the mainmast – and he, too, looked like a dog worrying fresh meat; his cheeks were smeared with dates.

Aye, we were hungry.

The boatsail kept our head up and our stern to the rollers, but we didn't have much headway, and as the storm mounted behind us, the waves grew steeper. This didn't happen immediately: in fact, I could tell this whole story as a transition from worry about our pursuers with little concern for the weather to worry about the weather with little concern for our pursuers.

About midday, the storm had risen to a point where the wind, which was now steadily westerly, was shrieking in the rigging, and the waves were so big that the little boatsail mast was only *in the wind* when our bow was going up the increasingly steep sides of the waves. We were all but becalmed in the trough.

At first, that was hard on us, but merely annoying.

Then the effect grew, and the moment where the wind caught the boatsail became increasingly perilous. The boatsail snapped and strained at its ropes, and the motion of the ship between my hands became ... alien.

Our two pursuers were close – too damned close. And with the wind behind them, their archers could loose at us and we couldn't hope to reply.

Luckily the wind was so strong that archery was not very effective.

The next change was to the steering – the ship began to accelerate down the steep wave sides. The waves were now as tall as the mast of a small ship, and as we went over the crest, the ship would *slide* on the far side. All this, while rain crashed down like a torrent of Persian arrows and the wind howled like the spirits of all the Titans sent to Tartarus.

It wasn't that any particular moment was perilous. The storm was not the worst I'd ever seen. It was the combination of all the factors: a single wrong decision, a moment's inattention at the helm, and we'd be dead.

I'm a fine man in a fight – none better. But fights only last so long. The sea is always there, and I am not the best sailor. Sailing, like smithing, requires patience.

Both of our enemies were away to the south, coming up on a very slight tack. *Amphitrite* was gone in the spume – perhaps already over the distant horizon. I couldn't even glimpse her.

When I could count the guy ropes on the bow of the nearest trireme, I cheated my own helm to the north at the top of a massive wave and we rode down that cliff of water like a boy surfing with his body in the fresh waves of a summer storm on the beach. I kept us slant on to the wave as much as I dared.

It worked. After three or four waves, I was on a north-west tack and the odd on-and-off action of the heavy wind on my sail seemed to drive us well enough.

At some point, the lead trireme slackened sail by lifting the hem of his boatsail. His lowest row of oar-ports was now exposed to the storm, and I'm guessing he was shipping water.

Ten more minutes, and he had turned west, putting his high prow to the rollers.

I'd like to say that I planned it all, or guessed it, but my turn was merely to put more water between us.

In another hour, we could scarcely see them, even at the top of the rise, and I had half my oarsmen pulling on the down slope of the wave. It took careful calculation, but it kept our course straight and – give me some credit here – it gave the oarsmen something to do.

By dark we had a sky full of lightning. The land was gone, the wind had risen again and now I brailed up the boatsail to a scrap. Half an hour later, with no order from me, Doola and Vasileos brailed it again, climbing out on the bow and wrapping the whipping, vicious cloth with sodden, slippery rope. But they triumphed, and we lived. Rowing became more important, too, as we needed a continuing impetus to stay stern on to the waves.

Perhaps they didn't grow larger with the dark, but they were far more terrifying, at least to me. I could just see the rising swell of the things at my shoulder: when a lightning flash came, I was always shocked at how high they were, how white with spume.

But I couldn't stop looking. The waves were terrible, like the pain of a wound that a warrior must keep testing, perhaps in the hope that it will diminish. That's my memory of that night – the constant, exhausting shock of the size of the waves.

Eventually, as it always does, night ended. It didn't end cleanly or evenly, with anything like a dawn. In fact, I remember doubting the evidence of my own eyes as I began to be able to see the white spray hell of the water to the west – that is, if we were running west. I had no stars and no sun; I was in an alien ocean.

I was cold, wet through, of course, and Vasileos stood at one shoulder and Doola at my other. In the night, they'd placed themselves with me in the steering rig. It took all three of us to hold the ship steady.

If one of the steering oars broke—

If the boatsail mast gave way—

If the rowers missed their stroke in the trough—

By midday – a meaningless name for a meaningless time, as we had no idea how much daylight had passed – I began to succumb to hopeless doubt.

What if the whole Outer Ocean were like this? Men said it was a circle of storms, girding the earth. Men at Marsala had said no ship could survive. I thought that they were fools – after all, Carthage came here.

But this was now the worst storm I'd ever seen.

Darkness fell again. It is possible that Doola and I shouted to each other, or perhaps Vasileos roared in my ear, but there was nothing to say.

The rowers – the fishermen, mostly – kept time by nothing but habit. Bless them.

And they rowed on.

The second night, we lost a fisherman's son overboard. He went to the cathead to defecate, and he was out there when a rogue wave buried the cutwater bow. The ram bit too deep, and, just for a moment, at the steering oar, I thought we would simply plunge to the bottom.

It wasn't until we'd bailed until daylight that we knew Aristos was gone.

And Bethes, one of the herdsmen, had gone mad. He shrieked and swore and leaped about until Vasileos led a party to trap him in the bow and tie him down.

'We're all going to die!' he screamed. 'Die! Make it *stop!*'

His screams were largely covered by the wind.

The second day of the storm dawned – if you could call it that.

Some time after the pale light showed us the roaring chaos of waves, Vasileos put a big arm around my shoulders. '*Sky – is – lighter,*' he bellowed.

A tiny, watery ray of hope penetrated my head.

More time passed. Someone cut the madman's throat; I saw it happen. His screams were ... the stuff of nightmare, and someone else couldn't stand it, shipmate or no. Remember that the herdsmen and the shepherds were different men from the fishermen.

Later, someone threw the corpse over the side.

The wind began to abate. The full-throated shriek of the wind in the boatsail mast's stays remitted until it was just a scream.

Poseidon's grip on my steering oars became a mere punch in the guts at the top of every wave.

Our boatsail mast had not given way. Our boatsail had not blown clear of its ropes.

But we'd been rowing for two nights and two days on a meal of dates, and the rowers were so far beyond done that our rowing was more symbolic than real.

I handed the steering oars to Vasileos – a process fraught with peril that revealed that my arms would not function properly and my legs were exhausted – but I struggled forward on a rope tied the length of the ship. At each bench, I stopped.

'Two more hours. We're going to make it.' That's the whole of the speech I shouted at them.

'Two more hours. Look at the light. Listen to the wind.' I shouted these words over and over. Men at one oar bench couldn't hear me on the next.

Hope is the most intoxicating drug, better than wine or opium.

Hope can make an exhausted man row two more hours; can cause a swordsman's arm to function for a few more cuts.

Those are the moments when the daimons that make a man's spirit prove themselves or fail. When everything is gone from you but that ray of hope.

A few failed. Most didn't. We rowed, and the wind abated.

The waves began to come in a regular cycle, and they grew less steep.

Then suddenly it was noon, on a blue sea with a stiff breeze.

And no land in sight, in any direction.

6

Other, better officers – Doola and Vasileos – had collected rainwater. We drank it. I served out wine from the cargo, and we consumed the last of the dates with handfuls of grain, and then the food was gone.

Despite our hunger and thirst, we threw a heavy handful of dates and a full cup of neat wine over the side to Poseidon.

I let us wallow on the waves until I was sure – *sure* – which direction was east. Despite the breeze and the sun, I knew that we were right on the edge of death, still. I didn't think we could survive two more nights at sea. I needed to find the land, find a beach and get my hull on it.

When the movement of the sun gave me east, my heart soared, and I prayed to Apollo Helios, Lord of the Sun, with a fervour I hadn't shown in many years. Apollo is not really a friend of our house. But that day, the track of the Golden Chariot across the sky revealed that the wind on my cheek was a gentle westerly, and our course was north and west. Vasileos and Doola and I had held our course all night. I'm sure that we went due west at times – the wind was west.

Since then, sailors on the Outer Sea have told me that westerlies are the gentlest storms beyond the Pillars of Heracles.

Let me never face an easterly, then.

Be that as it may, in the afternoon we took down the boatsail and we rowed north and east. It was back-breaking – not because of hard winds, but because we had a fully laden ship and we were exhausted.

After the briefest consultation with Doola and Vasileos, we began to jettison cargo. Four men were bailing all the time, and two more sought out the heaviest cargo with minimum value and threw it over the side. Sodden hides – from sheep and oxen – went. All the dyes, ruined in the storm, so that men's legs were dyed a vivid purple-black for days.

We drank the wine and threw the amphorae over the side.

We had a deep tier of amphorae and copper, and that we left. Virtually everything else went.

And still we laboured against a gentle headwind and our own fatigue. In our wake, a tragic trail of sinking cargo.

Evening came with no sign of land.

I slept the sleep of the exhausted, and woke to find that Vasileos needed me to take the steering oars. I slept between them – I'm ashamed of that, but I did us no harm – and awoke fitfully, and finally rose to consciousness with the dawn and the rise of an east wind.

We had rowed all night. Now the sky was darkening in the west, and the wind was coming *from* the west.

We raised the boatsail and then the mainmast. And lay about the ship, sleeping and talking fitfully. Men looked at the mass of clouds to the west from time to time, and then went back to whatever they were doing. Dice appeared. As darkness fell, a party moved about the ship, checking the tie-downs and making all fast for another storm.

In fact, I knew that if the storm caught us, we'd die. No one had any strength left. And to be fair, most of us were drunk. Not mutinously, angrily drunk; just drunk on fatigue and a little wine.

I roused myself – I wasn't any better than the rest – around nightfall, and went about the ship ordering men into watches so that we wouldn't run on the land. I had to believe there was land on our right hand, the starboard side, somewhere out there.

'Is it close?' I asked Vasileos.

He shook his head. His smiles were gone, and the lines in his face made him look forty years older. Even Doola had lines on his face.

Vasileos looked east under his hand and shook his head. 'No seabirds,' he said. He shrugged and took another hit of wine. 'In the morning we can cast the lead,' he ventured. More quietly, he said: 'We ran west for two days and nights. We ran as if Poseidon himself pushed our hull.' He shrugged. 'I would guess, in all this alien sea … who could know?' He shook his head again. 'Five more days?' he asked.

'We won't make five days,' I said.

Doola rubbed his beard. 'We might,' he said.

The next morning was clear and bright, and the wind blew strong from the west, and we ran north and west. I served out the lowest tier of amphorae – the best wine. Men drank it. We served out the rest of the grain, and men chewed on leather.

'Should have saved the dead man,' joked Kalimachos, one of the herdsmen.

Men paused, as if a collective shudder went through them all.

I thumped the side of the boat with my sighting staff. 'Not on my ship,' I said.

Everyone breathed.

And we ran on.

And on.

After noon, when I took a sight on the height of the sun as the Phoenicians do, and learned little from it except that I could calculate when noon passed – exactly – I worked my way to the stern and stood with Doola.

'Shall we turn the ship due east?' I asked, looking past my friend at the shipwright.

Vasileos was between the oars. He shrugged. 'Who knows?'

Doola looked forward. I followed his look. The whole crew was watching us.

'Stay on course,' I said, a little louder.

Vasileos met my eye, and his eye said, *It doesn't matter either way.*

We ran on.

Along towards evening, a pair of gulls attached themselves to our sternpost. They took fish out of our wake for a while, and then just sat there, defecating.

I took in the mainsail at full dark and we ran on, far more sedately. And when I took my trick at the helm, I turned the ship until the wind was stern on. Due east.

In the morning, everyone was sober and sullen, thirsty, and very hungry indeed.

There was no more wine to serve. That is to say, I knew there were twenty-four more big amphorae stowed forward, and I'd broach them rather than die, but we had a steady stream of seabirds now, and I was sure we were up with the land. In fact, it looked oddly as if the land was to our south, as well as our east.

An hour after dawn, when two men in the bow were demanding that we have a 'ship's meeting', porpoises appeared off the bow. They leaped and leaped, and the ship fell silent. Men fell to their knees, praying for Poseidon's favour.

We ran on, another hour. I got the mainsail up, aided only by three hands while Doola and Vasileos steered. The rest either wouldn't help or couldn't.

While I was taking the sight for noon, a group of the herdsmen gathered in the bow. I heard them, saw them, knew their intent. Their frightened ignorance was driving them. They thought—

To be honest, they weren't thinking.

They came forwards over the benches with swords and spears and clubs.

'Turn the ship around!' called the leader. He was the oldest of the herdsmen, and should have known better – Theophrastos. A good enough man.

'Turn the fucking ship around,' he said again, and some of his fear leaked through his voice.

I came to the edge of the small aft deck and stood over them.

'Back to your benches,' I said. 'You're all idiots. Do you think you know anything about sailing? There aren't any sheep here to herd. We survived the triremes and we survived the storm, and in a few hours we'll be on a beach.'

'We are going the wrong way!' shouted one of the boys. 'I can feel it!'

I looked at him, and almost died. Theophrastos stabbed at me with his spear. I had not reckoned on their deadly intent, and I almost missed the blow.

Almost.

Even as it was, his spear point caught me behind the ear and cut my scalp.

Without thinking, I got my right hand on his spear haft and jumped onto him from my higher vantage point. I stripped the spear from his hands and knocked him to the bilges.

The others stepped back.

One of the fishermen tripped the youngest herdsman and put his arms around him in a bear hug.

I looked around. The others were indecisive – not cowed, but unsure if they were willing to step up to violence.

I thought, too. We were hours from land – or so I thought. But I didn't have the strength to fight a mutiny, and—

And, as horrible as it sounds, these were herdsmen. Not my finest rowers.

Theophrastos, bellowing with rage, rose from the bilge.

I drew my *xiphos* and killed him. I deceived his reaching hands with a flick of my point and then cut back, hard, the full force of my right arm into his neck just above the collarbone. I didn't quite behead him. But close. And his blood fountained over his comrades.

They flinched.

I pointed my sword at them. 'He was a fool, and he died for it. Get back to your stations, or die with him. We'll be eating mutton tonight – or you can eat black air in Hades.'

That was the end of the mutiny, if it was a mutiny. It was really the rush of some panicked men, and I think now that killing Theophrastos was too much. I could just as easily have kicked him in the head. But I was tired, and afraid myself.

That's how it is, at sea.

My guilt for killing him increased all day, as little signs – a floating log, a wren – told us that we were coming up with the land. After midday, we saw land – a mountain range to the south. And then we saw the land to the east.

People cheered.

I felt empty, and foolish. I had earned their thanks, and then I had killed one of them. They all moved shy of me.

Even Doola.

The sun was just starting to sink when we came up with the land, and we coasted north, looking for a beach. We had to row, and that was difficult, as the men were weak and scared – scared of me, now.

But the closer we got to the land, and the more we could smell it, the more our hearts rose.

By sunset, we were within bowshot of land – a low and difficult coast. But just before full dark robbed our eyes, Doola saw a break in the coast, and we turned west under sail and passed over the bar of a river, and we saw huts – beautiful huts, with stone foundations and big roofs of thatch on the south bank, and two heavily built open boats riding a few ship's lengths out from a muddy beach.

I took down the sail in the last of the light, and we got the oars out with a slovenly motion that would have disgraced an all-slave crew on a Carthaginian. And we pulled badly – I say we, because I was on a bench. We caught crabs, and some men seemed incapable of effort.

We crawled the last hundred paces across the calm water of the estuary. Backing water to land stern-first seemed impossible.

But we managed, in a laborious and inefficient manner. We floundered the ship around, and backed water like boys rowing for the first time, and the stern grounded with a soft thump.

We'd lived.

I know I wept. Many others did, too. I lay over my oar, and I cried.

Landing stern-first means that the rowers are facing away from the land. So I was one of the last to notice that armed men were forming on the greensward by the river. It was Doola who alerted me.

Fifty men with spears.

Ares. I remember thinking that if they came to enslave me, I'd just lie down and take it.

But I rose, and moved perhaps by my killing of the morning, I seized not my spear but my staff, and I leaped off the stern to the riverbank and walked slowly, the land moving under me, towards the spearmen. It was just the last edge of a summer evening: the sky was still pink, but night was close.

I fell to my knees and clutched the earth, and kissed the grass.

Then I hobbled like a drunkard towards the spearmen. They watched me.

They looked utterly foreign. Many – most – were heavily tattooed. They had big, ugly bodies with fat bellies and hollow backs – men who didn't exercise properly. But they had big muscles, heavy thighs – trousers in checks and violent stripes.

Their hair was all the colours of the rainbow, even in the fading light.

Sittonax came up next to me, and he had a spear. He grinned at me.

He shouted at them, and two men shouted back. Both wore fine gear.

It was as if he cast a spell, or broke one. As soon as Sittonax called to them, their disciplined silence broke and most of them simply walked away. A few stayed to look at the ship, and one man, in a magnificent helmet with bronze wings and a gold torque around his neck, stood warily to the side. After a pause, he came and spoke to Sittonax, and when the two were done, they embraced like old friends and the man grinned at me and stood by.

'Your people?' I asked Sittonax. He gave me a look of pure annoyance in return.

'If we landed in a part of Sicily where they spoke Greek, would you be *home?*' he asked, which for him was a long speech.

'You speak to them well enough,' I commented.

He shrugged. 'These are Tarbelli. Their aristocrats speak a good form of my language – I can understand them.' He nodded at two spearmen who were looking at our ship. 'I can't understand a word from those two.'

'Oh,' I said, or something equally intelligent. 'You seemed to be talking ten to the dozen.'

'They thought we were coming to attack,' Sittonax said. He shrugged. 'Now they think we're here to trade. I had to explain that we aren't Phoenicians.'

I nodded. 'Tell him we're here to trade,' I agreed. 'And that we need food and water, or men will die. Tell them we've been at sea eight days in a galley.'

He nodded. He spoke to the man in the excellent war gear, who made noises in return.

He blew a horn, and the Keltoi moved quickly. My oarsmen stumbled ashore – it's amazing how unstable a man can be on dry land – and a local man showed Doola where we could set up tents. We had two big tents, built to rig on the hull of the ship. We had one up before the roast pig was brought down to us, and then no man could raise a finger for anything. They might have enslaved the lot of us in a matter of minutes, just for some pig.

I don't really remember much more of that evening. I ate and ate. I went to the ship, and Vasileos and I managed to get one of our heavy amphorae out of the bilge, and we broached it and served it to our hosts. And then I went to sleep – real sleep, for the first time in ten days.

I awoke to a rainy day and heavy swell out in the estuary. And to the thought that I had sailed out of the Pillars of Heracles, onto the Great Sea, and lived. You'd think I'd have been worried for *Amphitrite* and all my friends aboard. Let me tell you something about the life I led, honey. You had to trust your comrades and the gods. If they were dead, well, they were dead.

The first thing I did after rising was to pour a long libation and say a prayer aloud, to Poseidon, for their deliverance.

Then I went to find the tin.

7

There wasn't any tin at Oiasso. We sat with the lord of the town the next day, exchanging pleasantries, while his steward looked over our selection of wine and copper. Neither seemed to hold the least interest for the locals, and after some discussion I found that they had excellent copper down the coast in Iberia and that, while they enjoyed our wine, they had excellent wines of their own.

The *Amphitrite* had all of our other trade goods. I didn't have pepper; I didn't have silphium or anything else except for my own bronze wares – some helmets, a bronze aspis, some cooking pots and a bundle of swords. I won't say that they turned up their noses at my work.

I'll just say that they smiled and moved on to look at other items.

I had time to examine the chieftain's war gear. His bronze helmet with the wings was unlike anything I'd ever seen – almost like a Chaldicean helmet, with hinged cheekpieces and a low bronze bowl, but very different in appearance and marvellously well fashioned. It was decorated over almost the entire surface with beautiful repoussé – the work was very fine, even though the figures were, to me, amateurish. It took time for me to develop an eye for Keltoi work. To be honest, I still think they need some help with their figures.

Every man likes the art of his home, doesn't he?

That's not really the point. The point is that by the time the sun was high in the sky, I knew that I'd made an arrogant assumption about the north. They weren't ignorant savages ready to be impressed with the marvellous goods of our civilization. They were, in fact, impressed only by our pottery. They didn't really want our wines, but they wanted all the amphorae, and the empty one from the night before became our first guest gift.

The second thing we discovered was that the customs of the Inner

Sea didn't hold here. Or rather, it was like stepping back in time, to the century before my father's time, or even farther – to the world of the *Iliad* and the *Odyssey*. The Tarbelli aristocrat didn't *trade*. He hosted us and gave us gifts. Then he waited patiently for us to give him gifts, and the steward prompted us through Sittonax, who rolled his eyes.

'This is old-fashioned,' he admitted. 'But Southerners are old-fashioned.'

It made me smile, because for once, I was in my element. It was just like Crete, and I'd lived there. So I put myself in the role of the aristocratic captain and I disdained matters of trade, and Doola became *my* steward, and by dinner on the second evening, Tertikles – that's the best I can do with the local lord's name – and I were guest friends. We'd hit each other with swords, we'd raced horses on the dunes and I'd given him my second best helmet, which was, if no better than his own, no worse. He liked it.

Tertikles and Sittonax spoke together a great deal, and I left them to it when I wasn't required, seeing to the emptying of the ship. She'd stood nine days at sea, and she needed ... everything. We stripped her to the wood, scrubbed the bilge, recaulked the seams, and Vasileos wandered around her hull on the beach with a heavy mallet, driving pegs back into the hull and examining every inch with a professional eye.

I brought him a cup of wine. 'Good ship,' I said.

He beamed. 'She is, isn't she?' he said.

By the morning of the third day, Sittonax had his bearings, and he drew me a chart in the sand while the oarsmen scrubbed the hull clean.

'We came through the Pillars of Heracles,' he said, an eyebrow raised, 'as you call them, here.'

I nodded.

He drew a box. 'Iberia. As I understand it from Tertikles.'

I shrugged. No one at Marsala had ever been able to draw us even the vaguest chart of the world outside the Pillars.

'We're in this deep bay,' he said, drawing me the point where the north-western edge of the box intersected a long line he'd drawn with his stick that ran north to south. 'Somehow we ran all the way down this bay.' He shrugged.

Not a sailor. I knew *exactly* how it had happened. I just kept sailing east, expecting to find the coast of Iberia, and it kept escaping us.

'Those mountains,' he pointed to the long line in the south, 'are northern Iberia.'

'We sailed all the way round Iberia?' I asked. I'm a scientific sailor, but sometimes you just have to believe that Poseidon sends you where he wants you to go.

He shrugged again. 'Tertikles says that there is a Phoenician trading post – south and west, four days' rowing.'

I grunted. 'You think we could just sail in and *trade* for tin?' I asked.

Sittonax shrugged. 'No idea. But Tertikles wants to know if you'd like to join him in attacking it.'

'Attacking it?' I must have looked foolish.

Now, let's remember, my young friends – I had been a pirate. But by this time, I'd lived for years – *years* – on my own work and my own production and trade. It makes me smile, but at the time, I believe I thought myself too mature to engage in such foolishness.

'Oh, I don't recommend it, but he insisted I ask you,' the Kelt said. 'For my part, the Venetiae are farther up this coast – maybe six days' rowing. They'll have tin.'

'Are they your people?' I asked.

He rolled his eyes. 'No,' he said.

'Do you know them?' I asked.

'We trade with them, everyone does. They have the ships. They go to Alba. They control all the tin.' He looked the way a man does trapped in an argument with a small child.

'Will they want our copper or our wine?' I asked.

Sittonax shrugged. 'How would I know?' he answered.

That night, we sat down to dinner in the lord's hall. I met his sister, who was a year or two older than he – perhaps thirty. She was not beautiful, but rather strong-featured – a long, horsey face, strong teeth, a marvellous laugh. She had heavy bones like an athlete, and she was as tall as I am and perhaps as strong, too. I'd never seen a Greek woman who looked like her.

And yet I find I do her injustice. She was slim-waisted and wide-hipped and had deep breasts – just in a larger, stronger way than Greek women. She didn't have an ounce of fat on her. And her face looked ... ungentle. When she laughed, which was often, she laughed with the abandon with which men laugh.

But the longer I watched her, and the other Keltoi, the more I saw how different their women were. By the second night, their boldness had become proverbial with my crew – both for their straightforward propositions, and for forceful management when displeased. Thugater, that's a nice way of saying that when a Kelt woman didn't like the way you treated her, she had a way of punching you in the head.

And the gentlewomen – the aristocrats – all wore knives. They used them to eat, but they were not eating knives. Or so it appeared to me.

At any rate, her name was Tara, or close enough. She was far from beautiful, I suppose, but I wanted her the moment my eyes fell on her, and I suspected that the feeling was mutual. But she was the lord's sister, and that meant I needed to be careful.

Still, I taught her to play knucklebones our way, which was rather different from theirs. And she caught me peering down her marvellous cleavage, and she laughed. A Greek girl might have blushed, might have simpered; might have met my eyes for a moment and glanced away. Might have fled the room or gone stony cold, too. But she met my eye and roared.

When her brother came and sat with us, and Sittonax joined us, we could converse a little.

I have no idea what we talked about, but Sittonax became bored very quickly. Who wants to interpret for someone else's flirting? I mean, really.

Tertikles leaned in, then, and spoke vehemently – so strongly that I thought I was getting the 'this is my sister' lecture.

But she looked at me, licked her lips and nodded enthusiastically.

So I met her eye. She had wonderful, lively, expressive eyes. She was a person for whom the world was a fine place.

Sittonax looked at me. 'The lord just made a speech, and I'll say that he proposes – formally, and with a vow – that we go and attack the trading post.' Sittonax sat back. 'He's very serious.'

I'd had all day to think about it. I knew that Doola would be against it, but the rest of my people would probably go along with it. Especially the six 'marines' I'd picked up from Demetrios of Phocaea. And we had nothing to show for our adventures so far but bruises and welts. Nor were we well-found enough to trade; I'd learned that. It was a bitter lesson.

'What do they have in the way of defences?' I asked.

Sittonax raised an eyebrow at me. Again, I have to note that none of these people, except my marines, knew me as Arimnestos, Killer of Men. They knew me as Arimnestos, sometime merchant-captain and bronze-smith.

Tertikles grinned. He made a short speech, his arms moving dramatically.

Sittonax looked at me. 'He says that nothing will stand before his sword.'

About that time, Tara punched her brother in the arm.

They glared at each other.

I cleared my throat. 'Tell him that I'd be happy to join him, but I'm a greasy, wily Greek and I require things like scouting, surprise and a plan – as well as an agreement on division of the spoils – before I'd think of risking my ship. And what ship does he have?'

After some further discussion, Sittonax sat back, disgusted. 'He thought we could all ride in our ship,' he said. 'He said many interesting things. The Phoenicians have raided this place twice in the last ten years, for slaves. Their father died fighting the Phoenicians. So he has every reason.'

I nodded. I was looking at the crowd of my men and the locals who were eating communally, all intermixed. I was trying to catch Doola's eye, but he was gazing into the eyes of a blond Kelt woman and didn't seem to know I existed. Seckla watched him with undisguised jealousy.

Well, other people have complex lives, too.

Tertikles spoke again, waving his arms.

Tara watched him when he spoke, and then went back to watching me.

'How many warriors does he have?' I asked.

Sittonax nodded. He asked.

After a heated conversation, Sittonax turned back to me, his face flushed.

'He claims a thousand.' He shrugged. 'I think a hundred would be more like it. He's a hothead.'

This from you? I remember thinking. Sittonax had never had a practical thought in his life. He lived to eat, drink, fight and make love.

I caught Vasileos's eye, and he came up to the head of the hall. He looked embarrassed. It's funny what you remember. I never found out why. Who knows what the Kelt girl asked him? Or did. Hah! They were forward, and I saw them do things that I'd put weals on your back for, thugater. No, I won't tell you.

Fine. I'll tell you one. Kelt girls would, ahem, *measure* a man. With a stick. And then giggle.

No, you have to guess the rest for yourself.

I'm just an old man. Leave me alone.

At any rate, Vasileos came to join us, blushing like a virgin at a betrothal party. He sat beside me.

'Could we build a ship here?' I asked.

He shrugged. 'I'd have to see the timber in the hills,' he said. 'But if the pines up there are as fine as the two outside the fort, I'd say yes. I have my tools.'

'How long to build two more like *Lydia*?' I asked.

He shrugged. 'A month. I assume I will get all the help I need.'

Sittonax was shaking his head. 'You can't be meaning to stay here a month.'

'I'd like to give *Amphitrite* time to catch us up,' I said. 'And if he'll trade two ships for a month's food, and then some – well, we can go raiding with him.'

Sittonax shook his head. 'I want to get home,' he said.

'Want to get home rich?' I asked.

He kept shaking his head. 'You don't know my people well enough to do this, Arimnestos,' he said. 'Next week, Tertikles could be in love with a neighbour's daughter – or a horse – and your project will be forgotten.' He looked at Tara. 'And there are other complications. He's offering you his sister, in marriage. But it's not that simple. I need to tell you some things about the Keltoi. He's not her lord. She's more like his queen.'

'Just like that?' I asked.

'We're impulsive,' he admitted.

'Tell her yes.' I looked at her and winked.

And that, as they say, was that.

Marriage – at least, handfast marriage between mature adults – was a fairly informal affair, among the southern Keltoi. About a week later, we put our hands together over a copper cauldron of water, and her brother stirred honey into a poultice with a dagger of bronze that looked ancient. We both agreed – rather like farmers haggling over a cow – to certain conditions about how to raise any children, and under what conditions we'd part.

It was not a permanent union. In fact, it was more like a trade bond, or an *amphictyony*, as we call it – a league and covenant between neighbours. An alliance. And by the time her brother had said the words, there was a stack of big spruce trees by the beach and Vasileos had the lower strakes split. Twenty slaves and a dozen Keltoi craftsmen worked with him, and Sittonax sat on a log, translating, bored out of his head and resentful.

Our wedding night was great fun. The Keltoi are great ones for feasting – their notion of a symposium would recommend itself to the very richest Athenians – and our wedding feast was far more heroic than the ceremony itself. We drank and drank, and then my bride placed a hand on my thigh – very high on my thigh – and said, in beautifully accented Greek, 'Stop drinking.'

I almost spat out my wine.

She roared with laughter. 'Men – when they drink too much ...' she said, and made a motion with her finger that I shan't repeat.

Sittonax sat by me to translate. 'I've tried to teach her some Greek,' he admitted.

'You speak well,' I said to her.

'Not many things,' she said.

'She knew some Greek before,' Sittonax added.

'Ah!' I said. 'From traders?'

'Slaves,' she said, and shrugged.

Sittonax leaned forward. 'You know she's been married before,' he said.

'So?' I said. 'So have I.'

'They've all died,' he mentioned. 'In battle. All of them.'

'How many?' I asked.

'Six,' he said.

She met my eyes and smiled. 'You are a great warrior,' she said.

'She's practised that phrase a lot,' Sittonax said.

'I've been married before,' I said.

She smiled.

'My wife died in childbirth,' I said. Suddenly, I was crying.

She wrapped me in her arms. 'Bad,' she said. She was warm and kind.

I hadn't cried in someone's arms in a long time. And while some of my crewmen looked askance, none of the Keltoi so much as noticed. They're a more hot-blooded race than Greeks, and they show their emotions.

Later, we were alone. I won't bore you with details.

Hah! Maybe I will, later.

★

A week later, and Tara and I knew each other better.

I had never known a woman like her, and while I'm not sure I loved her, I *liked* her very well indeed. When *she* wanted to make love, she'd make love anywhere – in a field, in among the timbers of the new ships, on the mountainside where we cut the spruce logs, on our great bed in her brother's hall. But I swiftly found that it was her decision, not mine.

And there are tremendous advantages when you don't really share a language. We never argued – we didn't have enough words. And lack of language focuses you. I paid strict attention to her, and she to me. So I knew when she was annoyed, when she was delighted, when she was frustrated.

She was a good companion – the more so, as she was just as good a companion when we went up in the hills to cut more spruce as she was when we were using axes to cut; when we gathered firewood; when we swam; when we cooked. It's not that she was *manly*. It took me months in her company to put a name to it.

She was *free*.

But I'll talk more about that later. I like to tell these stories in order, and so I'll say that after we'd filled the beach with spruce trees stacked like kindling, hauled by heavy horses unlike anything I'd seen in Greece, we took council with Tertikles and his steward, with Doola who was besotted with a Kelt girl and scarcely able to think straight and with Sittonax, who wore a permanent scowl. It was a disjointed, spiritless meeting. Only Tertikles, Tara and I were interested.

In the end, I decided to take *Lydia* south and west, looking for the Phoenician port. Tara decided to come with me. I had a notion, too, that I might come across Demetrios and the rest of my friends. If they were alive, they were probably well to the south.

That seemed fine. Sittonax elected to come with us as well, and Doola stayed with Vasileos. Seckla came with me.

And off we went, into the Great Blue.

It's funny what you don't think of.

A day up the coast from Oiasso, and we hit a two-day storm. I had no Vasileos to rely on. It's an interesting facet of command – the ways you take the load off. I *knew* that I wasn't the best sea officer, and that I relied on Vasileos to take care of some of the routine ship-handling. But when I planned a four-day scout to the south, it didn't seem that important that he wasn't coming.

We didn't have *Lydia* off the beach before I missed him.

And the ship's name, *Lydia*. What had possessed me? Married to Tara, and a day at sea, and she asked me – between bouts of vicious seasickness – what the ship's name meant.

'Lie-dya,' she said. 'What is it?'

Sittonax grinned mirthlessly.

She's a woman I abandoned without marrying in my last port of call, I thought.

'It's a woman's name,' I said.

Tara spat over the side. 'What woman?' she asked.

I made some noises. 'A woman I knew,' I said. It sounded weak even as the words left the fence of my teeth.

'Wife?' she asked, in a matter-of-fact voice.

'No,' I said.

'Ah,' she said.

I let it go, and counted myself lucky.

I was still young, and I didn't know much.

Tara's seasickness went on and on. After a two-day blow that nearly killed us – it's not much of a story, and I don't wish to bore you – we found the coast again, sailed south for two days, and landed – at Oiasso. How Tertikles laughed!

We took on more water, more smoked pork, and sailed again. This time we sailed due east for a day with a perfect breeze, and made camp on an empty beach. Within an hour my marines were calling out, and a dozen locals approached carefully to sell us lobster and fish.

They weren't Keltoi and they weren't Greeks, and we didn't have anyone who could speak to them. They had an odd language, with grunts and clicks, or so it sounded to me. The men had heavy heads and muscles, and the women seemed about the same, to be honest.

Tara eyed them warily. 'Bask,' she said. She spoke rapidly to Sittonax.

'She says they are all witches, and we should be wary,' he said.

We were wary. We kept a good guard, but we ate their fish and paid in copper, and sailed away uninjured.

The next day there was no wind to speak of, and we rowed. Tara seemed disappointed when I rowed, but then she stripped off her linen shirt and took the oar across from mine.

The oarsmen whooped.

Tara grinned.

I'll tell you, short of having Heracles and Orpheus in your crew, a good-looking woman rowing with breasts bared does a great deal for morale. I'm not sure it wasn't the fastest rowing I've ever seen. It tired the men, but then, none of them would *admit* he was tired, which was useful in itself.

I rowed for a long time. I wanted my people to see I was with them, not just commanding them. They'd put up with two weeks of my aping the manners of the Keltoi aristocracy. I felt they needed proof I could still row. And I wanted proof I was getting my body back. Damn Dagon – he had nearly broken me, and a year, more, of exercise, rowing, sword practice and boxing had still not restored me to the level I'd been at when I fought at Marathon.

Damn him indeed.

So I rowed. And the next day, I rowed again.

Tara rowed every time I rowed. Well, as I say, that had positive benefits, but I realized that she would not stop until I stopped, and her arms and shoulders were strong – but not as strong as mine.

The second day, when we put our clothes back on – it was high summer, and I rowed naked – Tara pulled me by the arm. 'Did she row as well as I?' she asked.

'Row?' I asked. 'Who?'

'Lydia!' she spat. 'Did she row?'

Uh-oh.

Fourth day at sea, and the coast of Iberia, which had been like the broken teeth of an old man to our south, suddenly vanished. I turned from easterly to full south, and found the coast again after two panicked hours of raising and lowering sail. We landed at a headland and spent a fruitless day prowling what proved to be a deep bay, but eventually we were rewarded with an Iberian fishing port which had three things we needed – men who spoke Keltoi, fresh water and hatred for the Phoenicians who were, it turned out, just across the bay at Elvina, a day's row away. The Phoenicians and their local Iberian allies preyed relentlessly on Centrona, as our new friends called their village.

We got water. We traded copper for silver – they mined silver in the hills. And we got expert sailing advice from the local fishermen, who offered to show us the Phoenician port. I took two locals aboard who spoke Keltoi, and we rowed at their direction, coming up on the

Phoenician post with the sun behind us, so we were invisible, or so we hoped.

If it was a trade post, it was a very small one. There was what had to be a warehouse – the largest building, all heavy wooden piles and bark walls, and a slave pen – I knew what that was. Twenty huts, a single stone tower and a lighthouse.

And a warship drawn up on the beach.

Sittonax was tired of interpreting, and I was beginning to get the hang of the local Keltoi tongue and Tara was even better, so I talked to the fishermen through her.

'How many soldiers?' I asked.

Let's just say it took us some time to define what I meant by soldier.

In the end we agreed that I meant *armed men*.

'Twenty,' he answered. 'And more come in the ships.'

We crept north and west to stay out of sight, and then went ashore on the opposite side of the headland from the lighthouse, in case it was manned, and made our way up a long ridge that dominated the settlement.

It was a long time since I'd done all these things. But let me tell you, friends, it came back like the feel of a good sword in your hand.

We spent the day high on the ridge, with a woven screen of brush in front of us – me, Tara, Sittonax and two fishermen, as well as Aeneas and Alexandros, my two most reliable marines.

The warship on the beach was being repaired. I was pretty sure she was the trireme we'd damaged off the Pillars of Heracles, because her starboard cathead was a mess and there were injured men in the slave pen.

And the rowers were either slaves, or men treated as slaves.

'We can take them now,' I insisted to Sittonax.

He shrugged. 'Fine,' he said. But despite his bored face, he quivered with excitement.

Tara's eyes sparkled.

'Send to the ship and get everyone and have them arm,' I said.

Tara made a moue. 'What do you need them for?' she asked. 'Go and challenge their leader to single combat!'

Keltoi.

I grinned. 'I have my own ways,' I said.

★

147

We struck when the sun set, but the sky was still light. Working people would have been in bed.

I went straight for the tower. I had the marines and Sittonax and Tara, who had weapons and seemed to know how to use them. The eight of us would, I hoped, be enough.

Seckla led the oarsmen to open the slave pens and cow its occupants. Seckla had been a slave – I reckoned he'd be able to tell who might make a good ally among them.

Dogs barked and men shouted, and then I was up the ladder and in through the second-storey door to the stone tower. There was a man inside.

I killed him.

It had been some time. But the motions weren't unfamiliar, and neither were the smells.

I held the door for about twenty heartbeats, and then Alexandros was next to me, and then we were among them. I expect about half of them got to weapons before the real killing started, but they had neither armour nor shields, and their bedmates helped us a great deal. Girls – and boys – pinned the ankles of men, or trapped their hands, or simply kicked them from behind.

All told, it didn't take long. We slaughtered the guards and stormed the tower. There was a family living on the top floor – the only actual Phoenicians in the whole complex. I'm proud to say that we took them prisoner. The Keltoi don't rape, by and large, and Tara – whose right arm was covered in blood to the elbow – took the women and turned towards Seckla, who grinned and saluted her.

And that was that. The curly-bearded overseer's life wouldn't have been worth a brass obol had I let go of him, but he knew the *mathematika* of his situation the moment I took him, and he babbled out where the ship's crew was and his store of silver.

'Six marines! And the trireme's deck crew!' I shouted to my men. 'Follow me!'

But sometimes, the gods smile. I'd missed them sneaking in – they'd been quartered in a barn beyond the slave pens, and the trireme's helmsman had a house by the huts, but when Seckla freed the slaves – well, they tore the helmsman limb from limb. Which wasn't what I'd have wanted. A man who really *knew* these waters would have been a priceless asset.

Otherwise, it was all easy.

I sent Seckla to fetch *Lydia* around the point. We'd exterminated the opposition, and we didn't have to hurry.

We examined the stores of the little post. They were ample. The Phoenicians collected taxes from the whole district, even while taking their people as slaves. I suspect we'd have been quite popular if we'd stayed, but on the other hand, it was always possible the locals would see us as more of the same.

Which, of course, we were.

Slaves – African slaves – told Seckla that another ship had come in with the trireme on the beach and then sailed away. That's the only reason we missed a huge consignment of silver.

You can't waste curses on these things. We'd stormed the place with a boat's crew, and the worst injury was Giannis, the youngest of my herdsmen, who managed to lose the chape from his scabbard. In the attack, the point of his long knife rammed through the top of his thighs as he ran, opening truly horrible-looking wounds. No, I'm not making this up. We all teased him about it, and he took our teasing the way young men who want to be heroes react.

Good fun, really.

My crew were … blooded. There's no other way to put it. They killed together, and they were victorious together, and we had a small stack of silver bars and some tin that they all knew they'd share – together.

It all came back to me so easily. Kill the men. Take the women. Sell the cargo. Build morale in the crew. Train them to fight. Kill, and don't be killed.

Hardly worth the telling, really.

At any rate, we burned the slave pens and cooked pigs in the embers. The slaves liked that. Tara's admiration was candid. I liked that.

In the morning, I looked over the trireme. Her starboard cathead was smashed to splinters, and needed professional help. I remember standing there with two of my fishermen and Alexandros and Seckla. Seckla was a craftsman – the kind of man who's never happy unless he's working. He pushed and pulled and shook his head.

I agreed. I wanted that ship, but she was too damaged to use.

So I turned to my friends, the fishermen. 'Tell me about the weather the next four days.'

They prevaricated. But eventually, the older one admitted that it was unusually fine, even for summer.

Seckla glared at me. 'You *can't* be thinking we can tow this thing?'

Many things in my life have represented gifts from the gods. Briseis, despite the many ugly turns she did me – she drove me to heroism like a farmer drives an ox to work. My father's decision to send me to the old priest, Calchus, for training.

Four days' west wind.

I asked the former slaves for volunteers, and let's be frank – what choice did they have? Stay, and be enslaved by the Iberians? By the time the smoke of the slave pens was in the sky, there were already Iberian warriors prowling the ridges above the little warehouse town.

Before we'd been at sea an hour, they set fire to the lighthouse.

My Phoenician factor was a cringing coward. I might be, too, if a savage pirate and his tattooed mistress had my wife and children. But he was a fount of information as we sailed east on a perfect wind.

'We have no defences,' he admitted. He almost bragged it. 'It is fifty years since any of the interior tribes attacked us.' He looked at the sea. 'How did you make it past the squadron at Gades?' Then he looked at me. 'You – you were the small ship that Dadalos was pursuing!'

I smiled nastily.

'But – we took that ship!' He quailed at his own words.

I was older, calmer, more mature. So I didn't grab him by the throat.

'What ship?' I asked. I thought my tone was mild.

He grew very red in the face, like a maiden blushing. I took his hand and pressed my thumb and forefinger to a certain spot.

It was scarcely necessary. He shrieked. 'Days ago. Helitkon of Tartessos took a small sailing ship – no more than a fishing boat. Laden with goods from the Inner Sea.' He writhed in my hands.

'Where?'

'Helitkon brought him in to me. I supplied him – he sailed south!'

'Where's the ship? The crew?' I asked.

'He took them! To sell!' he was screaming.

It is sickening, I'll admit. His daughters looked at me with naked hate that transcended fear – they hated me more than they feared rape and death, which, all things considered, suggests they were brave. And they obviously loved him, which meant that, however much I wanted to see him as the enemy, as a piece of shit who dealt in human lives and stole and killed – he was a good father.

Of course, I knew that I dealt in human lives, too.

Time makes things difficult. Maturity – unless you are simply a killer, a thug – robs you of certainty.

I let go his hand. And I felt ... ashamed.

Tara watched me. She looked at me the way a cat looks at something it doesn't know. A cat is asking, *Is this prey? Or predator?*

Yes. Well.

I looked up at my mainsail, drawing well. I looked back at the long curve of the tow rope. I wished, for the hundredth time, that I had Vasileos.

But I sang a prayer to Poseidon that night, after I made love to my wife on the beach with the ancient pines.

The coast of Iberia had been Phoenicia's cash cow for seventy years, and it was naked before me.

Old thoughts boiled to the surface. I had enough silver from the one raid to make the trip a success. But—

But there could be more.

8

Oiasso welcomed us as victors, which we were. Tertikles was enraged, at first, that we'd stormed Centrona without him.

Doola hugged me on the beach, and introduced me to his wife.

One trick of leadership that I learned young was never to question a man's taste in bed-partners. No faster way to lose his faith, his loyalty, his courage. That said, though, I'd always known that Doola and Seckla were ... together. It wasn't a spoken thing. It just – was.

And then, one fine day, we landed at Oiasso, Doola fell for a Kelt girl and the next I knew, he was wed. Doola was my friend, practically my brother. It was not my place to even ask. I hugged him, kissed her and bade them every fortune.

But Seckla stood on the beach with death in his eyes. He was younger: tough, strong, tall and thin, and his love went to hate, all at once. I think he'd assumed that Doola would wake up one morning and be done with the woman. Instead, he married her.

And Seckla was also my friend. Seckla was touchier, more full of fire, perhaps less useful sometimes – but not on this last raid. Seckla looked at Doola, and I looked at Seckla.

Command. Leadership. A never-ending labyrinth of difficult decisions.

Tara got it all in one glance. Or maybe knew it from gossip. Either way, she was quick.

'They were lovers?' she asked. Actually, she asked something cruder. Her Greek was barbaric.

'Yes.' I was moving cautiously towards Seckla. I was afraid he'd kill his former friend right there.

She laughed. 'I'll find him someone,' she said. She laughed again. 'Men!'

★

Vasileos had finished both vessels. They were a little longer than *Lydia*, with beautiful lines, a slightly narrower entry, rather bluffer bows. The ram bow rose just a little at the tip, so that in heavy water, the cutwater would – perhaps – push the bow up, not down. Or so Vasileos theorized.

We sat down to our welcome feast, with Tertikles looking just about as happy as Seckla.

He was easy.

Tara told him that I planned to raid to the south, all along the coast, and he brightened.

A black-haired girl with a narrow face and huge eyes went to Seckla and hesitantly sat down with him.

Tara winked at me.

Seckla ignored her.

More fool he. But I had Vasileos watch him, and then I ordered Alexandros to watch him. Alexandros, like many other young men I have met and known, had discovered that he liked to be trusted – liked to be responsible. He was rising to command.

I felt old. I'd done all this before; none of it was new.

'What do we do with the prisoners?' Doola asked me.

'I'd like to ransom them,' I said.

We left it there.

Summer was slipping away by the time we got the cathead repaired on the trireme. And my nearly two hundred former oar-slaves created a certain chaos in the town – just feeding them strained Tertikles to the maximum. So all the silver and the tin from the raid went to paying for grain from other lords.

I gave up on trade and armed them with the helmets I'd made, and we used the rest of the hides to make plain spolas with yokes over the shoulders.

You might think that I'd be away south after Demetrios, Gaius and the rest, but I knew I was up against at least a pair of triremes with expert crews. And my prisoner told me that most of the slaves who went to the south were used in the silver mines above Olisipo on the Tagus, a river to the south of Centrona with a broad estuary, a dangerous bar and silver and gold in the mountains behind it.

He was very talkative.

I promised to release him with his wife and daughters on the coast south of Olisipo – *after* my raid. He didn't seem to mind.

Men can be stupid.

The grain was ripe in the fields and the apples were nearly ripe on the trees, and all four of my ships were ready for sea. I'd rowed my new warship up and down, and I'd roared myself hoarse in three languages trying to make the Keltoi obey, something at which, to be honest, they weren't very good. Keltoi don't obey, they discuss. Keltoi debate. Every man is the equal of every other man.

On the other hand, I ate well, exercised, trained men to use the sword and shield and made love every night to a woman who – well, who knew what she was about. It is very different for a man to make love to a woman who is the same size as he is. Very different. Very—

Athletic.

Ah, the blushes.

We celebrated the summer feast of Demeter – at least, that's what it was to me – and Tertikles sacrificed a slave, which was barbaric as far as I was concerned. He came aboard my trireme, because it was more comfortable. We had three triakonters, packed to the gunwales with Keltoi warriors in good armour, and a trireme with former Phoenician slaves, armed and ready to fight.

We were ready.

The gods had other ideas. We put to sea and sailed for little more than two hours before the wind turned round and headed us, and we were lucky to slip easily back into the estuary and land on our beach at Oiasso. Two days later, we rowed out past the headland and were back before dark – the wind was too fierce for the trireme.

Tempers flared.

Keltoi picked up their gear and went home. Oddly, this was balanced by late arrivals, who wandered down from the mountains as if arriving a week late was perfectly normal. Of course, they'd never rowed, and they resented being taught.

Tertikles became surly, and only his sister being there prevented violence.

We were windbound for ten days. I rowed in the estuary, and Vasileos kept them hard at it in the *Lydia*, but the other two ships did nothing but eat, drink and sleep. The season was getting on; we had our first cool night.

Seckla tried to kill Doola. It was quick, and carefully premeditated. But while Vasileos was busy, commanding his ship, Alexandros was right there, and he tackled the Numidian boy, tore the knife from his grasp and then knocked him unconscious.

The next day, I sat with Seckla in my tent, watching the whitecaps in the estuary and cursing the gods.

When his eyes opened, he looked at me for a moment and then rolled over so that he faced the wall of the tent.

'You are an idiot,' I said.

His silence was his only reply.

'If you had killed him, I would have killed you,' I said.

'Fine,' he said. 'Kill me now.'

'In a year, this will be a bitter memory. In five years, it will scarcely trouble you. In ten years, you'll make jokes about it.' I put a hand on his shoulder.

'No,' he said.

'Yes,' I said. 'I know. I *know*, lad. I have been abandoned, and I have abandoned others. It comes and goes.'

'When we were slaves,' he spat, 'you would moan in your sleep, and say a name. Always the same name. *Briseis, Briseis*. Always the same.' He rolled over suddenly, and glared at me. 'Tell me you have forgotten her, yes, old man?'

I shrugged. 'I have not forgotten her. But I don't burn. And neither will you.'

'My life is over.' He tried to turn back over.

I pinned him with an elbow. 'No, it isn't. And now you can be your own man, and stop being in his shadow.'

Silence.

The young burn so hot, and they have so much energy for hate, and anger. So I put a watch on him.

The next day, the wind pinned us to the beach, and Doola came to my tent. I hugged him, and he went into Seckla, as if Seckla was sick and needed visitation, which was true in a way.

Seckla had a knife. He slashed Doola's face, and then turned it on himself.

There are advantages to being a hardened killer. When a good friend tries to kill himself, you can disarm him without taking a scratch. I had the knife before he'd done much more than scratch his dark skin. He glared at me like an angry tomcat. I went to Doola and found that, while he was cut to the bone, it was really just a flesh wound. Face wounds bleed like – well, like face wounds. There seems to be enough blood to be fatal.

Hard to staunch, too. The blood went on and on.

Seckla watched – Alexandros was pinning him to his bed. 'Did I kill him?' he asked.

Doola got up with a linen towel against his face, soaked with blood.

Let me just say, the following conversation happened in a language I don't understand – well, mostly. Most of it was in their tongue. Despite that, I understood it fine, and besides, I've heard the story told a dozen times.

'Stop being a fuckhead,' he said.

'You betrayed me!' Seckla screamed.

Doola shrugged. 'Grow up. Be a man. It's time to leave childish things. I want a wife and children. We are free now. We can have anything.'

'I want you!' Seckla said.

'No, you don't. You want someone to take care of you. I want to be a free man. I'm still your friend.'

You get the picture. It went on for as long as it took a man to run five stades. Blood flowed down Doola's face, and he shouted at Seckla, and Seckla shouted back. Keltoi came and stood around, watching the entertainment.

Finally, they both stopped.

An odd silence fell, a sort of crowded hush as many, many people who had been listening all listened harder.

In the hush, I heard something. I had Seckla by the shoulders at the time. Vasileos, who had run to the sound of the shouting, stood in the doorway. He heard what I heard.

He ran out of the door.

I'm ashamed to say I dropped Seckla like a hot piece of meat and ran after him.

The sun was bright and the wind had dropped and now, a whisper of east wind blew across the hills like a lover's caress.

'Man the ships,' I barked. I knew that once we got to sea, all this foolishness would be gone. Nothing, nothing had gone well since we reached past the Pillars. I wanted to collect my friends, steal some silver and go home.

I was no less an idiot than Seckla.

Four days sailing and rowing brought us to the Iberian settlement across the bay from Centrona. They didn't give us a hero's welcome

– we had too many ships – but they sold us pigs and barley and we ate well enough.

'Ships come,' said the headman. With Sittonax to support me, we finally established that a few weeks before, a pair of triremes had come to Centrona, landed for a day and rowed away south.

That wasn't all good.

I bought all the grain I could, which wasn't as much as I wanted, and we rowed south.

We had to beach every evening. In a smaller boat, a triakonter, you can stay the night at sea. Right up to a fifty-oared ship, you can stay two or three days at sea and still have enough food to feed your crew, stowed in the bilges and under the benches. But triremes only carried food and water for one day. A trireme needs to make port – or beach – every night.

But I *knew* I needed a heavy ship. So we beached, and bought fish – fish for three hundred men. Grain. Rotgut wine, terrible small beer. At extravagant prices, and the haggling meant that the crew ate after dark, each night.

What was worse, I had to turn back every day to find the laggards. The two Keltoi ships always left the beach late and rowed slowly, if at all. The Keltoi were far too proud to row. If they didn't have a wind, they'd idle along.

I was starting to hate them. And Tara inevitably took their side.

Useless lubbers. No wonder they hadn't built their own ships.

Sittonax laughed. 'Wait until you meet the Venetiae,' he said. Then he made a face. 'Of course they never row, either.'

Six days we spent on the coast of Iberia. For an expedition that depended on surprise, we were the most incompetent squadron since Poseidon ruled the seas. We were loud, we spread over stades, we were visible from every headland. We never sailed before the sun – we were always caught on the sea by high noon. We ate late, and the Keltoi drank too much, any night that there was anything to drink.

Little by little, I lost control of the expedition. From here, I can see just how it happened. I wasn't interested in taking Tertikles on, day after day, night after night. He, on the other hand, was relentless in his lazy, shiftless, arrogant way. Every day, he would push his own authority.

After six days, he left my ship and moved into one of the two triakonters that were all Keltoi.

His sister went after me the next morning. 'You treat my brother like a slave,' she said.

'No, Tara. I treat him like a fool who knows nothing of war or the sea.' I wasn't taking this, even from her.

'My brother is a master of war. He has killed twenty men in single combat.' She was spitting mad. 'You cannot take the tone with him that you take. You speak as if to a child.'

'He wanted me to put the sail up,' I said.

'It was a simple request.' She stood with her hands on her hips.

'The wind was *against* us.' I shook my head. I hope you are seeing what I had to deal with.

She shrugged. 'So you say,' she said.

What do you do?

I just let it go.

Seven days, and we sighted the mouth of the Tagus.

I knew from my prisoner that the mines were in the mountains east of the river mouth – about a hundred stades inland, on the south side of the river. So I led my squadron out to sea, and we passed the mouth of the Tagus well to seaward, and then angled back east and landed on the soft sand south of the river mouth. Well south.

That night, I gathered my captains. Or rather, that's what I thought I was doing. Instead, when Tertikles and his war-captains joined me and Vasileos, Doola and Alexandros at the fire, the Keltoi refused to discuss plans.

Tertikles was in full armour. He jerked a thumb at himself with vast self-importance. 'I'll do as I think best,' he said. 'And I intend to attack the settlement.'

I thought about it for several heartbeats. It seemed to me that I had two choices: I could kill him, or I could submit to him. Both of those alternatives bored me. Or I could let him go his own way.

'So be it,' I said. 'Enjoy yourself.'

'You will follow my lead,' he said.

'No,' I said. 'No, we're quits here, Tertikles. You make your attack, I'll make mine.'

He was puzzled, a gleam of gold and bronze in the firelight. 'What do you plan?' he asked.

I grinned, my hand on my sword hilt. I may have been wrong – I never found out – but I suspected that I could have put him down before he could take a breath. 'None of your business,' I said.

Tara frowned. 'You must help my brother.'

I shook my head. 'No. Sorry, Tara. I never intended to attack the settlement. I'm not even going to scout it. It's defended – we'll never get as lucky as we did at the last one.'

'You are a coward,' she said.

It is funny how much some things hurt, and other things don't. Cowardice wasn't something I'd ever really worried about. So I shrugged.

Which infuriated her. 'Our marriage ends here, on this beach,' she shouted.

'Goodbye,' I said.

She followed her brother across the sand.

Dawn found us at sea. I didn't trust Tertikles not to burn the trireme out of spite.

But I turned south, not north. We ran two small coves down the coast and put in again before the Keltoi were even awake. We beached stern-first, and brought the ship well up the beach. Turned her turtle, in case it rained.

Then I gathered my whole crew, armed them and we marched inland.

Inland.

Why attack the settlement? The silver came from a hundred stades away. And that was where, in all likelihood, my friends were, if they were alive.

We marched across the plains south of the Tagus. It was hot here, and we raised dust as we marched, and there was no hiding the gleam of metal. By mid-morning, I was sure we could be seen for sixty stades.

There were farms, and plantations. We took water from wells, and I stole horses from the first really prosperous farm we passed, and more horses from the next. Only about twenty of us could ride and we spread out, to prevent surprise. I've never really loved horses, but they can be damned useful.

And Iberians have fine horses.

By late afternoon, my prisoner said we were halfway to the mines. We found a stand of trees, and my entire small army went into the trees and laid down, and in minutes most of my people were asleep. Even the stolen horses slept. Alexandros took four men and found a stream, and we filled canteens. I was too nervous – too *aware* – to sleep. So I helped carry water, and I climbed a tree and watched in all directions.

When the sun began to dip, I slid down my tree and ordered Doola to wake the men.

In the distance, there was smoke, towards the estuary of the Tagus.

I got my men together. We drank water, ate some dried pork and moved east, into the hills. There was a good road, and we found it quickly, and after that, I didn't need my prisoner.

We found the mines at dark. My herdsmen and shepherds crept around in the dark for a few hours, and came back and reported.

I had hoped that when Tertikles attacked the settlements, the slave guards at the mine would react. What I should have known is that a silver mine is much more important than a bunch of slaves and their families. I can be foolish like that.

The guards were alert and awake. They didn't actually catch any of my people, but we had the immense disappointment of hearing the alarm sounded – a man beating a copper plate and shouting, in Phoenician.

So much for surprise.

I slept for a little, and when I awoke I decided to have a look for myself. I climbed above the mine – actually a huge open pit – with Giannis and Alexios, another shepherd. Lights twinkled below us like orange stars.

Giannis had grown up during the summer. He lay on his stomach and pointed. 'I think these are the slave quarters,' he said. 'See? The largest building. Next to it – the tower. Yes? You see? And then – I don't know what this other building does.'

I did. I could smell it. They smelted in that shed. In the moonlight, I could make out pits and slag heaps among the shadows. I'd had a glimpse in the last light. It was the only time I can remember where my skills as a smith had tactical value.

I had a dozen archers, a dozen trained marines and a lot of oars-men. I couldn't afford a complicated plan; we lacked the skill or the trust. Neither did I have the time. On the other hand, the garrison couldn't be more than fifteen or twenty men.

And when push came to shove, I didn't really need to storm the tower. I wanted to – that's where the silver would be. But what I really needed were the slaves. If Demetrios and Gaius and Daud were here, they'd be in that slave pen.

Sometimes, you make complex decisions on the slenderest of evidence. It can lead to foolishness. Or brilliance.

I put a hand on Giannis's shoulder. 'I'm going for the slave pens,' I said. 'If I'm not back in an hour, tell Doola to come and get me.'

Giannis argued, but not for long, and then I was ghosting along through the darkness.

I am an old campaigner. I knew how to move well in the dark, even in a foreign place on foreign soil. I fell once, with a clatter. In fact, I fell, rolled and came up one twitch short of falling over a forty-foot cliff that would either have killed me or left me a broken man. But I got up and moved on, no worse for near death – there's a moral there – I stubbed my sandalled toes several times on the rock. But I moved slowly, took my time and in an hour I had gone down the slope and moved from slag heap to slag heap across the flat ground at the edge of the great black pit.

The slag was fascinating. I lay against one heap and smelled it, ran my hand over it. I even tasted a sample.

That slag heap told me more than my prisoner had told me. More than the slaves had told. It explained everything.

They didn't mine silver here.

They mined gold.

I crept carefully across the last of the open ground towards the slave house. It was quite big – a sort of hall of hides, with palisade walls – bigger than the largest barn in Boeotia, and it smelled. It smelled of men.

The timbers in the palisade were huge – big, resinated pines from the hillsides.

The hide roof was well up over my head.

I went to the door, first. It was at the top of a low ramp, up a set of steps, and it took me precious time to find.

It was latched outside, with a heavy iron spike driven through a shackle attached to a huge sliding bar.

I crouched, listening to the men in the tower. There were at least two on duty. They knew that someone was moving.

'It's a fox,' said one, with a deep voice.

'It's not a fox, you fool,' said a high-pitched voice. 'That was a man on the slag heap.'

'Wake the captain, then,' said the deep voice.

'You wake him, idiot,' said the higher voice.

And so on.

I sat on my heels in the shadow of the slave quarters and waited.

This had happened to me many times. I feel … it is impossible to explain … that I am waiting for a sign, a signal. There is no point in hurrying. I had no idea what I was waiting for, but I waited, and I prayed to Heracles, my ancestor, and to Poseidon, Lord of Horses, and the stars wheeled above me, mocking my pretensions to greatness. I thought of Briseis, and Euphoria, and Lydia. Of Phrynichus, and Aristides. For the first time in months, I thought of Miltiades.

It is an odd thing. I suspect that, when I am on the edge of life and death, perhaps I am closer to the gods. My mind is clear; I think well.

There, in the shadow of the doorway, I took stock, and found that I was wasting time. That my mourning for Euphoria was over. I missed Penelope; I missed Plataea. I didn't want to start again.

I didn't want to make a life of killing men, either.

It was a moment of great clarity for me. I remember it much better than I remember the landing on the beach, or the march overland. I believe that the gods reached out and touched me. I think that Athena stood by my shoulder, and helped open my mind.

I reached up and opened the iron shackle. It wasn't loud, but it made a distinctive noise.

'What's that?' asked the deep voice.

I began tapping on the door. We had tapped on Dagon's ship. If Neoptolymos was in there, he'd hear the tapping.

'I say we wake the captain,' said Deep Voice.

'And then he orders us to go out in the dark,' said High Voice.

Tap-tap-tap. Tap. Tap.

Thunk.

Well, that could be any slave. On the other hand, it scarcely mattered. I realized I was trying too hard.

I reached up and pulled the bar. It moved silently, the wood smooth.

The door opened inwards, of course.

There were fifty men by the door. Stinking, filthy and thin, eyes shining in the dark.

'Neoptolymos?' I whispered. 'Daud? Demetrios?'

Men were grabbing my arms.

Damn, I thought.

'He's in the slave quarters!' High Voice shouted.

Damn.

The men in the tower reacted far faster than I expected. They must have had a sortie ready and armed. The men on top of the tower shouted, and banged on a piece of copper. There was some more shouting.

The slaves around me seemed to hang back.

'Anyone speak Greek?' I asked. No need for silence now.

'I do, friend,' said a familiar voice.

And then the Phoenicians attacked.

There were a dozen. They sprinted across the yard – obvious in the moonlight. They had armour and spears.

Of course they did. In one glance, I knew they were Poieni, citizen infantry. Phoenician hoplites. It was, after all, a *gold mine*.

'Daud?' I asked.

'Arimnestos?' he asked. 'By the gods!'

And then the Poieni were coming at me.

They had to come up the short ramp and then the steps. And perhaps they didn't really believe that the intruder would be armed.

I got one for nothing. You usually do. My spear had not lost its purpose, and my hand had not lost its skill. My spearhead went in one eye, and he fell on top of his mates.

I wasn't going into the slave quarters. If I did, they could simply lock the door on me and hunt me down in daylight.

But I had the glimmer of a plan. So I took a step backwards onto the low platform just inside the log lintel.

They took a long minute to decide to come after me, though. And when they did, they came silently, their bare feet padding on the steps, fast and purposeful.

The first man came though the door with his aspis thrust well up ahead of him. I launched myself at him, and we went shield to shield in the near darkness. My spear was leaning against the wall, ready to hand. I had a short sword in my fist, and I cut over his shield. Then under it.

This man was good. He rolled with my shield slam and got free – got his shield down, and then up, while he shortened his grip on his spear.

I got my sword against his helmet – but not hard enough. Still, where a man's head goes, his weight goes, so I kept pushing, and he had to bend back.

But his spear started searching for me, wild pecks like a snake striking at a bird.

All in near-perfect darkness.

Something changed.

A man behind him thrust with his spear at my head, and some noise betrayed him. I wrenched my head to my right. My adversary's head cracked against the doorpost. Helmet and all, he fell away from me. The spear hit my helmet, but not a killing blow.

I got my weight under me, powered forward, got my right knee into my adversary's groin and then swung my aspis into his head – and by sheer luck blocked the next thrust from his partner.

There is no going back, in such combat.

I was too close to do anything but grapple.

I let the aspis drop off my right arm as my left arm swept past my new opponent's head, and I seized his aspis with my left hand, spun it and broke his arm, turned him as he screamed and *pulled*. I threw him in, through the door and in among the slaves.

'*DOOLA!*' I roared.

The third man came up the steps. I had his spearhead. Heracles gave it to me: suddenly it was in my right hand, which ran down the shaft even as he ran up the steps, and I turned it, slammed the spear across his aspis and then slipped it over his head and locked him by the neck. The fourth man thrust at me. The third man's face went rigid, and I backed up the steps, using him as a shield. I was strong.

Oh, I was strong. I laughed. I laughed at Dagon.

Break my body, will you?

My victim screamed, and I got the spear shaft under his jaw at last and broke his neck. Eager hands reached from behind me and grabbed him by the helmet and towed him into the slave quarters.

The fourth man was still in shock. He'd just seen three comrades die – one, judging from the man's skill, his captain. And then he'd stabbed his mate.

I got a deep breath into my body, seized my spear from behind the door and threw it into him so that he fell, the spear deep in his body. He thrashed, and the other men flinched away from him instinctively.

Men behind me passed me my aspis.

I had all the time in the world to get it on my arm.

I started down the steps.

The Poieni shuffled.

And broke.

I must have laughed. I'm laughing now.

Oh, the power.

I'd missed this.

They might as well have stood their ground. None of them made the door of the tower, because Doola was there, and his archers shot them down in the moonlit open ground. A few ran off into the slag heaps.

Some ruthless bastard in the tower slammed the door shut.

The slaves started to come out of their quarters. The door was open.

In the darkness, they looked like creatures from the underworld. They were too thin to be men.

I didn't know Neoptolymos when he stepped up to me. In Sicily, he had filled out into a solid rock, with muscles that stood out like a statue of Heracles. Now, the skin was stretched tightly across a skull-like head and his tow-blond hair was Medusa's in the moonlight.

'Brother?' he asked, his voice a sibilant whisper.

I thought he was some Iberian who spoke Greek. He didn't look like an Illyrian.

But I got it. Some interplay of light and shadow, something in the set of the mouth.

I crushed him to me.

'We knew you'd come.' He managed a laugh.

'Where are the others?' I asked.

He pointed towards the gaping pit, a black hole in the dark. 'They tried to escape and were caught, so they aren't allowed out of the pit. Gaius especially.' He grinned. 'He's a bad slave.'

'But alive,' I said. I feared the worst. This was insane. I'd heard rumours that the Athenians used slaves like this in their silver mines, but it made no sense, and now I knew that I should have come as soon as I knew where they were.

But that kind of thinking leads to mistakes. I shrugged it off. 'Let's go and get them,' I said.

'You have to wait for daylight,' Neoptolymos said. 'You can't even get down the ladders in the dark.' He shrugged. 'I tried, once.'

I reckoned it was two hours until dawn.

Doola came out of the moonlit darkness and hugged Neoptolymos. So did Seckla.

Neoptolymos laughed aloud. 'By the gods,' he said. 'You came. You came!'

There were a hundred or more slaves milling about in the darkness. Many of them ran off – I have no idea what happened to them. Many, of course, must have been Iberians, and found their way home. Or died.

But there were a hundred men who stayed: Greeks, Etruscans, Iberians, Africans from Libya and farther off, and Keltoi, too. Neoptolymos knew them – most of them by name – and he moved among them, giving orders – well, he had been a prince, once.

Meanwhile, Doola and I looked at the tower. Men at the top of it shot arrows at us, but I, who had endured Persian archery, didn't think much of their weak bows and their piss-poor shooting – in the dark, no less.

We walked all around the tower.

'If we burn it, every Phoenician in Iberia will know we are here,' Doola said.

I thought about it. There wasn't a hurry – yet – and I took some time to think.

'If they find our ships, we're fucked,' I said. 'But, other than that, do you really think they have two hundred soldiers? In this whole colony?'

Doola's eyes flashed in the dark. He laughed a cruel laugh. Doola was a gentle man; not a man who fancied killing, not a man who loved the feel of a spear in his hand. But slavery enraged him.

'You *want* them to come here?' he asked.

'We have the high ground, and their gold. They'd be fools to come for us. But if they do, we can teach them a lesson.' I grinned. He grinned.

We set fire to the tower.

It took time. It is one thing to say, 'The tower is made of wood', and another thing entirely to get it to burn.

Here's what we did. We stripped all the shingles off the livestock sheds, and then we broke down the sheds themselves and the big wooden structure where the smelting went on. We had a hundred pairs of willing hands, and it is literally *unbelievable* how much damage a hundred angry former slaves can do to their master's property.

Then we had ten of the strongest slaves, led by Neoptolymos, carry loads of flammables up to the tower, under the cover of twenty of us with aspides held over their heads.

The men in the tower understood immediately, of course.

We didn't lose a man.

Heh.

Six trips to the tower, and back, across open ground.

Then Doola lit a torch – one of ours from the ship. He was going to throw it at the pile, but I ran it to the pile and placed it well under. Nothing hit me, because it is really very difficult to shoot straight down in the dark with a bow.

The pile caught.

The tower caught.

The men inside died screaming. It should have been horrible, but instead, it was deeply satisfying. Make of that what you will.

Before dawn, the tower was like a lighthouse, a beacon, with flames ten times the height of a ship's mainmast roaring into the sky. One of the slaves, a man named Herodikles, sacrificed a ram from the pens and threw the carcass into the fire. He was an Aeolian, from Lesbos, and he'd been a slave for fifteen years, taken while on a pilgrimage to Cyrene.

There were a hundred such stories.

Men told them, while their oppressors tried to scream the smoke out of their lungs and failed. They smelled like roast pork as they burned.

In the morning, when the fire burned less than a mast-height high, and the sun was over the rim of the world, we climbed down into the pit.

They were all there, waiting. They were even thinner, and they didn't have darkness to hide the open sores, the flies, the ooze of pus. Despite which, they grinned from ear to ear. Gaius. Daud. Demetrios, who looked so bad I was afraid he would die before we could get food into him. I couldn't even figure out how he could stand on those legs.

They had been slaves for just two months.

The Phoenicians were ... I was going to say animals, but no animal except man treats another like that.

We rigged a sling, and lifted them out of the pit. Most of them were too weak to climb the ladder.

While that happened, I went and posted sentries. There was a new spirit among my men: the shepherds, the herdsmen, the fishermen's sons, the slaves freed at Centrona. We'd been victorious again; we were doing something noble. They were inspired, just as men can be inspired by a great play, or by the noble words of a godlike man like Heraclitus, or by the gods themselves.

I knew as soon as I looked at them. They were ready to do something great.

For the moment, all we had to do was to be alert.

We watched the plains all day while the tower burned. Men looked at me, and I smiled. I kept my own council. There was food in the sheds, animals in the pens, and I prepared a feast on the coals of the tower and served it to the slaves, telling my own men that they should go from slave to slave as if they were slaves themselves.

They did so with good will. The slaves tore into the meat, complained about the lack of wine and bread – mock complaints, although there's always some awkward sod who feels sorry for himself. But they ate and ate.

I saw no reason to leave so much as a goat alive, so as fast as they ate, we killed more.

And watched the plains.

About noon, we saw the dust cloud.

Seckla was my best rider. I gave him the mounted men, and clear orders. Up at the mine we had a view for fifty stades over the plain, so that I could point out his route – this stream, that copse of trees, that farmhouse.

They cantered away, and men cheered them.

The tower had just about burned out. So I asked the slaves to fetch water from the well, a bucket at a time, and pour it into the coals.

Steam rose to the heavens, carrying the scent of roast meat. Some of it was roast men, and the gods have never rejected such a sacrifice. I remember wondering at myself; I thought Tertikles a barbarian for sacrificing a man before we launched our ships, but I was secretly pleased to have sent twenty Phoenicians screaming to my gods.

Well.

It's true; I can be a vicious bastard.

When the dust cloud on the plain reached a certain point, I took most of my armed men and marched. We had full bellies and full water bottles, and we moved fast, going downhill, despite the full heat of the summer sun. My friends wanted to come – Gaius demanded it, and muttered words about honour.

I pushed a chunk of goat into his greasy hands. 'Honour this,' I said. 'I'll do the killing. You do the eating.'

We went down the mountain, crossed the stream at its foot and went along the ridge through the high beech trees until we came to the site I'd chosen on the way. When you are a warrior, you think about these things all the time. *That* field would make a good place. *That* piece of trail.

Ambushes come in as many different shapes as women. And men, too, if you wish. What would make one ambush perfect would be certain death in another.

I had very few missile weapons. So my ambush would be close in, a deadly, hand-to-hand thing. And since my men were on foot, we had to *win*. Because we were unlikely to outrun pursuit.

If we had had missile weapons – more bows, good javelins and throwing strings, heavy rocks – we might have chosen other sites.

Instead, we lay down among the trees, an arm's-length from the road. I took my place with Doola, behind a big rock that slaves and oxen had shifted. You could tell, because it stood clear of the ground, where all the other big rocks were half buried. It allowed me to see the road in both directions.

If you ever have cause to lay an ambush, whether you do it with a handful of mud for your brothers, or with a sharp spear for your . enemies, remember these simple rules.

Always have a clear line of retreat. Any other ambush is just an elaborate form of suicide.

Tailor your surprise to your arms and your enemy. If you have bows, you should wait at a good killing range, with an open field that won't block your archery. If you have time, plan your ambush so that your first flight of arrows panics your foe into a *worse* position. Don't drive him off a road and into an impregnable stronghold.

The moment anything goes wrong, including an hour before you sight the enemy – run. Men in ambush are absurdly vulnerable.

There, ladies. All my wisdom – wisdom I learned for myself, and not from Heraclitus. He was like a god, but I don't think he knew much about ambushes.

At any rate ...

We lay there. And lay there. An hour passed, and another, and the sun went down noticeably.

I had so much to worry about; a man commanding an ambush always does. Had they stopped and made camp? Taken another route, and even now they were storming the slave camp? They'd given up and gone home ... They'd slipped past us.

Another hour passed. Insects ate us, and men snuck away to piss and snuck back.

Men got the jitters.

And another hour.

And then we heard the sound. Hard to describe, but instantly identifiable. Men – a powerful number of them. Walking with a rattle and tinkle and clank. Talking.

They had two scouts. They were moving two hundred paces ahead of the column – walking on the road. When they came to the edge of our copse of woods, they stopped.

They talked with each other until the column had almost caught up.

Then they came into the woods.

My heart was pounding. The enemy had a hundred men – perhaps double that. It was difficult to count them from my hiding place, but there were many of them. They entered the woods.

Their scouts moved quickly. They were conscious that they'd allowed the column to close up to them too much, and they ran.

But just about even with me, one of them stopped. He was a handsome young man, wearing only a chlamys and a petasos hat and carrying a pair of heavy spears on his shoulder. He stopped from a sprint and looked into the woods. He wasn't looking at me, he was looking *away* from me, staring off into the woods.

His mate stopped running and looked back.

'See something?' he called in Phoenician.

The first man looked and looked, and then squatted and looked at the road.

'Men were here,' he said.

You have to imagine, they were an arm's-length from me. They didn't have to shout.

Behind them, the column came rolling along the road.

I saw Alexandros move, and I glared at him. Ambush requires patience.

'Escaped slaves,' the second man ventured.

The first man looked all around. He was young. That's probably what saved him. The young make piss-poor observers. He looked, but didn't see.

A commanding voice called from behind them on the road. I couldn't make it out, but it was doubtless their commander, telling his scouts to get a move on. Twilight was only two hours away.

The young man looked around again and shrugged.

He and his companion loped off.

I looked around. I could see Alexandros and Giannis and about fifteen other men.

I waited.

The column trudged forward.

Waited.

'She had tits like udders – Ba'al, it was disgusting!'

'He was an ignorant—'

'So I said—'

'I drank the wine.'

'I just want to ask this again—'

They were just men. Tall, short, weak, strong, smart, foolish – they were men, walking down the road on a summer evening, headed for battle. Nervous. Over-talkative, as all men are before a fight. As the tail of the column started to pass me, I saw the last two men of the first taxis nervously checking the draw of their swords while their phylarch told them that they needed to *stay together, stay together* in the fighting.

'Pirates! Just pirates. They won't have any discipline. Like the lot we took yesterday. Don't worry about—'

I rose from my place and roared my war cry.

We fell on the head of the column. They died, and the survivors broke and ran across the road for the shelter of the trees. Most ran a few steps into the woods before they died, because Doola and his men were on that side of the road, a little farther back.

The second taxis froze outside the woods, listening to the screams of their comrades and the sounds of one-sided hand-to-hand.

My dozen archers began to drop shafts into them.

Perhaps their officer was hit early. Perhaps he was a fool. Either way, they did the worst thing possible – they huddled like sheep and bleated, and the arrows fell.

A dozen good archers can do a lot of damage, even to armoured men, even trained men with good morale.

No one had trained men with good morale in a colony, ten thousand stades from home.

By this time, I was watching them. The fight in the woods was over before it really began – a hundred dead Phoenicians – mercenaries, in fact, mostly north Africans with some Greeks among them.

Men like me.

Heh. But not enough like me.

I started to get my oarsmen in order, and Alexandros was there, and Doola and Sittonax, his long Kelt sword red to the hilt.

I knew the second taxis would break the moment I charged it. You can read these things as easily as you read words on a page. It's like a woman's facial expressions. The nervous tick; the cold glance. So, by the same token, you can read the moving of spears, the shuffling of feet and the shaking of horsehair plumes. Nervous fidgets.

'Charge!' I roared.

We hadn't run six paces before they broke. They ran away from our charge, and many of them threw down their shields in the flight. The archers loosed and loosed, until our charge obscured their targets.

I didn't catch one of them. They ran so early that they easily out-distanced my people, all of whom had already fought in one combat – even an ambush is a combat – and by the time we'd crossed the clearing, it was plain to see we didn't have the daimon to run them down.

So we went around the darkening battlefield, collecting loot. There wasn't much. The weapons were average, the armour was leather and often already ruined, and most of the helmets were cheap, open-faced helmets or Etruscan-style salad bowls.

A few men had purses, most of them containing only copper.

Not much to die for.

At twilight, we gave up plundering the dead. There were no survivors, not even the two scouts, who'd been killed by the northern fringe of our ambush. That's the way of it, when an ambush works.

We left the bodies for the birds, and marched back towards the mine. When we got there, we ate some meat, drank water and watched the steam rising off the ruin of the tower. Then we went to sleep.

I remember that I forgot to post sentries. Luckily, Doola wasn't as tired, or as foolish.

Not that it mattered.

About midnight, Seckla came back. He had heads dangling from his saddlecloth, bouncing and frightening his horse. It was ghoulish.

I woke up long enough to embrace him and hear that he'd hit the survivors and harried them back to their settlement. And then I went back to sleep.

In the morning, it was grey, and the sun wasn't going to show. My men were surly with fatigue and reaction. I knew how to cure that.

I got a dozen former slaves and some of the stronger herdsmen, and together we moved the two largest of the charred beams from the stump of the tower. With shovels, we cleared the ash and the collapsed roof materials, but the fire had burned a long time, and almost everything had been consumed.

Except the gold and silver, of course.

It took two hours, and I was beginning to doubt, but there they were – a molten puddle of gold, and another of silver, about a yard apart. A fair amount of gold, and quite a lot of silver.

We took axes and hacked it up into manageable chunks, and loaded it on to our stolen horses. Morale soared.

We gorged once more on the dwindling stock of animals, and then we marched for our ships.

We all squeezed aboard, although the conditions were probably not much better than those in the slave pens. We had two hundred and fifty men in a trireme built for two hundred, and we had sixty men in a triakonter.

Off the Tagus, I signalled to Doola to lay alongside, and he agreed to take his shallower craft over the bar and have a look at the town. It was raining, and rowing the trireme was brutal, and I already doubted whether I could get the ship home to Oiasso like this.

Now that the derring-do was over, I began to consider what had happened to my wife and her brother, my erstwhile allies. I had to assume they'd been defeated. How badly? Badly enough, perhaps, not to make it home. Or worse, badly enough to make it back to Oiasso and close it against me.

Doola caught the morning breeze coming off the land and came back, my beautiful *Lydia* wallowing with so many people on board. He gave me a thumbs-up as soon as he was close enough to wave.

We went into the estuary at sunset. The moon was lost in the clouds, and the night was black, and we crept up the river, impeded by ignorance and by the current, which was absurdly strong for summer.

The town was twenty stades upstream. We found it, but it had a mole and the approach looked too hard to try in the dark.

On the other hand, there were a dozen small ships on the beach and in the channel on moorings. There was *Amphitrite*, and there were two more like her – tubby Greek-style merchantmen.

We took them. And for good measure, having silently acquired what we wanted, we set the rest afire. Then, on the dawn breeze and falling tide, we slipped away. My trireme was lighter by fifty men, and *Lydia* was lighter by thirty. Demetrios insisted on managing *Amphitrite* himself.

It took us ten days to reach Oiasso.

9

We were not welcome.

Tara came down to meet us. Tertikles sulked in his great hall of timber and let his sister tell us we were not welcome. Through Daud, because Sittonax wanted nothing more to do with the whole process.

'We need water and food. I'll pay.' I wasn't contrite – I thought that she and her brother had got what they deserved for poor scouting and planning.

'Pay with what?' she said. 'You little coward – running off and leaving us when there was a fight. Why would I give you food?'

'I have all the slaves we saved,' I pointed out. 'They need food.'

She spat. 'Not from us,' she said.

I liked her. And she was making me angry. The two, sometimes, go together. 'You want to blame me? Blame your brother. If he had followed me—'

'My brother? The *King*? Follow you, a foreigner?' She shook her head. 'A man like you does well to follow a man like my brother.'

I shook my head. 'Your brother is a fool. No one will willingly follow such a man.'

'And this should convince me to feed your *slaves*?' she spat.

I shrugged. 'Sell me food. Or I'll take it.'

She drew herself up as only a woman of good birth can. 'You think you can take us? You and your slaves?'

I nodded. 'Yes.' I pointed behind me. There were six ships.

She turned her face away.

Daud said something very quickly in Keltoi.

'We lost thirty men,' Tara said, in Greek. 'Half. Half our war party.'

'And accomplished nothing,' I said.

'My brother called out to them, challenging their captain to single combat. Instead, they shut the gates on us and shot arrows at us, and then the garrison marched out.' She smiled. 'We faced them. And charged them. We killed many.'

'At least a dozen,' I said.

'Hah! What did you do?' she asked.

I shrugged. 'We stormed their gold mine, killed the guards, took the gold, freed the slaves and came home. Oh – we massacred the town garrison, too. In an ambush.' I suspect I sounded smug.

She glared, and spat some words in Kelt.

Daud, despite his appearance, was recovering. He laughed. His laugh stung her.

'Give me food and water, and I'll pay in gold and leave. Or refuse.' I crossed my arms. 'And I swear to the gods I'll storm your town and burn your brother's hall and leave you for the ravens. You and your brother are amateurs. War is not a pursuit for amateurs.'

She shook her head. 'No. Fuck you. Come and try.'

She turned and walked away, and her spearmen backed off carefully.

I walked back to the ship.

'That didn't go well.' Seckla was laughing.

Doola wasn't. 'I want my wife.'

'We need food,' said Alexandros.

I scratched my beard. For all my big talk, I didn't fancy storming a former ally town. That smacked of impiety. We were guest friends. Oaths to the gods must have some meaning.

'I don't think your wife will want you,' I said to Doola. 'But take a file of marines and go and try.' I sent Alexandros to help. And to keep Doola from being stupid.

We had a hasty conference on the beach, Seckla and Daud, Gaius and me, Neoptolymos and Demetrios and Sittonax.

We knew enough about the coast by then to know that there were thicker, larger settlements farther north.

'We can make it one more day,' Sittonax said.

Demetrios shook his head. 'Some men have no fat on their bodies.' He shrugged. 'I am hungry, all the time. I am hungry while I eat. And hungry again as soon as I've eaten. And again, after that.'

Daud backed him up. 'Some of us cannot go a day without food,' he said.

I scratched my beard.

Doola came back, without his wife. He sat down like an old man and put his head in his arms.

Alexandros turned to me. 'She struck him. Said their marriage is dissolved.'

Sittonax shook his head. 'What do you expect?' he asked. 'You made them look like fools, and then you came back and rubbed it in.' He shrugged. 'Tertikles is a weak king. A bad king. But his sister is smart, and strong, and rules through him. And you have made him appear even more worthless, and made her look the same.' He glanced at the heavens. 'If we stay here tonight on this beach, Tertikles will attack you.'

'Heracles!' I swore.

'Sail away,' Sittonax said. 'In two days of fair winds, we can land on the isles of the Venetiae.'

'Our starvelings don't have two days,' I said.

I should have foreseen it. I had three hundred men to feed; I needed civilization. Good farms, on good soil, and men with an abundance to sell. Even for Oiasso, my three hundred would be a heavy burden.

On the ten-day trip north and east, my people had eaten fish in the villages every night. We'd emptied every village of meat and left silver in our wake.

I felt that it was all my fault. In the Inner Sea, it would have been easy. Or easier. Out here, it was as if we were at the edge of the world. Men were too few to support a trireme.

I thought of how smug I'd been, treating with Tara, and cursed my arrogance.

So I went back to her. With a dozen of my shepherds – now tall warriors in flashing bronze – I went to the gate of Tertikles' palisade and shouted for admission.

Tara came and opened the gate. She was in armour.

'So: the great hero. Planning to take our pigs with a dozen spear-men? Do they do your fighting for you?' She laughed.

I had decided how to play this out. I owed my men; I owed my friends.

But it left a bad taste.

'I offer gold for food and water,' I said.

She spat. 'You can have our flesh when you carve it from our cold bodies. And the only water you get is the water of my mouth,' she said. That is, I assume she said that. I only got one word in ten.

I walked forward. 'It doesn't need to be like this,' I said. 'I won. I took much plunder. You can say I'm dividing it with you. That your attack on the town was a feint.'

She waited while Sittonax translated. Then she came forward. 'You *used* us as a feint, didn't you?'

I shrugged. 'Does it matter? Your brother was going that way, no matter what I said.'

She turned her back. 'This is over. Go.'

I took a deep breath. 'I know you plan to attack my ships tonight,' I said.

She whirled.

'Give me food, or I will challenge your brother. And he will fight me in the morning, and die.' I spoke quietly, and Sittonax paused, looked at me and shook his head. And then translated.

'That will make me king. But by my customs, that will also make me an oath-breaker, because we are guest friends. Listen, Tara. These starving slaves – they are my *friends*. I told you I came here with other men. I will *not* let them die. I will kill to save them. They are my brothers. But we do not have to do it like this. Sell me food and water, and I will slink away tomorrow, leaving a tribute of gold on the beach, and you can tell any story you like.'

Her eyes bored into mine.

'I liked you,' she said slowly. 'But you are not my idea of a man.' She shook her head 'Too … greasy.'

I shrugged.

'Very well. Don't ever come back here. Don't ever cross that beach.' She took a deep breath. 'I will see to it that you have fifty pigs and grain and water.'

We ate, within a ring of guards.

I left her two pounds of gold, making those the most valuable pigs I've ever eaten.

And we sailed away north.

The coast of Gaul was kind to us. The sun kissed the water, and the breeze carried us most of the day. Demetrios tacked while we rowed towards evening, and we landed three hundred stades north of Oiasso by my reckoning. We ate sausage cooked on driftwood, and drank water from a spring, and in the morning we rowed away, leaving a handful of terrified shepherds. We killed twenty sheep and left them payment in silver. Pork doesn't keep in summer, but mutton does, even if not well prepared.

I was losing my taste for piracy.

By midday we could see the islands, tall against the low, swampy coast. We knew the first one was Olario, and we found the town on the landward coast – a fine town of slate-roofed stone houses, rising from the sea, with a good harbour, a stony beach and a natural mole of granite.

I sent Daud and Sittonax and my other Keltoi ashore with silver.

What followed was more like Sicily or Rome than what I expected from barbarians. Once again, my whole idea of barbarians was about to be stood on its head.

The Town of Olario was a Venetiae town. The warehouses were Venetiae, as were the piers and the stone roundhouses. And the enormous round ships – like a Greek merchantman built by giants. The town wasn't the size of Athens, or even Piraeus – but it would have been a good town in Attica or Italy.

It had sewers.

And customs officials.

They came out to our ships, and looked at my crews, at my emaciated stick figures, at my cargoes, and asked for bills of lading. This from a man in a frieze cloak with a bright saffron shirt, gold earrings and a magnificent gold neckpiece.

'Your slaves are in horrible condition,' he said. 'They might bring disease. You may not sell them here, nor may you land them.'

'They are free men,' I said. 'I have rescued them from the Phoenicians.'

The man had a fine red beard, with which he fiddled often, and watery blue eyes. He wore a magnificent sword and a pair of knives mounted in gold. I assumed, incorrectly, that he was the local warlord or king. 'Which Phoenicians?' he asked.

I waved at Iberia, eight hundred stades to the south by my reckoning. Really, by Vasileos's reckoning. He'd recovered from ten days of puking, and now had one of *Lydia*'s sisters, which he had named *Adelphi*.

My chieftain stroked his beard. 'By violence?' he asked.

You always know when questioning begins to go wrong. 'I have come from the Inner Sea to trade,' I said. 'The Phoenicians tried to take my ship on the sea. They seized my friends. I have spent months rescuing them.'

Red Beard nodded. 'We have no quarrel with the Phoenicians,' he said. 'We don't love them either. But we trade with them.' He looked around. 'You are Greeks, eh?'

I smiled. 'Yes. I am from Greece.'

The man smiled for the first time. 'Wonderful pots, you Greeks make. And stonework – there was a Greek man on Ratis, five years ago.' He nodded. 'An architect.'

It was stunning, to hear this barbarian use the Greek word for a man who built stone buildings. In fact, I was being mocked.

But then he offered me his hand. 'Detorix,' he said. 'I am the inspector for Olario. I will clear your cargo for sale. You will have to write me out a list of everything you have. Yes? Like any other port. And there will be taxes. There is a harbour fee.' He smiled. 'You expected painted savages, perhaps?'

I had to laugh.

It took me, Demetrios, Doola, Sittonax and Vasileos three days of sitting on the waterfront to count, number and list every item we had.

It was not entirely unpleasant.

For example, the *Amphitrite* had been inexpertly looted and left to sit on the beach. Her hull had a large patch of rot that was exposed when we careened her – where she'd sat on the beach, fully laden on the sand. We were lucky she hadn't sunk. On the other hand, most of her cargo was still intact, most of the bales not even broken. The bale of ostrich plumes was the most important. But our Greek fish oil and our Greek wines were still in the bilges of *Lydia*. We had nine packets of dyes, lovingly wrapped in pigs' bladders and then sewn in canvas. In fact, all they'd taken off the *Amphitrite* was the copper. The *Lydia* still had hers – twenty three 'hides' of copper.

We also had about a hundred water amphorae, which we would have kept for fresh water except that the Gauls offered such wonderful prices for them. And the Gauls had a cheap, high-quality substitute. The Gauls built water and wine containers of wood wrapped with cord, roots, or metal bands, called *barrels*. They made them in eight sizes – standard sizes, and every barrel-maker had a set of patterns to follow.

I tried to imagine imposing a set of standard sizes on Greeks. Or even standard measures.

You do know that the mythemnoi varies from town to town, don't you? And so does the dactyl and the stade. Oh, yes.

Where was I? Barrels. Wonderful. I loved to watch the Gauls build them. They were light and strong and when they were empty, you could pull the hoops off and they became a bundle of slightly curved boards that took up no space.

The locals were especially interested in my trireme. They crowded around, looking at her construction, her rowing benches, her ram bow and all the bronze there.

After two days of intense work, my crews had beached, emptied and careened our ships. Our goods had been sorted, dried, counted and in some cases, reluctantly burned or buried.

So, to my sorrow, were six men. Fifteen days at sea, even in high summer, are not the ideal anodyne to months or years of brutal slavery. They weren't my friends; they weren't men I even knew. But they had, however briefly, been my men.

We had a funeral feast for them, and we burned them. The Gaulish priests helped – they were surprisingly well-educated men, who knew the stars, and two of whom knew Greek, although the version they spoke was comically Spartan. They must have learned from some Laconian, some wandering mercenary or trader.

Herodikles, my Aeolian, said the words. He was recovering well. He had been an aristocrat, a priest from a good family. But by his own admission he had been a slave fifteen years, and some of that had been horrible. He flinched when Doola raised a hand in greeting. He ducked his head when Seckla let out a whoop of delight.

Demetrios was more cautious. Otherwise, he was very much himself. He smiled a great deal and didn't talk as much as other men. He was very sure of himself at sea, and less sure on land.

Daud had been a slave a long time. He survived the Phoenicians well enough.

Gaius was the most changed. He was deeply, passionately angry. It struck me that he'd have been the first to die if we hadn't come back.

'They treated us like *animals*,' he said one night on the coast of Iberia. I didn't bother to point out that we all treated slaves like that. But by the time we reached the Venetiae, he was better – his smile a little more bitter, but otherwise more like himself.

Detorix and a dozen other traders came to drink wine with us after I handed in our lading lists. They were like traders all over the world, carefully controlling their reactions, looking for advantage. Doola, who always handled these transactions, was not yet recovered from the loss of his wife. He wasn't interested in trade, or anything else.

Demetrios stood in for him, dickering, arguing, or being silent. I stood back, watching. We had decided that I would pose as the 'patron'. It was useful for Demetrios to say, 'Ah. Well, I must ask the patron.' And sometimes he would give a hurt smile, as if he wanted nothing better than to sell his ostrich feathers for a song, and he would say, 'Ah, but the patron—'

The food was good, and we paid in gold. We sat in actual wine shops and drank half-decent wine – too thick, unwatered, I felt, but there you go. Each to his own taste.

It was good to drink wine at all. And I bought great barrels of the stuff for the recovering men, because wine is the very best thing for a man recovering from ill health. Wine, and apple juice, both of which were available.

And meat.

And bread.

They were getting rich off our need to feed hungry men. But they were traders, and they had the foodstuffs to sell, and we had nowhere else to buy.

I had about enough gold to keep all of them for a month. They weren't, strictly speaking, my people. But—

The Gauls left almost immediately, after coming to me with their thanks. A dozen of them stayed: they weren't Gauls at all, but Albans, from another one of the islands. They also came to me, in the first days among the Venetiae, and asked if I would sail them home.

I said I'd consider it.

Our third evening on Olario was beautiful, and we sat in our wine shop on the waterfront, watching small boys fish in the harbour. Watching three young women posture for Seckla, who was diving naked from a rock. With the exception of the African, all my friends were there, and other men, like Alexandros and Vasileos, who had earned their right to be included. It was like a mix of democracy and oligarchy. Command always is.

Demetrios shrugged. 'It's a good news, bad news kind of thing,' he said. 'The tin doesn't come from here.'

Sittonax shook his head. 'Thieving bastards. I worked for them! They said the tin comes from the islands.'

I laughed. 'Ever seen a tin mine?' I asked. 'I haven't, but I know what the ore looks like. Any bronze-smith does. And it won't come out of sea-rocks.'

'So they don't have tin?' asked Gaius.

'They do. It's their principal export.' Demetrios sat back and played with a loop of beads. 'It comes from somewhere near here. I get that much.'

'Is it worth finding the source?' I asked.

Demetrios shrugged again. 'I don't know. But they drive a hard bargain. They want all our amphorae – and they offer a wonderful return. All the wine, all the oil. I think they only want the jars, but why should we care? In each case, we make five or ten times what we paid.'

My turn to shrug. 'A profit we might match at Marsala, and save ourselves danger and labour and travel.'

Demetrios nodded. 'I thought the same. It is worse for our copper – they offer no better than the Inner Sea price. They say there is copper all along this coast, and in Iberia.'

'That's what the Iberians said, too,' I admitted. Heracles and Poseidon, the weariness of it, transporting copper halfway round the aspis of the world, only to find that it is worth less there than at home.

Vasileos spoke for the first time. 'Makes good ballast,' he said wryly.

'We have the gold,' Gaius said eagerly. 'We could just go home.'

I looked around. Seckla was drying himself with his chlamys, to the complete approval of three young Keltoi, who had never seen anyone quite so like an ebony Apollo.

'How exactly are we getting home?' I asked.

That set the lion among the sheep.

Demetrios nodded. 'I wanted to talk about that, before we start trading,' he said. He looked at me.

'We don't want to go back through the Pillars,' I said. 'And for certain sure, we don't want to go home that way with heavily laden trade ships.'

Vasileos nodded and leaned forward. 'That squadron at Gades is fully alert, now,' he said. 'Even if they were asleep, when we come to the Pillars, the current runs *outward*. Without a perfect wind?' he made a motion with his hand. 'We just wallow around waiting for their triremes to snap us up.'

'It is worse than that,' Demetrios said. The Sikel was smiling, but it wasn't amusement. More like courage. 'There's a rumour that came in with the fishing boats this morning that there is a Phoenician squadron on the coast south of here. Burning its way north.'

I hadn't heard that. 'Poseidon's spear,' I said.

Vasileos nodded. 'You had to know they'd strike back,' he said. 'All we did was singe their beards. And they must have taken some of the Keltoi.'

I felt foolish. 'Of course,' I said. 'They'll strike for Oiasso,' I said, standing up.

Vasileos took my hand. 'If they did, they hit it days ago. And our one trireme won't save it.'

'And we don't exactly owe King Tertikles anything,' Sittonax said.

I sighed and sat. Doola raised his head. 'My wife!' he said, and put his head down again.

'Jupiter's dick,' Gaius said. 'I'd love to put a spear into some Phoenicians.'

Seckla, coming in from the water, grinned. He sat by Doola – Alexandros watched him like a hawk – and put and hand on the older man's shoulder. 'Did I hear someone suggest we could kill Phoenicians?' he asked.

'We're trying to reckon how we can make it home,' Vasileos said.

'I, too, wouldn't mind a chance to kill some of the slavers,' Daud, usually quiet, smiled.

'That won't get us home,' Vasileos said.

'Yes it will!' Gaius said. 'We strike their squadron and then slip past it, and they keep going north.'

I thought about that.

'The good sailing is over in a few weeks,' I said. I looked at Vasileos, of course – I never made a statement about weather or sailing without his consent. He nodded.

'If we … sail south,' I shrugged, 'it can be done. But not with *Amphitrite*. Only rowed ships will make it into the Pillars in one go, unless we have the luck of the gods, and I don't think we can count on that.'

'Detorix wants the trireme,' Demetrios said. 'He wants to buy it.'

'Then I'd have no ship!' I said.

Demetrios shrugged. 'I'm just saying,' he protested. Then he looked around, as if afraid of being overheard. 'The Venetiae are in fear of the Phoenicians coming here,' he said. 'If you plan to go to sea and fight, you don't want to tell them that.'

I gave him the look men give each other when they mean they weren't born yesterday, nor the day before, either.

I looked around. 'What do you think?' I asked Vasileos.

He shrugged. 'Are we traders? Warriors?' He met my eye. 'I want to go home alive. With a little silver. I do not need to be a hero.'

Daud shrugged. 'I am home,' he said. 'I can walk to my father's farm in ten days.' He grinned at his stick leg. 'Two weeks.' He looked around too. 'But if you were going south to fight the Phoenicians, I'd come.'

Seckla smiled at me. 'I'll go wherever you go.'

Gaius was sharpening an already sharp knife. 'I want to kill Phoenicians.'

Neoptolymos said, 'I am very strongly of Gaius's view.'

Doola raised his head for the first time. 'I want to try and rescue my wife,' he said.

Alexandros looked at Doola. And at me. I didn't give him anything – my thoughts were running like an athlete in a race, and I wasn't sure what I wanted.

He didn't say anything, but sat back.

Demetrios took Doola's hand. 'I will come with you to get your wife. You came and got me,' he said. 'But I am with Vasileos. I am no hero. I want to trade and go home rich. I have been away from home too long. I am scared all the time, even with all of you, my brothers, around me. This sea is not my sea.'

Sittonax looked at me, and then around at all of them. He kicked his long sword out along his leg and leaned back. 'You're a pack of fools,' he said.

We all looked at him.

'It's autumn, or near enough. If Doola's wife isn't a slave tonight, she will be tomorrow night. Or not. And she's not *your wife*. You foreigners never get our ways. She broke the pact. She's gone.' He shrugged. 'But that's not what makes you fools. I think we only made it into the Outer Sea by a miracle. I want you all to think of that storm.' He shook his head.

'Four days north of here is the delta of the River of Fish – the Sequana. One of the largest of the Venetiae communities is there. They hire guards there, and ship tin across the mountains.' He looked at us. 'To Marsala, you fools. Up the Sequana to my people's country, and down the Roan to Marsala. You can be home in five weeks. It is what the Venetiae *do*. They run the tin trade to Marsala.'

Sittonax *had* told us all about the tin route, back in Marsala. And now we were on the other side of it.

It was almost funny.

Vasileos pulled at his beard. 'We aren't going to get our ships over the mountains,' he said.

'Sell them,' Sittonax said.

Now I leaned back and scratched my beard. I was looking at Sittonax. He was cleaning his nails.

'We can do both,' I said.

Often, the smallest and least consequential things become the greatest complications. It is the hand of the gods in human affairs.

I chose to represent our going to sea as my willingness to give the escaped Alban slaves a run across the waves to their homes.

Detorix spoke to them rapidly in Greek, and then in one of the Keltoi tongues – too rapidly for me to follow. And then he smiled. 'They should stay here,' he said.

It was a surprisingly false smile. I liked Detorix. He loved gold, but he was as friendly and as plain-spoken as a trader ever can be. 'Why?' I asked.

Detorix frowned. 'We will not allow you to take them home,' he said. He shrugged. 'Please do not press the point.'

He withdrew from the meeting like a man who had overplayed his stones in a game of polis.

Something was wrong, and I didn't have time to figure it out.

What made *no* sense is that he couldn't actually give orders. As far as I could tell, I had three hundred armed men and he had ... a dozen other traders, and none of them struck me as deadly blades. I understood – from Sittonax – that all the coastal tribes feared the Venetiae; they had many large ships and the money to hire warriors. The Keltoi had mercenaries, like everyone else.

Sittonax sought me out. 'The Albans have something to say,' he said.

'Best say it quickly,' I said. Detorix was approaching with a long tail of fellow Gauls: six of them had spears.

Behon, the healthiest of the Albans, came and took my hand. He said a few words.

Sittonax waved his hand. 'He pledges his undying loyalty, and so on,' he said. He sounded bored.

'He says the Gauls don't want you to cross the little sea because that's where the tin is.' As he said the words, Sittonax's intonation changed, and he became more excited. 'But of course!' he said. 'Now it is I who am a fool. Of course the tin comes from Alba.'

Behon's grey eyes bored into mine. 'You be my chief, and I will be your man,' he said. At least, that's what Sittonax said for him.

His brother, who had a name something like our *Leukas*, took my other hand.

Detorix came to a halt. 'Foreigners,' he said formally.

I gave both Albans' hands a squeeze and let them go. 'Yes?' I asked.

Detorix pointed at our ships. There were men aboard them. And they were being poled off the beach and into deeper water.

'I have seized your ships. Temporarily.' He smiled a troubled smile. 'I am sorry to be so high-handed. But without meaning to break the law, you have threatened our trade. I had no idea you had these Albans aboard; nor that you had any intention of making the crossing. I cannot allow it.'

I looked out over the water. 'You are taking my ships,' I said.

Detorix shrugged. 'Only until you swear the oaths and offer some surety that you will not sail for Alba.'

I want you to savour the irony, thugater. I had never intended actually to sail for Alba. I had intended to go down the coast, rescue Doola's wife, if it could be done, and kill a few Carthaginians.

It amused me that there were barbarian bureaucrats, too.

I laughed.

The Albans got behind me.

Detorix resented my laugh. How could he not?

But it was funny.

He looked at me, and I laughed. And finally I pointed at the men behind him – about thirty men, fewer than half of them armed.

'Detorix,' I said. 'I don't want to make threats. But you have taken my ships. Why shouldn't I kill the lot of you and storm the town?'

He swallowed sharply.

I shook my head. 'Detorix, there is no reason for us to be foes.'

Detorix nodded. 'I cannot allow you to sail for Alba.'

'I'll give you my word not to sail for Alba.' That was easy. And I wasn't some Persian truth-teller. I'm Greek. I can lie when I please.

He started to nod, and a man behind him said something sharply, in one of the many Keltoi dialects.

'I will have to send for instructions,' he said. He licked his lips.

I was glaring. 'How long?' I asked.

He didn't know. He was sending to the capital.

I turned to my friends. 'If we kill any of them, I have to assume there will be no further trading,' I said. 'And that screws us, if we want to take Sittonax's route to the Inner Sea.'

Doola spat.

Gaius crossed his arms. 'You have to assume that his *instructions* will include several boatloads of soldiers.'

'If we're going to fight, the time is now. We have every advantage,' Neoptolymos said.

Sittonax shook his head. 'You *can't* fight. These are the Venetiae. Their reach is long – longer than … anyone's. No one will sell you grain. Every man's hand will be against you.'

'Not if we kill them and sail south,' I said.

But the moment had passed.

It is odd. Five years before, I'd have wiped the town off the face of the world, sold the women as slaves and killed the men. Or died trying, which, as events proved, was the more likely.

IO

I slept badly. My dead troubled me, but my living troubled me more. I was uncertain as to whether I had treated Tara well, I was deeply aware that I had treated Lydia badly, and the combination ran through my dreams and into my waking life.

It is odd to be haunted by a living person. Everywhere I went, I saw Lydia – in Keltoi girls washing their clothes in the stream by the beach; in women at market, standing by the well.

Why? I really hadn't thought of her in months. I suspect that I had behaved badly, and Heracles sent these thoughts to torment me. So evil is punished in the world. But it may be that opening the bales of goods – so carefully packed in another world, on Sicily and at Marsala – carried some hint of her. I don't know.

I do know that I felt a surly failure when I awoke the next morning. I went for a run with Neoptolymos and Seckla – Neoptolymos still a stick figure, but eating like a horse, and Seckla now probably the best athlete among us. My wound still troubled me, so I ran carefully. And slowly. Which suited Neoptolymos, but Seckla simply ran off into the *khora*, the countryside.

Of course, we ran naked. And nudity is a shameful thing among Keltoi, or at least, it is not as common as among Greeks. We, of course, thought nothing of it. While we ran out along the muddy roads between low stone boundary walls, we were untroubled, but as we poured the daimon of competition into our aching muscles to sprint the last few stades into town, there were men with staves.

We ignored them and sprinted past.

They closed in behind us and followed us to our tents. They were grumbling angrily, and we, of course, hadn't any idea what they were on about.

Luckily, Sittonax was up, and he laughed at us with them, if you take my meaning, and soon enough they dispersed. As a foreigner, it is always better to be an object of gentle derision.

Detorix came to us at mid-morning. I was organizing some contests, because my morning run had improved my mood and reminded me of what was important in life, and I had decided – again, between one heartbeat and another – to be responsible for the rowers and not simply send them off into the world.

Let me digress, thugater. The truth is that if I released them – or, more likely, drove them away – they would be slaves again in no time. One of the problems with slavery is that it allows a certain kind of man to cease to be, in almost every way. It extinguishes his willingness to be ... well, free.

Which of us does not long to be taken care of? Which of us does not desire – at least in old age – children and friends to wait on us and help us walk and piss and eat? Eh?

And the slave – is this not why we call them children? A slave with a soft place, a good master and acceptable work is spared so many decisions, is he not?

Heh. Had you going there, for a moment. It can be quite comfortable, as a slave. If only you are willing to give up everything that makes life worth living.

But once a man has been a slave a certain time, it takes time to make him free. He has to *learn* to be free.

If you save a man from starving, can you then leave him to starve again?

If you rescue a drowning man, do you push him back in the water? So.

So I was sitting under an awning on a crisp late-summer morning, while two men – one of the Albans and one of the Greeks – fought with padded sticks. The sticks represented swords. Now, Greeks scarcely ever fight with just the sword, but Polymarchos, back in Syracusa, had taught me a great deal based on using the sword alone. He had introduced me to the *theory* of combat, much as Heraclitus introduced me to the *theory* of living your life. A man may be a good man and live a righteous life and never hear a word of philosophy – but for most of us, some education in the theory of living – which we'll call ethics, just for the sake of completeness – is a great aid. And likewise, now that I'd been introduced to Polymarchos's remarkable theories on fighting – on body posture, on balance, on control – I saw how all fighting could be governed by these principles.

If I wanted to digress all night – here, fill the cup full, pais, and don't stint – if I wanted to digress all night, I'd tell you how deeply linked the two theories are. Control, moderation, inner examination—

Right – the Ionian boy is falling asleep. Back to the story.

I was watching two young men demonstrate that the Greek saying that every boy is born knowing how to use a sword is pig shit. They swung wildly at each other and cringed away from every blow. Detorix came up and leaned on his staff.

'I need to talk to you,' he said.

'Come to take my goods as well as my ships?' I asked.

He managed to look pained. 'It will all be returned to you,' he said.

'Sure,' I said, or words to that effect.

'Your people need to remain clothed at all times,' he said.

'All times?' I couldn't help myself.

'I have had complaints. You ran naked—'

I laughed. 'Sittonax says the Keltoi fight naked,' I said.

Detorix glared at him with fixed disapproval. 'Madmen fight naked.'

I shrugged. 'Greeks take off their clothes to do heavy labour,' I said. 'And to bathe. Something we like to do often, even if the sea is as cold as rejected love,' and my friends laughed.

Doola nodded to Detorix politely. 'Fishermen say the Carthaginians are in these waters,' he said.

Detorix looked away.

'If they catch our ships in this harbour, we'll lose everything,' he said.

Detroix didn't look at us. He shuffled his feet. In fact, for all that he was a tattooed barbarian, he might have been any gods-curse Athenian bureaucrat, unwilling ot take responsibility for a decision.

But as I spoke of bathing, I had a thought. And the thought made me smile.

'Very well,' I said. 'We'll only be naked when we have to be.'

Detorix stomped away, if a man in light boots can be said to stomp on a gravel beach. He rattled away.

I turned to Doola. 'We're going to have a swimming contest,' I said. 'I've counted days. The Carthaginians could have been here... two days ago. We need to move.'

Doola nodded.

I watched some more bad swordsmanship, and I went out on the gravel and began to give lessons in the most basic elements of sword-fighting – or boxing, for that matter. I walked up and down the beach, speaking to every group of men, pairing them off until every oarsman had a partner of roughly equal experience. I got Alexandros and his mates – the six men with the most experience of fighting – to coach with me; Gaius and Neoptolymos and Sittonax joined them, although I had doubts about the way Sittonax approached swordsmanship.

And as I went from group to group, I outlined the day's activities.

We formed two long lines, and shuffled back and forth across the sand. I was content for a while just to let them move, practising the most basic footwork of shield-fighting – or, as I say, boxing or any other combat sport. We advanced and retreated, we cross-stepped, we jumped.

After a while, I sent them off to get sticks. Three hundred men take a great many sticks. On the other hand, we were in a merchant town, and they were anxious to sell us anything, including seasoned ash and oak.

In half an hour, two men had broken fingers and one had been knocked unconscious. Pretty good, for three hundred amateurs.

When men were drooping and all learning had ended, I gathered them in a big huddle and gave them a long, rambling speech about comradeship and good spirit. Long enough for them all to rest.

Detorix and his six spearmen and a goodly number of his people were watching all of this from the edge of town.

'And now – *swim!*' I said. And we all ran into the water.

Only about two-thirds could swim.

The men who couldn't swim just ran into the water and cleaned themselves, cooling their muscles and relaxing.

Those who swam well, however, ran down the shingle, took long leaps into the surf and swam powerfully out to sea. We swam as fast as tired arms could manage, on the prearranged route – out to the big rock off the beach, and then north. I remember watching Doola swim a remarkable stroke – with just one hand, while the other hand held something out of the water.

To the trireme.

Fifty of us went up the side together. The two men left aboard as anchor watch weren't so much overwhelmed as mocked.

It was, if I may say so, one of my better plans. No one was injured, and in a single burst of enthusiasm we retook all of our ships, all of our weapons and all of our goods. The ship-handlers were sent over the side.

It was, I confess, my intention to gloat. But that didn't happen, because as I settled between the steering oars to turn the bow, Doola gave a great shout. He'd shimmied up the boatsail mast to check the sail, which had been left furled for two days in the rain.

He dropped to the deck by sliding down the forestay and ran along the catwalk.

'Six triremes!' he shouted.

There was only one reason there would be six triremes in the offing.

There was a wind blowing off the land – the mainland across the straight. A westerly.

'Hull up or down?' I asked.

'Hull up.' That meant that with low ships like triremes, they couldn't be more than twelve to fifteen stades away.

'Cut the cable,' I ordered. Seckla, shining with water, used an axe – the forward-anchor cable parted in one blow, and the ship was alive.

Half my rowers were frolicking in the surf on the edge of the beach, and I needed them.

'We beach stern-first. Touch and go.' With half our complement of oarsmen, this was going to be a complicated tangle. But Doola and Vasileos were up to it. In moments we were around, helped by the current.

'Steady up!' Doola roared amidships. 'Back oars!'

I felt the steering oars bite, and then I felt the stern touch under me, and in moments the oarsmen were pouring in. To my left, Vasileos had the *Lydia* in the surf. To my right, the *Nike* took in her rowers.

How I wished we had a signalling system; anything. But we didn't, so I lay with my stern on the beach for long heartbeats with my rowers switching places – the swimmers hadn't always taken the right benches, of course – while the Phoenicians became visible to the south.

Demetrios got the mainsail up on the *Amphitrite* with the anchor still down. Her head came up, and he pointed the craft due north – it looked as if he'd run aground on the north harbour entrance. Then he plucked up his anchor stone and shot away.

Lydia couldn't lie close enough to the wind to use the west wind to run north. She rowed off the beach. *Nike* followed at her heels, almost falling afoul of her, and I watched with my heart in my mouth and my stomach doing backflips.

Someone was screaming my name.

It was Detorix.

My rowers were *almost* ready. *Lydia* had thirty rowers, and I had one hundred and eighty. A hundred and eighty men take a certain time to get themselves organized.

I stepped out from between the oars. 'Carthage!' I shouted. 'Phoenicians! Six galleys!'

That shut him up.

'I'll lead them away!' I shouted. 'They want me!'

Detorix looked as if he might want me, too, but at that moment, Doola ordered his rowers to give way.

I was back between my steering oars in a flash.

In two more heartbeats, I had that feeling – one of the finest, in a crisis – that the ship was a living thing.

I gave Doola the nod I always gave him that meant we had steerage way. The stern was off the beach in fine style.

In ten strokes, we were catching up on *Nike* hand over fist. A hundred and eighty men can row a great deal faster than thirty men.

All was not well, though. The trireme was not at her fastest, because she was meant to be beached and dried after every day at sea, and her timbers were heavy with water.

I consoled myself that the Phoenicians were in damp hulls, too. They had to be, to have made the Venetiae Isles in twenty days from Gades. That was my guess – still is.

We raced for the harbour mouth. The lead Phoenician trireme was six stades away or closer. Even as I watched, *Amphitrite* shaved the northernmost rocks. Demetrios sailed *between* the outermost big rock and the headland, trusting that a fully laden merchantman was still shallower than the water.

He was a great sailor.

He made it with about an arm's-length to spare and he was running close-hauled, his mainsail brailed and heaved right round, using the west wind to urge him up the channel.

Lydia followed him under oars, also cutting inboard of the big rock, white with gull droppings.

Nike shaved the headland, and lost the stroke for a heartstopping moment when Gaius misjudged the turn and his port-side oars brushed the gravel. But he had enough way on to make the turn, and then his men were rowing for their lives.

I didn't think I could shoot the gap. I steered outboard of the rock. By this time, the *Euphoria* was almost up to cruising speed, and we shot out of the harbour entrance even as my marines armed and my archers wiped down their bows and shook their heads over bowstrings left exposed for two days and nights.

Even as we ran out of the harbour, we were passing the *Nike*. That's how fast a trireme can be.

Behind us, we could hear the drum on the lead Phoenician. He was moving to ramming speed.

It was going to be close.

Doola was serving out bowstrings. He – steady, sensible fellow that he was – had his strings in a pouch at his waist. All the time. Even ashore, even mourning for his lost love.

Bless him.

I used our relatively slow speed to advantage, making a sharp turn to starboard – head up into the wind, almost across the lead Phoenician's course, making him turn. A trireme at ramming speed has some very limited options for turning.

I caught Doola's eye. He was stringing his fine Egyptian horn bow, his eyes all but bulging with the effort. But he nodded.

'Full speed!' he called. One of the Alban boys started to beat the new tempo against the butt of the mainmast with a stick.

Now, we were in a waterlogged hull – a Phoenician galley is a heavy trireme to start with, heavier lumber, a much heavier bow. Of course, I now knew why: they built them for the Outer Sea. But they weren't as sleek or as fast as Athenian triremes on their best day.

Add cargo.

Add too many marines.

Add our mainmast, sail furled, lying down the central catwalk. Ships planning to fight leave the mast ashore.

We were heavy, and slow.

Luckily, our opponents were in the same shape. Plus their rowers had been rowing since dawn, I'll guess. Almost head on into the wind.

It was a curious sort of race – tortoise versus tortoise.

Ahead of us, we could see the coast of Gaul – the mainland. The channel – the strait, if you like – would turn west in about six stades. I had a plan for that, too.

The Phoenician fetched my wake and turned – very slightly. I could see his archers going forward into the bow. The bow went down, and cost him some speed.

The first flurries of arrows fell well short and were blown off to the west.

But we were almost in bowshot. A stade or two.

I cheated the helm to port.

It wasn't enough, but it was something.

The Alban boy smacked his stick faster on the mainmast.

We began to pick up speed.

In the time it takes to tell this, the Phoenician closed from three stades to two, and then the rate of her catching us slowed. Behind her, the other five triremes trailed back – two were right up close, and the other three were well back, almost a dozen stades.

I cheated my helm to the west again.

We were five stades from the channel's turn to the west.

Doola appeared in the helmsman's station. Alexandros was beside him, in armour. 'Let me have the helm while you get into your kit,' the young man said.

Seckla had my armour. So I handed Alexandros the steering oar, and Seckla buckled the straps of my thorax under my left arm.

We had passed all of our own ships. They lay right against the coast – I thought Demetrios was insane, but I had problems of my own. The Phoenicians, naturally enough, were throwing everything at me. I was, after all, the pirate rowing along in one of their ships.

Doola stepped up on the bench, leaned out over the curving strakes of the stern and loosed.

I couldn't even see where he was shooting.

'Duck your head,' Seckla said.

I did, and unseen hands put my helmet over my head.

I stood up, and Behon put my aspis on my arm.

Doola loosed again. And again. And again.

In a stern chase, the pursued has one advantage – the running ship has all the timbers of the stern, which rise like a temple roof above the helm. It is like a shield for the running ship. The pursuer's bow is lower, and open, so that arrows from the running ship can pass the length of the pursuer, hitting oarsmen, or anyone.

Three of Doola's archers stepped up and began to loose arrows with him, taking turns on the port-side bench. It was difficult shooting, with the wind, the angle of the bow and the motion of the sea.

On the other hand, they must have loosed an arrow every three beats of a man's heart.

A few were coming aboard us.

I was armed, and I left the oars and ran forward along the mainmast to the place amidships from which I sometimes commanded. Men were grim-faced with exertion. Full speed – ramming speed – can only be held for so long. A man can row flat out for about as long as a man can sprint at full speed.

We'd already done that.

Alexandros yawed – a moment's inattention, and we turned slightly to starboard, and there they were, a spear's-throw aft, their beak reaching for our stern.

'Everything you have! Be free men! Nothing at stake here but our freedom!' I called. '*Pull!*'

The next six strokes were better.

But the Phoenician had matched our turn, and now I couldn't see a thing.

Aft, Doola stepped up onto the stern bench and loosed. Some flicker crossed his face – a smile? – even as he jumped down and one of our Greeks stepped up on the bench and loosed.

And then, *there they were*. The trireme appeared from behind us like a sea monster broaching the waves. But this sea monster appeared because it was wounded – it had turned too hard, or a chance arrow had slain an oarsman, causing the man's corpse to let go his oar and foul his mates, so that his ship turned suddenly on the drag.

In a flash, we were ten ship-lengths ahead, and the enemy ship had lost all his way and was headed due west, into the stony beach. She was turning and turning, and the port-side oars were in chaos.

She struck bow-first. I doubt that the beach did a bronze obol of damage, but oars were splintered, and when men take a heavy oar in the teeth, things break.

'Cruising speed!' I called. The Alban boy looked at me with wide, frightened eyes. I made myself smile.

'Slow them down, boy.'

He tapped his stick more slowly. He had a wonderful sense of tempo.

Men on either side of me all but collapsed on their oars.

I leaped onto the unstepped mainmast and ran along it aft. I stepped up on the starboard-side helmsman's bench, where the archers weren't – shooting on that side would cramp their bow arms – and looked aft.

The second Phoenician was making up the ground lost by the first. She came on with beautiful symmetry, the three banks of oars flashing in the blue and gold sunlight like a fantastic dragonfly skimming the waves.

He was three stades back.

I leaned forward.

We were three stades from the turn in the channel. Already, the wave action was heavier on the bow.

'Deck crew – ready with the boatsail.' I gave my aspis to Seckla. 'Steering oars,' I said to Alexandros. 'Well done.'

He nodded, a serious young man. 'Steering oars, aye,' he said. I got my hands on them, he ducked out and I was between them.

The second Phoenician elected to wait for the third. Their tactic showed immediately, as the lead ship yawed to the east a few horse-lengths, obviously intending to range alongside my starboard side. The trailing Phoenician would go for my port side.

But when the leader elected to wait for the next ship in line, the initiative passed to me.

'Cables to the masthead,' I said, but Seckla already had them laid.

A good crew is the only advantage worth having.

Even as I watched, the cables went over the crown of the mast and were made fast. Four men began to haul them tight – tighter and tighter, and then they were belayed forward, and the job was done.

We were less than a stade from the turn in the channel.

I was watching the Phoenician coming up our port side, wondering when his rowers would flag, and she was just passing the one that had run aground. And *Lydia*, forgotten, came up on the Phoenician from close to the beach and rammed her.

Vasileos, bless him.

The sound of his ram going home carried over the water. The little triakonter wouldn't ordinarily have done much to a trireme, but a trireme anchored by having its bow buried in the shale of the beach was a very static target, and her beak opened the timbers.

Lydia had changed the engagement in a single action. Now she was backing oars, and *Nike* swept past her, under her stern, and as they passed the stranded trireme, they threw fire into her stern.

The trailing Phoenicians now put their bows to the troublesome small craft and went to ramming speed.

I couldn't see *Amphitrite* anywhere. My first, heart-stopping worry was that she'd been rammed and sunk while I was looking elsewhere, but after a few glances – I was steering as small as I could – I couldn't find a ship in the geometry of sea combat that might have taken her.

I looked over my right shoulder, and there she was – she'd tacked, and was now hard against the coast of Gaul.

And, of course, the Phoenicians had to assume that Demetrios was just a local coaster running for sea room.

Doola was still loosing arrows at a magnificent rate, and his apprentice bowmen were hard at it. The newest of them had stopped shooting and was now simply handing arrows to the others. But as the two Phoenicians overhauled us, we started to take hits.

Seckla took the first arrow.

He fell, face down, and screamed. Alexandros stood over him, holding his aspis to cover.

'Prepare to turn to port!' I roared in my best deep-blue voice. 'At my word, port oars back water!'

I watched the horizon, glanced at the trailing Phoenician. It was going to be close. If we lost too much speed, we'd be rammed.

Doola and his archers all put a shaft on their bows and waited. Just for a moment, we would lie across the bows of the trailing ship – at less than a stade.

'*Now!*' I cried.

The port-side oarsmen backed water, laying on their oars for two strokes.

The ship pivoted on the stern.

The port-side Phoenician seemed to shoot at us like an arrow from a bow.

'Ramming speed!' I shouted. I think I screamed it.

Seckla rolled over and said something to Alexandros, who called out – and the deck crew dropped the boatsail off its yard. The breeze filled it instantly, and the ship leaped ahead.

The archers loosed – all together.

If they hit anything, I didn't see it. You can't always have a miracle on demand.

Our turn, on the other hand, took the Phoenicians by surprise, and our boatsail gave us a tiny advantage in speed but a wonderful, instant advantage in stability.

We were now running north-west, with the wind on our starboard quarter.

The port-side Phoenician came closer.

Doola's archers got off another volley. Then they cheered. Then they shot again.

And then the port-side Phoenician stopped gaining. Her beak was so close: Poseidon, I can still see it, the waves pushing against it, the eyes on either side wicked with battle lust, the beak itself so close I could have leaped to it.

For three heartbeats, we were a spear-length apart.

And then we passed them, shaving her beak. I'd love to tell you there was a tiny thump as the beak touched our stern – but I don't think it happened like that.

And we were away. Now we were running easily, and they had to slow to make the turn.

By the time they made it, we were ten ship-lengths ahead.

Seckla was propped up in the bow. He was pointing at the mast and giving orders, and before I felt I had to go forward and sort things out, the mainmast began to rise. It, too, had cables run to the crown. It went up and up, and seemed to take an hour, and astern of us, the Phoenicians started to gain. Again.

Far astern, over by the island, *Lydia* made the turn in the channel and *Nike* appeared in her wake. *Amphitrite* was somewhere to the north, and I'd lost her again against the low-lying coast.

'We cleared their archers,' Doola said. 'There's not an archer left alive on that ship.'

I wasn't sure that made much difference.

Again, if I'd had a signalling system – a way of telling *Lydia* what I intended – I might have made a fight of it. I was confident that I could take any one of the Phoenicians; I was pretty sure that, given the favour of the gods, I could take both, with the *Lydia* and the *Nike* ranging up on their sides.

But the risk would have been immense, and the gain very small. Because as the mainmast went home in its box and the chocks were pounded in with mallets, I knew that, barring a weather change, my trireme was safe. None of the Phoenician ships was faster. That was vital. We were all about the same: the second Phoenician had a small edge in speed, which she had squandered waiting for her consort.

Now both ships were five ship-lengths back, and too far to the north. Neither had started to raise their mainmasts, and their rowers were flagging.

Five stades behind me, *Lydia*'s mainsail spread like a pale flower turning its face to the sun. *Nike* followed suit.

The three rear Phoenicians still hadn't made the turn in the channel.

'Mainsail!' I called. I put the helm down, used the steering oars to bring the wind right aft, and then the mainsail was sheeted home and Doola was ordering the oarsmen to get their oars in.

I raised my arms and prayed to Poseidon, right then and there. I sent the Alban boy, whom I christened Tempo, for wine. And I poured it into my favourite bronze cup and threw it over the side, and oarsmen cheered.

It took the Phoenicians a quarter of an hour to get their sails up, and they lost ground with every heartbeat, so that by the time their big striped sheets were hung, they were halfway back to the horizon, and we were running free. Behind them, a nick on the north-eastern edge of the bowl of the world, was *Amphitrite*, I assumed.

But the bastards didn't give up.

We'd run off the beach with no food and almost no water – remember, we'd sold our amphorae.

Now, with parched rowers drinking the little water we had aboard, fresh water was an immediate crisis. And as if they knew our ill planning, the Phoenicians dogged us, well to windward but always close enough to snatch us up.

I summoned Doola and Sittonax. I thought longingly of the wine I'd just thrown over the side. Did Poseidon even know this sea, with its horrifying ten-foot-high rollers and whitecaps in every weather?

Sittonax pointed at the long line of low-lying land to the north and east. I could already see the promontory that marked the extreme westward end.

I hadn't marked what it meant, but before Sittonax spoke, I realized that this must be the westernmost point of Europe.

We were sailing off the edge of the world.

'What's north of here?' I asked. 'How far to your Sequana River? The *River of Fish*?'

He shook his head. 'A long way.' He shrugged. 'I've never been there. But it must be four days – maybe six.'

Detorix had mentioned the Sequana like it was near at hand.

'And the main islands of the Venetiae?' I asked. They were three days' sail, or so Detorix had said.

Sittonax shrugged, palms up. 'I'm not a sailor,' he said. 'I'm a guard. I was hired inland. On the Sequana, where the big ships unload.'

'Poseidon's rigid member,' I swore. I remember, because Doola looked shocked. It made me laugh, which in turn lightened the tension.

Behon was working on the deck crew, and he came aft eagerly. He spoke rapidly to Sittonax, and pointed north and west. With the wind.

'He says we can make Alba in a day on this wind. To Dumnonia, among his own people.' Sittonax looked deeply sceptical.

I tugged at my beard. 'Ask Behon what he did before he was enslaved,' I said.

He looked at me. 'Fisherman,' he said in Greek.

Aha.

'Very well. Doola, how's Seckla?' I asked.

Doola leaned forward. 'Gut shot,' he said softly. 'It went about three fingers in. Oozing blood. He's fine for the moment.'

We both knew what a gut shot meant. Sepsis and a nasty death.

'Go and stay by him,' I said. I turned to Alexandros. 'Take the helm.'

To Sittonax: 'Ask him whether this wind will hold.'

'Two days.' The Alban made an odd motion with his lips, as if tasting the wind.

'Ask him what the coast is like in his Dumnovia.' I was weighing my non-existent options.

'Rock, and more rock.'

I swore. 'We're going to run on that coast in the dark.'

He shrugged, as if to say that all of us were in the hands of the gods.

In late afternoon, the wind changed two points – to the north.

As the sun dropped towards the endless Western Ocean, the wind rose and we had to brail the mainsail. Seckla was up and moving – I'd have gathered hope, but I had seen this before. Men with gut wounds got better for a little while, and then—

Apollo came with his deadly arrows, and took them.

As the red ball of the sun fell into the Western Ocean – by the gods, daughters, to look west at the setting sun, and see *nothing* but open ocean is perhaps the most terrifying sight I've ever had within the orbit of my eyes. Somewhere out there were the Hesperides. It was like—

Like living in a myth.

While being chased by slavers.

We weathered the great promontory of Gaul at sunset; the sky was already full of stars, and the swells lifted our bow and it fell, and the sail was too full for my comfort. Far astern, *Lydia* and *Nike* followed me, and *Amphitrite*, who could sail better on any wind but dead astern, had ranged up and lay five stades away, as close to beautiful as she would ever be in the red, red sunset.

We buried the Phoenicians over the horizon, but when we were at the top of a wave, our lookout on the mainmast could see their mainsails flashing red to white in the setting sun. And far, far to the east, a column of smoke caught the last light where the lead Phoenician galley burned.

I don't want to say that I thought I could take all six of them.

I'll only say that, had I had drinking water aboard, I might have tried.

But my men were already desperate, and if we had had to row, even for ten stades, I think that they might have started to die. Remember, I had men who were a few days out of desperate bondage. A third of my rowers were strong enough, but as thin as young trees.

But the knucklebones were cast, the sail was brailed, the helm set and we ran north, and the sun set in the Outer Ocean like an evil eye into an alien sea of blood, and we could all but hear the hiss as it plunged red-hot into the sea. It had an evil look, and by the gods, we were all afraid.

Dawn, and I was still at the steering oars. I sucked on a piece of old bread to get saliva into my mouth. Men drank more questionable things: water from the bilge, urine mixed with seawater. Next to loss of breath, thirst is the fastest way to bring a man to desperation. Try it sometime. See how long you can go without water. You can go a day, but after a few hours, it becomes the sole focus of your thoughts.

The worst was that the sun found us alone. When you run at night without lights, it is easy to lose your consorts. There were no landmarks – no rocks, no coast. In fact, the very worst of it was that once we lost sight of the coast of Gaul, we didn't even know which way north *was*.

That's right. Think about it, friends. What magical device would give us direction? All I knew was that the helm was the same way I'd left it, and that the sun rose in the east, give or take a few degrees. But a few degrees at sea can be a great distance.

Alone, on the Outer Ocean. No sails, no land, a few gulls.

On and on we rode at a breakneck pace on a freshening wind.

'How far?' I asked Behon.

He rubbed sleep from his eyes. 'How would I know?' he said through Sittonax, who naturally was very happy to be awakened to translate.

'You used to sail here, remember?' I asked.

Behon shook his head. 'No one but a fool comes out on the Great Blue,' he said. 'I never leave the coast.'

He drew lines on the deck with a charred stick, showing me how the coast of Alba ran east to west, with the coast of Gaul like the hypotenuse of a shallow triangle, so that he would sail east into the rising sun across the south coast of Alba and then touch on Gaul – far, far from where we were. If we were anywhere. If his chart was accurate – the drawing of an ignorant man who measured distance in vague notions of time – then we were south of Alba, west of Gaul. And more than a hundred stades from any land.

It would have been more terrifying, if I hadn't been so thirsty.

We ran north, and north. One of our Africans sprang off his bench at about noon, took his oar in hand, ran to the side and jumped.

He was gone in a few moments.

The sun was relentless, for autumn in the north.

I tried to sleep. Tried to daydream. Tried to imagine sex – Briseis, Lydia – or combat. Anything that would lift me and take me from water. But a dream of Lydia's lips became my tongue questing her mouth for water, and a daydream of fighting Persians became a picture of drinking their blood.

About noon, Doola and a pair of our fishermen rigged the charcoal fire amidships and began to boil seawater. They took the biggest cauldron they had and got it boiling, and the vapour that rose off the boiling water they collected in a tent made of Doola's bronze breastplate. They collected it as rapidly as they could, and in an hour's work they got about two cups of drinkable water.

They accomplished very little, except that they made everyone *feel* better. And the water was passed around. One man – one of the

Greeks – tried to drink the whole cup, and when one of the Albans pulled it away, he spilled it.

Alexandros drew his sword and refused to let the oarsmen gut the Greek. The young man was becoming an officer.

Doola went back to boiling water.

The coast of Alba resolutely refused to appear.

On and on we ran north, and I lost my ability to tell time. Time passed. Eventually, the sun set again. Towards last light, I thought I saw sails in the south, but I had sparkles in my eyes and I had already spoken twice to Heracles by that time. I don't think these were true visions, but merely phantasms of my waterless brain.

And then came the night.

Had I been in my right mind, I would have been afraid of running on a rock-bound coast, but perhaps I no longer believed in the coast of Alba. Yet I could think of nothing but water, and if I slept, it was fitful, and if I woke, I was not fully in the world. I think that at some point in the night a sea monster, or just a whale, broached near us and vented, and I was not even scared, but merely curious with the lethargy of the dying.

I could go on, but I shan't. Eventually, the sun rose.

And revealed the coast of Alba. Rock girt and grey, even on a bright day, Alba rose from the sea like my monster, and my heart with it.

I don't remember saying anything to anyone, but in moments, the deck was astir and everyone was awake. Behon staggered aft and stood with me, and muttered – whispered – things. Sittonax came aft after him.

'He says you'll make a fine landfall,' Sittonax whispered.

Behon pointed a little east of north. 'The island of Vecti, he says. Foreign ships come there.'

I put the bow at Vecti and we ran on.

By the time the sun was clear of the eastern horizon, the island was obvious, set away from the coast, and I could make out the eastern headland.

'I assume the beach is on the landward side?' I asked.

Behon shrugged. 'Never been there,' he said, through Sittonax.

And then the last hour. Two men were dead – slumped at their benches, gone in their sleep. We put them over the side, and the deck crew went to their stations as if they, too, were dead.

I was going to have to turn west into the channel between Vecti and the mainland of Alba, and then land stern-first on what I hoped was a beach. I would need the rowers to row.

We made the turn, and the mainsail came down in a rush and tangled the rowers, and for minutes we rose and fell on the swell, unmoving, crippled by our own fatigue and our timing. And then, as slowly as a snail on a log, we got the sail clear and the rowers began to row, like small boys trying to row for the first time in a fishing boat.

Pitiful.

An hour passed.

Another.

Now I could see the beach, and there seemed to be people gathered there.

Slowly, like raw beginners, we turned the ship, got the bow to the channel and backed her onto the beach, catching crabs with every stroke.

If the people on the beach hadn't rushed to our aid, we might have lost the trireme at the every last. The port-side oars failed – men simply stopped rowing. Perhaps they thought we were home and safe. And the tide and waves caught us and threatened to throw the hull up the beach and break us.

But Albans waded out, grabbed our ropes and got our stern aground. Behon called out to them, and Tempo, and they waved.

And water came aboard, in skin, in light wooden buckets and big bronze beakers and shallow bowls – every man, woman and child on the beach suddenly had water, and I had the discipline to watch as men drank, and then I couldn't stop myself. A light-eyed man gave me a tin pail, and I drank and drank. And paused, and drank again.

And drank and drank.

Perhaps the most amazing thing about thirst is how very quickly you recover. All that is required is water. In moments, your head is clear; the lassitude falls away.

If you have been without water too long, there may be cramps.

I had cramps.

I slumped to the deck and looked at the tin bucket, and what I realized after a few breaths was that I was looking at a bucket, a household bucket, perhaps for feeding cows, and that it was made entirely of *tin*.

II

The wind came up at midday, while we were still in an orgy of drinking the water. The blow began from the east, and as the wind went around the points of the compass it rose and rose, and when it settled as an easterly, it shrieked along the beach like a racehorse.

We got rollers under our keel and moved our black ship up the beach. I was afraid of storms, but I was more afraid of being caught by the Phoenicians with my keel in the water where they could just tow her off.

And then, full of water, we were given a meal – and we went to sleep. I'd love to tell you that we posted guards and acted like good sailors or even good pirates, but we passed out, and it was twelve hours before most of us were up.

I had the energy to help a dozen other men pitch a tent – to pull Seckla into it, lie him on blankets and curl up by him with Doola on one side of him and Sittonax on the other. It was cool in mid-afternoon, and promised to be cold at night.

In the morning, Seckla was moaning on his bedroll. I knew what came next. In the dawn, I considered putting a knife in him. Gut wounds are horrible. I'd watched a few.

But Doola's eyes were open, and I knew he'd never forgive me.

But again, Behon worked to our rescue. He found a doctor – one of the Kelt doctors, who were also priests, men of learning and often musicians – and led him by the hand to Doola's side.

'Good morning,' said the white beard, in a passable imitation of Attic Greek. Then he rolled Seckla over and examined his stomach wound for some time.

'No food,' he said. 'Nothing but water. I'll be back.' He picked up his heavy staff and left our tent.

Seckla moaned, but he didn't scream. Yet.

Outside, we could hear rain on the tent, and I went out. We were two hundred men in four tents, stacked like cordwood; the easiest way out was to crawl under the edge. It was wet, and cold.

I found Behon standing in the rain, and Sittonax. We walked through the downpour to the water's edge, and looked out into the mist. The wind was from the south, and moderate enough.

Sittonax led me up the beach to the warehouses. There were six of them, built of timber and thatch, and a pair of stone roundhouses, not unlike the Venetiae houses; not unlike a military tower in Boeotia, either, except that the stones were smaller and completely unmortared.

The first warehouse contained about a hundred ingots of tin, and each ingot was shaped like a capital eta, H, and weighed as much as a grown child.

I laughed.

I laughed and laughed.

'This is where the tin comes from,' I said, satisfied.

Behon said something quickly, and laughed.

Sittonax nodded sagely. 'Not quite. He says the tin comes from the land opposite, and farther inland. They gather it here, to sell to traders. Phoenicians, Venetiae – anyone who comes.'

'Pray for *Amphitrite*,' I said.

But it was *Lydia* who appeared. Vasileos brought the triakonter in, and we watched his crew make all the mistakes we'd made. We scrambled out into the freezing surf and helped the smaller boat land, and pressed water on them.

They'd started with full water amphorae – lucky them – but spent two additional days at sea.

When Vasileos had water in him, he pointed south. '*Nike* is somewhere out there, and we saw *Amphitrite* at sunset,' he said. 'We smelled woodsmoke and I followed it. Then we met a fishing boat who gave us all his water, and here we are.'

'The Phoenicians?' I asked.

Vasileos shrugged. 'How far can they chase us?' he asked.

'The ends of the earth,' I said. 'We attacked their gold. And their prestige.' In fact, I was coming to terms with the notion that by raiding their mine, I'd started a war.

I had no qualms. The Phoenicians got what they deserved.

Between my trireme and *Lydia*, I had most of the remaining gold we'd taken, and all the silver. *Amphitrite* and Demetrios had the rest of the gold.

Keltoi love gold. So I traded all the gold for food, bad wine and tin. I traded the amphorae in *Lydia*'s hold for more tin – and for barrels.

On our fourth day ashore, I sent *Lydia* with Vasileos to search the coast for the missing ships. My sailors stripped my trireme to the gunwales and dried her and recaulked her, and then we stowed the tin as ballast. I could only buy about seventy of the pigs, but that was enough.

The barrels went fore and aft, into the bow and stern. I'd never had so much drinking water.

I bought dried fish in enormous quantities, and dried meat and dried berries.

After a week, Vasileos came back with *Amphitrite* limping in at his heels. The two ships landed just ahead of a purple-black sky that swept out of the north, and we had six days of violent rain and high winds.

Demetrios drank the bad wine and smiled a great deal. 'We are the greatest sailors in the circle of the Ocean,' he said. 'I saw *Nike* a week ago. She lost her mainsail in the blow, and we passed them fresh line and they were rowing north. They'll be well off to the east. There's a current. We lost our reckoning.'

'East?' I asked. 'The wind was from the east?'

'I've been up and down this coast,' Demetrios said. 'Fishermen said there was a big island full of foreigners, but I couldn't find it.'

Whereas we'd sailed right into it. Since Demetrios was the best seaman I've ever known, I have to assume we had the will of the gods with us.

We sat out the blow and rested our crews, and fed them regularly. The locals were friendly, even when we'd spent our money and our trade goods. A surprising number of local ladies began to sport ostrich plumes. African beads were wildly popular.

I think we added to the population.

After two days of fine weather, Vasileos and Demetrios pronounced *Amphitrite* ready for sea.

We finished lading our ships, had a dinner of roast pig and leeks to celebrate, spent the last of our trade goods, saving aside only a few pots and some weapons, and rose to a red sun and the promise of three days' good weather.

We left Vecti with the ever-present wind in our teeth, but it was gentle, and we rowed due east, with *Amphitrite* tacking far to the south.

I wouldn't let the men touch my hard-bought supplies. We landed that night and killed sheep, and didn't pay for them, like sea rovers. The next day we met three fishing boats, and the men aboard hugged Behon. He came aft to me, knelt and took my hand, and I pulled him to his feet and embraced him.

'Thanks!' I said. It was obvious he was home, and these were his folk. They had a look to them that was similar. Dumnoni.

He climbed over the side, and the fishing boats followed us into the beach, a fine harbour with miles of beach, and we feasted on their catch.

They told us that *Nike* was farther up the estuary, patching a sprung bow.

The wind was rising, and I wasn't unhappy to go up the estuary. We found *Nike* towards nightfall, and Gaius was as happy as you can imagine. But he'd brought his people through in fine order.

He threw his arms around me. 'You'll never guess what I've found!' he said.

'Tin?' I asked.

'Spoilsport!' But he laughed.

The next day, we said our farewells to Behon. Leukas, his brother, elected to stay aboard. Perhaps it seems an odd decision, but we promised to take him over the mountains to the Inner Sea, and to send him home the same way. And Leukas was – and is – a fine sailor – handy in a way Behon was not, and Seckla liked him and began to teach him to tend the sails.

Seckla ... who appeared to have recovered. I don't know whether this was the science of the local priests, or his own healthy flesh, or the will of the gods. I can't remember exactly how deep the arrow went. But Seckla made a full recovery, and had a little bump on his chest he used to scratch.

We had water. We had two days' food, our holds full of tin and we had exact sailing directions for the northern Venetiae islands and the mouth of the Sequana River, which we were told was two days away.

We were five weeks from home.

It was glorious.

We set sail with the dawn, and we had to row out of the estuary as the wind had shifted all night and then settled back into an easterly, but the oarsmen – every one of whom was going to get a share of all that tin – rowed steadily, slowly, but with a will. And our ships were clean and dry, and we moved well enough.

We found *Amphitrite* hurrying towards us in the early morning, her mainsail and boatsail set, slanting up from the south and east.

We watched them and chuckled, because they weren't going to reach us on that tack, and they'd be all day following us if they lost ground. There was a certain rivalry between the men who had to row all day and the 'mere' sailors.

At our closest point of approach, perhaps ten stades, they dropped all their sails.

That meant something.

'I think they're waving,' Doola said.

I nodded. Already my eyes weren't what they had been at seventeen.

'Let's go and speak to them,' I said wearily. They were downwind – easy to get there, harder to row back.

The boatsail mast was rigged, so I gave the rowers a rest and we ran downwind, and *Lydia* and *Nike* lay on their oars.

When we were a stade away, they started to yell – Demetrios and a dozen other men all yelling in unison.

I got it immediately.

'PHOENICIANS!'

As soon as Demetrios knew that I understood, he put his helm over, raised his sails and ran back west.

Even as Seckla's men raised the mainmast and the two triakonters followed suit – you don't always need signals – the first shark's fin nicked the southern horizon in the sunlight.

By the time we had our sails set and we were all running west, there were five of them.

12

I was thousands of stades north of the Pillars, and the Phoenicians had sent a squadron to track me down.

In a way, it was flattering.

But the immediate crisis was one of navigation. The wind was blowing off the coast of Gaul, and it was going to blow us west. West was the tin island, but after that – nothing. I'd seen glimpses of that nothing: a grey, rock-bound coast stretching away into the setting sun.

There is a saying in Plataea that the frog would rather be alive in the desert than dead in the pond. It's not a pretty saying, but it is a true one. My oarsmen grumbled and looked west with desperate anxiety, but as long as we sailed west with the world's wind at our backs, the Phoenicians were not likely to catch us.

So I sailed west. I had a plan, one that depended on my being a little more cunning than my adversaries. I sailed west, and planned to double back around the tin island and leave them all a-stand in the channel. I didn't expect it to work, but I wanted to try.

We sailed west a day, and made camp in an estuary – not a place I'd been, of course. Leukas told us it was safe to land.

He insisted that if we beached and drew our ships up, the Dumnoni would protect us.

'Of course,' he said with a shrug, 'it would have been better if you'd sailed north into the heart of our country.'

It was late, and we had a dozen small fires burning behind the dunes that separate the cold beach from the sea. I had as many men on watch. All the Phoenicians had to do was to catch us against the beach and we would either be dead men, or we'd spend the rest of our lives on Alba. All the natives said it was an island. An island with three hundred stades of sea between it and the mainland.

I don't think I went to sleep that night. It wasn't just the ships. The truth was, with Vasileos – possibly my greatest weapon – I could *build* more ships.

No, it wasn't ships. It was the cargo. The tin, the silver and the gold. If we abandoned or burned the ships, we lost the cargo: no two ways about it. There was no way to keep thousands of pounds of tin – or even a couple of hundred pounds of gold and silver. And I hadn't come all this way to lose it.

Long before dawn, I stumbled around in the dark until I had located Doola, Seckla, Gaius, Neoptolymos and the rest. I had heated enough wine to fill my old mastos cup, and above us, the stars wheeled across the sky – bigger and farther away, I think, than they were back in Greece.

I had built up a fire and I handed the cup around, and they pulled their cloaks as tightly as they could. Beyond the circle of the fire, men were rising from sleep – and none of them was happy to rise so early.

Doola looked at me blurrily over the rim of my cup. 'So?' he asked.

'I see two choices,' I answered. 'We can burn the ships and lose the cargoes. Go inland, find Leukas's people and wait the Phoenicians out.' I looked around. 'We have three hundred men, and they rely on us. We'll have to feed them, or risk having them either turn on us or to banditry.'

I looked around. Demetrios shrugged. 'You took them,' he said.

'I did, so they are my responsibility,' I agreed. 'But we are in this together, and that cargo is our cargo.'

Doola nodded.

Neoptolymos shrugged. 'Let's fight,' he said.

'That's a third option,' I agreed. 'We could put to sea and fight: five triremes against one trireme, two triakonters and a tub of a merchantman – all brilliantly handled, of course.'

Demetrios shook his head. 'Suicide,' he said. 'We'd just die.'

Seckla grinned. 'No, the gods will make a way for us.' He looked at me. 'Because Arimnestos has the luck of Hermes.'

Gaius was staring out to sea. 'You have another option?'

I nodded. 'We run west. According to the Dumnoni, it is a long promontory. Then we run north, around the north end of the island.'

Demetrios whistled. 'How far?' he asked.

I raised my hands to the heavens. 'How would I know? Leukas

says ten days' sailing, but – let's face it – he doesn't really know any waters but these right here. Just like all the other Keltoi.'

'Except the Venetiae,' Demetrios said.

Doola handed me the cup. 'If we run all the way around Alba – and stay ahead of the Phoenicians all the way – where do we get to?'

'The coast of Gaul,' I said. I drew them a chart, as best I could, in the sand. 'Alba is a triangle, about three days' sailing by ten,' I said. I remember saying that. Laughable, but the Venetiae had said it, and Leukas said it. I believed it. I drew the long line of the Gaulish coast – another angle.

'North around Alba, then east to Gaul, looking for the estuary where the Venetiae have their homes,' I said. 'We sell them our ships, and move our tin over the mountains and down to Marsala.'

Demetrios was looking out to sea. 'And all we have to do is stay ahead of the Phoenicians all the way.'

I nodded. 'It's true.'

He shook his head. 'Listen, I'm a good sailor, and not a good warrior. But that plan seems foolish to me. Fifteen days' sailing – twenty days', more like. Twenty days for them to catch us on a beach. Twenty days where we have to find a safe route and a site to camp, and all they have to do is follow us. It is a landlubber's plan, that depends on our navigation being perfect. One error, one blocked channel, one day of adverse winds – and they have us.'

I rubbed my beard, chagrined. 'Do you have a better plan?' I spat. For all my vaunted maturity, I didn't really like to be questioned.

He shrugged. He was watching the ocean. 'Do we all agree we can't run the Pillars again?' he asked.

He looked around, and we all nodded.

'So: we have to make the coast of Gaul. Right?' He was very serious. He leaned forward. 'I say we sail west – yes. But as soon as the wind shifts a few points, we sail *south* into the deep blue. *South* for Oiasso. Right across the hypotenuse of the triangle – right, Ari?'

I had been teaching him basic geometry. There's a lot of time to kill when you are at sea, or camping on headlands every night. And teaching your best navigator some geometry can prove quite valuable.

Seckla nodded, and even the cautious Doola looked pleased. 'This is a better plan,' Doola said.

Neoptolymos and Gaius and I felt differently. 'This plan is all luck and seamanship,' I said. 'All the Venetiae fear the deep blue. They say ships *die* out there. We've already ridden out two storms, Demetrios – I don't really want to face a third.'

Neoptolymos nodded. 'Ari's way keeps us on a coast all the way,' he said. 'If the Phoenicians catch us, we can abandon the ships and run inland.'

Gaius agreed. 'Demetrios, you have a ship that sails closer to the wind than mine. You have a deck for men to sleep under. And – honour requires me to say this – you are a far better sailor than I. You could weather a storm that would kill me.' He looked around. He was a proud man – who is not? But he hung his head. 'When I lost you, I was afraid. Afraid right up until I found you again. I want a plan that keeps us together.' He shook his head. 'Or I want to give my command to someone who is ... better at it.'

Seckla, of all people, put an arm around him. 'You command very well,' he said.

Gaius shrugged. 'Outwardly, perhaps. Inwardly—'

I looked at Demetrios. 'But surely that is how command is for all men,' I said. 'You worry for them. They row for you.'

Well, at least that line won me a laugh.

Demetrios came and stood by me. 'Your plan is the plan for the warrior-landsmen. My plan is the plan for the fishermen.' He made a rocking motion with his hand. 'Either might work, or be disastrous. But I agree that you have the luck of the gods, so I will do as you desire. Choose!'

'I held this council so that I would not have to make this decision alone,' I said.

Seckla laughed. 'Nice try. Let's get moving, before the Phoenicians solve the whole thing by hitting us in the dawn.'

I agreed, but first, I explained my plan for losing the enemy around Vecti. And Gaius and I wrote out a simple signal book on wax tablets and handed them around.

We got off our rocky beach in fine style, and we were out in the rollers before the morning raised the wave height and made launching impossible. And we were at sea for three hours and hadn't seen a sail, and hopes were beginning to rise.

And then, they were there. The first sail nicked the horizon at mid-morning, and by noon all five were visible, and gaining. We were sailing at the speed of the slowest – *Nike*, I'm sorry to say. They had long-hulled triremes that cut the water like dolphins, and they ran off three stades to our two.

The sun had passed its zenith, and I poured wine over the leeward rail and put the helm down for Vecti, now visible – at least, to anyone who had been there before – on the starboard bow. By the will of the gods, the timing was perfect. They were well up with us, and it was late enough in the day that a cautious trierarch would be scouting the coast for a place to camp.

East by north. An hour, and the island filled the horizon. And then I turned and ran due west again. The Phoenicians were now hull up, perhaps twenty stades away. Perhaps less. Honey, hull up is when you can see the hull of a ship over the rim of the world – the horizon. With a stubby merchant ship, you can see a glimmer of his hull at thirty stades or more, but a low warship is invisible until he's close – unless his mast is up.

Seckla had gone aboard Gaius's ship, to support him. He'd left me Leukas, who was becoming one of us – sea time bonds men quickly, or leaves them enemies. So it was Leukas who stood by me at the helm. Doola was amidships. Everything was laid by, ready for action. Every man aboard knew that the easiest solution to our problem was to weather the island of Vecti and leave the Phoenicians gasping in our wakes – and run for Gaul.

Doola came astern, about an hour before I'd have to execute the heart of my plan. He looked out to sea and made a motion, and Leukas smiled and walked amidships down the catwalk.

Doola wouldn't meet my eye. 'I want to sail south,' he said. 'I confess that your plan is better – safer. I agree that Demetrios is pretending that all of us have his knack for weather and sailing.'

I nodded.

'But I want my wife,' he said. 'If it was ... Lydia ... left at Oiasso. If it was your Briseis, of whom you speak in your dreams—' He met my eye. 'I am the old, mature man. I am the solid man, the one whose shoulder you all cry on. But I want something. I want my wife.'

I had sworn to live and die with these men. They were my brothers. And what, exactly, were we? Were we merchants? Were we warriors?

What would Heraclitus say?

Well, he would most likely have said something dark and mysterious and difficult to make out. But he insisted to a group of us once that in friendship, men came closest to the gods because friendship was selfless. He gave a eulogy once for a boy who died protecting another boy from dogs – he said that this fiery soul had gone straight to Elysium, because there was no finer death than giving your life for your friends.

I didn't stand there pondering it.

I just want you to understand that there was no way that I was telling Doola *no*. In three years, I don't think he'd ever asked me for a single thing.

We were slanting down on Vecti, on a quarter-reach, with the wind a few points off the stern.

'Everyone ready to row,' I called. Everything would now depend on the ability and willingness of my friends to trust me and read the signal book.

Because I was throwing the plan out of the window.

There was one advantage to having the smaller ships. We were lower in the water.

What I was about to try was insanely risky. It made me smile: in fact, as soon as I'd made my decision, I began to grin uncontrollably. There is a feeling you get, as a commander – a feeling you get when you know you've made the right choice, even if you fail.

I had it immediately.

I grinned at Doola. 'We'll get your wife,' I said. We were six stades off Vecti, racing for the westernmost point of the island. In the old plan, we should have dropped our masts and turned north to row through the channel.

'Signal that we will turn to the SOUTH.' I pointed at the Great Blue.

Doola had the signal tablet, and he began to flash my bronze-faced aspis. We had an alternate signal system with lanterns, and another with cloaks. The sun isn't as common in northern waters as he is at home.

Amphitrite signalled that they understood.

Euphoria signalled that they understood.

But Nike shot in under my stern. Gaius leaned far out over his curved stern. '*South?*' he bellowed.

'South!' I called. 'Trust me!'

Gaius shrugged, and his ship dropped astern.

'Signal again,' I said.

One by one, the three ships acknowledged.

'Sails down on the signal!' I called. Doola repeated it in three flashes. This, we had practised.

'Do it!' I roared.

Leukas's men sprang into action, and our sails dropped to the deck, our masts came down with a rush and no one was killed. The deck crews grabbed the billowing canvas, trapped it against the deck and sides and began folding it aggressively. The triakonters had the harder job – no real deck crews, less space, no deck or even a good catwalk.

But the sails were gone in the beat of a heart. Even a nervous heart.

Before the way was off us, I had turned my trireme south by west – out to sea, and headed for the deep blue.

We were going to spend a night at sea, in the most dangerous waters in the world. On the positive side, the sun was golden orange and there wasn't a cloud in the sky.

Against the coastline, our low hulls ought to have been invisible, and we were rowing west and south out into the open ocean. If the enemy saw us, or deduced our course, we'd be caught. On the other hand, we'd know almost immediately when they figured out our ruse because they would have to turn – to tack across the wind, and with their sails up, that would show at quite a distance.

I watched those sails the way a coach watches his runner at the Isthmian Games, or the Olympics. My heart was in my throat. It beat twice as hard and made my gut ache.

On and on we rowed – not at racing speed, either. I knew we were in for a long haul, and the wind was still blowing from east to west. It should have favoured us, but we wanted to go south, and our sails would give us away. Even poor *Amphitrite* had to row, and she was a pitiful rower.

After an hour, I cast her a tow. My two hundred rowers were her only hope. Otherwise, her twelve oarsmen were going to burst their hearts.

Passing the tow cable used some time. And we rowed some more, and I watched those ships.

And then they all took their sails down.

It was late afternoon by this time. If our plan had worked, then they had 'followed' us into the channel between Vecti and Alba. They'd have had to take their sails down, to row east into the channel.

But one ship kept her sails up. And as I watched, that ship tacked across the wind and came down towards us.

I cursed.

Doola came aft.

'He's not onto us yet, but the Phoenician trierarch smelled a rat. He's sending one ship south, just to have a look.' I watched him. 'When he's hull up to us, then he can see us. We'll know the moment he catches us: he'll turn back north and start signalling like mad.'

'And then what do we do?' Doola asked.

'We raise our masts and pray to the immortal gods,' I said.

It was two hours before he caught us – late enough that we began to hope darkness would creep over the rim of the world and save us. But the gods were not with us, and we saw him suddenly spin about on his oars, and we knew the game was up.

Every one of our ships had his masts laid to, with heavy hawsers already laid to the mastheads. The masts went up; the sails came out like the rapid blossoming of flowers and the oarsmen relaxed with muttered curses. Men rubbed their arms, or each other's backs, and we ran towards the setting sun at a good clip.

But the moment the sun touched the horizon, I put my helm down and headed south. Due south. The wind had backed a few points, and we were committed, now. And there was no way the Phoenician scout could see us. We should be lost in the dazzle of the setting sun, or the gods hated us.

About midnight, the wind dropped altogether. I had stars by which to navigate, and I kept the north star over my shoulder as best I could – no mean feat when there's a roof of wood covering your navigational aid, let me tell you. I kept giving the oars to Leukas and running forward to take another sight.

How the gods must have been laughing.

The moon was full, and we ran south over a ghost-lit ocean. I could see the other three ships well enough, and whenever we threatened to get ahead, I would order the sail brailed up.

It was my second night awake, and I must have fallen asleep between the steering oars because some time not long before dawn, when the air goes through that change – from cool to warm, I think, hard to define, but the moment when your mind, if awake, begins to hope for dawn – something was wrong, and I awoke as if a trumpet was being played in my ear.

We sailed on for twenty heartbeats, and I couldn't place it but my heart was beating a Spartan marching song, and then I caught it.

It was an unmistakable sound, even to a lubberly sailor like me. Surf.

'Leukas!' I roared. And threw my body into the oars, turning the bow to the north as hard as I could. The wind had swerved to being almost due south, and I wanted to get the head up into the wind and drop the sail – the fastest way to get a ship to stop.

Leukas had his deck crew on the sail instantly. The sail came down, even as Doola roused the oarsmen to their duty and the oars started paying out of their ports. We were losing way – the steering oars wouldn't bite – and I could hear the ocean pounding on rocks to starboard. I left the steering oars and leaped onto the rail, looking south.

I couldn't see a thing – and then I saw water shooting into the air, perhaps as high as the top of a tall temple – due south. It was hard to make out: that's what it looked like.

Just astern, *Nike* was following my lead, head up into the wind. Oars were coming out.

Euphoria had made the turn.

Amphitrite had been last in line, and now she had turned all the way to the east and was still under sail, but she could make way with the wind almost amidships, and we could not. She began to come up on us, hand over fist.

When my rowers got their oars in the water, I was all a-dither about what to do – had we discovered an island? What rocks were these? What lay beyond them?

I couldn't see enough to tell, and as minutes led into hours, I realized that our beautiful weather was gone and now we were running east, slowly under oars, and the sound of surf crashing on rocks came from astern.

It was dawning a grey, grey day with fog, and I couldn't see a thing.

We ran east for three hours before the fog burned off, and then we couldn't believe our eyes.

Due south, across our path, was land.

I summoned Leukas. 'What the *hell*?' I shouted. I was angry – the anger of fear.

He shook his head. 'I think ... that is, I—' he looked around, as if perhaps Poseidon would come and save him from my wrath. He shrugged. 'It has to be Gaul,' he said.

We had taken eight days, or so I assumed, to sail from the coast of

Gaul to Alba, and we'd done the return trip in the same number of hours. Or so it appeared.

Thugater, the truth – inasmuch as I'll ever know the truth – is that the Venetiae had lied to us about the shape of Alba and the shape of Gaul. Why should they tell us their navigational secrets? So we spent days running along the coast of Alba when we might have been safe in a harbour in Gaul.

We landed at noon, and bought some bread and some good wine, and got sailing directions for the mouth of the Venetiae river – the Sequana. That night, we made camp on a good beach – one of six or seven in a row, almost as fine as the Inner Sea. It was easy to land, despite the rising swell. We purchased fish from local men, and we ate well. Oarsmen need food.

I posted guards on the headlands and ordered a day of rest. We'd been at sea five days straight, and the oarsmen had worked every day. There's a limit to endurance, especially with men who have been kept under cruel conditions. Although I was also happy to see how Neoptolymos and Megakles were both filling out, their emaciated bodies starting to remember their form. I had been through the same process when I was recovering from Dagon's tender mercies.

That bastard. Sometimes I wondered if he was aboard one of the ships that were trailing us, but of course it was unlikely. Nor did I think he was a good enough sailor to survive in the Outer Sea.

We slept a lot that day, and the locals flocked to see us and sell us food. I had silver, and by midday, the local war chief came in his chariot, and looked us over with lordly disdain. That was fine with me. Neoptolymos wanted to challenge him to single combat. He was young.

Mornings were starting to be cold. I didn't feel young.

After the local aristocrat was driven away by his charioteer, I found Doola. He was stretched out under a sail, staring at the canvas over his head. I handed him a cup of wine.

'We're in Gaul,' I said.

He nodded.

'I meant to sail south to Oiasso,' I said. 'But either my navigation is very bad, or the bastard Venetiae lied to us about the shape of Gaul.' I shrugged. 'The local chief says that your wife is about nine hundred stades south of here.'

He actually laughed. He got up on an elbow and patted my arm. 'Now that's an error in navigation,' he said.

I shrugged. 'We're all alive,' I said. 'And we have our cargo on the right side of the channel. Even if the Phoenicians catch us now—'

He put two fingers to my lips. 'Naming calls,' he said.

'I plan to sail north another two days, to the mouth of the Susquana. There's a Venetiae town there.' I fingered my beard. 'If you want to take the warriors and go south, I'll buy horses for you – and I'll wait for you.' I shrugged. 'It's the best offer I can make.'

Doola nodded. 'I'll take it,' he said. He picked himself a half-dozen fighters – Alexandros, of course – and Neoptolymos, which was no surprise. I traded a full ingot of tin for a dozen good horses, with tack, and some dried fish, dried meat and wine.

In the dawn, there were still no Phoenicians in the offing, and we prepared for sea. One of my fishermen from Marsala – an older man, Gian – took Doola's place as oar-master. My marines rode away south, with a local guide. Sittonax went with them, leaving Leukas as my sole interpreter.

We got off the beach beautifully – Gian seemed to know his job immediately – and despite heavier waves, we made good time. The coast was low, with some beautiful small islands – one was a magnificent rock rising out of the water, and as we sailed by, we could see that it was dry at low tide. Tides here ran very high, insanely high by the standards of the Inner Sea.

We camped on another fine beach of beautiful white sand. In the night, someone attacked my guards, and we all stood to arms, waiting for the Phoenicians to descend. But in the morning, it was obvious that we'd been raided by a half-dozen young men, because their tracks were clear in the sand.

I sighed for my lost sleep, watched the cliffs carefully and ordered my ships to load. I was suffering from a nagging fear by then, that we were simply too far from home. The men were hungry, and our feast day of a few days earlier was already just a memory.

But early afternoon showed me an opening in the coast – it *had* to be the estuary of the Sequana. But I couldn't run into the estuary in the dark, so I stood off.

We spent a brutal night at sea. The wind rose, and I began to wonder if I was going to be wrecked just when all seemed safe. Dawn found me too close to land, with a rising westerly that threatened to drive me hard to shore. I had no choice but to run into the estuary, and once I did that, I was at the mercy of the Venetiae.

On the other hand, I had three warships, one of which ought

to be the biggest in local waters – well, of course, there were the Phoenicians. But I hoped that they were well to the west.

I ran into the estuary with a gale rising behind me. The estuary of the great river runs east to west, and we ran east for hours in the odd light, with the sky to the west growing blacker. But the water of the estuary was calm and shallow – almost too shallow.

Amphitrite had trouble tacking back and forth, and she parted company to travel long boards to the north and south.

We had to row, and my unfed rowers were increasingly unhappy. I had no more wine to give them. I walked up and down the catwalk, promising them a life of ease once we reached the town. I had only other men's word there *was* a town. The estuary seemed to go on for ever, and by the end of the day, despite the rising storm behind us, we had slowed to a crawl because *Amphitrite* had no more room to tack and had to row. Everyone was exhausted. No one was making their best decisions.

Late in the afternoon, Gian spotted what seemed to him to be a line of masts to the north. We turned towards the north bank of the estuary and rowed slowly, and as we rowed, it became clear that the fisherman was right. The masts developed hulls – big, high, round hulls like Athenian grain merchants'. And to our delight – well, to mine – there wasn't a single trireme among them. In the darkness of my thoughts, I'd expected to find the whole Phoenician squadron here ahead of us, trapping us against the storm at our backs.

There was a town, later we knew it was called Loluma, and the first lights were starting to twinkle on the storm-laden air as the sun set. I could see a line of three stone piers, and another pair of wooden ones built, it seemed, of enormous trees. Tied up along the piers were lines of large open boats of a type unfamiliar to me – dozens of open boats, ten yards long and only one yard wide. Closer up, each boat seemed to be carved of a single giant tree.

Beyond the piers and docks was a broad beach – more of a mudflat, or so it appeared. The tide was high – let me just add that by now, I was beginning to learn to judge their fickle and titanic tides.

We stirred a great deal of interest. A pair of small boats launched from the piers while the light was still good. I wanted to beach all my ships; Demetrios came up under my stern to tell me the same.

'It's going to be bad,' he said.

We lay on our oars, watching that pretty town – big wooden houses with thatched roofs, muddy streets, open fields, cows and the smell of woodsmoke, which to a sailor is the smell of home and hearth. I don't know what the oarsmen thought, but I know what I thought. I thought about what the Venetiae would say. Now that I was here, I wasn't sure that the Phoenicians hadn't burned the other Venetiae settlements behind us. That they hadn't decided to arrest us.

In fact, we'd gone and bought tin from their source.

The first man up the side of my warship was Detorix.

In a way, seeing Detorix was a relief. He was a known quantity. He'd done right by his own lights, and at least I wouldn't have to explain from first principles. I saluted him gravely, and then offered him my hand.

He took it and clasped it like an old friend.

'We thought you dead,' he said. He smiled. 'And some of us thought that was the better way.'

'Still alive,' I said. 'How is Olario?'

He nodded. 'Untouched. The Phoenicians were so busy trying to kill you, they passed us by. How many of their ships did you destroy?'

I shrugged. 'One,' I said. 'At least, that's all I know of. I lost the rest of them on the coast of Alba.' I thought I might as well get that in right away.

'I took my round ship to sea behind you and ran north to Ratis,' he said. 'But the Phoenicians stayed on you out to sea.' He raised an eyebrow. 'So: you found Alba.'

'Yes,' I admitted. 'No thanks to you.'

He shrugged.

'Listen,' I said. 'I have a cargo of tin. I want to take it all the way south to Marsala. I'll pay the freightage – in ships. I'll sell you these four ships for the freight on our tin and other metals. You don't need to worry about my coming back for your tin – I won't have a ship on the Western Ocean.'

He smiled. 'I do want your ship.' He ran his hand down the steering oar. 'A warship.' His lust was evident.

Who was I to stand in his way? And I'd thought it through. This way seemed to me to cause the least chance of resentment. The last thing I needed was for the Venetiae to have me killed to protect their tin monopoly. I wasn't ever coming back. I was prepared to swear oaths on any god they named.

'Well?' I asked.

He shrugged. 'I can't say,' he prevaricated. 'But I imagine something can be arranged along those lines. I don't have the prestige to negotiate such a big trade in one go. I'll need partners. No one will want these smaller boats—' He pointed to the triakonters. 'It's a miracle they've survived as long on our coast as they have. And I imagine you want to land tonight, and not fight that storm.'

This was the part I had been dreading.

'Yes,' I admitted.

He nodded.

Leukas translated what we were saying for the other man – another aristocrat, taller, older and wearing a torq of solid gold. I bowed to him. He was introduced as Tellonix. He had the only cloak I had seen among the Keltoi that was dyed with Tyrian dye, bright purple – like a tyrant or a king or an Aegyptian priest.

He looked at my ship. 'How many ingots of tin do you have?' he asked in Greek.

In the Inner Sea, we like to chat a little before we do business – but there, with the lights of the town behind us and the gale beginning to blow down the estuary, I was happy to negotiate in a hurry.

'Seventy,' I said.

He twirled his moustaches, which were heavy.

'Land your ships as our guests,' he said. 'You have my word you will not be seized here.' He gave Detorix a significant look.

The younger man was unabashed. 'What was I to do?' he asked. 'He had three hundred fighting men.'

'And he still does. And yet he has come back to us in peace,' Tellonix said in Keltoi, which Leukas translated.

Well, I knew I had nowhere else to go, but there was no reason I had to say so aloud.

We got our keels up the beach – as I say, it was more mud than sand. Men's feet stank when they got ashore, and we were so far up the estuary that the water was scarcely salt. We pulled the ships even higher up the beach – at high tide, my trireme was ten horse-lengths onto the *grass*. We had help from a hundred willing Keltoi – men and women.

We got the ships ashore, and we got our cargoes off and under our tarpaulins, and then the rain started and we ran for shelter. I think that in all Gaul, only the Venetiae had the facilities to sleep three hundred sailors, and even so, we had to raise our tents – in a blustering, squall-laden wind. It was hard work, but our feet were on

225

dry land and we were filled with spirit, like Heracles.

In the morning, the weather was, if anything, worse, but I woke in a fine wooden house – a little smoky, I confess, and cold, but outside a gale blew over the town, and even the water of the estuary looked deadly.

Breakfast was an oddly shaped squash full of good butter and honey, and we ate with gusto and drank the thin local beer. Demetrios raised his small beer and said, 'May the gods protect all sailors on a day like this. Even the poor Phoenicians.'

I don't think Neoptolymos would have drunk to that, but he was away south.

We slept and ate for three days while the storm blew itself out, and then the serious trading began.

We had been unlucky in some things, and lucky in others. In our favour, the winds that had seemed adverse to us had allowed us to bring a cargo of tin before the last convoy left the mouth of the Sequana for the interior. Winter closed down the tin trade, as it closed everything else, and we had arrived in good time to make the trip.

Our ships were not as valuable as I had hoped. Freighting three hundred men and seventy mule-loads of tin overland to Marsala cost me all four ships and all my silver. 'My' silver. That's a laugh.

And my gold was spent keeping us all in Marsala while the convoy prepared.

It was only in the mouth of the Sequana, at Loluma, which is what the Venetiae called their trade town there, that we really saw the power of the Venetiae. It wasn't just that they had ships – and they did, ships as large as our Inner Sea grain ships, capable of carrying thousands of mythemnoi of grain in a single cargo. The Keltoi built barrels – as I've described – to standard sizes. And they built the open boats – the ones I'd seen at the piers – also to standard sizes, so that the barrels rolled easily aboard, right down the gunwales to the stern. It was a superb design: a Gaulish riverboat could load on any bank, and unload right back up the bank with a few strong men. They could row or pole, and they drew so little water that they could run up quite a small stream, or pass a dam or a fish weir.

They had a particular flat barge for carrying tin. Each boat took three ingots, and had a crew of two. Tin was so valuable, even here, that each boat had a curiously carved log on a rope, and the log was threaded into the ingots. I asked Tellonix what it was for.

He smiled. 'If the boat capsizes and sinks, the little piece of wood floats to the surface and shows where we can retrieve the tin,' he said.

They usually hired out guards – men like Sittonax. Detorix wanted my oarsmen, but I wasn't willing to sell them. I did convince him to treat them as free men, and offer them wages. Few of them were willing, at first, but after an idle week and some descriptions of the trip we were going to make, more and more of them signed to row for him – almost a third of the former slaves. None of the men from Marsala, of course. We were almost home, or so it seemed to us, and most of the fishermen assumed we had about ten days' travel before we got there.

I spent many fine evenings in the tavernas of Loluma, talking to Venetiae captains about their routes. They were careful, circum-spect, but sailors have a natural tendency to brag to each other, and Demetrios was the very prince of navigators – he had brought us through the Pillars of Heracles and all the way to Alba, and his exploits loosened their tongues. They told us fabulous tales – tales of islands west of Alba, and north, too – of islands of ice that glittered in the sun, and shoals of cod so thick a man could walk on them.

One captain had made a dozen trips to the north of Alba, for slaves and gold. He laughed at our notion that we could sail around Alba in ten days.

'Thirty days,' he said, shaking his head. 'And even then you would need the gods at your helm.'

Demetrios gave me a long look.

What could I say?

We Greeks gathered in a circle of standing stones, and Herodikles said the prayers for the autumn feast of Demeter. We gave a horse race, with prizes, for Poseidon, who had favoured us and let us live. It pleased the Keltoi, too, because they loved horses, even though theirs were, to me, the ugliest horses I'd ever seen: heavy, ungainly and short-legged. But they raced them, praised them, called them names like Wind and Spirit, just like our horses at home.

We introduced them to the idea of a night-time torch race on horseback, which they liked a good deal. We paid for a feast.

Our convoy was completed. I was taking a little over two hundred men home. All I needed was Doola.

13

Ever waited for someone in the Agora?

Ever sat by a stream, waiting for a girl who promised to walk with you? Or by a door, because she said she'd be there in a minute?

Ever waited and waited, and been disappointed?

At what point do you walk away?

For me, the issue was winter. The Venetiae were unfailingly polite – even a little oily, which is not how one thinks of barbarians, is it? But they wanted us gone. They feared that the Phoenicians would come, as did I – and they feared that we would make trouble, which wasn't so far from possible, either. And they feared that we might try to seize our ships back. They feared too that my freed slaves might eat them out of house and home.

I feared the cost. I wasn't living on charity, but I had made a deal – for the whole journey – and I knew that sooner or later, Detorix would sidle up to me *very apologetically* and demand that we get under way. I didn't really have to care, but there might come a further point where the Venetiae would simply refuse to perform their part. Or that the passes would close, and we'd be stuck for another winter in the north country.

Something had happened to me. And the longer I spent in the pretty town of Loluma, the more thoroughly it happened. I was turning back into Arimnestos. I still mourned Euphoria, but I was merely sad. I missed Athens. I missed Plataea.

I was sorry that I had made such a mess of Lydia, and Sicily, but I was determined to go back and set it right.

I was going back to being the man I had been. With, perhaps, some changes. I did not seriously consider, just for example, threatening the Venetiae with the burning of their town, just to keep them in awe.

Of course I'm smiling, thugater. Things change. People change. But some things remain the same always, as you'll see if you stay with me another hour.

About two weeks after we landed – to be honest, the whole period is a blur of activity to me – a round ship crept up the estuary under oars – eight long sweeps handled in a fairly seamanlike manner – and I sat in my favourite of the three waterfront tavernas, drinking a wooden bowl of the excellent Gaulish wine and watching the ship come in.

She was a trader, of course – a Venetiae ship that had just made the passage to Alba. Not a tin ship, or not this trip – this ship had been far to the north along the east coast of Alba, collecting hides and selling wine.

The captain, whom I'll call Accles because that's the closest I ever got to his name, sat with me for a day, recounting his adventures. He was eager to meet me, because he'd met with the Phoenicians off Vecti and spoken to them.

'You have made them very angry,' he said.

Detorix was sitting across from me. Spying, I think – or at least, watching. Leukas translated for me – translated some. By then, my Gaulish–Keltoi wasn't bad.

'The Phoenician trierarch said that you ... were a pirate who came from Greece just to prey on Phoenician shipping,' he said.

I smiled. 'I have no love for Carthage or Tyre,' I said. 'I have sunk many of their ships, and killed or taken many of their men.'

Detorix and Accles exchanged a look.

'Have they asked for you to hand me over?' I asked.

'They will,' Accles answered. 'I mean, I had no idea who you were until I came ashore here.'

I nodded. 'Will they come here?' I asked.

Detorix gave me an odd look. 'We don't allow them to come here,' he said.

I looked at both of them. They both watched me.

I resisted the impulse to place a hand on my xiphos hilt.

While we were all staring – or perhaps glaring – at each other, a woman came in. She was a matron – a year or two older than me, I expect. Keltoi women are very fit, like Spartan women, and you can't always read their age in their bellies. But she had the wrinkles of laughter in her eyes, and the way she carried her head spoke of dignity combined with, shall we say, experience?

She wore a sword, but that wasn't so rare among aristocratic Kelts. She looked at me with appraisal – perhaps even challenge – and sat by Accles.

'Is this the pirate?' she asked.

Accles pretended to laugh.

'Yes,' I said. 'I am. But not of Keltoi. Merely of Carthaginians.'

She raised an eyebrow. She had red-brown hair and a long, straight nose and wore a gold pin on her wool cloak that was worth ... hmm ... a small ship.

'I'm Arimnestos of Plataea,' I said.

She looked at Accles. 'Well?' she asked.

Detorix leaned forward. 'He's on his way south with a cargo of tin.'

'Stolen tin?' she asked Detorix.

Ten years before, I'd have slammed my fist on the table and said something like, 'I'm right here.'

Instead, I sat back and had a sip of wine.

'He purchased the tin at Vecti,' Detorix said.

'With spoils taken from the Phoenicians?' she insisted.

I snorted.

She ignored me.

Detorix looked at me, though. 'He says not. He says that he brought trade goods from the Inner Sea.'

'And the Phoenicians, our most reliable trade partners, are lying – is that it?' she asked.

Detorix shrugged and didn't meet her eye.

She turned to me. 'The Phoenicians landed north of Vecti, burned a village and killed a handful of people,' she said slowly. 'My people.'

'And took fifty of them as slaves?' I guessed.

She shrugged. 'Yes, I have reason to believe it.'

I nodded. 'When I stormed their town, I opened the slave pens. There were hundreds of Keltoi.' I shrugged. 'And I rescued them and brought them home. Ask around.'

'Your attack may have provoked a war,' she said.

'They attacked me first,' I said.

She shrugged, as if the rights and wrongs of the issue didn't interest her much. And there was no reason it should. As I found out later from Detorix, she was the queen of three tribes, and she needed to keep her peoples happy and well fed – which meant a constant tin trade, reliable alliances and open communications – with the Phoenicians.

'Wouldn't it make more sense to burn a couple of their ships to teach them not to enslave your people?' I asked.

She went back to talking to Detorix. 'If we just send them his head, will that be enough?'

Detorix shook his head. 'They don't even know what he looked like,' he said.

Well, there's barbarian honesty for you. They discussed taking me, executing me and sending my head to my enemies – in front of me. It's honour of a sort.

'I'm not sure there are enough men in this town to take me,' I said, conversationally.

She looked at me the way a man would look at a pig, if the pig talked. She smiled. 'Southerners don't even know how to use a sword,' she said.

'Really?' I asked. 'I don't expect many of our swordsmen come this way. The way I hear it, you get architects, tin vendors and wine merchants.'

She smiled; it was amazingly condescending. Briseis could have taken lessons.

'And are *you* a swordsman?' she asked.

Damn it, I was being played. She knew what I would say, and I was being manoeuvred into giving a display of skill so that I could be killed. And Neoptolymos wasn't close.

I had a boy – a pais – named Ajax. He was tiny, underfed and fast. He was around me all the time, fetching me wine, carrying my purse – you know, a pais. He wasn't a slave – or rather, he had been a slave and now he was free, and I'm not sure he had noticed a difference.

'Ajax, run and fetch Gaius, will you, lad?' I said. The boy ran out into the afternoon.

The great lady leaned forward. 'Are you going to show us your swordsmanship?' she asked.

I frowned. 'Against whom? You?'

She smiled. 'You are as far beneath me as the pigs who eat rubbish on my farms, foreigner. Why not fight one of them first?'

I leaned back – I'm a Greek, not a Kelt. I was being bated, and I knew it. And I wasn't fifteen years old, either.

We were sitting on three-legged wooden stools at a wooden table in the open, under a linen canvas awning that stuck out from a timber building. When I leaned back on two legs, I could put my back against one of the supports that held up the awning.

I pointed a finger – my left hand – at Detorix as if I was going to make an accusation. And then my left hand darted to her right arm and pinned it down, and I drew my kopis and laid it on her throat.

Her eyes were fairly large.

'Leukas, tell this woman exactly what I say. Are you ready?'

Leukas swallowed. 'She's my queen, boss.'

I nodded. 'Good. Tell her, she can fight me herself. I don't see any reason to fight the pig, the pig-keeper – you getting this? The pig-keeper's boss, her warlord, her top swordsman – no, I'll wait until you're done.' I kept her pinned in place. She tried to get to her feet and I slammed her back down on the stool.

'Or, I'll just cut her throat and burn the town and steal what I need to get home,' I said to Detorix. 'Understand me, Detorix? You tried to take my things and my ships once before. Call me pirate? What you lack here is the *force* to carry out your will. Understand?'

The silence went on a long time.

Gaius came in. 'There's some very unhappy barbarians over there. I think they are sending for archers,' he said.

'You will be my second in a duel,' I said.

He shrugged. 'Detorix?'

I let go of the queen and backed away.

She looked at me with pure, unadulterated hate.

I smiled. 'You haven't met a swordsman, lady. I know, because a swordsman wouldn't have let that happen. I don't think you want the humiliation of facing me with a sword in your hand, but unless you apologize to me, now, and swear an oath to the gods that you will not harm me, you can fight.'

She stood straighter. 'Fight,' she spat.

I turned my back on her and walked out into the sun.

Leukas followed me. 'Aristocrats – all they do is fight. And practise to fight.'

I was looking at her sword, which was long and straight. 'Ajax, go and fetch me my long xiphos,' I said.

Six burly Kelts in heavy leather came and stood around the queen. I smiled at them. None of them smiled back. Two were huge, and two were quite small – thin and wiry. Such men can be the most dangerous.

Detorix came towards me, hesitating with every step. 'I really need to stop this,' he said. 'This is not our way. This woman is a guest. You are a guest.'

'And we have agreed to play a little game,' I said. 'Gaius, ask her if she wants a shield.'

Leukas asked the question. No one answered him.

Ajax ran back with my longest, slenderest xiphos. I had taken it off a Carthaginian, and I rather liked it.

I walked in the sun, a little way along the gravel, turned and drew the sword. I put the scabbard in my left hand, and threw my chlamys over my left arm.

She had a shield. A big shield.

I saluted and she did not. I stepped in, flicked my blade up and she raised her shield, and I kicked it and her to the ground with a pankration kick which she didn't see coming because I was too close, and she'd raised her shield and thus couldn't see.

I stepped back and let her get to her feet. When she set her stance again, I shook my head. 'No, you lost. There is no second chance. If you want to send another man, so be it – but you lost.'

She glared. But she walked over and tapped one of the big men.

His sword was as long as my arm, and longer. He took the shield.

It didn't look thick enough to be stable. It was oddly shaped and too damned long, and his arms were like an octopus's arms – too long and too fast.

He came at me, whirling his sword in front of his shield.

Polymarchos had made me practise against this sort of thing, which he called the whirlwind. I made myself relax, moved with him, backing away, letting him slowly close the distance. He had a tempo to his spin, and I moved with it, almost as if we were dancing.

I had my strike prepared, but he surprised me, leaping forward with a shriek, the sword cutting up from below my cloak. I got my scabbard – my heavy, wooden scabbard – on his blade, and he cut right through it and into my chlamys. The blow didn't cut into my arm, but he almost broke my arm with the blow.

Of course, he had a foot of my steel through his head. A little punch, a hand-reverse to clear his raised shield – one of Polymarchos's best tricks.

He was dead before he hit the ground.

I hadn't intended to kill him. In fact, it's worth noting that he was too good. If he'd been worse, or slower, or less long-limbed, I'd have let him live.

And he was certainly trying to kill or maim me.

I stepped back and the pain of his blow hit me. I stepped back again, and one of the little bastards came for me.

He leaped the corpse of the big man, and swung his heavy sword with two hands.

I cut his sword to the ground and pinked him in the hand.

He roared and cut at me again.

Again I cut his sword to the ground with my lighter weapon, and this time I skewered his right hand. But he raised the sword with his left, so I ripped my point out of his hand and brought the blade down on his left forearm. And then stepped in and kicked him in the crotch.

And he slammed his maimed right hand into my face.

Kelts: they're insane.

He didn't break my nose. That was lucky.

I was blind with pain for a moment, so I slashed the air in front of me to keep him back. I connected with something, but most of my long xiphos was scarcely sharp and all it did was raise a welt, I suspect.

He leaped at me again just as I got control of my head. *He didn't have a weapon.* And he was as fast as a fish in the stream. His wounded hands were up, and he was reaching for my blade.

I had to kill him, too.

Now I was breathing like a bellows, and I fell back.

I wanted to say something witty and insulting, because I was angry – full of rage, like Ares. But all I could do was breathe.

It didn't feel good.

In fact, I felt ... wretched. These two men had never done anything to hurt me – well, except to attack me at the behest of their mistress – and now they were dead.

She looked at me, and at the four men beside her.

I breathed hard. And waited.

Gaius nodded. 'That's it, then,' he said, in his aristocratic Greek. 'Tell that woman that it is over, or it is war, and if it's war, we have two hundred men and she has four.'

I looked at him. I hadn't expected him to step in. But that's what friends are for.

I turned to Detorix. 'We will leave in the morning,' I said. 'Let this be an end to it, and don't let me regret not walking over and killing her.'

Detorix nodded.

That was good. I was done with the Venetiae.

So we left without Doola, and that didn't make me happy. Nor did I trust our hosts any more, or our boatmen, or anyone.

We had to pole our boats north. Some of the oarsmen were quite good at this, and some were not. We had a pair of guides and interpreters, but otherwise we were on our own.

After the first night, we built a regular camp by the river and we put brush all the way around it and stood to, fully armed, an hour before darkness and an hour after dawn.

The third day, we saw horsemen on the horizon as we poled upstream.

By the fourth day, we were quite aware of the horsemen, who scarcely troubled to hide themselves. And the river was a snake, swimming on the sea – an endless curve and back-curve. Sometimes we could see a town or settlement a dozen stades before we reached it. Some settlements were on both sides of a peninsula, so we'd pass the town twice. And it did seem like we paddled or poled twice the distance that we'd have walked – or that our shadows rode.

I'd had about enough of the Keltoi by then. And I was unhappy with myself – the more I thought on it, the more I decided I'd allowed myself to be ruled by Ares in the taverna. I didn't need to show her my arête. I didn't need to fight. I could be Odysseus instead of Achilles. And the two dead men were powerfully on my conscience.

But even as I thought these thoughts – thoughts largely fuelled by Heraclitus, of course – I also thought like the pirate I often was. I considered setting an ambush for the riders. It was foolish to let them pick the time for an attack.

But it would be worse to fight them. Once we fought, we'd be the enemy to every barbarian on the river, and that would be the end of us and our tin, too.

I thought about it for another day, as we poled on and on and seemed to make very few stades.

That night, Gaius and Seckla and I took Herodikles and one of the younger shepherds, Leo, who was growing as a man and as a leader. The five of us slipped downstream in a small boat, and we floated silently in the darkness until we came to a campfire. We landed well upstream, and crept carefully down on them.

Eight men, a dozen horses.

It was the work of two minutes to cut all the hobbles of the horses and chase them off into the darkness. They roused themselves, and we were gone.

The next day, we had no contact with them.

We poled on. We were low on food, and I had to bargain with a fairly hostile village of Kelts who lived in reed huts that stood on stilts in the water. We bought grain for silver, and got the worst of the bargain.

Two nights later, one of our interpreters tried to run. He was surprised to find that I was right there, waiting for him.

Three more days poling, and I was sure we had slipped our pursuers. The poling had become quite difficult, as we were travelling into the upper reaches of the river.

Let me add that although I was sick to death of barbarians and their neck collars and their feuds and their superstition, it is beautiful country, and those Gauls could *farm*. The banks of the river were cultivated – not everywhere, but long swathes cutting through the forests. The towns were prosperous, if hag-ridden with aristocrats.

Another thing I feel I must mention, although this is not meant to be a tale of marvels encountered in travel – traveller's tales are all lies anyway – is their priests. They were all men, all representatives of the aristocratic classes, and they could perform prodigious feats of memory. I met a priest on the Sequana who could recite the *Iliad*. I didn't stay to hear the entire piece – I'd have been there all winter – but his memory seemed perfect to me, and he could start wherever I asked him: I could name a verse or an event, and he would begin to recite. I found this very impressive, and told him so.

Yet these learned men seemed to me more like magpies than like true priests. They absorbed a great many facts – it was from a Keltoi priest that I first heard of Pythagoras, for example – and they knew everything about plants, herbs and medicine, but so does any decent doctor in Athens or Thebes.

For moral philosophy, they were merely barbarians. They had no great code of ethics, and their laws were mostly learned by rote and not reasoned, or so it seemed to me. In behaviour, too, the aristocrats seemed to do every man as he wished, and when the wills of two such clashed, there was war – petty or great depending on the status of the contenders. Twice as we poled our way up the Sequana, we passed villages burned – the second was still smouldering.

Greeks could be just as bad. So could Persians. But there was something … ignorant about the Keltoi. Of course, I'm a Greek, and that may just be my own ignorance speaking. And you must remember that I was seeing all this through the eyes of a man who had suddenly begun to see the uselessness, at some level, of violence. The Keltoi queen – Nordicca, I knew her name to be, of the Dumnoni – was typical of her breed. The truth is that I had found her quite attractive, sought to impress her and ended up behaving like a posturing adolescent, and men were dead. I won't say they haunted me – they had died with weapons in hand, striving against me – but I will confess that I knew their deaths to be unnecessary.

But I digress. Fill my cup, pais.

I had my two interpreters watched very carefully, night and day. Demetrios managed our boats, and Gaius managed the interpreters. We made sure they knew they'd be well paid, for example. I was quite sure they were supposed to desert us, but we promised them enough silver to make them modestly wealthy men.

In truth, Detorix had taken some precautions to make sure we never came back. I might have hated him, but life had taught me that merchants will act to protect their trade the way farmers act to protect their crops. They will make war, or commit simple murder, to keep others off their trade routes. The Venetiae were no different in kind from the Phoenicians, except that they weren't quite such rapacious slavers. When I look at how Athens behaves these days, I have to admit that apparently Greeks are just as bad. Or perhaps worse – more efficient.

The younger of the two interpreter guides was Gwan, and he was a warrior, an aristocrat, and not a merchant. Over the course of a dozen stops on the Sequana, I gathered that this was a great adventure for him; that his father was deeply in debt to the Venetiae, and that his service was part repayment. He was of the Senones, the people who ruled the great river valley.

He loved horses, and he was the most profligate lover I think I have ever met. It was difficult to find time to talk to him, he was so busy lying with women. The men that Gaius sent to follow him always blushed to tell of his exploits. He was neither particularly clever nor particularly handsome, and yet, in every village, one or two young women seemed to leap on him with an enthusiasm that might have made me jealous, if I hadn't been so busy.

What was his secret?

I have no idea.

At any rate, after twenty days we were in the upper reaches of the Sequana, and poling was hard, the current was fast even in autumn and we were all tired at the end of the day. Gwan rode ahead on horseback, and was waiting for us on the riverbank. We put up our tents in the fields, already harvested. Men and women with baskets were making a small market, an agora, for us to buy food.

Gwan was good at his job.

His partner was an older man, a fisherman. He was not an aristocrat, and he didn't speak much. Or have the pure enjoyment of life that Gwan had. His name was Brach, and he was dark, tall and silent, and he walked with a stoop that looked sinister to a Greek.

Gaius and I were poling together with Seckla and a pair of Marsalian fishermen. I don't even remember their names, but I remember they were both cheerful companions. We were singing hymns – Homer's hymns, all we could remember. Seckla was laughing at the words – his gods were otherwise, and he found ours odd.

Brach was sitting in the stern. He'd poled for an hour, and it was his turn to rest. He was watching the bank, and I was watching him. He seemed alert, and afraid. When I stooped to get my wooden canteen and have a drink, I happened to stumble by him (try retrieving anything on a barge that is ten times as long as it is wide, and you'll see why I stumbled). I got a whiff of him, and he was afraid. He smelled of fear.

'What's the matter?' I asked.

I could see Gwan standing on the bank, and I could see fifty or so farmers and local peasants with their baskets of produce. None of them was a warrior. You can disguise a warrior, but not if you pay attention. Men in top physical training stand and move differently from men who work the land for others. Men at the edge of violence have a different look on their faces. Not that I thought all these things at the time – merely to note that I was conscious that we had more than seventy giant ingots of tin and a lot of gold, too, and that in my heart I knew the Keltoi would try for it, sometime. I couldn't see *anything*.

'What's wrong?' I asked.

Brach glanced at me, his face a dead giveaway, and shrugged. He stared at the water.

'Armour,' I ordered. I shouted the order sternwards to the next boat, and reached for the heavy leather bag with my thorax.

We were armoured and ready for anything in a quarter of an

hour, and the farmers stood on the bank, puzzled, anxious and then downright fearful. They abandoned the bank, and many packed their goods and fled the market. When we landed, we looked like a war band.

Before the sun had set another finger, a dozen chariots appeared, and fifty Keltoi on horseback. I had forty men with spears and shields out as guards while we dragged downed trees to form an abatis – a wall of branches. Not a great defence, but enough to discourage casual looting and easy predation.

The local aristo had an eagle in bronze set on top of his helmet, and wore a knee-length tunic of scale – not a style of armour I'd ever seen before – and it looked as if it would weigh far too much for use in combat. Of course, the great gentry of Gaul travel to war in chariots. I wondered if this was what Lord Achilles looked like.

He spoke to Gwan, saluted and his driver rolled to a stop an arm's-length from me. I had my pais offer him a cup of wine, and he took it, poured a libation like a Greek and drank it off.

'Tell him that I apologize for frightening his people. Tell him, as one warrior to another, that I received a sign – perhaps from my ancestor, Heracles – and had my men get into their armour.' As I spoke, I indicated the plaque that showed Heracles and the Nemean Lion that was affixed to the inside of my aspis.

He listened. And I'd say he understood, as he gave me a sharp glance, dismounted and offered me his hand to clasp. I took it.

He spoke slowly, paused, took off his helmet and spoke again.

'He says, warriors must learn to understand and obey such signs. He says a party of armed men passed his outposts this morning, travelling quickly on horseback, and he has been in armour all day. He says, perhaps your ancestor is not so wrong, after all. He gives you his word that no harm will come to your people tonight.'

I let go his hand. Let me say that sometimes, between people, there is a spark of understanding. It can lead instantly to love, or friendship; to treaties, to alliances, to marriages. This man was clear-eyed and honourable. I would have staked my life on it. Gwan said his name was Collam.

We passed a few minutes looking at each other's war gear. His scale mail was beautifully wrought: the scales were fine, the size of a man's thumb or slightly smaller, and I'd say, as a bronze-smith, that there were four thousand of them in the whole tunic. His helmet was superb: very different from the helmets I made, and he took mine, put it on and moved like a fighter, trying it, while encouraging me with motions to try his.

I found his interesting – airy, open. The cheeks were hinged, the bowl was shallow, the neck curved down like my father's to meet the armour at the back, like the tail of a shrimp or lobster, except without the articulation. There was a narrow brim over the eye, which, even late on an autumn day, kept the sun from my eyes.

Collam made a motion and grinned. He had bright blond hair and enormous moustaches – I don't think I'd ever seen a man with so much moustache.

'He wants to trade,' Gwan said. 'My father is his sister's husband's brother – does that make sense? We're not close, but he's a famous warrior and his words are true.'

I hadn't needed Gwan to tell me that. I loved my helmet – I had made it with my own hands. It fitted me perfectly, and I trusted it.

But when you can't give something away, you are a slave to it. And generosity is one of the virtues. Besides, his helmet was a magnificent piece of work – the eagle on top was an artwork.

I grinned. 'Tell him it is his.'

We fed him. The farmers came back at dusk, when they saw their lord sitting on one of our stools, drinking our wine, and we bought pigs and grain. We also bought some dried fruit and meat.

I was so interested in Collam that I lost track of Brach, and so did Gaius. Collam was the sort of man that Gaius loved, and he sat with us. The Latins are not entirely Keltoi, but they have many words in common, and Gaius's Keltoi was far better than mine, good enough that he could almost converse without Gwan. I missed Sittonax, and I missed Daud.

Play it as you will; it was morning – the night passed uneventfully – when we discovered that Brach was missing. Collam came down to the riverside with his corps of charioteers and cavalry to see us off. I was in my armour, watching the men load the barges and keeping an eye on Gwan, while Seckla and Gaius searched the fields and woods around our camp. Seckla could track. So could a number of the herdsmen.

When Collam came up, we embraced.

'He asks if you'd like to sell any of your tin,' Gwan said.

He was on the main tin route, but then, of course, he was wearing ten pounds of the stuff in his harness. His war band probably ate bronze.

'How much do you want?' I asked.

He shrugged. 'One pig,' he said. Eighty pounds. The value in Marsala would be almost eighty ounces of gold. Twice that in Sicily.

Gwan turned to me. 'He won't – well, trade, precisely. If you give it to him, he will make you gifts of equal value. This sort of thing frustrates the Venetiae—' He smiled.

But I had approached Collam as a warrior. So we were bound to behave like heroes.

Fair enough: I'd been a hero before. Herodikles had a team of men who had just wrestled a pig of tin to the riverside. I waved to stop them from loading it into Herodikles' barge.

'Yours,' I said in passable Keltoi.

That was one-eightieth of all our profits. I was going to look like an idiot if he didn't give me something in return.

He went and lifted it – by himself. He grunted, grinned and put it in his chariot, and the leather and rawhide stretched, and the whole light vehicle sank a little into the riverbank. The charioteer looked as if he might cry.

I said, 'I'm missing a man – a Gaul, lent to me by the Venetiae as a guide. He has wandered off. And I would like to know anything you know about this party of armed men.'

Collam nodded when this was translated. And Gwan grew pale and looked at me.

In Greek, I said, 'Gwan, I suspect you were told to betray me. Yes?'

Gwan couldn't meet my eye.

'Do you want me to tell this famous warrior that you are a hireling of the Venetiae? That you have been paid to lead me to an ambush?' It wasn't quite a shot in the dark.

'They have my father,' he said.

'Gwan, the world is not always as dark as it seems. When Detorix knows that I am gone away south to Marsala and won't return, he'll release your father. Or you can come and find me, and I swear by the immortal gods I'll come back with thirty warriors and take your father back.'

Gwan looked at the ground. Collam asked him something – asked him what was wrong, I think.

He looked at Collam and spoke for a long time.

Collam grew angrier and angrier.

It can be very difficult as an alien in another culture. Coming upon the Keltoi from the sea, it was easy to assume that the Venetiae were typical of the breed – indeed, that they were the lords of the whole people. I had fallen into this trap, and that morning, on the Sequana, I realized that I knew almost nothing of the Keltoi. Collam was no more like Detorix than Detorix was like Tara. Briseis and Euphoria and Aristides and I are all Greek, and yet four more different people could not be imagined. One wants to typify a people, but they are always too diverse to be typified.

At any rate, Collam began to ask questions, and Gwan hesitated to answer, and I began to suspect that Collam was going to injure or kill Gwan on the spot.

'What's the problem?' I asked.

Gwan went on talking to Collam.

I stepped in between them. 'Speak to me,' I said.

'He is angry because ... my father had no right. He says my father had no right.' Gwan was on the edge of tears.

Collam was shouting. His charioteer had his hand on the knife at his belt.

I put a hand on Collam's arm. 'Tell him I'll fix it,' I said.

Collam looked at me.

'He says, what business is it of yours?'

Warriors are all alike, in too many ways. Most of those ways are dark, but not all.

'Gwan, are you my man, or do you serve the Venetiae?' I asked.

Gwan met my eye. 'Yours, my lord.'

'Then tell Collam that I say, "Gwan is my man. I will see to his father's debt".' I offered Collam my hand.

Collam listened. He took two or three deep breaths, and took my hand.

I thanked the gods that I had just given him a small fortune in tin. It had to sway him; he had to accept that I was an aristocrat like him, not a venal river trader.

He drove away in his chariot, and I doubled the guard and told Seckla and Herodikles to hurry the loading. And I took Gwan aside.

'You'd better give this to me straight,' I said.

Gwan shrugged. 'I'm supposed to leave you at the first portage,' he said. 'That would be tonight or tomorrow night.'

'And then what?' I pressed.

'My father's people will put together a caravan of donkeys and horses to go across the hills to the next river,' he said. He shrugged.

'I don't know what happens next. But I can guess.' He looked miserable. 'I think they will ambush you in the hills. Or perhaps—' He shook his head. 'Perhaps my people will ambush you.'

I nodded. 'I think you should come with me, all the way to Marsala. Take a share of the profits and come back and buy your father's freedom.' I looked into his blue eyes. 'You really think your people want to fight me and two hundred of my men?' I asked.

He shook his head.

When we had most of our boats loaded, a pair of heavy wagons came down to the waterside, and two chariots. Collam leaped off the lead chariot as it drove by and landed cleanly on his feet. He was a pleasure to watch, and I would have liked to wrestle with him.

The wagons were full of barrels, and the barrels were his gift to me. We had twelve big casks, and each weighed as much as a pig of tin. I laughed, embraced him and told him through Gwan that Gwan would go with me to Marsala and return rich enough to retrieve his father's debts to the Venetiae. In effect, I involved Collam in an alliance to preserve Gwan's honour – and my convoy.

Collam shook my hand again, and through Gwan, told me that fifty horsemen had crossed his lands the night before and that as far as he knew, Brach was gone.

Fifty horsemen. I laughed. 'They'll need a lot of help,' I said.

Collam offered me twenty warriors, but I patted his shoulder and told him not to worry.

We swapped belts, there on the shore. It was a little like living in the *Iliad*. And then we were away, into the late morning, poling hard upstream.

Gwan usually rode ahead, but I kept him by me – the best way to avoid temptation is to avoid temptation, in fact – and I sent Seckla, who was a brilliant rider, to lead a dozen other men who could run. I've already said that the Sequana runs like a snake: a few men, running and resting, can easily pace a convoy of boats.

It was mid-afternoon when we ran out of water. There were good landing stages; this was the point from which the Venetiae transshipped their own cargoes. A big town stood there, well fortified with heavy palisades and a stone socle under the timber ramparts.

Gwan's father was a minor lord in these parts. But the men who were to form our donkey train didn't seem to be part of a conspiracy: the animals were already assembled, and they had panniers sewn to hold the big pigs of tin. There were eighty animals in the train, with forty men to handle them. The whole assemblage cost us four pigs of tin.

In the town, which was both smelly and quite marvellous, I found a gem – a goldsmith whose skill, while barbaric, was still very fine. I traded him a small amount of our gold for a pair of arm rings such as the local gentry wore. I liked them, and I needed to wear my status. It is often that way, when you are among foreigners. In Boeotia, they would know who I was even if I was naked and covered in soot from the smithy. In Gaul, I needed a pair of heavy gold arm rings. Herodikles mocked me for turning barbarian, but I think the arm rings stood us all in good stead.

We drank wine, ate well, and a day later, we were away. In any place we lingered, we spent too much. I had almost one hundred and eighty men, and they cost me an amount of gold equal to the size of your little finger *every day* just to keep in food and wine. Let me put it this way: we took a rich treasure from the Phoenicians, and two hundred slaves. The treasure, every ounce of it, about paid for the food. It had been the same when I served with Miltiades – there isn't much economy to piracy.

On the other hand, without two hundred hungry men with an absolute loyalty to me, I doubt that we'd ever have got so much tin over the hills.

At any rate, we enjoyed Agedinca. Gwan was feasted, and through him, Seckla and Gaius and I met the lords of the Senones, the people who controlled the upper valley of the Sequana. They were rich in good farmland, and in the possession of the trade route, and their halls were full of armour and magnificent plates and cups. Their women wore more jewellery than Persian princesses.

We camped well outside of town, and we rotated a guard of forty men on our camp. By now, every former slave had a sword, a helmet, a spear or two and a shield, and I drilled them myself, teaching them the dances of Ares each day. I had two reasons for my care: first, that they might fight well, if we had to fight; and second, to keep them busy. They were oarsmen, and they had every reason to be bored.

When our donkey train was ready to cross the hills, the King of the Senones came to see us off. He admired my warriors, and offered me a hundred more men.

I bowed respectfully and refused them. I didn't want to have to trust him.

He shrugged. 'The Aedui are our enemies,' he said. 'They often attack the tin trains. Be wary.'

Gwan nodded. After we had started up the valley, he rode up to me – we had two-dozen horses – and pointed up the pass. 'If the Venetiae are going to ambush you,' he said, 'They won't do it themselves. They'll pay someone to attack you. The Aedui are the obvious choice – they attack trains all the time.'

'And yet the king said nothing of the fifty horsemen,' I noted.

Gwan looked away. 'He is my cousin,' Gwan said. 'But not a friend to me or to my father. I think perhaps he takes your tin to build your train – and takes silver from the Venetiae to allow your train to be ambushed.'

Gaius said, 'If that's so, then the baggage-handlers and the teamsters will all desert. Or attack us.'

Gwan shook his head. 'That would be hard to work out,' he said.

I wanted to trust Gwan, but there was a barrier between us, deeper than the cultural divide. I truly wished that I had Daud or Sittonax with me. Leukas was Alban, and too far removed from the politics – if I may call them that – of the Gauls. Leukas distrusted Gwan all the time. Leukas was also jealous of Gwan's continuing success with every maiden – I use the term loosely – on the river.

People are very complicated.

Men told me that it was six days over the hills to Lugdunum, the town at the head of the Rhodanus River that flows into the Inner Sea. The first night in the hills it was cold, and men pulled their cloaks tight around them and lay closer to other men, or built their fires higher. We had camped at a traders' campsite – so it was stripped of all useful wood, you can bet. I sent fifty men off into the hills for wood, and another ten armed men to watch them. We built big fires, and shivered, and Gaius and I went from fire to fire, reminding men that we were ten days from Marsala and the Inner Sea, to encourage them that if we had to fight, it would be worth doing.

At a fire, one of the original crew of the *Lydia* asked me what the shares of the tin would be. It was a fair question, and one that had occupied me.

We'd started as a half-dozen men with a dream. We were coming home with more than a hundred freed slaves. Only sixteen men had died on the whole trip through accident, quarrels and Apollo's arrows, and the men who were almost home had begun to wonder what they might receive.

And, of course, the men who had started from Marsala thought they were more worthy than the men who had been rescued from slavery. Gian told me point-blank that the former slaves now had their freedom – that was their share.

'And weapons!' shouted another Marsalian shepherd.

Greed. They'd been like brothers when we were rowing for our lives in the fog, but ten days from home—

I assured everyone that the shares would be fair. There was probably some half-truth to my statement, because I had yet to think of a simple, logical mathematical solution. But the mere promise that there *would* be a payout was enough.

The hills were magnificent; greener and more heavily wooded than hills in Greece. I thought they were quite high, until we climbed over the summit of the second pass and arrived at a mighty hill fort set at the top of a rocky crag and surrounded by stone walls built like any fortress wall in the Ionian Sea. It was a puzzle of giant rocks, as if the whole wall had been built by Titans. From those heights, I could see a range of mountains to the east that rose like jagged teeth. I had never seen mountains so high, even on the coast of Asia. They were breathtaking, at least in part because they were so far away. The Senones all told me they were the Alps. The hill fortress was a capital of the Aedui, but they offered us no violence. In fact, the lord of the place – I forget his name – told me that a Greek had designed his walls and taught his people to build them. I thought about what it would be like to be working so far from home. It cost me a whole pig of tin to feed my people across the hills. They had their own gold and silver here. They wanted tin.

And then we were down the other side of the pass, down the path into the high valleys of the Cares River. Fewer farms, and more trees.

My pig of tin had purchased more than just food. It purchased six more horses and some information, and I was aware that there were fifty horsemen ahead of me on the road. North of Lugdunum, where the Cares flows into the Rhodanus, we marched down the valley and I saw the sparkle and sun-dazzle of Helios on naked steel, and I knew.

I trusted my Senones by then. They didn't seem shifty enough to be traitors, and they laughed a lot and drank hard. It is difficult for a Greek to distrust such men. Despite which, I had a former oarsman stand with every Senone in the train. And then we all armoured ourselves.

You may say that I was broadcasting to the ambush that we knew they were there.

I was. Why fight? If they wanted to slip away into the hills, I wanted to let them. My guides and my drovers swore we were a day from the navigable waters of the Rhodanus. I didn't want to fight. In fact, all I wanted to do was to get home. The charms of travel and exploration had faded; I was beginning to feel old. In fact, I was thirty years old that autumn, and the age of it was in my bones.

I watched the hills, and the steel moved, but it did not disperse. Whoever was up there had enough men to fight my two hundred.

When we were armed, I sent my dozen horsemen to scout. As an aside, Greeks are not much good as scouts. Greek cavalry tend to fight other Greek cavalry – it's like any other Greek contest – and the losers don't go back to tell their friends what happened, I can tell you. But Seckla's people have different notions of scouting, and Seckla led his boys down the valley and across the fields on a long sweep while I got my train organized and pushed my main body of spearmen out in front of it. I left eighty men with the Senones – a fine reserve, and at the same time a good baggage guard. My other hundred pushed forward in a line four men deep, a small, shallow phalanx that nonetheless covered the train behind them. They weren't closed tight – the ground was far too broken – but they were close enough to support each other, ebbing and flowing around the patches of woods and rocks like a stream of hoplites.

Seckla sprang the trap, if it could be called a trap. He encountered a blocking force at a small bridge and rode away before they could throw javelins at him – then found one of the flank forces moving along some hedges to the right. He rode back to me as we closed on the low stone bridge.

He pointed. 'Sixty men at the bridge, lightly armed. At least a hundred to the right in the woods. Those horsemen must be somewhere, but there's no dung on the road and no horse signs to the right.'

Friends, that's a scouting report. Honest, factual and terse.

I had put Demetrios in charge of the baggage train, and I took command of the phalanx myself, with Gaius and Gian as my deputies. I got them all together, quickly. 'We're going right over the bridge,' I said. 'We'll smash them and move across, and then the spearmen will switch from advance guard to rearguard while the train moves as fast as they can. We'll be out of their reach before their flanks can close on us.' I pointed at the bad going – the fallow fields, the marsh on our right. 'Don't lose your nerve. Just keep going. My only worry is that they have more men in ambush on the other side of the stream. Seckla, that's your part – as soon as we clear the bridge, ride through and look down the road. Everyone got it?'

Everyone did.

I rode to the head of the phalanx, dismounted and gave my horse to my boy. '*Philoi!*' I shouted. 'You are better men, and you are better armed. See the men by the bridge? We will sweep them aside like a woman sweeps dust off the floor. And then we will go *home*.'

They roared.

I was glad that they were roaring, because my stomach was somersaulting like a landed fish. My quick count was that the enemy – I had to assume they were the enemy – had three hundred warriors and another fifty cavalry. Odds of three to two sound heroic, but in a small fight, a few men are an enormous advantage. The ground was passable for cavalry; hardly ideal, but fifty Saka archers could have destroyed my whole force. Luckily, Gaulish noblemen don't use bows. Ares be praised.

I took my place in the ranks and raised my spear. 'Let's go!' I said. And like Miltiades at Marathon, I called: 'Let's run!'

We ran at them.

The entire time I held my command meeting and gave my little speech, the men on the right flank had been moving forward cautiously. It is a thing men do – they sort of *pretend* to cling to cover, even after they have been discovered.

My archers – the same men who performed the role on board ship, but without Doola's magnificent archery – began to drop shafts among the more confident men on the right. I don't think they hit a man, but they slowed the right flank of the ambush to a literal belly crawl.

We ran forward to the bridge. The Aedui were in a shield wall, about forty men with javelins, big shields, a few well-armoured men in front. Gaius and I took the centre of our spearmen into them, and our flank men went right down into the stream and up the other side. In spring, I'm sure the stream was full and the bridge was required, but in mid-autumn, all they lost was their close order as they poured over the streambed.

I didn't have time to watch. I ran forward, and despite the old wound in my leg, I flew. When I reached the Aedui shield wall, it was just me and Gaius.

We had never really fought together.

Perhaps we sought to impress one another. But neither of us would give a step, and neither of us slowed, and so we hurtled straight into their ranks. I got my aspis up and forward onto the spears and I let them slow me, and then I leaped as high as I could and threw my spear – hard – into the front rank, and came down without getting a spear in my foot or knee or head – alive, in other words.

Gaius must have thrown a pace farther out, because a man fell, and for a moment, their ranks rippled—

I put my shoulder into the back of my aspis as I landed, head down, and my impetus slammed a man back even as I got my kopis out of the scabbard. The long swords the Gauls used only hampered them, this close. I know, because one rang off my helmet immediately. I was in their ranks, moving among them, slashing right and left. I doubt I killed a man, but I'll wager I *hit* six in as many heartbeats.

And about then, the rest of my spearmen hit their shield wall, and they folded. They began to break from the front, not the back, and suddenly they were dead men – just like that. Let me say, we outnumbered them four to one, and we had every advantage: terrain, flanks, depth and armour. But their shield wall couldn't hold *two* of us.

It is a difference in attitude, eh? As many Persians would have killed us. Hmm ... Or perhaps not, eh?

I burst out through the back of their shallow line, and my flankers were climbing the bank and I was almost across the low bridge. To the right, a hundred men or more were coming at the flank of the tin train. It would be close whether they got to it, or it got across the bridge.

To the left, the river guarded my flank. Or so I thought. But when I looked, there were fifty armoured horsemen swimming the river. The same low water that had allowed me to cross the streambed—

Well, I can be a fool, sometimes.

And my spearmen were running the Gauls down and killing them instead of stopping to rally.

Oh, for a hundred real soldiers! Even real pirates.

Men in victory are as irrational as men in defeat. Only a veteran knows the truth – that it's not over until it is over.

Seckla hadn't crossed yet. I held up a hand and stopped him.

'If there's an ambush, the spearmen will find it,' I said. 'Stop the horsemen. And take the archers.'

Seckla nodded and rode off, and I ran – in armour, damn it – back to the donkey train. They were trotting along the road. Demetrios was at their head.

'Move!' I roared. *'Move!'*

I looked to the right. The archers lofted another volley, and hit not one but two Aedui warriors, and the rest fell on their faces. My archers turned and followed Seckla, and the Aedui rose to their feet and came forward – slowly at first, and then with more spirit.

I had been far too confident.

Panicked men do not make good animal-handlers. Panicked men lead to panicked animals, and panicked animals run. In all directions.

In a matter of heartbeats, an easy victory had become a disaster. My train didn't cross the bridge. It ran off, away from the charging Aedui and towards the river. A donkey with an eighty-pound ingot of tin doesn't run all that well, but it will run as fast as it can.

The horsemen were almost across. The archers were starting to engage them. The range was close, and the archers had time and felt safe, at least for the moment.

Horses and men began to die.

Behind me, the Aedui from the bridge were dying. But my precious spearmen had run too far, all but Alexandros's marines and maybe a dozen others.

I could have screamed in my frustration. Even Gaius had run off after the Aedui. Gwan – I could see his Gaulish gear – was beside him, halfway down the valley.

On the other hand, when the animals broke for the river, the eighty men in reserve ceased to matter as baggage guards. That's how it goes.

'Demetrios!' I called. He did not look like a great warrior; he wasn't very tall and his helmet looked several sizes too big. 'Face to the right!' I called. I ran to his men.

I'd like to say that the enemy didn't expect us to abandon our tin, but they were not under anyone's control either, at this point. I put myself at the head of Demetrios's baggage guards and we charged the Aedui on foot, who had been pricked by the archers and crawled across the marsh.

A few of them died, but the rest chose to run, evading our short charge and running back into the marsh. There were some desultory spear casts from both sides.

I needed a decisive result.

I wasn't going to get one.

'Hold them here,' I said to Demetrios, and ran – panting, now, with effort – back to my marines and Giannis and a few comrades.

'Follow me,' I spat. I ran down the slope towards the river.

The cavalrymen were trying to kill Seckla, and Seckla was refusing to be drawn into a fight, and the archers were running around, trying to stay alive and occasionally launching a shaft. I only had six archers, and they were the balance of the fight. The cavalrymen didn't seem to know that, though. Phokis, one of the former slaves and a fine archer, died from a chance javelin throw, but he was one of the few.

At any rate ... I charged fifty cavalrymen with twenty infantry.

I didn't have a spear to throw.

It was foolishness. They were brilliant horsemen – as good as Persians – and one of them saw me, and all by himself he turned out of the chase for Seckla and rode at me. I should have stopped running, but I didn't. I ran right at him.

He was grinning. He had a scale shirt down to his thighs, a fine helmet and two javelins. He threw one just before he reached me. It bounced off the face of my aspis and then I sidestepped and his horse sidestepped – he struck with his javelin, hitting me in the head. My sword licked out and caught his leg, and then he was past me, and I was alive.

I shook my head, and the eagle fell off.

A dozen more of their cavalrymen turned, now, eager to emulate their fellow. And he was circling wide behind me, coming back for another try.

'Form on me,' I croaked, and set my feet. I remember praying to Heracles, and feeling like a fool. I had come all this way, and I was losing my train of tin. And perhaps my life or my freedom.

I gritted my teeth.

A dozen cavalrymen may not sound like much. After all, I was a hero of Marathon! I had faced down a hundred Persian noblemen – the finest horsemen in the circle of the world.

But the Gauls were, man for man, marvellous horsemen, perhaps the equals of the Persians, and they were fresh, delighted to be fighting, dangerous men on well-trained horses. I was tired, and defeat has its own fatigue. And we were losing.

Behind me, the Aedui infantry were gaining courage, and working their way forward.

Far to the south, I could see Gaius's Etruscan feathers waving on the brows of his helmet. He was rallying my phalanx. He would only be ten minutes late. In time, perhaps, to rescue my corpse.

My marines and some shepherds pressed in around me.

'Spears up!' I remember roaring.

There's a belief that horses won't face a spear point, or a well-ordered host of men. I don't know – perhaps it becomes true at some point, if the host is wide enough. Certainly, I've seen five hundred Athenians turn the charge of the very best of the Persian noble cavalry, the horses turning away before a single man had died.

But the Gauls trained their horses differently. The Gauls came at us in no particular order, but one man, on a beautiful white horse, was in front, and he came at me at a dead gallop, and when he was a few horse-lengths away, I realized that he was not slowing down and that I was literally trapped between my comrades.

So naturally, I leaped out and charged him.

What would you do?

I got my aspis up – no low blows from a horseman. I was on the cavalryman's bridle-hand side, so he had to cut cross-body at me, and I took his blow on my sword – held high over my head, across my aspis face – and I let the blow roll off my blade like rain falling off a temple roof, turned my hand and struck. It was a short blow, but I had plenty of fear to power it, and he had no armour on his thighs, and then the next horseman hit me in the back and I went down.

My cuirass took the blow, but I went face down over my aspis and I stunned myself on the rim of my own shield. A horse kicked me as I fell, right on the point of the hip.

I *thought* I'd got a spear through my armour. I assumed I was dead. I was down, and the pain was intense, and when I tried my legs, they didn't work.

My legs didn't work.

I don't know how long I lay there. I was conscious, but I had taken two bad blows and a light ring to my head, and I had every reason to think I was raven's food.

Then a riderless horse came pounding across the ground at me, and without conscious thought, I rolled myself over to avoid it.

With my legs.

Thought is action. I got my feet under me and powered to an upright position. My sword was lying there. My helmet had twisted on my head. I remember standing there on a stricken field, unable to decide which I should do first – retrieve the sword? Fix the helmet?

Aye, laugh if you like. Pain and fatigue and desperation make you stupid.

My marines had scattered. Giannis helped me get myself together.

Six of the Gauls' cavalrymen were down. And Seckla was leading the others in a merry dance.

Suddenly, we were in a stalemate. A *stasis*. I muttered to Giannis, and he began shouting for the men to come to me.

Other men pointed at me.

Demetrios had all of the reserve together, and they came to me in a block. The Aedui infantry were still hesitant.

My archers were in a patch of brush, down by the water, and they were carefully loosing at the bolder Gaulish horsemen. They didn't hit many men. But they hit a great many horses. And the Gauls are tender on their horses.

When I went down, we were losing. When I got up, we weren't.

War's like that. I made a good plan, and it failed. The enemy plan was foolish, and it nearly succeeded.

But now we had some advantages. So I ignored that dull, metallic ache in my hip, and I picked up a fine Gaulish spear and pointed it down the field at the riverbank, where our donkeys and horses were pinned by a handful of mounted Gauls.

'There's our tin, friends,' I said.

'Arimnestos!' shouted Giannis. I thought he was trying to get my attention, but Demetrios shouted it too. In a moment, a hundred men were bellowing my name as if it were a war cry.

I'm not ashamed to say I almost burst into tears. And when we charged, I had the feeling – that old feeling – that I was invincible.

That's the daimon of combat, thugater. One moment you think you are dead, and the next, you are full of of piss and vinegar, ready for anything.

I've seen a few defeats, but far more victories, and men die in defeat faster than they do in victory.

We slammed into them. No, that's a lie, friends. We ran at them, and most of them ran from us – into the river. The men chasing Sekla were cut off, well up the ridge to our right. And in a few moments, we were all around our pack animals. The stubborn panic of the average donkey is a two-edged sword. They ran from us, but they weren't going to tamely submit to our enemies, either.

If men hadn't died, it would have been like comedy, Thugater.

We'd run around in all directions, our bandit enemies had largely run around us, and now they were running away. I'm not sure if that counts as a battle or not. We lost nine men, dead and badly wounded, and the worst part was killing off our own wounded – Garun, a Marsalian fisherman who's been with me since I poured bronze for the ram-spur, and others just as good, or just as deserving of life. But when a man has a spear right through his guts so that the head comes out the back—

—Best he have brave friends.

The Aedui infantry on our side of the stream faded the moment it became clear that their noble cavalry wasn't going to fight. We took eight of them, too – tired men who didn't have the muscles to run away.

The enemy had about thirty dead and wounded and twenty captured. A dozen of the captured were cavalrymen. They couldn't cross the gully to freedom, and Gaius closed the bridge, and Demetrios and I worked with Sekla to herd them into a circle. They were mostly very young men, and all the fight had gone out of them, and I think they'd have surrendered sooner except that they got the idea we were going to execute them.

Did they think we were fools?

We used them as hostages, of course. We sent the youngest, a boy of seventeen, up the ridge to tell his lord that we had them, and then we made camp. We spend two hours on our ditch and our abatis, and then we collapsed in exhaustion. A fight – even an easy fight – takes it out of you, and the affray at the bridge on the Rhodanus was a sharp fight with a bad bit.

The next morning, we rose and packed our animals carefully, and marched with a strong advance guard – twenty men. After all, we'd captured a dozen horses. And we now had a dozen men in fine scale shirts.

By evening, we were camping within bowshot of the walls of Ludunca. The town had hundreds of timber houses and some dozens of stone houses, as well as four temples and a stone outer wall. We paid a fine for camping in someone's field.

Gwan and his Senones unpacked the donkeys and the horses and the carts, and turned them around for home. Their part was done. At Ludunca, all of our tin was loaded onto barges. These weren't made of a single tree trunk like those on the Sequaana. These were made of planks – as few as three very wide planks, or as many as nine. The sides were formed of single, heavy planks that fitted perfectly to the strakes of the bottom. Again, the boats were designed to take the standard barrels, but could also hold our pigs of tin.

Vasilios was fascinated. He told us all, several times, that the way they built boats depended on the available timber. He was especially impressed with the way the Galles used iron nails to clench the timbers to cross supports – very alien to the Greek construction method, but very strong.

He showed me one in particular that impressed me. The floor of a particularly large and heavy barge had cross beams to support the side of the boards and to keep them together. These boards had holes drilled in them and then in the supports, and pegs of oak were driven into those holes, and then iron nails were driven into the pegs, forcefully expanding them against the wood around them. The result was watertight and as strong as – well, as iron. And oak.

We loaded for Marsala even while we negotiated with the local Aedui for the release of our hostages. They were all important young men – not the infantry, no one even wanted them back, but the horsemen. In the end, I released them all for a pound of gold and some casks of ale.

I don't think I've mentioned that we figured out that Callum had traded us twelve casks of bee's wax for a pig of tin. I had no idea if that was a fair trade, but people had begun to make offers on the bee's wax already. Without Doola, I was helpless to guess the value. Demetrios said it would trade well in many places, because it was so clear and white.

I have to smile. I had a picture in my head of Arimnestos, the Killer of Men, standing in front of a group of unwed maidens – perhaps at the temple of Artmeis at Brauron. I was holding up a ball of pure white beeswax, and telling them that it was the very thing to use on their best white linen thread.

Well, I think it's funny.

The trip down river from Ludunca was uneventful. We reached the Inner Sea at the old Phoneician port at Arla. I'm not ashamed to say that I threw myself down on the beach and kissed the sand and the water. I was not alone. We ran up and down the beach, and then we ran again, until the running became a kind of celebration.

The boatmen were cautious about the edge of the sea, but they got their barges all the way along the coast to Massalia, almost one hundred stades, poling along the beaches. It is a protected part of the sea, but it seemed dangerous to me, perhaps because I had been through so much that I feared the loss of everything at the very end.

But one fine day in late autumn – just the edge of winter, with a bitter wind blowing out of the west, and a chill in the air that could make a man ill – we sighted Tarsilla. People came down to the water's edge, and we landed on the beach, landed our pigs of tin, our little remaining silver, our bee's wax, Gallish wine, hides and all. We moved them all into Vasilios's shed that he had used to protect our ship when he was building it.

We had a feast on the beach, and the next day we celebrated the Feast of Dionysus in style, with wine and song and even a play done by one of the teams of actors from Massalia.

Two more days, and Demetrios of Phokia arrives with sixty men and a pair of oxen to kill, and gave another feast for our return. We spent two days telling him of our travels.

He spent both days telling us of war with Carthage.

Carthage had struck at Sicily in our absence. And not just Sicily – the Carthaginians were using force to get absolute mastery of all the trade routes in the western Inner Sea. Carthage had been involved in wars on Sardinia for fifty years – and had squandered armies and fleets attempting to dominate the stiff necked peoples of the island. By the time Telesinus was Archon in Athens, Carthage had at last dominated the Sardana, and was now attempting to use her new ports to attack Greek colonies like Massalia – and Syracusa.

But the Greek world had not stood still during the year I had been away. Gelon, the Tyrant of Gela and Naxos, had seized power in Syracusa.

That was news. I knew a Sicilian Greek aristocrat named Gelon – in fact, I had enslaved him. It couldn't be the same man – the Sicilian Tyrant had never been any man's slave – but I wondered if my Gelon had made it home.

At any rate, Gelon – the tyrant – was unifying the Greek cities of Sicily and Magna Greca against Carthage. Not everyone joined him. Rich cities like Himera on Sicily and Reggium in southern Italy chose to remain independent.

Really, it was the Ionian Revolt played out in miniature. It had been going on for years – as one or another Greek state rose to prominence and led the resistance against Carthage, and was conquered or bought off, another would come. But Gelon of Gela – a right bastard, if Dionysius the Phocaean was to be believed – had at least achieved the building of an alliance.

I wondered what his conquest of Syracusa meant.

We were lying on the beach – it was still warm enough to be outside with a bonfire – eating beef and lobster. Dionysius the Phocaean was licking his teeth. 'There is no side I want,' he said. 'I don't want the Carthaginians to enslave me, and Gelon is a horror. He enslaved half of the free population of Syracusa – you know that?'

My blood ran cold.

'Women, children – sold off or put in brothels. Men made into oarsmen, or forced labour on farms. Gelon won't allow a lower class – a Thetis class. Claims they destabilize the state. He insists he'll have only aristocrats and slaves, like Sparta.' Dionysius picked his teeth and looked at me. 'I don't like either side.'

I lay on my straw paliase, using a metal pick to get the meat out of the body of a lobster and drinking wine. 'I owe Carthage something. I'm of a mind to trade my share of the tin, take a ship while I have a crew – a fighting crew—' I paused. I hadn't been aware that this was my intention. But suddenly it was.

I nodded. 'But first, I'm going to have Demetrios here go sell the tin, while I go back and find my friends,' I said. 'Doola, Daud, Sittonax, Alexandros – they're probably right behind us on the road. And I owe something to young Gwan there.'

'Winter will close the passes,' Demetrios said. 'And I won't be selling any tin this winter, either.'

As if to prove him right, a cold gust of wind blew down off the mountains at our backs.

Part III
Massalia

ἔτι δὲ τούτου καταγελαστότερον, εἰ Φωκαεῖς μὲν φεύγοντες τὴν βασιλέως τοῦ μεγάλου δεσποτείαν, ἐκλιπόντες τὴν Ἀσίαν εἰς Μασσαλίαν ἀπῴκησαν, ἡμεῖς δ᾽ εἰς τοσοῦτον μικροψυχίας ἔλθοιμεν ὥστε τὰ προστάγματα τούτων ὑπομεῖναι, ὧν ἄρχοντες ἅπαντα τὸν χρόνον διετελέσαμεν.

Even more should we deserve the ridicule of men if, having before us the example of the Phocaeans who, to escape the tyranny of the Great King, left Asia and founded a new settlement at Massilia, we should sink into such abjectness of spirit as to submit to the dictates of those whose masters we have always been throughout our history.

Isocrates, *Archidamus* 84

14

I didn't go anywhere that winter. I sat in Massalia with my smithy and a supply of tin the other bronze smiths envied, and cast a pair of light rams – carefully designed and carefully cast, according to my own theories. Around the headland at Tarsilla, Vasilios laid down the keel for a trieres. She would carry one hundred seventy-two oarsmen and each oarsmen would have a dactyl over two cubits in which to breathe. I had copper, and I had tin, and I traded Dionysius a competed ram for all the timber. I told the oarsmen that I would need them in the spring, and that the payoff for the tin adventure would happen at the spring feast of Demeter.

Gaius stayed the winter with me. He disdained working in the forge, but he would sit in a chair and chat with me while I worked, which made the time pass pleasantly enough.

Winter passed slowly.

It was interesting, the experience of being rich. Some men were jealous, and some were openly admitting it. Of course, I had two hundred 'clients' in the form of the former slave oarsmen, the marines, the shepherds and the fishermen. None of them seemed to want to go back to work.

Piracy has many ills, and the greatest may be that when you teach a hard-working boy that he can steal and kill for gold, he may feel that hauling nets is dull.

And there was an element of comedy to my riches. After all, the tin ingots were still stacked in the warehouse, and before midwinter, when one of the ingots showed signs of the tin illness, we brought them into the house we'd built and kept them warm, which seemed to help.

You probably don't know about tin blight. Tin, when it gets cold and wet, can develop an illness like wheat – it grows a white mould, and once the mould spreads, the metal can be ruined. Indeed, if you leave the tin long enough, one day you'll walk in and find your fortune in tin is nothing but a small pile of white dust. This was one of the reasons smiths couldn't build up stores of tin. As a smith, I knew a few tricks – I knew to run over the outside of the pigs with flax tow and pork fat; I knew to keep them warm. But I spent my winter in a constant anxiety about the tin.

And that wasn't my only anxiety. Again, my riches were more apparent than real. We had some gold – the ransom of the Gaul aristocrats, the gold we took all the way back in Iberia – but it was only really enough to pay for food and wine for the oarsmen who remained.

It was the *rumour* of our wealth in tin that made us rich. Some men thought we had thousands of mythemnoi of tin – other men thought we'd discovered a new source. All ascribed to us an almost heroic level of wealth.

As the winter wore on, and I worked in my shop in Massalia, I began to fear what those rumours might sound like out on the Great Blue. Somewhere, I feared that men just like me were hearing of the fabulous wealth we'd won. And were fingering their swords.

After the midwinter festivals, I laid out the rest of my hoard to have my oarsmen build a pair of towers down by the beach. And I put the word out in Massalia that I was looking for archers.

Massalia isn't a big town. At most, there are a thousand free men, with their families; another thousand slave men, or perhaps a little more, and then another few hundred Gauls, mostly jobbing labourers or craftsmen. While there are caravan guards working the tin trade and the wine trade, there aren't enough professional soldiers in the town to make a company, and when I enquired around the wine houses for more archers, most men shook their heads. Archery isn't all that popular among the Gauls.

In fact, as Dionysius said one evening on a kline in my townhouse, I already had the biggest body of soldiers in the town. He didn't sound jealous.

His new ship, *Massalia*, was being built in a stone ship shed down by the beach. He was planning to go to sea to prey on the Phoenicians, and to protect the Massalian trade. Increasingly, as winter passed and we talked, I was of a mind to join him. But only after

I'd found Doola, who I hoped – and prayed – was wintering with his wife, somewhere on the other side of the Alps.

Spring came late, after a great deal of rain. My new ship – which I called *Lydia* despite some superstitious qualms – was taking shape. But Demetrios's new merchantman, *Sikel Herakles*, was almost complete.

We were standing on the beach in the rain, looking at the hulls.

'I'll take her to sea as soon as she's ready,' Demetrios said. He licked his lips as a boy does when a girl shows a bit of thigh or breast – sorry, girls. These things happen, and I'm sure they are all errors, eh?

'With the tin?' I asked.

He nodded quietly.

'Where do you plan to sell it?' I asked.

'Syracusa. Or just possibly Rome.' He shrugged. 'I'd like to have Doola back.'

'I'd like you to wait for me,' I said. 'Seventy pigs of tin – a rich prize for a pirate, and everyone's had the winter to hear of our success.' I shook my head. 'Please wait for me.'

He narrowed his eyes.

'I was trading these waters before I ever knew you,' I said.

We looked at each other. 'Listen,' I said. 'I'm not *telling* you, I'm asking. Doola will want to be here for the sale. He has contacts; he understands things—' I paused. I could tell I was going the wrong way.

'I was trading tin when you were off being a pirate in the east,' he said.

'And because I'm an excellent pirate, I want you to consider that in every little port on the Inner Sea, men like me are gathering over cheap wine and entertaining themselves with stories of how Arimnestos of Plataea and his friends went and got a thousand mythemnoi of tin.' I shrugged. 'Do what you like, Demetrios. It's as much yours as mine.'

'I *know* it's as much mine as yours,' Demetrios said quietly. 'Do you?'

I crossed my arms. 'What's that supposed to mean?'

'Equal shares for the seven of us. And all your oarsmen's pay comes out of your share. They aren't my men. They don't work for me.' He spat. 'They don't get a dactyl of my tin.'

To say I was taken aback wouldn't do justice to my feelings. 'We wouldn't have any tin without them,' I said.

He shrugged. 'Says you.'

'Demetrios!' I shouted. 'What— We swore by Zeus and Heracles. Don't be like this. We need everyone together to decide on the shares.'

He turned away. 'Doola and the others are dead.'

'Why do you think so?' I asked him, following him along the beach.

'If they were alive, they would be here.' He kept walking. 'It is you and me and Gaius and Seckla. But Gaius and Seckla are *your* men, not my friends.'

Riches. The root of all evil, if you ask me.

So I spent the winter worrying about Doola and Daud and Alexandros and the rest, and about pirates taking my treasure, and tin blight and friendship. Not the best winter.

I also looked for love, and found nothing. I bought a slave girl I fancied, and she was temperamental, anxious, ill used and mostly not very interested in what I purchased her for. Her name was Dais and she was Iberian, and she hated my pais and he hated her, and she was jealous of everyone in my life and at the same time demanding and lazy. She had a beautiful body. She had been badly treated. I felt for her; I caught her slashing her arms with my bronze razor, once. I had enough to worry about. Nor did I feel that by freeing her, I'd do her any favour. She couldn't take care of herself.

Before the winter was over, I hauled her by the ear down to the market and sold her to a temple priest. Chastity was better than Dais.

The rains came and went, and in late spring, well after the first feasts of Demeter, I gathered my archers and marines – sixteen men – and we bought good horses and headed up the coast to Arla. I left Gaius with Demetrios, and that was a hard parting. Demetrios had left our shared house and moved in with a Sikel slave woman he'd bought, and he was making it fairly clear that we were not friends. He was openly offensive to Seckla, and cautious with Gaius.

Tilla, his slave woman, was just as difficult as he. She seemed to feel we were all in a state of near war. Perhaps this is a Sikel thing, but she wouldn't unbar their door when I came to say goodbye. She shouted that she knew I'd come to kill her.

By Zeus, I was angry.

I went to embrace Vasileos. He and Gaius were laying down another keel – Gaius had decided to order another trireme before mine was even complete. He was going to go home a rich and powerful man – if he could find oarsmen.

Vasileos heard my tale about Tilla and shook his head. 'She is a witch,' he said. 'She has turned Demetrios into a very small man, and now she seeks to poison him against the rest of us.'

I shrugged. 'It's the tin. I've seen this with soldiers and pirates – enough money makes men go mad.'

Vasileos shrugged. 'Your ship will be ready when you return.'

Gaius hugged me. 'I'll watch Demetrios.'

As my little cavalcade rode out of town, I happened to see Demetrios watching from the window of his house. So the bastard *had* been home.

By comparison with Tarsilla, life on the trail was easy, pleasant and adventurous. The wet early spring had given way to an early summer, and the ground was dry. We had two horses for every man. I had Seckla, of course, and Giannis, and Megakles, the eldest of the fishermen who had made the voyage with us and who showed no inclination to go back to his nets. He was old to be a soldier – well over forty, and not much of a fighter – but he was one of those men who can do or fix almost anything, and he was unbelievably tough. He never complained about rations, never minded the weather and never minded work. If I don't mention him often, it's because he seldom spoke, but he had a smile – a wonderful smile when he was happy, and a slightly ironic smile when he felt that someone wasn't pulling their weight. His entire ethical system seemed to revolve around how much work a man did. He seemed to think highly of me, but he wasn't above mutely handing me a sharp knife and a lot of raw pork with a silent look that said, 'Hey! Don't be a pompous fuck. Do some work.' A very expressive look, for one small smile and a slightly raised eyebrow.

The first night, we stayed on a farm west of Tarsilla. The second night we were in Massalia, drinking wine with Dionysius. He wished us luck, and despite some hard heads, we were away in the dark, picking our way across the tracks to Arla, going up the ridges past the shepherds and into the high hills. It only took us two days to make Arla and I truly hoped – I don't know why – to find Doola there, or some rumour of him.

After Arla, we became a war band. We rode every day in formation, with three scouts well in front, a main body, a rearguard.

Twenty men in armour on horseback is a lot of men, in the high country behind Arla. The Greek homesteaders feared us, and the Gauls barred their doors. We slept in the open, and when it rained, we were wet. Several of my marines had taken Gaul scale shirts – Anchises, one of Dionysius' men from Lade, and his brother Darius (and what an unpopular name *that* must have been during the Ionian revolt). When we had been on the trail a week, they were in despair over their shirts, which were turning brown despite relatively good weather.

'What you need is a dozen slaves apiece to keep you polished,' I said.

Megakles showed them how to use ash, tow and olive oil to polish iron, but the amount of work involved staggered them.

Living outdoors is a different skill from sailing on ships. Horse care, all by itself, can become a full-time job. Every man had two horses, and they had to be curried, blanketed, picketed out and fed – every night – and curried and fed in the morning. And being horses, we had one down sick before we left Massalia and another lame at Arla. Between maintaining armour, cooking food and caring for horses, every one of us was fully employed from dawn to dark.

Horses. Really, if there was only a way to live without them. They don't love me, and I don't love them. I'm a passable rider, and a passable charioteer, too – I was trained to chariots in my youth, as some of you may remember. And I love the look of horses, but, may Poseidon forgive me, I'm a bad aristocrat, because mostly I think they're the stupidest animals that a man has to deal with every day, unless he herds sheep. What other animal will run off a cliff? Eh?

At any rate, we were five days going north up the valley of the Rhodanus River to Lugdunum, and another two days there in a fine house that took travellers – a large stone house with its own stables, where thirty merchants could eat, sleep and rest. Despite excellent weather, ten days' travel had tired us out.

We had a spot of trouble in Lugdunum. The second night there, Seckla and I went out to a wine shop to drink. We were unarmed, because the town was well governed and the Aedui lords didn't allow men to wear arms openly. We were on our third bowl of the excellent local wine when a group of young sprigs came and sat on the trestles. It was all open-air; there were twenty men and a few women all sitting under the vines.

One of them, a curly blond in purple trousers, kept looking at me and glaring. He had gold earrings and was heavily muscled – a lord.

Almost too late, I figured out how I knew him. I'd cut him out of his saddle and sold him back to his father, that's how I knew him. I can't remember his name.

He and his friends began the usual way – looking at us and laughing.

Now, thugater, I was no longer eighteen. In fact, that year I was thirty years old. My blood didn't seem any cooler, and yet a group of Gaulish boys catcalling from an adjacent table didn't spark me to violence the way it might once have done.

Seckla, on the other hand, began to flush under his dark skin.

I put my hand on his. 'Let's just drink and go,' I said. We didn't have weapons, and this was an Aedui town.

But Purple Trousers couldn't let go, and when we rose to leave, he got up and blocked our way to the outside.

He said something, and all his friends laughed. I assume he thought I didn't speak any Keltoi, but of course I did. He made a statement about what I did with Seckla. I laughed. I suspect he alleged what Seckla might himself have preferred, if you take my meaning, and again, among Greeks it's not a killing insult, but I suppose it is among Gauls, which is funny all by itself.

Then the man turned to face me, and his face was already transformed – that look men have when they switch from rational creatures to animals. And his fist went back, and there was a dagger in it.

I caught his dagger hand in my left, thumb down, and I broke his arm and took the dagger. And I punched him six or seven times until I broke his nose – all the while clutching his broken right arm in an elbow lock. He slumped, and I kicked him, hard.

I looked at his friends. In Gaulish, I said, 'He attacked me with a dagger. Next man, I kill.'

They followed us into the street. And down the street. And to our lodgings, gathering friends as they went.

About an hour later, they got torches. Our landlord was none too happy, and sent for the lords of the town, who sent a dozen warriors. And the archon, whatever they called him, ordered me to pay a fine of twenty silver coins – about fifteen Athenian drachma.

When I explained in my not very good Keltoi that I had been attacked, he just shrugged.

So I paid.

Gwan didn't play any part in this, because as a Senone, he was only going to make trouble here.

We rode out the next day, followed by thirty or so Aedui gentry. But we had food, two horses to a man and pack animals, and they didn't, and if they wanted a fight, I wasn't interested. We took the west road over the passes toward Rhodumna and the upper Senones country, and we outdistanced them easily. But I began to wonder how I was going to get back.

Now I hoped to find Doola in every town and village. When we reached the limits of the Senones country, I sent Gwan and his two retainers out ahead, to arrange food and to scout and ask around. But by the time we'd been twenty days on the trail and we rode our tired horses across the divide and down into Agedinca, we hadn't seen or heard any rumour of them, and a black man should have been easy to find in Gaul.

Two days later, we guested with Collam, and I brought him some Persian saffron and some pepper from the beach market in Massalia. He offered to let my little war band stay for some time, and he sent riders out to the south and east.

I passed a very pleasant week. We hunted deer and wild boar, and I showed him how the Greeks hunt rabbit and he laughed himself silly. Even when I came back with a pair of coneys, he was still laughing. No Gaul aristocrat will do anything on foot if it can be done on horseback, and the sight of me running the trails of his forest naked was apparently the very height of Gaulish humour.

Summer was coming, and the grain was ripening in the fields, and all I could think about was the tin, and Demetrios. There was a girl in Collam's hall – well, I was quite taken with her. She had beautiful big eyes and a wonderful laugh. She was by no means a great beauty, except in a lithe, flat-chested sort of way … Ah, I beg your pardon, girls. But she made the time pass quickly, and the enthusiasm with which she opened the pins on her dress and let it fall—

Ah, blushes all round. I really shouldn't tell these stories. I merely want you to see that I was coming back to life in every way. I'm ashamed to say I don't remember her name, but she was no slave. One of the very finest things about the Keltoi is the freedom of their women – in that respect, there's a great deal the Hellenes could learn from them.

Collam's son came back from the south with a rumour that there was an early cart train coming up from Korbilon, which, after some talk, proved to be a town on the mainland opposite the Venetiae islands. I was worried that the Venetiae might hold a grudge, although, if you've been listening, you'll know that we did them no harm. But as I have said elsewhere, merchants guard their trade routes the way farmers guard their fields. Dicca, as I called the lad, told that over the hills, men said the cart train was guarded by a black man with magical powers.

That seemed hopeful.

Sophia! That was her name. Or perhaps that was her name in Greek. At any rate, I was enjoying her, and in no hurry to leave, once I knew that Doola was coming. My host had tribal problems – a fractious neighbour, and Gwan's father still owed the Venetiae, and was still a hostage with them.

Collam sat down with me – we'd been there a full week, and perhaps more. We'd eaten a feast of pork, and the wine bowls were passing. I was sitting with Sophia, my arm around her waist – the Keltoi encouraged such behaviour in public, whereas in Greece it would have excited comment, to say the least.

Collam looked at Sophia and nodded. 'Be sure you get a boy off him,' he said.

She threw back her head and laughed. 'I'm past all that,' she said. But she smiled at me.

Collam leaned back against the table and twirled his moustaches. 'Let me make you a proposition,' he said.

'Don't listen to him,' Sophia said. 'He wants you to fight.'

She grinned and Collam frowned.

'I want you to fight,' Collam admitted, and tossed the woman a false glare. They weren't brother and sister – I never fully understood their relationship, but it was deep. He looked back at me. 'Listen – I can help you, and you can help me. The Venetiae, they want to move their goods without paying a toll. And my brother-in-law,' he paused, 'is willing to make concessions to them. Concessions he shouldn't be making. But they are buying him against the rest of us, instead of paying their tolls.'

'Ahh,' I said, or something equally intelligent.

'He's assembled a strong force: he has Venetiae cavalry and his own charioteers and several hundred infantry.'

'And you want to take him on,' I said.

Collam nodded. 'He's a rich man – far richer than any of us. But if the smaller lords band together, we can take him. And you are a famous warrior. And you have twenty warriors at your tail – a fine company. If you fight beside me, I'll give Gwan any Venetiae prisoners to trade for his father.'

I shook my head. 'I didn't really plan to come here and make war,' I said. 'I need to find Doola. I won't do anything to annoy the Venetiae while Doola is still on the river or the road.'

It was a good thing to say, but the Lord of the Biturges had other ideas. I suppose he heard that my host was making alliances and causing trouble, because Genattax of the Biturges marched against us with twelve hundred men, and he came almost without warning.

I might have wondered why Collam was so glad to see me that spring, or why he was so eager to send scouts out to the south. In fact, his son and his other horsemen were watching every road and path for Genattax all spring, and my search for Doola was merely fortuitous.

But I wasn't going to ride off and leave Collam in the lurch. And the rumour was that the black man and his convoy were ten days away. Maybe less.

Why did things have to be so complicated?

Collam used me as a recruiting tool, showing his Greek warrior off to his neighbours. He had me demonstrate pankration with Seckla, and sometimes with some unlucky Gaulish lad. I felt as if I had become some sort of slave prizefighter, but by the time Genattax came at us over the hills, we had a thousand men, almost a third of them cavalry.

Seckla was hesitant, but the rest of the men were game to fight. Fighting for strangers can be a testy business – you don't really know who can be trusted, and there's always the possibility of out-and-out betrayal, but I trusted Collam.

We dismounted and fought with his tribal infantry. I'm not very good at fighting on horseback, and I thought that I could do something to stiffen the javelin-throwing peasantry.

We formed on a hillside, with the enemy in full view, also forming – chaos, really. Men wandered up to the battle, and when they formed their phalanx, each man chose his own place. It was alien, and yet somehow familiar – after all, even in Plataea, men generally stand beside their brothers and cousins. I wanted us to form quickly and attack across the valley while the enemy was still forming, but Collam laughed at my notions of tactics and said that such a fight would decide nothing. So instead, both hosts formed, and moved carefully down the ridges towards the streambed at the bottom. It wasn't very full. There was marshy ground to our left, and all of our cavalry formed on our right. All the enemy cavalry was there, too. They had more cavalry than we did, and more chariots, and we had more infantry.

May I say that war looks a good deal less necessary when you are fighting for strangers? As far as I could tell, the differences between Collam and his brother-in-law could have been resolved in an hour over a cup of wine. Perhaps a Gaul would have felt the same about Datis and Miltiades. At any rate, I didn't feel fired with enthusiasm for the conflict, and as morning wore into afternoon, I was increasingly aware that the enemy's mounted flank outnumbered ours and also overshadowed it, as their line went well beyond ours to the right.

But they wouldn't cross the stream, and neither would we. I understood why we wouldn't – we were outnumbered. But they had the numbers, and that trickle of water wouldn't have slowed their cavalry.

After some discussion, I found that it was only my ignorance. The *chariots* couldn't cross the river, and that meant neither side was anxious to engage.

Well, they aren't professional warriors. They have their own ways, and they are, after all, only barbarians.

We stood across the stream from them for hours. They would chant, and our side would chant. Sometimes a lone man would emerge and bellow a challenge.

I stood with Seckla and watched.

As the sun began to go down, a big man with a red beard emerged from the enemy infantry and whirled his great sword over his head and smacked his shield boss with it. I remember thinking – why not?

In fact, I dared myself. I had never been so close to conflict and felt so little.

I was afraid – afraid I was losing my taste for war. I was going to become one of those old men who love babies.

Who knows what I feared. I am now an old man, and I love babies. Hah! The things young men fear.

At any rate, I kicked off my sandals and walked to the edge of the stream. He came down – I don't think he was delighted to have his challenge taken up, after an afternoon when no challenges had been answered.

Since he hesitated, I jumped the stream. Immediately, a great shout went up from our lines, and men clattered their spears on their shields and roared.

He was obviously surprised. Nor did he have a spear, and I did. He backed and backed, and we began to circle.

I tried some old tricks to draw and attack, but I began to fear that I was dealing with a very experienced warrior. He would not be drawn. He wanted me to commit to my attack so that he could counter it, come inside and hit me with his sword.

I wasn't sure his strategy was sound – I wasn't sure that his long sword could even hurt me through my armour. He wore no armour – just a silver torque and trousers.

We circled again, and men shouted insults. They wanted us to get on with it. Easy to say, when you aren't the one facing three feet of Keltoi steel.

And then, he crossed his feet – a foolish thing to do at any time – and dropped his shield just a bit. We were ten feet apart, and he thought I couldn't hit him.

I stepped forward and threw my spear; he raised his shield and I was already drawing my sword, and my spear went in *under* his shield and into his thigh, and he grunted. I use heavy spears, and the blow went well in, and he couldn't get it out.

He screamed and fell to his knees, and of course that hurt him more.

I carefully pinned his sword hand with my shield – dying men are dangerous – and cut his head off with my kopis.

It was a good stroke, and he was positioned for it, and Ares himself held my hand. I have cut men's hands off before, but I don't think, until that moment, that I had ever beheaded anything but rams in sacrifice. Blood fountained out of his neck, and his body twitched and fell forward, and his eyes *blinked* from the severed head – I swear it. It shook me.

Our whole phalanx set up a wild bellow of approval, like so many oxen.

I went and retrieved my spear. And then, well. Apparently my interest in war had not waned. I started walking towards the enemy.

'Send me another hero,' I shouted.

The enemy phalanx was not very tightly formed. As I have said, every man stands where he will, and their spacings are not ideal, and men who dislike each other leave gaps, as do strangers. All in all, they form at something more like our *fusin* or normal order, not the *sunaspismos* or close order that a phalanx more typically fights in. I walked forward slowly, and the men opposite me shuffled back.

Well.

A young man without a torque came out. He was probably someone's bondsman, and although he was well muscled, he didn't know much about using a spear.

I killed him.

A tall man with heavy moustaches came out. He had a magnificent torque and a shirt of scales, and a helmet with a pig on top. His shield was long and narrow, like two boards together, with a long central boss. He had a good spear, and he crouched like a boxer as he approached me.

He tried to shield-bash my aspis. He hadn't fought a Greek before. The round face of my shield ate most of his energy, and the willow splits resisted the rest, and he backed away. I stabbed for his feet and got one. My spear came away bloody, and he roared in pain and leaped.

I wasn't prepared. No one had ever leaped into the air in front of me before, and instead of gutting him in the air, I ended up slamming my spearhead into his helmet – better than nothing, but he came down on my shield and we went down in a tangle. I went over backwards, my legs trapped under me, and something snapped – very painfully – in my right foot as I went down. I was under him, but he was just barely moving, and I had time to get the knife out from under my arm and put it under his chin.

By Heracles, my foot hurt. When I looked down, my toes were swollen. I'd broken it.

What an inglorious wound.

The next man was already dismounting from his chariot. By Greek standards, the Keltoi have very little sense of honour. I'd put three of theirs down, and they just kept sending champions. This new one was somebody – his men cheered, and he had a long shirt of polished scales and a beautiful helmet with eagle's wings – real ones – on either side of his head.

I got my aspis back on my arm and I sheathed my dagger, and my kopis, and got my spear back.

He stood by his chariot and shouted his lineage – descended, apparently, from the War God.

I was breathing like a horse after a race, and he was fresh.

He picked up his shield, hopped once and hurled his spear like Zeus's thunderbolt.

The hop gave him away, however, and I deflected it with my aspis.

He reached up and his charioteer handed him another spear, and he threw it.

I began to get angry. And his second throw wasn't any more decisive than the first.

And he reached for a third spear. The bucket in the chariot had six.

You can run on a broken foot. Really, you can.

I didn't run at him. I ran at his horses. They wanted to shy, but the charioteer held them.

I killed one.

Heh.

Then I killed the other one.

Then I killed the charioteer. He was yelling at me as if I'd committed some sort of foul.

Kelts don't kill charioteers, apparently.

Then I turned and started hunting the lordling.

His daimon had already left him. He tried to keep away from me. And he was yelling – demanding that I stop, that I had broken the laws of a duel.

At least, that's what I think he said.

Eventually, when he was pressed almost back to his own foot soldiers, he stopped. We went shield to shield. I used mine with a push of the shoulder to roll his down, and I pricked him with my spear – I got him, but his scales saved him from the worst of it.

He stabbed at me, but I had turned him with my stronger shield and he stumbled away.

My spear licked out and struck his helmet.

He stumbled.

I struck his right foot with my spear.

He gasped, but his shield was still steady as I leaped forward, and our shields went *crack* as we struck at each other. My spear went into his throat, and his spear rang off my helmet.

I stumbled back. If I had not killed him, he would have had me then.

Now their line was backing away from me.

Seckla came across the stream at my back. He rightly assessed that I was hurt.

But he didn't come alone. The rest of my men crossed with him

– and Collam's infantry. Although they owed me no loyalty, they apparently thought that this was a signal and then began to cross, and suddenly, our whole line was crossing the stream.

But the enemy were falling back.

Our cavalry didn't move. They sat on their side of the stream and watched our infantry push the Biturges up their ridge.

They began to run.

The Senones leaped forward like hungry wolves, gave a bellow and it was over.

Well, except for the actual battle.

The infantry didn't decide Keltoi battles. Cavalry decided Keltoi battles. The Biturges cavalry watched their infantry run, and they turned on us.

I couldn't keep up with the runners. My foot hurt too much. So I was standing, breathing, leaning on my spear when the Biturges cavalry charged into the Senones infantry. It was an insanely stupid thing to do – they abandoned the streamside and charged our victorious infantry out of loyalty to their own infantry, I assume.

The way Collam tells it, he couldn't believe his eyes for several long breaths of a man. It seemed to good to be true.

But as the last of the horsemen cantered uphill away from the stream, he decided it must be true. And he led his cavalry across the stream, and that, my friends, was the end of the battle. Collam captured half a hundred noble cavalrymen and twenty chariots.

Of course, the Biturges cavalry had had ten minutes to chew on us, and I missed the end because I was lying face down in the grass.

I missed everything. Doola came upriver with ten more pigs of tin, his wife and twenty barrels of wine, as well as three hundred Gaulish refugees looking for a new life on the Inner Sea.

Collam made a treaty with the Venetiae on his own terms, and traded them six of their merchant aristocrats for Gwan's father and his debt.

I was two weeks returning to consciousness, and I had headaches and black depression – the result, a Greek doctor told me later, of a bad blow to the head. I never saw the man who put me down – I was alone, and a great many of them came for me because, of course, I'd downed their champions.

My recovery was slow. I caught something – one of Apollo's arrows – that made me drip at both ends, and my foot swelled and got purple so that I thought it would have to come off. And then I lost more time – off my head, I think, with a fever.

Doola nursed me. Bless him, and his wife. I was a hero to the Gauls, but with so many prisoners, so much loot and the trade negotiations, I was largely forgotten.

It was a month before we left. Even then, I'd lost weight, and I could just barely ride, and it was Doola, not me, who led us back across the passes to Lugdunum. We had many parting embraces and declarations of friendship, and I had enough golden torques given me to start a collection.

And in fact, gold is always good.

When Doola rode south to find his wife, he found Oiasso destroyed – the villages burned, the hall flattened. But the people were scarcely touched; they simply retreated into the hills.

The Carthaginians encouraged the local Iberians to attack again. And winter set in with no crops harvested. The whole community of Oiasso had to depend on relatives in neighbouring communities for food.

As soon as the hill thawed, Neoptolymos and Alexandros led a hundred men on a counter-raid into the mountains, and they took flocks and grain. And tin.

Doola convinced them that they should pack their belongings and leave. It was a fine tale, and one that I heard told several times and never fully understood. I did learn that Tara and her brother died defending their hall; that the Phoenicians had come back twice, and had four ships the second time and five ships the first time.

'They were hunting us,' Doola said.

We said goodbye to Gwan at Lugdunum and rode south, moving in easy stages. I was still recovering, and our Gaulish horde needed food and rest. But it was a fine summer, and we had Doola's tin to trade – ill-gotten gains from the Iberians.

Midsummer saw us at Arelata, and men said that Phoenician ships had been on the coast all summer. And there had been raids.

Massalia had been attacked, and had repelled the attack.

My stomach clenched, and then rolled. No one at Arelata knew where Tarsilla was, but they all agreed that the Phoenicians had attacked every town on the coast that was Greek.

At Arelata, we prepared for the last dash to home. We elected to do it by land, because everyone at Arelata said the coast was too dangerous. There were no tin shipments moving into – or out of – Massalia.

And Sittonax and Daud were leaving us. They had helped get the convoys out to Arelata, where all of Tara's people were planning to settle. There was good farmland all the way up the hillsides, and these were people used to terracing.

But the last night, Sittonax and Daud both changed their minds. Daud and I embraced, and we both wept a little.

And then he said, 'Fuck it. I'm coming.'

Sittonax looked at him as if he'd grown an extra head. And then shrugged.

'Fine,' he said. 'I'll come too.'

So we all drank more wine. The next day, we offered sacrifices for our own safety and for that of our friends at Tarsilla, and we headed for home.

15

Tarsilla was not a smoking ruin. We came down the steep ridge behind, already aware that the town was safe from our friends among the herdsmen and shepherds, but still peering over every hill for a sign.

The timber temple of Apollo was still there. The theatre – a small one – was still there.

There were ships on the beach.

I knew *Lydia* as soon as I saw her. She was perfect – the finest trireme I had ever seen. Vasileos had outdone himself. And her twin sister was next to her. Gaius's vessel, and although I did not know it at the time, she was at that moment just a day old, all complete, the traditional ceremony just complete, the oarsmen sleeping off the festivities under awnings.

Gaius called her *Iusticia*. Justice.

Demetrios's house was closed and boarded. The wine shops certainly looked as if the Phoenicians had landed and smashed the town, but the rest looked good, and our house was secure, the main gate closed. Giannis opened the gate and embraced me, and we were home.

The thing I remember best about that homecoming was Doola and Seckla. Doola had brought his wife, of course. Seckla helped her down from her mule, and we all knew – right there – that all was well. She smiled at him, perfectly aware that this was an important moment. Then Doola went and embraced him. Seckla cried.

Well, lots of us cried. But we were home, and we'd done it.

We had done it.

I haven't mentioned Neoptolymos. Of course he was with Doola. He had done great deeds of arms in the south, with the Vascones, and against the Iberians. And when I recovered from my wounds, I found him as big as ever, his frame filled out, but calmer and happier, too. He had married a Vascone woman, Brillix, who was as much the opposite of the blond Illyrian as a human being could be. Where he was tall and pale, she was small and dark. He was taciturn and morose, and she was cheerful, funny, endlessly talkative. I've heard that opposites attract, but Brillix was the most opposite I could imagine to my vengeful Illyrian friend. And she made him – better. She made him happy. Happiness is better than revenge.

Nonetheless, she also gave him a reason to want both wealth and security. He was no longer a sword for hire. He was a husband and, it was obvious, about to be a father. Brillix was as close to perfectly spherical as a woman could be when pregnant.

We drank a lot of wine that day, and handed out more to the oarsmen.

It's not all war, my friends. Sometimes, life is just sweet. The next few weeks – oh, there's no story to tell, except that watching Brillix wander the house, cooking, cleaning, feathering her nest – watching Doola and Seckla rebuild their friendship, with Doola's wife as an ally – caulking and preparing our triremes for sea, training our oarsmen, drinking at the edge of the Middle Sea—

It rivals any time in my life. I missed having a love of my own, but to be honest, watching Neoptolymos and Brillix, or Doola and his wife, I was not interested in buying a slave and pumping away at her. I wanted a wife.

I wondered if Lydia were still available. But it had been more than two years. And to a marriageable young woman—

Still, one of the things my teacher, Calchus, had taught me over and over again, when I was a boy at the *tholos* tomb above Plataea, was that you never know until you ask. I had thought about Lydia many, many times in two years. I had behaved badly – shockingly badly, really, by my own standards. But her father was not without error, either. It began to occur to me that in my new status, as a rich shipowner, I might have a certain appeal.

Other things were occurring to me, as well. Riches – real wealth – the wealth to buy and maintain a ship, retainers, warehouses – have a cascade of effects.

Have I mentioned that I knew by then that Miltiades had died? Pointlessly, of a minor wound, in prison? The fucking Athenians – pardon me, thugater – had imprisoned him for failing to take the island of Paros. Heh. That's what they said, anyway. I loved the pirate, but he was scheming to make himself tyrant, I guarantee it, and I wasn't there to save his aristocratic arse.

Themistocles was building Athens a mighty fleet. All the Inner Sea was talking about it, because the Phoenicians were rumoured to be allied to the Persians. In Massalia, over wine, Dionysius told me that two sets of Persian envoys had come and gone from Carthage.

And everyone in the Inner Sea knew that Persia was going for Athens. Again. But this time, not with a provincial satrap and a hastily raised army. The word was that the Persians were going to throw a thousand ships and a million men at Greece.

Well, that's what Dionysius said, anyway.

And Demetrios was gone.

He'd taken *Sikel Herakles* to sea as soon as I was gone. He'd also taken a quarter of the tin.

And he hadn't come back.

There's time for rage, friends. Time to swear revenge and get it.

There are other times to shrug and call it a day.

It was only tin. There were fifty-six pigs still under the floorboards of our house, and another eight we'd brought all the way from the Vascones' land. Interesting that Doola insisted we all share, even though he and Neoptolymos and Daud had done all the work.

So we had sixty-four pigs left, less four pigs that Gaius used and four I used, sheathing our ships and our rams, and two more that we sold in Massalia to cover expenses and to do favours for bronze-smiths who helped us. That left us fifty-six pigs. We sold ten pigs – a *lot* of tin – to Dionysius, both to keep him sweet on us and to raise the cash to pay my oarsmen and hire oarsmen for Gaius. In the view of all of us – except, unfortunately, Demetrios – these were group expenses.

We ballasted our triremes in tin – twenty-four pigs each ship. It was a lot of tin.

Those forty-eight pigs were pure profit, and every man of us was due one-sixth in cash.

At the same time, I threw all my remaining silver and all the gold torcs I'd earned into the common pot. Doola and Neoptolymos had loot, too – and in it went. That came to a tidy sum. Vasileos was voted a full share of the tin, and so was Sittonax, which reduced our shares to one-eighth.

Getting all this? Merchants are always surprised at how well soldiers can divide profits, but listen, honey – the rules for dividing spoils are in the *Iliad*. We're good at maths. I had run the tin as a profitable military venture, not as a trading concession – or at least, that's how it had ended. Vasileos was deeply moved to be offered a fortune, and Sittonax laughed. He just laughed.

Of course, we had one last task – to sell the tin.

Forty-eight pigs of tin was enough to wreck the trade in a small market, or make other men rich in a large market.

Doola had other plans. He wanted to sell the tin at the top of the market, a month or so before the yearly convoys from Iberia reached Carthage. He studied such things, and he sat on the beach at Massalia and listened to the merchants – no Phoenicians this year – and made his plans.

Sometimes, you wander lost in life and you feel abandoned by the gods, and you move fecklessly from one day to another without purpose. Other times, it seems as if the hand of the gods is on your steering oars, and no matter what you might plan, the gods point you to a certain act, or in a certain direction. That is how I felt that summer. We had four glorious weeks of preparation, and then, after a night without wine and a good sleep, I rose in the dark with all my friends and all my people, and we got the two new ships manned, and friends – shepherds and fishermen – pushed our heavily laden ships down the beach and into the sea. And as the sky lightened to the east, we pulled our swift ships over a calm sea, bound for Sicily and Syracusa and the largest market for tin in the Inner Sea.

We rowed east and south, and stayed on open beaches with a heavy guard. Fishermen fled us, but when we managed to convince one we were safe, off Etrusca, he reported that a heavy Carthaginian squadron was operating in Sardinian waters.

We rowed south the next day, giving Sardinia a wide berth by continuing down the Tyrrhenian coast. We seemed to push the trade right off the seas – we did, after all, have a pair of sleek warships, and everyone ran. Which was just fine with all of us.

We passed the Tiber without entering the estuary. Gaius didn't want to go home until the tin was sold, and I appreciated his willingness; we didn't want to stay at sea with our cargoes. We wanted to get to the Sicilian market as soon as possible.

Let me wander off my topic to say that by this time I had begun to consider returning to Plataea. Euphoria's death was far enough behind me now, and I had begun to think of taking my tin and going back to start again. So I did mention to Doola that the very best market at which to sell our fortune in tin was Athens.

Doola just shrugged. 'I don't know Athens,' he said. And that was that. Listen – when the storm was roaring, we listened to Vasileos and Demetrios. When there were spears drinking blood, they all listened to me. When there were things to be traded, we listened to Doola. That's what made us strong.

We had three days' bad weather south of Tiber. We were headed by winds and the seas were short and choppy and a misery for the oarsmen, and I did something I hate – I turned tail and ran for a beach, landed and spent two days watching the weather. I remember so well, because without it—

Well, talk about the hand of the gods. The gods had me in both hands, that summer.

Two days later, we weathered Pelorus in a fine west wind, passing Charybdis under sail with the rowers making jokes about their godsend of a vacation. With the wind under our sterns, we ran west as far as we could, tacked, rowed and did it again. I mention this because it was a tactic I used to work up a rapid response in my crews, and always have – it's neither faster nor slower than rowing, but it does give the men a rest, and it also trains them in the rapid switch from sailing rig to rowing and back, which is essential to survival. Well, I laugh – survival as a pirate, anyway.

Both of our ships had the new Tyrrhenian rig which men now call the *triemiola*, so we no longer took our mainmast down – ever – and we had a half-deck aft instead of a catwalk making for a heavier, but more stable, ship; a wide platform for our marines and archers, and a permanent station for the deck crew who worked the sails. Again, none of this was revolutionary. There were a hundred triemiolas in the Inner Sea. But we had a pair, and we had trained our crews the way the best military crews were trained. We'd been together a long time, too – the core of our crews were the men who'd gone to the Outer Sea and back.

You can tell we're coming to a fight, can't you?

Heh.

We were tacking and rowing our way down the Strait of Messina, with me in the bow watching our tacks and trying to decide whether I was going all the way to Syracusa, or whether to make do with Regium on the port side – the mainland side. I passed the city, noting three triremes in the harbour, yards crossed and ready for sea, and we crossed the strait one more time and ran south along the Sicilian coast, watching for the beaches north of Katania as Aetna grew to starboard to dominate the horizon. The wind abated – blocked by Aetna – and we found the beach I remembered. I missed Demetrios, and that's the truth; he knew these waters like a pilot, and I was a mere duffer by comparison. But we got our heavy hulls ashore, and we hired rollers from the fishermen and ran our hulls right up the beach to give them a good drying. Wet hulls are heavier and slower, and when you have a ballast of tin—

We set a heavy guard. I was a day short of my goal, with a fortune in tin, and there was a heavy Carthaginian squadron at sea. I was no fool. I had marines on either headland, and by all the gods, that night I considered hiring a hundred donkeys and walking the ingots to Syracusa, I was that afraid.

I was afraid of more than that. The Tyrant of Syracusa was becoming renowned by then for his treatment of merchants. He was a bloody-handed aristocrat, a man who had risen to his place by a long string of military victories. Gelon hated merchants and 'little people', as he called them; he exacted heavy taxes to pay for his wars, and despite all that, Syracusa was more prosperous than ever. Maybe because of him. He had restored Syracusa's military power. Carthage was not going to find Syracusa an easy nut to crack.

But I might. Former slave – tin merchant. I was more than a little afraid of his customs officers.

And as we sat on the beach at Katania, returning to talk to Lydia seemed stupider. It seemed like foolish romantic claptrap.

Cowardice is the sum of the whispers of the weaker daimons in your soul, my friends.

The sun rose, and I didn't buy the donkeys. I got my oarsmen onto the ships, put on my finest chiton, my armour, my best cloak. I arrayed myself as Arimnestos of Plataea, lord of men. I took a deep breath and reminded myself that Gelon of Syracusa was a parvenu from Magna Greca, and I was a son of Heracles.

I prayed, too.

We got off the beach in fine style, and I sacrificed a fine silver cup and some superb Sicilian wine to the sea god, and then we were rowing south. When we were clear of Aetna's shadow the west wind was unleashed, and we began to make leeway to the west – virtually a stade west for a stade south. It was a strong wind, raising a phalanx of whitecaps that made the water look like the Outer Sea.

'Any stronger, and we'll have to run west,' I commented to Giannis and Megakles, who were sharing the steering oars.

Megakles grunted. Giannis smiled – he was about to go to Syracusa, and he was excited.

I remember looking up from Giannis to find that Seckla was pointing at the bow, and I followed his pointing finger to see the low shape of a ship nicking the horizon to the west on the opposite course.

And another astern of it.

And another.

They were all of them triremes, or so they appeared at this distance. A word for you virgins – a warship is low and crewed by rowers, virtually invisible until you are within fifteen stades or so, and even then difficult to see. A heavy merchant is not longer, but it is rounder, higher out of the water, heavier in its masts – much easier to see, in any weather. So we could see that the ship closest to us on the horizon was a trireme or a big bireme, and the ships astern of her were not merchantmen.

Also worth noting is that there are a hundred things a sailor learns in one look at a ship – even a ship on the horizon. Listen, girls: when you are going to the fountain-house with your friends and your slaves, you know it is young Eustacia bending over the well long before you can see her face, right? You know her from her clothes, from the shape of her hips, from the indefinable way she bends her body ... isn't that true?

Just so, at sea. One glance, and you know.

So, the lead ship was Greek.

The two ships behind were Phoenician.

There are these moments in every man's life – women, too – in fact, whole cities and nations – that define them. And are defined by them. There are moments where you act because you are what you are, and not because you have some finely realized philosophy to justify your actions.

I turned to Megakles. 'Hard to port,' I said. Doola was a few steps away on the half-deck. All I had to do was give the signal to raise the mainsail, and it was in motion.

We heeled a little as we turned.

The mainsail raced up the mast, and we had the wind astern, and we were tearing downwind at the two Phoenicians. It feels to me now as if we turned before the words had left my mouth, but in fact it must have taken some minutes, and many breaths must have passed my lips.

None of them questioned me.

Let me say this – with a smile, I hope. I had two ships laden with treasure, and I was a few hours' sail from the port where we would realize our fortunes, and when I ordered us to turn, the Phoenicians were far too committed to the chase of that Greek ship to pay us any attention. We'd have been in Syracusa by late afternoon.

I turned off our plot to run downwind on a pair of well-armed enemy warships with professional crews, for no better reason than that I hated them, and that they were chasing a Greek ship, and every one of us had been a slave on a Carthaginian.

I threw it all away.

Hah!

Beat that.

We ran down at them; they were well trained and saw us almost immediately, with our heavy sails set. No reason that they shouldn't.

But they were nearly up with the Greek galley, and they began to range up either side, archers shooting into the crew. The Greeks were resisting. Then, one of the Carthaginians dropped astern, and with a magnificent effort got his crew to row double hard, and he rammed the Greek ship in the stern – a difficult ram in any conditions, and twice as difficult in that sea. The Greek ship's bow fell off the wind, and she was caught broadside and rolled. The Phoenicians rammed the Greek, but their attacks were oar-rakes, and they may have killed rowers but they couldn't get their beaks in.

All this time, and we were racing down the wind. And then we saw why they were so bold.

There were two more triremes rowing up in the eye of the wind. Two more Phoenicians.

This *was* the heavy squadron.

I laughed.

I mean, I had committed my treasure and my ships . . . right down their throats.

We were under sail, so I manoeuvred my hull right alongside Gaius. I got up on the swan-neck of wood that protected the helmsman, and he climbed out to meet me. We were only a few feet apart.

'Want to run for it?' I called.

He laughed. 'No,' he said.

That was our command meeting.

Two stades out, we got our sails down. We were racing along faster than a horse gallops, a heady speed that fills the senses, and we had new-built ships with strong bows and new timber. And tons of tin. And new rams, just cast by me. I trusted Vasileos's work, and I trusted my own.

Ah, the moment.

We were going so fast that when the rowers put their oars in the water, they slowed us, and we threatened to fall off our course as they touched the choppy water.

The two nearest Phoenicians were on either side of the Greek, boarding from both broadsides. Because they'd made shallow oar-rakes from astern, they had both grappled with their bows just about amidships to the Greek ship, so their sterns projected.

We came at them like arrows from a bow, an oar's-length separating us, my *Lydia* just astern and to the starboard. We struck their sterns almost together. *Lydia*'s beak struck through the enemy ship's timbers like a man punching through a house wall when his house is afire, and timber flew through the air. It was the most decisive strike I have ever seen. Most ram attacks turn a ship over, and the wreck floats. But the target was stationary, held by the grapples, and couldn't turn or roll. And we hit hard – hard enough to stove the bows of most ships.

But not my *Lydia*. We ripped the stern right off, and the Phoenician filled and sank as fast as I can tell it.

Two hundred men died in the next minute – drowned, slave and free, Phoenician nobleman and Greek victim.

I watched them die as my rowers cheered and backed water.

Gaius blew right through his – probably an older ship, or one with the Tenedos rot, because he tore the stern off and his hull slid *over* the wreck and he raced on, leaving his victim to sink. I admit that I watched his standing mainmast spring forward the length of a horse as he struck, and I feared it would rip through his bottom – but it didn't.

The Greeks cut their grapples desperately, because the weight of two sinking ships was dragging them down like one of Poseidon's monsters.

The Greek was in rough shape. He had a dozen Phoenician marines on his decks and a great many dead oarsmen, his stern was badly damaged and his ship was sinking under him.

That was too bad, because I wasn't leaving Gaius to fight two angry Phoenicians alone, and I wasn't about to put my marines onto a sinking ship. Doola shot one of the Phoenician marines – a beautiful arrow – and we were away, and that was all the help we offered him. Well, aside from sinking both his enemies, of course.

The two oncoming triremes were under oars, and they had had a long pull – they'd been far to windward. You could see from their rowing.

We had standing rigging, remember. We didn't have to take our masts down, even after a collision like the one we'd just had. Now we had them aloft again, just as fast, our victorious oarsmen resting.

I laughed. I felt like a god of the sea.

I would have fought fifty Carthaginians, if they had come at me.

The ones to the west of us turned on their oars and raised their mainsails and ran.

It was the right decision. We'd evened the odds in one headlong rush, and now we had the fresh crews and the edge that victory brings, and they knew it.

Now, in sea terms, we were supposed to let them go. It is not for nothing that we say 'A stern chase is a long chase'. When you are astern of an enemy, you have no advantage of wind direction. You have only the speed of your ships. For the most part, Greek ships are faster than Phoenicians, but we were heavily laden.

And when they turned away, we had won. It became our duty, by the laws of hospitality, to rescue the Greek ship.

But the closer Phoenician had lingered in his turn – bad ship-handling. The westernmost one had issues, too, and got around before his sails were well set, leading to some yawing.

Megakles looked at me. He had his grin on his face. 'That guy is a fool,' he said, pointing with his chin at the nearer Phoenician. 'Bad crew.'

Seckla was all teeth. 'Let's take him.'

Doola had just unstrung his bow. Without demur, he restrung it.

It was like that.

The oarsmen grumbled.

But, as I pointed out, we were under sail.

We ran about six stades, and the sail began to shiver. The wind was changing, the sun was clouding over and the air had that taste it gets when there's a storm over Africa. We got our sails down long before our prey, and they wallowed in the gusts as the wind changed and we were coming up on them hand over fist.

Gaius was well astern of us, and five stades to the north. This was a natural consequence of the weather change, and if the pattern of wind gusts had been different, he'd have come up with the third Phoenician and we'd have been left to the south – but there came a point when he was no longer in the fight.

That decided me on my tactics. We crept up the last three shiplengths, using the boatsail to give us an edge, and then we went to ramming speed, our ship shot forward and we caught their steering oars. The enemy ship yawed, and all my archers shot into the command platform.

We ran farther west because we could only turn so fast, and it was then, as the second enemy ship ran like a rabbit, leaving the one we'd just struck to its fate, that I saw Dagon. He was a stade away, and I knew him in a moment.

And every shade of fear and hate struck me, all together.

Ever see a woman you have loved? A boy you wanted and lost to another girl?

You know what I mean. All that, in one moment. I swear, I had all but forgotten his existence, until I saw him.

My ship was already turning under me. The orders were given, the sails were down, the rowers fully engaged. I was not going to catch that galley that day. But I watched him from my command deck until we turned back to our prey.

I don't think he saw me.

Damn him.

The wounded Phoenician surrendered. He hadn't a chance: I had a consort on the horizon, and he had lost his steering and most of his officers in one pass. And as soon as we came alongside, some Greek dragged a Carthaginian down into the benches and strangled him.

I put Doola and Megakles and all my marines into him, and we rowed his bow around while Megakles rigged a jury steering oar, and then we were rowing across the new, choppy African wind. Darkness was falling when we came alongside Gaius. Gaius had run west ahead of us. He was the one who came alongside the sinking wreck of the Greek ship and rescued her crew and her oarsmen, filling his ship to a dangerous degree, knowing that I was right behind him. And I was. I came up beside him, and at the edge of darkness, lashed together, we transferred a hundred desperate men. A trireme can only hold so much, and then it won't float. Or it folds in the middle. But bless Vasileos, he built good ships, and we ran for the coast, rowing as well as we could with so many extra bodies on board.

But they helped, sometimes three men sitting on the same bench. I put forty Greek rowers into my capture, and at about midnight we were off the beach at Katania. Seckla swam ashore, roused fishermen and got beacons lit, and one by one we got our ships landed, stern-first. It wasn't that the seas were high, or the current treacherous. It was merely that we were exhausted. It was dark. Mistakes were made.

Men were injured.

But we didn't lose a ship, or an ingot of tin, and in the end we got fires lit, and men fell asleep naked on the summer sands.

16

I dreamed of Dagon. They weren't pleasant dreams, but on waking they reminded me of how much I hated him, and how deep he was in my soul. He had made me feel weak. He had hurt me.

I wasn't going to forget. And all my vaunted philosophy wasn't going to change that he needed to die. I'd like to pretend to you that I felt some greater urge – that I wanted him dead so he couldn't kill any more preganant women. Something noble.

No. He hurt me. He hurt my image of what I am. I have spoken to women who have been raped. We share this. He hurt my *soul*. I wasn't going to let him go.

He'd passed within two stades of me. But Tyche had decreed that his ship got away.

I rose, shivering, and got some warmed wine. I heard the sound of a woman shouting.

I knew there were women aboard the Greek ship; I'd seen them as we swept by. As the sun rose, I found out who they were. There were five of them: a free woman and four slave attendants. They were swathed in cloaks and shawls – like any woman who travels at sea with two hundred men – and in the lukewarm and rosy brilliance of a Sicilian morning, they looked like drab flowers.

Scared, angry flowers.

They had their own firepit in the sand, but no wood. The free woman barked orders, slapped a slave and carried firewood herself, boldly walking to the fire my archers had going and taking from theirs.

I watched all of this, a horn cup of wine in my hand, while Doola sold an ingot of tin to the local bronze-smith's guild. There were, apparently, six smiths in Katania, and they banded together to raise the money for a full ingot.

Their spokesman was a big man with a heavy beard. He might have been a Plataean. He nodded to me, and we gripped hands and his eyes widened.

'You work metal?' he asked.

I nodded, and pointed at *Lydia*. 'I cast the rams,' I said.

He walked down the beach, and we examined the rams. He was interested in my design. I served him a cup of his own local wine – Sicilian wines are superb – and we walked back up the beach to Doola.

'You are clearly sent by the smith god,' he said. 'We haven't seen this much tin in two years.'

It is deeply pleasing to make another man happy, is it not? And this was a worthy man, the sort of tekne whose craft pleases the gods. It was a fine start to the day, as was the silver that Doola took.

All the while, I watched the women. I was curious, I suppose. The free woman sent a slave girl to borrow a copper mess kettle from the archers, which she did with a flirtatious twist visible from half a stade away, and smoke rose from their fire. They were a competent bunch.

Gaius came, and Doola, Seckla, Daud and Sittonax, sitting on stools or on their cloaks in the sand, and we ate sardines and olives and new bread. Despite, or because of, yesterday's exertions, we were all in fine spirits, and we broke our bread with the gusto of the victorious.

Gaius saw me watching the women. 'She was taking passage to Croton,' he said. 'No great beauty,' he added dismissively. 'Tall as an Amazon, though.'

Doola raised an eyebrow, and chewed on his bread in a way that rebuked Gaius quietly.

Gaius snorted. 'Marriage didn't make *me* an expert on women. Why did it make *you* one?'

Doola ate an olive. 'I live with mine?' he said. 'You visit yours in the holidays?'

Gaius spat angrily, but anger never sat long on him. 'Now what?' he asked, after we had all chewed more food.

'Syracusa, I think,' I said. 'We can be there by nightfall.'

Everyone nodded, and slaves appeared to fold our scrap of a tent and our stools, but I told the officers to assemble all the rowers, and I paid every man a silver tetradrachma of Syracusa from the store of silver – ten days' pay. They filed past Gaius and Neoptolymos, one by one, as Doola read their names from his tablets and made a mark in the wax. Most men grinned. A few bit their coins, and one fellow immediately handed his to another. He looked at me sheepishly. 'Dice,' he said.

I spent two hours rearranging the crews. The Greek ship was a fast merchant out of Croton. The master was Achilles son of Dromos, a professional sailor. His ship was owned by one of Croton's super-rich aristocrats. Achilles didn't seem too concerned.

'You saw me make a fight of it,' he said. 'If it comes to court, I have your testimony, and the lady's. I'm not worried.'

His eyes were on our Carthaginian capture. 'Going to fit her out?' he asked.

I laughed. 'I don't know if we can afford a third ship,' I said. 'But at least today, we'll sail her into Syracusa.'

He nodded. 'I can command a ship like that,' he said. 'Not every-one can.'

I was entertained. My people called me trierarch, which in Athens was the commander of a ship, but in Magna Greca, the trierarch was a rich and often useless member of the crew, if he shipped at all. Achilles, a short, balding man with a bent back and a permanent sneer, took me for a rich aristocrat.

'I can,' I said. 'And any of my friends can, as well. We've sailed the Outer Sea.'

He stepped back. 'Meant no offence,' he muttered. 'I'd just like to have a job.'

Between his oarsmen and the freed captives from the Phoenician, we had a full set of rowers for the captured ship. We – the six of us – had a quick meeting and handed the command of the ship to Neoptolymos, with sixteen pigs of tin. We offered Achilles the post of helmsman.

He wasn't exactly eager, but he took it, in the end.

By the time we'd shifted ingots of tin and made repairs to the former Phoenician, we'd wasted the day. Evening fell, wine appeared and men drank. Neoptolymos and Seckla had the duty, and they visited the watch posts on the headlands. Giannis had, in a somewhat circuitous manner, become the commander of the marines, and I took him aside and asked him to have men watch the women's fire. Wine and women are a fine mix, as long as everyone is in agreement about the whole thing, but these women were ... different.

Sure enough, before the moon rose, some of my recently freed slaves attempted to carry off one of the slave women. The archers pounced, and my evening was interrupted by an angry virago, a pair of archers and a struggling, very drunk Greek.

I was sitting on my stool, trying to tune my *kithara*. I think I've mentioned that I had become determined to learn to play it. This determination ebbed and flowed, and never seemed to result in my getting anywhere. If Gaius or Neoptolymos tuned it for me, I could play a few tunes – like a small boy, as Gaius liked to tell me. But I couldn't seem to tune it.

The slave girl was black, and had lost most of her wrappings, and her body instantly put me in mind of just how long it had been since I'd felt such smooth skin under my hands. Hah: I really shouldn't tell you girls such things. On the other hand, better you know what men really are like, eh?

Heh.

She was scared, her eyes everywhere, wild, her mouth slightly open. Her mistress had her arm around her.

'Is this your version of a rescue?' she shot at me. Her Greek was perfect – Attic Greek, the way a lady would speak it – Jocasta, for instance.

I rose, put my kithara on my stool and shook my head. 'I'm sorry, Despoina. But no harm has come to the girl. And it *is* my version of a rescue.'

'If these archers had not happened by—'

Demetrios the archer, a Cretan, grinned. 'We didn't exactly happen by, either,' he said.

She turned and looked at him. It wasn't a glare – just a carefully judged look.

He fell silent.

'I demand better protection. And how many days are we going to stay on this beach?' she asked.

There are situations it is very difficult to resist. 'The food is good, and the company suitable,' I said.

She surprised me by smiling. 'I think perhaps our views on suitable company might differ,' she said. Her voice was deep, almost masculine. Her face was veiled. She was tall – as tall as I am, and that's saying something. Later, in fact, I noted that she was a hand shorter than me, but she always left the impression of great height. Something about her voice and posture suggested she was my age or older – not a young virgin, by any means, but a matron. Her figure was good; a man can become quite expert at judging women through enveloping robes, and I find that my skill in this regard is inversely proportional to the length of time since I last saw a woman unclothed – hah, a mathematical joke. You young people have no notion of humour.

'Would you join me for a cup of wine? And Seckla, take a file of marines and remind the oarsmen that these women are off limits, yes?'

Seckla rolled his eyes and walked off with two of Giannis's men, as well as the slave girl and the prisoner.

My guest watched them go. She turned to me. 'It is a long time since I have been alone with men while drinking wine,' she said. 'I would like one of my women to attend me. Not Tessa. She's in shock. Send a man for Antigone.'

Send a man for Antigone. She issued the order with a slight wave of her hand. The delightful thing was that she had every expectation of being obeyed. Complete assurance.

Doola laughed, and went. Gaius rose from his stool and inclined his head. 'My lady,' he said. 'We thought you were some merchant's wife.'

She was very tall. 'I might well be some merchant's wife,' she said. 'Wouldn't that entitle me to your best treatment, anyway?'

'You are too well born to be a merchant's wife. Rather, the Queen of Croton.' He bowed.

She laughed. 'Croton does not have a queen. And you?' she said back to him.

'Gaius Julius Claudius,' he said with a fine bow. In his own barbaric tongue he said, '*Civis Romanus sum.*' He grinned. 'I'm from Rome.'

'Oh,' she said, with instant dismissal. Croton and Sybaris were two of the richest cities in the world. We still call the lifestyle of the very rich 'sybaritic', and such people 'sybarites'. Croton was just as rich, and full of scholars and poets, too. Rome was, by contrast, a town full of cows and chickens.

Gaius was abashed.

She turned to me. 'Are you a pirate?' she asked.

I nodded. 'Yes. All my life.'

She had just drawn breath to launch into a speech – I could read her, and her reply was predicated on my denying the title of pirate. My acceptance of it caused her to step back and throw an arm across her body.

I smiled. 'Nonetheless, we will land you unharmed at Syracusa tomorrow, if the gods will it so.'

It can be hard to talk to a human with no face, a woman swathed in veils. I couldn't tell what she was thinking. She raised her cup and drank, and I saw a hint of a strong jaw and a long face.

'You speak well enough, for a pirate,' she said.

'And you are brave enough, for an aristocrat and a woman.' I smiled and held out my cup to my pais for more wine. 'What brings you to Syracusa, Despoina?'

She shrugged. 'That is my business, I fear,' she said.

Few things kill conversation so effectively as telling someone to mind their own business. I bowed. 'I hope we can make you comfortable, Despoina. Is there anything you need? You built and maintained your fire very well, I noted. Do you need food? A cooking pot? Some wine?'

She nodded. 'Wine is never amiss. And I note that your sailors have straw for bedding. The sand is cold, and women have hips. We would appreciate some straw.'

The reference to women's hips was clearly an attempt to warm over the conversation, but I was done. She hadn't even bothered to thank me. I knew her kind; or thought I did.

'Gaius will see you back to your fire, and ensure you have wine and straw,' I said, in dismissal.

'I will?' Gaius asked. 'Oh, right. Trierarch, and still functionary. Follow me, my lady.'

'I have offended you,' she said suddenly. 'I didn't mean to. I am not good at this. I do not ... mix with others.'

'Then you mustn't be surprised that others do not seek to mix with you. Good night,' I said. I walked off into the darkness; not that I had anywhere to go, but I didn't need to talk to her any further, just then. Arrogant woman. *Mix with others.*

We are seldom so offensive as when we seek to make apology.

We put to sea with the dawn, three warships under easy rowing. It was a hundred stades to Syracusa, and the weather was turning bad – the wind from Africa was in our teeth, and the southern sky was dark, and the wind held a hint of sand.

The rowers had to earn their bonus.

By midday, they were pulling full strength to gain us a few dactyls at the stroke, into the teeth of an African gale. This was the one point of wind at which the new triemiola rig was inferior, and the Carthaginian capture, with her mainmast stowed between the benches, offered less resistance to the wind and kept pulling ahead, despite the relative inexperience of her crew. Our masts took the force of the blast and caused the bows to fall off course over and over, until I finally surrendered to the inevitable and began to make short boards, steering south-east and then south-west. That eased the ship's motion and helped Gaius as well. I watched his bow to gauge the effect on my own, and saw the woman standing there, her shawls streaming behind her in the wind.

Yes, she had a fine figure. I had decided that I disliked her, and I was anxious to be rid of her.

To be honest, I must have been suffering from the reaction that always sets in after a fight, even such a one-sided fight as we had had the day before, because the storm seemed to me to be the last straw. I felt, just at that moment, as if we were never going to make Syracusa, and that the woman was the curse.

Oh, I can be a fool, too.

Sometime after noon, Doola came aft and Megakles stood in the helm oars and we shouted at each other. They wanted to turn back. I did not.

It's not worth repeating the argument, which was probably rendered comic by the wind. None of us could understand each other, and we all wanted to be heard.

It was one of those times when men are reminded why only one man can be in command, at sea. Because divided councils result in compromises. In assembly, or when directing the affairs of a great merchant, such councils are essential. At sea—

I was determined that we would continue, even in the dark, if for no other reason than that I feared what would happen if we tried to turn. The seas were high, and our sleek warships had high bows but very shallow waists, and the rollers coming from Africa would wash clear over us, amidships. I feared to lose a ship in the turn – along with a third of our precious treasure and a third of my friends. Care and work would get us into Syracusa.

I'm making this too long. It is a curious facet of reminiscence, my friends: I exaggerate those things that were important to me, and I skip over events that might have had far more importance to others. If Seckla were telling this tale—

Bah. I'm an old man. That was a hard afternoon, and a hard night, and I was proceeding against the advice of my best helmsman into the teeth of a gale, sure I was right. I had become a far better captain in the Outer Sea, and now I was willing to hold my course against their advice. That's why I remember.

It was close on midsummer, and the sun was out there, somewhere above the cloud. It was dark by mid-afternoon, and darker still at what should have been evening, and the dust coming off Africa was in our eyes. But after the wine had been served out to the oarsmen, Seckla caught sight of a glimmer to the south-west, and shortly afterwards, it was visible on every rise.

I relieved Megakles, and he went forward, looked for himself and reported that it was the outer lighthouse at Syracusa. Bless him.

The rowers were filled with confidence, and in an hour, we gained fifteen stades on the wind and the harbour entrance was clear enough. I cheated the helm to the west, so that we approached the entrance at a shallow angle from the north. The great breakwater wasn't built in those days, and the lesser breakwater only protruded a stade from shore.

About a stade off the entrance, I noted that there was a current running inshore – from the sea west, into the harbour. Twice, I had the rowers row to hold us in place – bow into the storm – while I ran amidships to peer through the murk at the harbour lights. We had a lantern – three lanterns – over our stern, and another at the masthead, and despite all of that, Neoptolymos almost ran us aboard, his ram shaving past our port-side oars, and he was gone, heading fast into the harbour. His ship turned far too fast, the starboard rowers backing water, took a wave right over the counter and shot into the harbour.

It was ragged, but he was in. I had intended a somewhat overcareful approach, using the current to push our bow into the harbour which my rowers held steady, but Neoptolymos's success emboldened me, and I waved to Megakles. I was less bold: I let the wind push our bow around, our rowers gave five rapid strokes, as if we were ramming an enemy, and we were in. The change in the sea was instantaneous – we went from a howling wind and steep waves to glassy calm water and no wind in five strokes.

A ship's-length aft, Gaius made the turn. Later I understood that he left it late and his port-side oarsmen actually struck the rocks with their oars, but close enough *is* close enough – he weathered the headland and we were in the harbour.

It was moving, to sail along the beaches of the harbour front where I had spent so much time. I wondered if Anarchos still lorded it over the waterfront. I wondered what Gelon was like. I wondered where Lydia was.

Doola came and stood at my shoulder, as we slid down the calm water towards the waterfront. 'We are coming back,' he said.

I smiled. 'We said the same at Massalia,' I noted.

There was quite a crowd on the waterfront. It was nigh on full dark, but three warships passing the harbour mouth in a storm was something worthy of comment. Perhaps a thousand people watched us land our ships. Doola leaped over the side and went up the beach to find lodging and food for six hundred sailors and oarsmen. I was busy getting the crew off, guiding the stern of a heavy ship well up the beach and setting a night watch on our fortune. My oarsmen were all aware of what they'd been rowing in the bilges beneath their feet, and in an hour they'd have told every petty criminal in every brothel on the waterfront.

Gaius's passenger disembarked. He provided her with four marines under Giannis, and she vanished into the darkness. I missed her going, but I wasn't sorry. To be honest, now that we were ashore, I was foolishly eager to find out what had happened to all my friends – and foes – in the town. And at the same time, suddenly apprehensive all over again. I feared Lydia's scorn.

I feared her father's scorn.

I also feared thieves, and I slept aboard, my head pillowed on my cloak and my feet on the helmsman's bench.

I rose in the morning, swam in the sea and then walked up into the city to find an open bathhouse. The Temple of Poseidon maintains one for travellers, and I emerged clean, massaged and feeling alive and virtuous.

On return to my ship, I found Doola surrounded by merchants, none of whom was familiar to me. I looked in vain for Anarchos. Instead, I saw a cloaked herald approaching, and I ran aft and changed hurriedly into my best clothes and jewels. As I expected, I was summoned by the Tyrant of Syracusa. He sent me a dozen gentleman hoplites and a polite messenger named Dionysus, son of Anchises. The messenger was a beautiful young man with hair so blond he might have been a Gaul.

The message was a polite command to attend the tyrant *at my earliest convenience.* 'I am ready,' I said. I sent a messenger for Gaius and asked him to accompany me. He was obviously a gentleman. Remember that I had heard that the tyrant was against commoners.

We walked up the twisting streets to the citadel through a city that was far quieter than the Syracusa I had known three years earlier. There were few men and no women in the streets, and those men I saw did not meet my eyes, but merely hurried by.

I had mistaken the hoplites for local aristocrats, but after climbing a few streets, I realized that they were beautifully kitted-out mercenaries.

'Anyone here from Plataea?' I asked cheerfully.

None of them was, but there were men of Thebes and Megara and even little Thebai.

'Are you from Plataea, then?' asked the escort officer, a phylarch from Hermione in the Peloponnese.

'I'm Arimnestos of Plataea,' I said.

He stopped dead. 'You're not.'

'I am,' I said.

He shook his head, and then gave his spear to another man, took my hand and shook it. 'A pleasure to meet you. Why didn't you say? The Tyrant would have sent a better escort.'

I laughed. It is good to be famous.

The other mercenaries pressed around me and shook my hand over and over.

One of them, a short man with short hair and an Attic drawl, laughed. 'I was there too,' he said. 'At Marathon. With Miltiades.' He shook his head. 'Great days.'

'I understand Miltiades is dead,' I said.

He nodded. 'Where have you been?' he asked. 'He's been dead nearly five years.'

I shrugged. 'It's a long story.'

Gaius stood by and rolled his eyes. Well – no one is very famous to his friends, which is probably just as well.

The Palace of Syracusa is, to me, an exercise in hubris. It is built like a temple to the gods, and yet its only purpose is to house men. It towers over the town, on top of the acropolis, where there ought to be a temple and instead there is a citadel. As far as I'm concerned, that citadel is the reason that Syracusa succumbs so easily to tyrants – always has and always will. The man who holds the acropolis holds the city. By placing the gods on the acropolis, Athens makes it much harder for a mere man to take their houses – and any man who does such a thing is an obvious blasphemer. The Peisistratids had houses on the Acropolis, but no one but priests dwell there now.

I digress, again.

High above the town, we emerged on a path with a marble railing, lined by statues of women who were holding the railing. The view was breathtaking, and the storm off towards Africa was a pronounced darkness, like a bruise in the sky. My escort halted at the end of the path, where the statues gave way to a garden, open on one side to the city, and closed on the other three by deep colonnades.

All this for the pleasure of one man.

Gelon was standing among his roses; he had a small, sharp sickle in one hand and he was pruning, cutting dead flowers, slicing away buds past their promise.

Hah! It all appeared a trifle contrived, to me. Gelon, the great aristocrat, tamer of the commons, pruner of the high and the low. Something like that.

Nonetheless, I bowed.

My escort commander said, 'Lord Arimnestos of Plataea,' and saluted with his spear. To me, he said, 'Lord Gelon of Syracusa.' He caught my eye as he turned, and his escort marched away smartly.

Gelon, the Tyrant of Syracusa, was a tall, deep-chested man with deep, dark blue eyes, the kind of eyes usually painted on by amateur statue-painters who have access to too much lapis. His eyes were arresting.

His gold hair, almost metallic in its vitality, was arresting, too. He had a touch of silver-grey at the temples, well muscled arms and legs – he looked, in fact, like a big, handsome man in the very prime of life and condition. And I have always thought that his looks were part of his success. He looked like a statue of a god, like the best statues of Heracles or Zeus. He dressed simply, as had become the fashion since the teachings of Pythagoras began to sweep over the Greek world, and he wore no jewellery unless he wore a cloak.

At any rate, at the mention of my name, his eyes widened ever so slightly.

'Are you *really* Arimnestos of Plataea?' he asked.

I bowed. What do you say to such a foolish question?

'Well,' he said. 'Welcome to Syracusa. I gather that your ships bring a cargo. And I gather that you have quite a story to tell.'

'You have the better of me, then, my lord,' I said. 'I have a cargo of tin, which my factor is even now selling.'

'Of course I have the better of you,' Gelon said, a trifle petulantly. 'It is my business to know such things. I gather that you had an encounter with ships of Carthage.'

'We encountered them,' I admitted.

'Such encounters are my business. Tell me, please.' He snapped his fingers and a pair of slaves appeared. One reached for my cloak. The other handed me wine.

I removed my cloak in a fine swirl of Tyrian red, and both slaves fell back a pace. Gelon paled – or rather, as I was to learn with him, his lips grew redder.

'You are armed,' he said.

'At all times,' I said cheerfully, and tossed my cloak to the nearer slave. 'See to it the pin's still there when I get it back,' I said.

'My slaves do not steal,' he said.

'Good,' I said. 'I found three ships of Carthage pursuing a Greek ship north of here – practically off your harbour mouth. I sank two and took the third.'

'Under whose protection?' the Tyrant asked. 'Do you act for Athens? Is that why you feel you can take ships on the high seas with impunity?'

I laughed. 'I doubt that anyone in Athens even knows that I am alive,' I said. 'I need no man's permission to take ships on the seas but my own.'

'Dano says that you told her you are a pirate,' he said.

'Dano?' I asked.

'The woman you might recall rescuing,' he said with a slight smile.

I shrugged. 'I served Miltiades too many years to call myself anything else,' I said. 'And I was bold enough to assume that I would be welcome here, for making war on Carthage.'

The Tyrant pulled his beard and nodded. 'You are correct. And yet, it might have been better had you asked me, first. Carthage has a mighty armament off my coast, and I am not yet ready to contend with them.' He shrugged. 'Where did you acquire so much tin? Preying on Carthage?'

I shook my head. 'No. And then, perhaps they would tell this story differently. We sailed into the Outer Sea and they hounded us unfairly. After a while, I attacked their shipping and their trade, yes.'

Gelon nodded. 'There have been rumours of a Greek pirate in the

Outer Sea,' he said. 'Well done. Now that I know you are the famous Arimnestos, it makes more sense to me, as the earliest rumours said you were some bronze-smith with a taste for war.'

I was feeling perverse. 'I *am* a bronze-smith with a taste for war,' I said. 'I cast the rams on my ship's prows, I can make a better helmet than any smith in this city and I have fought in a dozen pitched battles on land and sea, and in fifty skirmishes. Heracles is my ancestor. I led the Plataeans at Marathon.' I smiled. 'My ships carry more than forty full ingots of Alban tin, which Sicily needs.'

He nodded. His godlike face split in a smile. 'You need to put me in my place because you have heard that I hate the tekne,' he said. He shrugged. 'Men – lesser men who cannot understand me – say such things. Indeed, I love fine things, and I honour the artisans who make them. Yet I know that they lack the skills and education to serve as citizens and voters. Their dedication is their craft, as women's dedication is their children. They are too busy to direct the affairs of the city.'

'You should meet my friend Aristides,' I said. 'You two would have much to discuss.'

Gelon shook his head again. 'Debate with me, if you disagree.'

'If cities were directed by craftsmen, perhaps there would be less war and more art. The exercise of craft – the excellence of making things well – is, I maintain, as sure a guide to arête as excellence in rhetoric or athletics. What excellence does a man have merely by birth?' I nodded out to the south, towards Carthage. 'I have seen more courage from Keltoi slaves, sometimes.'

Gelon was not angered, nor was he stung. He was no straw tyrant. 'Well said, if full of possible holes. What if a man makes things all day and has no idea of what has gone on in the assembly?'

'When did your assembly last meet?' I asked.

The sound of a woman's laughter pealed through the garden. I knew her laugh immediately – the laugh of a deep-voiced, deep-chested woman.

She came along a gravel path with the grace of a goddess. She was tall, as I have said. Her face was ... magnificent, but not beautiful. The angles were too sharp, her nose almost like a beak, her eyebrows fierce, her mouth a long slash. And yet—

Dano of Croton was, and remains, as enigmatic as her father.

'He argues like a sophist, changing his ground as fast as you change yours,' she said.

'I practised debate as a boy, when I was learning to be a swordsman,' I said.

Gelon raised an eyebrow. '*Learning* to be a swordsman,' he said, with gentle contempt. 'Any well-born boy is born knowing how to wield a sword. It is an innate skill. Like virtue.'

He truly believed what he said. It is important that you understand this to understand the complexity of our lives. He was a great man: a great mind, a deep thinker, a superb general. And yet he truly, utterly believed that the well born were superior in every way – far more like the gods than, say, one of his Sikel or African slaves.

But my growing respect for him couldn't stop the sneer from touching my face. 'Would you care to put one of your well-born young men against me?' I asked.

He shook his head. 'You claim descent from Heracles,' he said. 'Naturally, you are a better warrior than other men.' He smiled. 'Even if you waste your talents working bronze.'

It was like the feeling of a heavy Persian arrow hitting my aspis.

'Would you care to put one of your well-born gentlemen against a slave of my choosing?' I said.

He shrugged. 'There are always exceptions. But in general ... Come, you won't deny that the well born are handsomer, with better bodies and more aptitude for anything. It doesn't surprise me that you are a fine bronze-smith. Any gentleman will excel at any of the lesser trades. But this is like an adult stooping to enter the boy's events in the Olympics. Let the lesser men work bronze. A gentleman should work with men.'

'If this is true,' I said, trying once more, 'why are so few gentlemen any use at the helm of a ship in a storm?'

Dano of Croton laughed. 'He doesn't know, and you should stop trying to beat him. And Gelon, be a good host. This is the man who saved me from the Phoenicians. Even now my great height would be fetching a stunning price at some brothel in Carthage.' She smiled at me. 'I failed to thank you at the time, Arimnestos. I was ... disconsolate. It is difficult to explain. I do not live in a world of ship battles and pirates. I read about such things.' She shrugged.

Well. It is rather difficult to harbour resentment against someone thanking you in front of the ruler of a tenth of the known world. She offered her cheek to be kissed, and I kissed it.

The Tyrant laughed. 'Do you know who she is, son of Heracles? She's Dano of Croton. Pythagoras's daughter. One of my best friends. I owe you immeasurably for her rescue – but we had no notion of what kind of man you might be. I had imagined a much blacker pirate.'

I shrugged. 'I have been a black pirate. I imagine that the darkness of one's acts is often judged differently, depending on which end of the sword faces you.'

Dano shook her head. 'I confess that you rescued me, and I am grateful. But despite that, I believe that all violence makes men lesser – more like animals.'

'War is the king and father of all; some men it makes kings, and others, slaves,' I said. 'Peace begets nothing but dull care. Strength comes through change. The wise adapt.'

'Heraclitus!' she said. 'That charlatan.'

'He was my master and teacher,' I said. 'And he honoured your father.'

'My father did not honour him,' she said. She paused. Her voice had begun to grow coloured, heated, and she took several breaths. More than any Pythagorean I ever knew, Dano controlled herself at all times.

Now the Tyrant laughed. 'Brilliant!' he said. 'I have a follower of Heraclitus to debate with my daughter of Pythagoras; we can form a three-sided triangle of discussion. Arimnestos, be free in my city. I may have a matter of ... hmm ... policy to discuss with you, now that I have met you. I'm sure many people here will want to meet you. Do you wish me to give you a guide?'

'I know the city well,' I said.

Gelon gave me an odd look, and said, 'Very well. I will have rooms assigned to you in the palace.'

'I would be too afraid of being murdered by fanatic Pythagoreans,' I said.

She started to bite back, and realized she was being mocked. Instead of glaring at each other, we found ourselves smiling. It was an odd interaction. I was quite sure that I didn't find her attractive, so I wondered at the readiness of my unintended smile.

The pretty young Dionysus, son of Anchises, reappeared to lead me out of the palace. We didn't leave the way we'd come, but went up into the main apartments so that he could show me, I suppose, the sheer magnificence of the palace, and then we headed down a grand outside marble stair that wrapped around a small temple platform to Nike. A priestess was just emerging from the temple; her sheer gracefulness caught my eye. She wasn't tall, but willowy and her neck rose from her sheer white chiton—

It was Lydia.

I stopped on the steps and almost fell.

She looked at me, put a hand to her chest and then turned and went back into the temple of Nike. Without intending it – indeed, without any conscious thought – I ran back up the steps to the temple, but Dionysus caught my hand.

'You cannot go in there,' he said. 'Gelon would have you killed.'

I saw that the temple doors – well-worked bronze, the height of a man, with deeply inset panels that showed scenes from the triumph of the goddess – were slightly ajar. She was watching me. Or watching for me to go.

'I know her,' I said. It was, all things considered, a foolish thing to say.

Dionysus looked at me. 'I must suggest that you are mistaken,' he said primly.

The next few days passed in a pleasant, but confusing, whirl. Doola was busy selling our tin, and through him, our inn became a hive of mercantile activity. Gelon might disdain merchants, but his factor made it clear that Syracusa needed tin.

I received invitations to the palace, which I accepted. I dined with Gelon and the nobility of Syracusa. Lydia – if it was Lydia I had seen – was nowhere in evidence. I shared a couch with Gaius, and we were bored. I didn't see Dano. Of course, I was back in civilization and women didn't, in general, dine with men, especially in conservative, aristocratic Syracusa.

Dull.

After two days of it, I couldn't stand the inaction. At first I wandered the waterfront. I met men from Athens and Croton, from Rome, from all the cities of the Etrusca, from as far away as Tyre. The Tyrian, a senior officer of a merchant on the beach, looked me over carefully from the deck of his ship and then beckoned to me.

'You are the great Greek pirate,' he said. He grinned. It wasn't a real expression – more like a dog showing its teeth. He sent a boy for spiced wine, and we sat on bales of his linens from Aegypt and he told me without preamble that Darius, the Great King for all of my life, was rumoured to have died at Persepolis, which was about as far from Syracusa as I could imagine in distance. His successor was Xerxes, or so my Phoenician helmsman informed me.

He talked about Persia's determination to conquer Athens, and after a while we moved up the beach to a taverna. Men came and went, asking his leave to buy one thing or sell another. After some small talk about his family, he got to the point. He leaned back, stuck two fingers in the top of his linen kilt and smiled.

'Now I have told you something, yes? So you tell me. You make war – sea war – on Carthago, yes?' He smiled, but the smile didn't reach his eyes.

'Carthago enslaved me,' I said mildly.

He nodded. 'You have killed many of my people. Many. Yet I sit here and make the talk with you, and you do not seem like a monster. Why so much war, eh?'

I spread my hands. 'It seems to follow me,' I said.

He nodded. 'So tell me this. Is it true you went to the Tin Islands? All the way into the Outer Sea?'

I was watching him carefully. I didn't think it impossible that the Phoenicians would murder me in cold blood, for all sorts of reasons – but first and foremost because I knew the route to the tin. 'Yes. All the way to Alba. And back.'

He smiled, leaned forward and extended his hand. 'I'm Thato Abn Ba'al. I, too, have crossed the northern seas.' He grinned. 'I tell them, at home, that we could publish the route in every city in the world and do ourselves no harm, because only a *great* sailor can make the trip. That the squadron at Gades is wasted.' He nodded. 'You have prisoners, I believe.'

I am a man of the world, and I like most people. I have come to an age where I can say that in truth, there is no one truth – that no man is much better than any other, and that Greeks are not handsomer or smarter than Persians. No race has an edge in courage, or discipline, or ship-handling.

But I cannot abide Phoenicians. Maybe it is bred to the bone after years of war, or perhaps they really are rotten to the core of their child-killing society. Eh?

So all this, this whole pleasant morning of conversation, was a preamble to asking me if he could ransom my prisoners.

'I have a few,' I said. My annoyance was already rising.

'Give them to me, and I'll see what I can do to get you trading privileges in Sidon and Carthago,' he said with a smile.

'Why would I want to trade there?' I asked. I was already getting to my feet.

'The richest trade in the world? The finest entrepôt, the best warehouses, the most imposing array of products, the best craftsmanship?'

'Athens, you mean?' I said.

He laughed, but his laugh was more false than an old whore's smile.

'Athens is a nice little town,' he said. 'Sidon, Tyre, Carthago – these are the finest cities in the world, and you should beg to trade in them.'

'Why?' I asked. I leaned forward. 'I can take whatever they have to offer whenever it suits me.' I nodded. 'Like that ship right there.'

'It would mean war between Carthago and Syracusa. A war that Syracusa would lose. Carthago can put a hundred thousand men in the field.' He stood up. 'Slavery has eroded your manners as well as your sense of right and wrong. I sought to do you no harm, Greek. I want to buy your prisoners.'

I nodded. 'I'll send you my factor,' I said haughtily. In fact, I wanted rid of them, and money is always nice. The problem with anger is that it can get in the way of common sense. I didn't need him or his ship, or the international complications that would arise. Even as it was, my possession of the hull of a captured Carthaginian warship and the freed Greek slaves roaming the streets spending their pay was making trouble for my host, who in turn was increasingly distant to me.

Piracy. Always a complicated matter.

I turned to leave Thato Abn Ba'al, and had another thought.

'Do you know a Greek in Carthago's service called Dagon?' I asked.

The Phoenician rolled his eyes. 'Yes.'

'Insane?' I asked.

The Phoenician shipmaster shrugged. 'A bad man. And not one of us, whatever you say.' He spat.

'Will you see him? In Carthago?' I asked.

Thato narrowed his eyes.

I shrugged. 'I am not after your ship. I spoke in heat.'

He splashed some wine on the floor. 'Make me your guest friend, and I'll talk to you about it.'

A guest friend is a sort of sacred trust, like brotherhood. If you make a man your guest friend, you accept responsibility for him in your house and your city – but you also, in effect, swear to support him and not to harm him, ever. Sometimes guest friendships are passed down from generation to generation.

'If you wanted my prisoners, why not just say so?' I asked.

'It is rude to start a conversation with a demand,' he said. 'I am a gentleman. I heard that you are, too, despite your violence.'

I sat again. Poured a little more wine. 'Guest friendship is a door that swings both ways,' I said.

He spat thoughtfully. 'I am not a barbarian,' he said. 'Make me your guest friend, and we will share the rewards in the eyes of our gods. And men.'

Despite all, I liked him. So I got up and swore the oath to Zeus, and he swore by Ba'al and Apollo, and we clasped hands. Some bystanders in the taverna witnessed – a big Athenian helmsman I didn't know came and slapped me on the back.

'Then take the prisoners,' I said to my new brother. 'No ransom.'

He was genuinely surprised. Unaffectedly surprised. 'You mean that?' he asked.

I led him to where Neoptolymos sat under an awning, drinking wine. He had six Carthaginian officers, and a pair of our marines watching them – and making sure our former slaves didn't gut them for old times' sake.

'Neoptolymos?' I said. 'Let them go. This man will take them home.'

Neoptolymos nodded. He was an aristocrat, too; he rose to his feet and bowed to our Phoenician guest.

Thato started to lead them towards his ship, they clutching his knees and patting his hands and weeping. As well they might. But he pushed the youngest one away and turned to me.

'I may see Dagon in Carthago,' he said. 'I can't stand him, but I see him all too often.'

'Tell him you met Arimnestos of Plataea.' I smiled. 'Tell him that when I find him, I will break him on an oar and crucify him on my mainmast.'

Thato nodded and pursed his lips. 'I will,' he said seriously.

I was busy in other ways, as well. The Athenian helmsman – a former slave named Simon, like my hateful cousin – was almost fully loaded with Sicilian wine and copper ore and three ingots of my tin, and he was headed east to Athens. Since I had already begun to form my plans to return to my own life, so to speak, I asked him to see if he could find Mauros, or any of my other friends in Athens or Piraeus. I wrote a letter to Aristides, sometimes known as *The Just* who had led one of the Athenian taxeis at Marathon, and another to Themistocles, the leader of the Athenian *demos*, asking them to see to it that if my ship still sailed the seas, it came to me at Massalia.

I wrote another letter to my sister Penelope.

I had decided that it was time to return to my home.

But first, I had a military operation to plan.

And I had to know about Lydia.

I completed my letter-writing, visited Doola's mercantile exchange and sat down to listen to him dicker with a pair of Sybarite merchants.

It took me a moment to realize that he was *buying their tin.*

This made no sense to me, but I smiled at Doola, who was clearly having a fine time, and walked outside, where, to my confusion, Seckla was leading a pair of donkeys loaded with tin out of the inn's yard.

He smiled at me and walked on, attended by a pair of slaves.

Perhaps we delivered.

I fortified myself with one more cup of wine and walked up the town, to the shop where I had worked for a year. I sent a slave in for Nikephorus. But I already knew that the forge was silent, and when the mistress of the house emerged, she looked at me, face carefully blank.

'Where is Master Nikephorus?' I asked.

She looked away. 'He died.'

'And his wife?' I asked.

The woman looked at the ground. 'She died first.' She finally met my eye, and hers held rage. 'You have nerve, coming here. After what you did. You don't think I know you? I know you.'

This was what I had imagined, when I imagined the worst possible outcome of my visit. And I didn't know her.

'You ruined her. Turned her head – made her a whore.' The woman spat at my feet. 'My curse on you. I pray for your destruction, every day. May the sea god suck you down. May the Carthaginians take you.'

I confess that I stepped back before her rage.

'I wanted to marry her,' I said weakly, knowing that this was not precisely true.

'Did you?' she asked. 'I'm sure you still can. She might make a good wife, between pleasuring gentlemen at parties.' She stepped forward. 'My sister *died*, of a broken heart. Her husband died when the fucking Tyrant took his citizen rights. They took you in, you fuck. Gave you work. You *ruined* them.' She was screaming now. I was backing away as if she were three swordsmen. Or perhaps five.

Five swordsmen would not have made me feel like this one middle-aged woman.

What do you say? To the screaming harridan in the street? *I meant no harm? We were just playing? I play with girls all the time? I'm a warrior, and it is my right to take women as chattel?*

One of the effects of age is to realize that most of society's rules – even the most foolish – exist for reasons, and are broken only at someone's peril. From the comfort of this kline and across the distance of years, I doubt that I wrecked Lydia alone, or that her mother died entirely of my actions. Nikephorus could have been less intransigent. As I discovered, he threw her from the house. She was a prostitute by the next morning. That's the way of it. And she came to the attention of the man who became Tyrant, and he took her for his own. As you will hear.

Well.

How much of that is my responsibility? Eh?

When the night is dark, and the wine is sour, it looks to me as if it is all my responsibility. All of it. I played with her life, and I broke it. That's hubris, my daughter. Treating a free person as if they are a slave.

I never promised you a happy story.

I left the street and walked down the hill, and sat on the beach over the headland from the citadel, and I wept. And then I went back to town along the waterfront, looking for a fight, and didn't find one. You never do, when you really want one. So I drank, and I walked, and I wandered.

It grew dark. And there was Doola standing in front of me, and he walked with me a way, and then it was morning, and I awoke with a hard head and a general sense of hopelessness.

I went downstairs and sat with my friends. Because they were true friends, I told them the whole story. Doola knew some, and Neoptolymos most of it, but when they heard the whole story, they gathered around me and Seckla hugged me, and Doola just stood with a hand on my shoulder.

'You owe the girl,' he said.

'She must hate me,' I said.

Doola nodded. 'I don't think that will change. You must help her, anyway. Take her away from here, to where she can start again.'

'Perhaps she likes it here,' I said; a fairly weak thing to say, really.

Doola just looked at me.

Neoptolymos said, 'Let's just take her.'

I didn't see any solution. But Doola insisted I had to see her, and I determined to try.

I began by asking any staff I met when I went up to the palace. Rumours of the Tyrant's *hetaera* were everywhere in the town, but there was no one at the palace who would even mention her. At my third invitation to dine, I went and sat on young Dionysus' couch – it was crowded, I can tell you – to see what he would tell me, but the party was growing wilder by the moment and I couldn't even get his attention.

I have seldom felt such an utter depression of spirit as I felt that evening. I sat in the Tyrant's beautiful garden – he'd had the couches arranged outside – and the sun stained the sky and distant clouds a magnificent orange pink even as his roses scented the air. It was an intimate dinner – perhaps thirty guests, with superb music and very good food. I remember none of the dishes, because I didn't want food.

I sat alone on a couch, ignored by the other guests, a mere oddity, a foreigner who had sailed a long way and nothing more. I was thirty years old and more. I was a famous man – in a way. But that way was not the kind of fame any man seeks. I had the reputation of a killer. A pirate. A thug. I had abused a girl half my age, and because of it, her family was disgraced or dead and she herself dishonoured. And nothing could make that right. There was no one to kill.

I am not a fool. I was trained by one of the greatest minds in the history of Greece, and I have a brain of my own. I could, and did, see the difference between what my emotions said I had done and the actual responsibility I bore. But that didn't matter, any more than the various excuses I make myself for the oceans of blood I have shed with the edge of my sword.

I was more than thirty years old, and I had neither wife nor children; no permanence, no hope of continuity. If an enemy spear took me, I would be gone like a bad smell in a powerful wind.

I still think these thoughts, thugater. Nothing makes it better. It is dark, and it can go on for days. There is nothing joyous about murder. The thrill – the contest – of war is only half the story, and the other half is remembering all the men whose lives you reaped so that you could have their gold.

I decided to go. If I had been feeling better, I might have been bold enough to walk off and search the palace, but dark spirits do not raise your courage.

Gelon came and sat on my kline just as I was about to leave. 'You are like the spectre at the feast,' he said. 'Is my food bad? Do the musicians displease you?'

'No,' I said. 'I am not in the mood for food. I should have declined to come, my lord. I am poor company.'

He furrowed his brow. 'I expect better of my guests. Come: tell us of sailing the Outer Sea.'

Another man – one of the horse-breeders who seemed to be Gelon's favourites – clapped his hands together. 'Tell us!'

Another one of them, a taller man with ringlets, looked at me curiously. I suddenly knew him – he was one of the wealthy men who had evicted me from the city gymnasium some years before.

Had I been in a different mood, that might have roused me, but in my present mood, it only served to make me tired.

'Another time,' I said wearily.

'I insist,' said the Tyrant.

Well, he was the absolute lord of Syracusa, and my ships were in his harbour. 'Very well,' I said.

He held up a hand. 'Let me send for Dano,' he said. 'She loves any physical science. She will want to hear this herself. In fact, she insisted.'

I lay back, while slaves rearranged the couches so that I could tell my story to the party.

Theodorus – his name came to me – came and stood by my kline. 'I think I know you,' he said hesitantly.

'I was a slave,' I said. 'And you didn't want to know me.'

He frowned. 'You probably shouldn't be in the palace.'

I nodded. I found that I was growing angry easily, that I wanted to quarrel with this relative nonentity. Which was foolish. Anger is always foolish.

'Why don't you tell him, and we'll see how he reacts?' I said.

Theodorus looked at me. 'How does a former slave own three warships?' he asked me.

'Good question,' I said. I smiled.

He went and said something to one of his cronies, and then the Tyrant was back with Dano. She wore a veil and sat in a chair.

Theodorus cleared his throat even as Dano raised the edge of her veil and gave me the sweetest smile. It wasn't the smile of a flirtatious woman, but merely a smile. In that moment, it was as if she read my mind – my anger, my hurt.

She was a good woman. A *good* woman.

I tore my eyes away from her to find Theodorus standing by Gelon. The Tyrant was listening to him speaking, low and urgently.

Despite Dano's presence, I was content to be thrown out. I didn't like Gelon, and his cronies seemed to me to be the opposite of proper aristocrats. Instead of tough, educated men who could lead war parties or talk about the affairs of their city, these seemed to me to be soft-handed sycophants.

But Gelon laughed. 'Theodorus, do you actually think that men like us are bound by petty notions like slavery?' His laugh was real, and it rang, loud and full, and again, the Tyrant gave me the impression that he was like the Lord Zeus. It was the laugh of the king of the gods. 'If the Lord Apollo fell to earth and was enslaved, would he be any less a god?'

Some of the others looked at Theodorus, and some looked at me. I'm not sure that the Tyrant convinced them, but after a moment, it was obvious that I wasn't going to be conveniently thrown out of the palace, and would have to sing for my supper, so I began to tell the story.

I thought I'd tell it fairly, so I started from Syracusa, with our first boat. They were true nobles – they were fascinated by the way that small men make money. The tale of the purchase of our second boat fascinated most of them in a way that the tale of my trip beyond Gades did not.

When I mentioned Anarchos, the tyrant slapped his thigh and laughed. 'I know him,' he said. 'He is precious to me.'

Well, well.

By the time I had the ships off the beach at Massalia and off the Inner Sea coast of Iberia, two-thirds of my listeners had lost interest. The Tyrant and the Lady Dano, on the other hand, were rapt with attention, and young Dionysus gazed at me with genuine hero-worship. When I told the story of running the mill race at the Pillars of Heracles, he clapped his hands together and said, 'Odysseus, come to life,' and Dano's eyes shone.

Let me tell you a secret. No matter how far down you are, the admiration of a handsome woman will almost always bring you up in your own estimation, and some male hero-worship doesn't hurt, either.

Not at all.

I took them up the coast, out to sea in storms, in raids on the Carthaginians, up to Alba and all the way home. The sun was gone, the lamps were lit and half the guests had left when I was done.

I took a long drink of wine.

Dano threw back her veil and drank some wine. She looked, not at me, but at Gelon, who nodded.

'Indeed, for an hour, I was the King of the Phaekeans, listening to the Man of Sorrows tell his tale. If you ask me for a ship to take you home, I will have to give you my treasure. That was a great tale.'

Dano raised the communal cup. 'How my father would have loved you,' she said.

I smiled. 'I eat meat,' I admitted. 'I don't think I could give it up.' Sorry – that quip was aimed at her, because the secretive Pythagoreans didn't let outsiders know anything of their practice, but everyone knew they didn't eat meat.

She shrugged. 'He loved men who do things, and men who learn things. It seems to me you are both. And that was a marvellous story. What will you do with the rest of your life?'

I shrugged. 'You overwhelm me with so much unmerited praise.' I slid off my couch and stretched.

Gelon rose and crushed my hand in the two of his. 'Stay here with us, then. Be one of my captains. Persia and Carthage are combining to extinguish the Greek world: a single great war to dominate the earth, or so my spies tell me. Come and help me stop them. This is the richest city in the Greek world; we can have a grand fleet.'

Dano made a motion with her hand. 'Athens has built more than a hundred triremes in the last three years,' she said.

I whistled.

'I can buy and sell Athens,' Gelon said. 'A commercial city ruled by a squabbling assembly of proles. They will never rise to greatness. Men require to be led, and well led, by those who are better. Syracusa will be a greater city, because those who rule her are themselves greater.'

I shrugged again. 'Men on ships require to be led,' I said. 'Men on farms require only to be left alone.'

Dano laughed. 'May I quote that? It's brilliant. And you say you studied with that fool Heraclitus?'

'He was not a fool, but a great thinker and a brilliant man, humble before the gods, capable of solving almost any problem. And yet he studied other men's thoughts and learned from them, too – in Aegypt, in Persia. Even your father, who he viewed as the greatest mathematician of the age.' I had a thought, then, of sitting in the garden of Hipponax's house, teaching Briseis from a book of Pythagoras, watching her beautiful fingers work the geometric figures with the compass I had made her.

Gelon smiled. 'Can you work any of Pythagoras's solutions?' he asked me.

'Several,' I said. 'I can find the value of the hypotenuse given the lengths of the two other sides.' Seeing his surprise, I said, 'I use it every day to figure my dead reckoning at sea. If I am rowing twenty stades an hour to the south, and wind and current are moving me six stades an hour to the west, what is my true course and speed?' I asked.

'A little less then twenty-one stades an hour, south by east,' Dano said, clapping her hands together.

'What do you do when your course and the current aren't at perfect right angles?' Gelon asked.

'Guess,' I said, and he laughed.

'And how do you measure the speed of your cross-current? Or the wind? Or even your own speed through the water?' Dano asked.

'We cast the log for speed – it is guesswork, but accurate guesswork. My young friend Seckla can cast the log for a ship's speed and he'll be accurate within ... well, within my tolerance, anyway. Currents: more guesswork.' I waved my hands.

Gelon nodded. 'It is experience, is it not? That gives a mariner the ability to make these guesses?'

I sensed I was entering into another argument.

'But you could teach another person to do it, could you not, Lord Arimnestos?' she demanded. 'I am reckoned intelligent – could you teach me to command your ship?'

'Or could she teach herself?' asked the Tyrant. 'Could she work it all out from first principles and then put to sea?'

'My lord, my lady, I have the feeling that I am caught between Scylla and Charybdis here. But I would say that yes, I could teach Lady Dano to command or to pilot; and yes, she might even teach herself, although she might also die in the attempt. But I would insist that while she might learn to be a brilliant navigator by practising mathematics, seamanship is a great deal more, and requires years at sea. I started late, and my helmsman Megakles, for example, a fisherman born, has a deep understanding of waves and weather – and I do not. So I ask him, often. Nor have I learned his knack. Yet I can pilot a ship from here to Gades with a few landfalls, and the sun, moon and stars, and he would have to coast the whole way. There are many skills at sea, just as on land, and not every skill is acquired the same way.'

The Tyrant's laugh boomed out again.

'You don't lose an argument often, do you?' he asked. He rose from his couch and went to be gracious to other guests, and I gathered I had annoyed him.

Dano sat on the edge of my couch. 'I wonder if you could come and speak about navigation for our school in Croton?'

I was flattered. 'I would be delighted,' I said. 'But I understood that your father was exiled from Croton, and no longer had a school there?'

'Oh,' she said. 'That was many years ago. Members of our ... group—' She looked up and met my eye. 'Men can be fools, no matter how well born and well educated. Indeed, it sometimes seems to me that well-born, well-educated Greek men are the greatest fools in the world.'

I laughed. 'Such speech must endear you to all such men.'

She shrugged impatiently. 'It is foolish to speak in generalities,' she said. 'Indeed, you make me garrulous, when I would prefer to be silent.'

'Because women should be seen and not heard?' I asked.

She glared, and then saw that I was smiling. 'Because a philosopher learns more from listening than from talking,' she said.

'You are a philosopher?' I asked.

'Everyone is,' she said simply. 'Only a few mortals have the leisure to devote the time to it that it deserves, but everyone who travels the face of the world is a philosopher – unless they sink to become animals.' She smiled, at her own vehemence, I think. Pythagoreans eschewed displays of emotion.

'I think I must agree to that, or be characterized as an animal,' I said.

She looked at Gelon, with the last of his guests, and said, 'I love it here, but I am merely a curiosity. I came for the friendship my father bore Gelon. I have been well received, but Gelon imagines that I am a woman, and sends me yarn. Will you take me back to Croton? I can pay.'

I nodded. 'With pleasure.' I wanted out of Sicily.

And I had remembered Anarchos.

The next morning, sober and of sounder mind, I wandered the inner harbour – not where the big foreign ships beached, but where the local trade came. It took me about two hours to find one of Anarchos's enforcers, and an hour later, I was with the man himself.

He looked at me over the rim of his wine cup, and toasted me.

'Here's to success,' he said. 'The greatest mariner of the age, or so I hear it.'

'Here's to your friendship with the Tyrant,' I said. 'He told me that he loves you. In just so many words.'

Anarchos looked around. 'He said that? Out loud?' He snorted. 'I'll be lynched.'

'I gather he's none too popular with the lower classes,' I said.

Anarchos leaned back. 'He stripped everyone but the richest six hundred families of their voting rights. Set against that, he's lowered taxes, and he has kept the Carthaginians at bay.' He motioned over my shoulder. 'Nice ships. You have become an important man.'

'Again,' I said.

I smiled.

'So what do you want?' he asked. 'Of me? You don't need me any more.' He shrugged. 'I try to be realistic about these things.' He nodded. 'Or do you need me after all?'

'Where's Lydia?' I said.

'Ah,' he said. In fact, he knew what I was there for from the moment I walked in. Anarchos was a man who bought and sold weakness. And he knew mine.

Our eyes locked. 'You walked off and left her,' he said.

'I offered to marry her,' I said in instant defence. Foolish, wasted words.

'But her father turned you down. I remember. When you left, her father threw her into the street.' He licked his lips. 'I took her up.'

His statement cut me like a sharp sword.

He spread his hands. 'Don't pretend you cared! We are men of the world. You had your turn, and I had mine.' He laughed at my face. 'But I lay with her, which you hadn't the balls to do. And she liked it.' He smiled. 'I didn't rape her. Hah! You are a fool. And my men are all around you. If you draw, you'll be dead in a moment.'

I couldn't help myself. Rage, jealousy, self-hate – what a stew of low emotions I was. I got to my feet and men crowded in close, and I felt the prick of a knife through my cloak.

'When I was tired of her – just as you tired of her, no doubt – I arranged for Gelon to meet her. Beautiful, well spoken, hot on the couch and cool in debate – the perfect mistress for the Tyrant. He couldn't have some low-born porne, could he?' Anarchos laughed. 'You still think that you are better than me, lad.'

It is chilling that, in the moments that most matter, we don't think of our great and noble teachers and their fine thoughts, but instead we think like animals. I wanted to kill him.

Because, of course, he was completely correct. His contempt was merited. And he had probably dealt fairly with her, by his own lights.

But as a man, I didn't see any of that. I burned – oh, Zeus! – I burned with rage.

Anarchos laughed again. 'Will killing me make you a better man, hero?' he asked. 'Get you gone.'

He stood up.

I stood too.

It may not strike you as one of my boldest, bravest, strongest moments – but it was. I stood up, and I mastered myself. I clamped down on the rage. I told myself that I was not responsible for his actions, but only my own.

'Tell me how to reach her,' I said. I kept my voice low.

He looked at me as if I had slapped him.

'I want to talk to her,' I said. 'That is all.'

He narrowed his eyes. 'Why? I mean, why should I help you?'

I took a deep breath. 'You and I have a great many things in common.' I met his eyes. 'So I'm going to assume that some of the things you do are difficult to live with. And that once in a while, you have to do something to help someone, or become a monster.'

Anarchos paled, but he made himself laugh. 'I can't remember when someone last appealed to my beneficent nature.'

I shrugged. 'I intend to offer her a path away from here, and a great deal of money to start again somewhere.'

'She hates you. And she won't hate you less.'

It's odd. I knew that, but hearing Anarchos say it – in a matter-of-fact voice devoid of sarcasm or deliberate malice – brought home to me that it was true. It made me feel a little sick, the way a man feels when he first discovers that he has a fever.

'I accept that,' I said quietly.

He nodded. 'If I can arrange something, it will be on my grounds and you will be in my hands,' he said.

'You'd be a fool to have me killed,' I said. 'But I expect you'd weather it.' I nodded. 'You know where to find me.'

He nodded. 'I think you owe me money,' he said. He actually smiled. 'The amount might not even be noticeable to you—' he laughed.

I had to laugh, too. He was right.

He extended an arm. And I clasped it. Somewhere, he and I had taken each other's measure. I couldn't manage to hate him.

On the way back to our inn, I saw Seckla with a dozen of our oarsmen, loading mules with ingots of tin – our tin – at a warehouse well above the water. I looked at him, and he shook his head.

'Don't ask,' he said.

I waited for Doola to be done with his latest transaction. Then I sat down and told him everything I'd learned from Anarchos.

He nodded. 'You behaved well,' he said.

Gaius shook his head. 'Well?' he asked. 'Let's go and gut the crime lord. I've always wanted to do him, the bastard. Kill him, grab the girl and go.'

Neoptolymos nodded. 'I, too, have always wanted him dead.'

Gaius grinned. 'Think of all the other little people who'd bless our names. He's a complete bastard. And he raped your woman? Kill him.'

I sighed, because part of me wanted the same thing. I looked at Gaius. 'Someday, I hope you get to meet my friend Idomeneus.' I motioned to my pais for a cup of wine. 'You can't kill everyone you disagree with.'

'Says who?' Gaius asked. 'If Doola ever finishes dicking around with these merchants, I aim to be the richest magnate in Rome, and if men annoy me, I may well kill them.'

'I hope you will all come with me one more time, first,' I said.

Gaius smiled. 'Where?'

I looked at Neoptolymos. 'Illyria. I promised to put Neoptolymos back on his throne, and I will. And I intend to kill Dagon.'

Gaius shook his head. 'But not Anarchos.'

I shook my head. 'No. It is different.'

Gaius narrowed his eyes. 'You think too much, brother.'

I have neglected, I think, to mention that all Syracusa was a field of Ares; that men were drilling in the squares, dancing the various forms of the Pyrrhiche, running in armour to harden their bodies. The shops on the Street of Hephaestos were thriving, and helmets, thoraxes, greaves, ankle armour, even armour for men's feet and elbows poured forth. A lot of it was crap – I walked down the street, and was surprised at how poor some of the work was – but some was magnificent.

And the best work was that of Anaxsikles, who had more than fulfilled his promise. I had known him as a young man, and now he was a man, and a master. I think I mentioned that he was the second son of Dionysus, the master smith at the top of the street, and his work was ... god sent. He had his own shop.

His work struck me like the shock of a nearby lightning strike; like full immersion in icy water. There were three things that distinguished his work: his absolutely perfect planishing, so that even the most complex curve of a helmet or a greave was as smooth as a mirror; his elegance of form, so that I could pick his work out when I paused to lean on my staff and watch the youths drill, because his armour made a man look like a god, whereas other men's work could make a man's legs look shorter, or their torsos broader. Anaxsikles' work had the opposite effect; and finally, the almost total lack of decoration. He was, in his way, a genius, and he had perfected his forms to the point where embellishment was unnecessary. His greaves were completely smooth; his torso cuirasses followed the musculature of the body without the complex hip extensions or the acanthus whorls that were standard on most breastplates.

I stood in the street, watching him work under an awning, and my heart was torn in many different directions. I wanted to be working. I wanted to be as gifted as he. He was younger than I, and already a better smith.

Age brings its own humility as well as its own relaxation. When one is young, one strives to be best against all comers. The best in war, the best on the kithara, the best at reciting poetry, the best at smithing.

Time passes, and some men are revealed as swordsmen, and some as kithara players, and some as smiths – greater and lesser, according to their merits. Heraclitus taught us that no man need do any more than to strive to be the best he can; that arête lies not in triumphing over others, but mostly in triumph over yourself. So he told us, but which of us believed it? Not I. I wanted to be best of all men. I still do. Humility is not yet my portion.

But standing there, I had to acknowledge that this young man made armour on a plane that I would never reach, not if I put down my spear and did nothing but work at an anvil until the end of my days. It was a curiously painful discovery, and yet liberating.

All this in as little time as it takes one man to greet another on the street, and then Anaxsikles raised his head. And smiled.

That smile was worth a great deal to me. I was afraid – well, that my behaviour with Lydia had poisoned everything.

He put his hammer carefully into a rack at his side, handed his mittens to a slave and came out of his shop to embrace me. That was pleasant.

Spontaneously – mostly to show him how highly I regarded his work – I asked him how much he would charge for a full panoply.

He grinned. 'You can make your own!' he said.

'I want yours. Yours is better.' I nodded at a pair of greaves on the display bench – the pure form of a man's lower legs, without any decoration beyond the beauty of the body. 'I can't make those,' I said.

He laughed. 'Flatterer,' he said. 'I learned to make armour from you. You were the one who taught me that there should be nothing on which the point can catch. I have thought about our duel a hundred times.'

'You've created a style,' I said. 'I see men in your armour every day. You are the best armourer I've ever seen.'

He beamed. 'And you?'

I laughed. 'I've made some simple helmets. I spent a winter learning to cast larger pieces.'

He nodded. 'Yes, that's an important skill. I haven't tackled it yet. What did you learn?'

I won't bore you. I talked about casting ship's rams, and he came down to *Lydia* and looked at the ram and smiled when he saw the name. 'So you still love her, too.'

I shrugged. 'Most of what happened is my own fault,' I said, with an honesty that surprised me. 'I loved her. I think of her often.'

He nodded. 'I always loved her,' he said. 'I would have married her – after you left.' He paused, looked at me. 'Many hold you responsible. I don't,' he said.

'I am, though,' I said.

He shrugged. 'I would have married her,' he said quietly. 'Even after her father cast her out.'

'Really?' I asked.

He shrugged. 'Men are fools. Is a hammer the worse when another's hand has touched it, so long as I wield it well?' He shook his head. 'Even now, I would marry her.'

'You wouldn't be able to live here.' I said it with flat certainty.

He nodded. 'I never expected to be talking to you about this. I, too, failed her. When her father cast her forth, I allowed my father to convince me that she was worthless.' He shook his head. Gone was the master smith, and in his place was a very unhappy young man.

I thought for a few heartbeats. 'I'm trying to contact her,' I said. 'I thought to offer her a dowry and a trip to somewhere else. Athens, perhaps.'

'She would never take anything from you,' Anaxsikles said. 'I'm sorry. But—'

It is hard, to hear that someone you have loved hates you utterly. And yet – how could I have expected anything else?

'If I arranged a meeting,' I said, 'would you go?'

He nodded. 'Of course.'

I took a deep breath. 'I never expected this as an outcome. I went to your shop to tell you what a fine smith you've become.'

He nodded. 'The gods walk the earth,' he said.

'Indeed,' I agreed.

I didn't tell Anarchos what I had planned. But my heart was lightened. I told only Doola, because of all my friends, only he seemed to understand me. My plan was simple; I intended to reunite Lydia and Anaxsikles and then get them transport to Athens – Lydia's dowry would set Anaxsikles up in a shop under the Temple of Hephaestos. It was a good plan, and it deserved to succeed.

But Anarchos dragged his feet, explaining that he only had one clandestine method of contacting Lydia and it was complicated, depending on a Saka slave in the nursery, where Lydia seldom went, as she had no children of her own.

I tried to see her on my next visit to the palace. I wandered as if lost, looking for her, but the slaves were too afraid of their master and too helpful, and I was quickly escorted to the Tyrant, who laughed and made quips all through dinner about the navigator of the seas who got lost in his palace.

That night, he invited Dano to join us. She shared my couch in the Italian way for a while, and when it was time for her to move – and I can't pretend I didn't enjoy her warm femininity next to me – she smiled. 'I'm ready to leave,' she said. 'When can you depart?'

I thought about it. It was a four-day run to Croton, unless the weather turned nasty; a week and a half round trip. Doola was all but done with his sales; we accused him every day of playing with the Syracusan merchants the way a cat plays with mice. The Syracusan armament required bronze for everything, from armour to ship's rams, and bronze needs tin.

'Day after tomorrow,' I said.

She grinned. It was a lovely grin, and made her beautiful. 'Wonderful,' she said.

An hour later, Gelon sat on my couch. 'You are taking my Dano home,' he said. 'I had thought to keep her longer.'

I shrugged. 'She asked me,' I said.

He nodded. 'But you will return?' he asked.

'Of course,' I said.

'People tell me you are having armour made by Anaxsikles,' he said.

I smiled. 'He is perhaps the finest armourer in the Greek world,' I said.

Gelon frowned. 'He is, after all, just a smith. I understand you have spent time with him. Why? Does his conversation fascinate you?'

Dangerous ground. *We're plotting to steal your mistress.*

'He was once my apprentice,' I said.

Gelon recoiled as if he had been struck.

'I am not only a merchant and former slave, but I am a master bronze-smith,' I said.

'You are a man of many faces,' he said. He was clearly displeased.

His displeasure meant little to me. And it occurred to me that if he discussed me with Lydia, he might learn a little too much.

'I have had complaints about your black man,' he said.

My black man? That wouldn't go over well, even as a joke, in our inn. 'My friend Doola?' I said carefully.

'If you must. The African merchant.' His contempt was so deep-rooted as to be offensive. 'He charges outrageous amounts for tin. I have been asked to seize your cargo and sell it at a fair price.'

'Would that be the Carthaginian price?' I asked.

He laughed. 'You know full well that they are boycotting us – ahh, I see. You make game of me.'

I shrugged. 'Yes and no, my lord. I wonder if the merchants who want our tin understand the risks we took to get it. Or would be willing to take those risks themselves.'

'Yet my understanding is that your Doola now holds all the tin in the city, and demands almost twice the Carthaginian price.' He shrugged. 'The mechanics of trade bore me.'

'But the adventure of it would not, my lord. We sailed the Outer Ocean and made war on Carthage every day to take that tin.' I knew what he admired and what he would accept, too.

He smiled – just a little. 'This is why I will allow no merchant to vote in the assembly. They are men without a single noble thought.'

Whatever I might have felt inside, I merely nodded.

It was the only role I played in the sale of the tin, yet I suspect it was important enough.

While I worried about Lydia, and spent money on armour, Doola had not merely sold tin. He had followed a strategy like a military campaign, selling tin only to traders who were leaving the city with their cargoes, like the Athenians, and using the profits to buy *all the other tin*. There wasn't much, but he bought the Illyrian tin and the Etruscan tin that trickled into the city. He bought most of it on credit, because when you have fifty ingots of tin in your warehouses, everyone is willing to give you credit.

While I lay on a kline with the Tyrant, talking of politics, Doola owned all the tin in Syracusa – almost all the tin on Sicily. And then, in the decisive battle of the campaign, he sold it – to six buyers, as he had up the coast at Katania, selling simultaneously to each of them at the same price.

The next morning, I was up late. I walked up into the town, and found the craftsmen's gymnasium. It had been closed by order of the Tyrant, it turned out. Allowing little men to exercise was apparently as wrong as allowing them a voice in government.

I asked around for Polimarchos. Eventually I gave up and asked Anarchos, who shook his head. 'The fighter?' he asked. 'No idea. I had forgotten him.'

So when I stood on Anaxsikles' shop floor with his apprentices measuring me with calipers, I asked him.

He thought a while. 'I wonder if he didn't go off to Sybaris,' he said. 'I think I remember him getting an offer from a rich man to train him in arms.'

'Oh,' I said, or something equally foolish. When you are young, you expect everything to remain as it was while you change. As you grow older, you realize that nothing stays the same.

'Ten days,' Anaxsikles said. 'I'll work on it myself.'

'Ten days?' I said. 'A helmet alone will take that much time.'

He grinned. 'Ahh, now who is the master? What colour do you want your horsehair?'

'Red, black and white, you ungrateful pup.' Truly, Anaxsikles made me feel better, and I can't explain precisely why.

I made the rounds of the town. I bought myself a new sword and a pair of spears, and I bought arms for Giannis – better and finer than what I'd made. I armed Megakles as a hoplite, I put Seckla in a fine corselet. I met Neoptolymos going into Anaxsikles' shop as I was coming out, and we both laughed.

'You said we were taking me home,' Neoptolymos said. 'I thought it was time to look the part. We're all rich, or so I understand.'

It was great fun to spend money like water on beautiful things.

17

The run to Croton was beautiful all the way. The weather was start-
lingly fine, as it can be on the east coast of Sicily, once in a while.
The moist haze lifted, the skies were blue and the wind mostly west
of north, so that the rowers had little of which to complain. We
coasted to Katania and ate lobster; coasted again until we were opposite Rhegium, and then crossed the straits effortlessly, as if such a
thing was easy. Next day we coasted east along the base of the boot
of Italy. There are rich towns all along that coast, and we lived well,
paid silver, and even the oarsmen, I'll wager, enjoyed the trip.

I have said before that few things are as good for a crew as an
attractive but unavailable woman. Dano was a fine sailor, delighted
by every aspect of life at sea, and she insisted on rowing one afternoon, simply to see if she could; two of her ladies joined her. She
didn't strip to the waist, to the disappointment of the crew. At night
she sang, and men came from all the fires to listen to her, or to her
slaves and ladies. Pythagoreans make no distinction of rank when
they eat or speak, so she discoursed on philosophy to any oarsman
who approached her. The food was good, the wine was better and
the company excellent. Doola was as pleased as a craftsman at the
completion of a noble work, and we were all as rich as Croesus.

Great days. It was a different greatness from Marathon, or the
heady days of the Ionian revolt.

I remember lying one night on a beach – I think we were a day
east of Rhegium – and thinking, as I passed the wine to Doola, that
this was how life was supposed to be.

'Friends, whatever will we do next?' I asked. 'We're too young to
lie on our laurels.'

Doola laughed. 'Home to Massalia, and make babies,' he said.
'Buy a farm, and get fat.'

Gaius joined his laughter. 'I have two fine daughters who barely know me,' he said. 'And enough money that I need never leave them again. I will build a temple, and restore my family's power and prestige.'

Neoptolymos nodded. 'I will take back my castle and my people, and raise strong sons and raid Greeks,' he said.

Daud shook his head. 'I don't really want to go home any more,' he admitted.

'Settle in Massalia, then,' Doola said. 'Lots of room.' He looked around. 'Doesn't anyone but me miss Demetrios?'

I nodded. 'I do.'

Daud said, 'We should find him. Make peace.' He looked around. Not everyone agreed.

Sittonax fingered his beard. 'I'm not ready to settle down.' He smiled. 'And what of you, Ari? Are you done? Will you stop being a sea-wolf?'

I remember smiling around at them. 'I would that it could be like this for ever. Triumph after triumph; adventure after adventure. But, I am growing older, and my sword hand will slow. I think I will go back to Plataea, after Neoptolymos is safe in his mountains, and see what awaits me.'

Doola looked blank. 'You won't return to Massalia?'

I shrugged. 'Who knows what the future holds,' I said.

Dano was good company. I admit that some days I wanted to bed her, and then other days I thought of her as a companion, not a woman. Hah! Make of that what you will.

At Croton she was very nearly a queen. She feasted us in her home – seven warriors eating vegetables, because, as everyone knows, the Pythagoreans eat no meat. She spent an evening telling us what the Pythagoreans do believe, which is complex and made me vaguely uncomfortable: it seemed to me, and still does, faintly blasphemous. At the core of their beliefs lies the tenet that the human soul – the very essence of a man or woman – is indestructible, and endures from aeon to aeon, so that a man is reborn again and again in a different body, with different parents – perhaps Greek in one generation and Aethiopian in another.

That much is easily understood, but after that it grows more complex. They believe that the reward of a good life is to go on to a better life, and that the curse of an ill-lived life is to go down the ladder, as they say, so that a bad man might be reborn as a dog. Of this, I have the greatest doubts; how can one cow live a life more filled with cow-arête than another cow, and thus earn a higher step on the ladder? Perhaps I needed to sit longer at Dano's feet and worship.

On the third night, we stayed late, and I sat at her feet quite literally. Some of her followers and friends had come to meet me and the others, and they were brilliant people, well educated, handsome – and very un-Greek. Men and women lay together on couches for dinner, and after; men lay with men and women with women, and all of them seemed like family to all the others. Yet at the same time they didn't seem to me to treat their slaves any better than any other group of people; they were all rich, at least by the standards of Plataea, and had many of the vices and attitudes of the rich. If their women were freer than Greek women, let me add that Greek aristocratic women are also very free.

It was pleasant, but far more alien than a similar visit to a Keltoi hall or a Cretan lord. Many of them owned all their belongings in common, which sounds remarkable, but in truth, they had so much, and so much surplus, that I doubt the sharing was ever very onerous.

I ramble. I was delighted with Dano, but not with her world. I didn't enjoy eating vegetables without meat – indeed, I slipped away every day and ate pork in a taverna by my ship.

But that last evening, as I lay beside Dano, and she was facing her friend Thanis and had her back to me – her hips pressed against mine – she took my hand, as she never had before. And pressed it against her stomach while chatting.

The invitation was clear.

Later, while most of the guests were leaving, she took me aside.

'You could stay here and be one of us,' she said. 'You are a natural aristocrat – a man of worth. Leave the world, and join us.'

'I am not sure I could stop eating meat,' I said.

'Pah!' she said, and wrinkled her nose. 'I can smell it on you, even now. But despite that, I think you might find compensations. You have, all by yourself, changed my view of your Heraclitus. You have a good mind, and good discernment. You could be one of us. With me.'

I kissed her. It was—

Not enough. It didn't move me, particularly. I am hard put to explain what was wrong; my body found her attractive enough. My mind found her mind attractive enough.

328

Perhaps I had grown too old for love. That is certainly what I thought. I kissed her, my tongue roving automatically, my performance barren of meaning.

Oh, the horrors of age. I cursed inside at my lack of passion.

She broke away. She seemed as ... unmoved as I. 'It is your decision,' she said with a smile that was a little more brittle than before. 'You would be welcome here.'

The next day we sailed for Syracusa, and she didn't see me off.

Anarchos had nothing for me. I confess that I threatened him. Something about my failure – my failure even to make love to an attractive woman – made Lydia's happiness more important. Perhaps I was cursed by Aphrodite – that was Seckla's opinion.

He was unimpressed by my threats. He laughed in my face.

Well, there you are. Two bad men, locked in a pointless contest.

I went back the next day and apologized. 'I can save her,' I said weakly.

'So can I,' Anarchos said bitterly. 'But I don't. Because she won't save herself.'

'Does she love the Tyrant?' I asked.

He shrugged.

I sighed. 'I'll return in the spring,' I said.

He nodded. And extended a hand. 'I hear you are very rich, now,' he said.

I laughed. 'Now. Or, perhaps again.' I reached under my cloak. 'Here's your initial investment. With a sizeable return.'

He eyes the leather bag. I'd given him gold for his silver, and a magnificent Alban pearl I'd picked up. He rolled it in his hand. 'Congratulations,' he said. 'I admire your fights with the Carthaginians.'

'You could come along sometime,' I said. 'I'll be fighting in the spring.'

He patted his waist. 'Not likely. But I might build a privateer to go with you. Would you stomach that?'

'If his captain obeyed,' I said.

We shook on it.

I collected my armour from Anaxsikles in the same hour that Neoptolymos tried his. Men said we were like Achilles and Hector standing side by side. We glittered with all the new bronze.

Now, if you consider, in all my life I have been armed in the arms of dead men, or in my own work. This was the first panoply I'd ever had that was all the work of one man, purpose-made for me.

Glorious, like the sword and the spears that went with it.

I had thigh guards, and arm guards, upper and lower, and ankle guards, rendering me proof against any chance blow in a ship fight. A solid-bronze thorax and a helmet with folding cheekpieces, and greaves that fitted up over the knee like a bronze skin.

A shop boy held a mirror, and I looked at myself – a man of bronze.

I ran up and down the street in it, to the delight of a hundred small boys. Despite the old wound, I ran well, although Neoptolymos ran better. And we threw our spears and even fenced a bit with our swords, and the crowd roared with pleasure. Remember – this was a society at the edge of war with mighty Carthage. They were afraid. Afraid they would lose. And seeing us – friendly foreigners who would help – gave them heart.

Ah, it was glorious.

Last of all, I went to see Gelon. He seemed scarcely to remember me, which was odd. I explained that I was returning to Massalia, and he was uninterested until I said I would be back in the spring with five ships.

'It is my intention to strike the Carthaginian trade in the Adriatic,' I said. 'If you prefer, I can touch at Rhegium rather than here. I know your relations with Carthage are delicate.'

He nodded. 'Oh, come here,' he said. 'Will your five ships support me when we are at war?'

'Yes,' I said.

He nodded. 'Then let us not mince words. We are at war with Carthage now – and with Persia. There is a rumour that Xerxes is now Great King – and has sent an ambassador to Carthage to demand they make war against us. To destroy the Greek world.'

I nodded. 'I have heard this rumour before,' I said. 'It is something men say. I doubt the Great King even knows where Syracusa is.'

He frowned. 'Yet Athens intends to send an embassy here to ask for our support against Persia,' he said.

My eyebrows shot up.

'Oh, yes, Plataean. It has come to that.' He drank wine. 'Athens has more than a hundred ships to put in the water, all triremes. Yet I have half as many again, when all the cities of Magna Greca support me.' He nodded. 'I will be Hegemon of the League against Persia. Wait and see.'

I couldn't see this idealist being invited by Athens to command a rowing boat in a race, but he believed himself a great man. And indeed, despite my dislike of him – yes, I had decided I disliked him – he had greatness in him.

As for promising my ships to support him, I assumed that we would. How could I have seen how it would all fall out? The truth is that, like many Greeks, I never imagined what was coming. To men of my generation, Lade and Marathon settled everything – Lade gave Persia the upper hand in Asia, and Marathon denied them Greece. That business was finished.

In retrospect, I should have known, of all men, where we were headed, and at what speed.

We sailed for Massalia near the end of the season, rich, fat and sleek. Gaius went back to Rome, and we feasted with him and his delighted wife for three days before dropping down the Tiber and racing north. We worried every day and every night about a Carthaginian squadron, and we met none.

Massalia seemed very small after the summer in Syracusa. Dionysus was delighted to see us; he had taken three merchantmen over the summer, and was eager to take part in our Adriatic adventure in the spring. He was, as ever, a hard drillmaster, and our rowers cursed him all winter as they sat on benches on a freezing beach, lifting weighted oars and doing other exercises meant to keep their bodies hard. We trained, too. I tried to remember all that Polimarchos had taught me, and I had men lifting heavy stones, fencing with sticks, practising taking and defending ships large and small. We had two months of heavy, icy rain and Dionysus kept us at it. I think some of the oarsmen would have killed him, if they thought they could have got away with it.

But it was not all work. We celebrated feasts like rich men; we built the first stone temple in our small settlement, and many of our men rebuilt their homes in stone. Vasileos rebuilt our Carthaginian capture, making her a lighter ship and slightly longer. We hired more marines from all over the Tyrrhenian Sea – most of them Etruscans. We had some Latins, too – big, tough men.

I threw myself into exercise. It appeared to me that this was my last adventure. I felt old that winter, with aches in my hands and knees that wouldn't go away. I had no interest in women, and little in wine or song. It seemed to me that the compass of the world was drawing in, smaller and smaller, and that after one more raid, I would go back to Plataea and be an average smith, and die there.

And that seemed to me just.

How the gods must have laughed.

18

Just before the spring feast of Demeter, Dionysus rode over from Massalia to tell us that a Sikel fishing boat had come in with rumour of a heavy Carthaginian squadron cruising our coast. So we got our hulls out of their ship sheds and into the water – my *Lydia* and Neoptolymos' *Eleuthera*. I had Megakles as my helmsman, and Neoptolymos had Vasileos. Our crews were veterans and our marines were, if I may say so, superb – all fully armoured, and all in the peak of training.

We couldn't wait to get our beaks into some Carthaginians.

We rowed out for a stormy day, our bows into the wind, and came home lashed by rain, and never had a sniff of the Carthaginians. Of course, we never had more than a six-stade sight line, either, so it would have been Poseidon's will if we had seen them.

But we slept dry at home, with sentries on the headlands and food and wine, which was more than any raiding squadron was getting. And we were off the beach again the next morning, when the air was still brisk and the sun not even a streak of salmon pink on the eastern horizon. We ran along the coast to Massalia, and landed at noon. Dionysus was ready with two ships.

We spent three days training – rowing out towards the northern point of Sardinia until we could see the headland, and then performing manoeuvres – line to column, column to line; changing stroke, changing direction, reversing benches. My oarsmen were openly discussing killing Dionysus. It was Lade in miniature, except that I was a much better trierarch myself, and knew that the standard Dionysus set was perfectly reasonable.

Listen, thugater. It's like this. If you take a warship to sea, spend the summer rowing up and down the coast looking for the enemy and raiding his pastures, and then finally meet up in the fall – well, your rowers and your marines have, in fact, spent three or four months training. Getting hard. Every direction change, every squadron manoeuvre gets them better.

All Dionysus did was to insist that we be as good as autumn sailors in the spring, by packing a lot of drills into the first week at sea. But such things were innovations, then. Young Phormio does it all the time, these days, or so I'm given to understand.

As usual, I digress. But it is important to understand how *untrained* crews were, usually, in the spring. We'd worked all winter – I suspect I was the only pirate in the whole circuit of the Inner Sea who paid his crew through the winter. I had never really done it before. When I worked for Miltiades, we fed our oarsmen all winter but we didn't train them. They just drank and, er, did what oarsmen do, when there's a town available.

Anyway: three days at sea, and never a sign or report of the Carthaginian squadron. We went back to our home ports for two days' rest, and then we were at it again. This time, we cruised west along the coast, the mountains rising away to the north and the sea spring blue and clean beneath us.

Two days west, and we sighted a pair of warships to the south and gave chase. They fled, and we rowed like madmen – all of us, even me.

Oh, how I remember that chase! Two days at sea, and we rowed and rowed, and we were the better men.

Finally, they turned west just at sunset the second day and ran ashore, and we were so close behind them that we landed in the froth of their oars and had our marines ashore before they could draw up their ships.

But they were Etruscans.

How we laughed, there on the beach! They laughed too, with the sudden relief of men at the edge of death. We were poorer by the value of their ships, but that two-day chase put us in fine condition. Most men will only train so hard when there's no real threat, but offer them a prize on the horizon—

We were already a third of the way down the coast to the Tiber, so we camped with our Etruscans for a night and set off south in the morning, now a powerful fleet of six ships. The Etruscans were Veii, and ostensibly at sea to protect their city's shipping. I suspect they had in mind a little piracy.

We left them at the mouth of the Tiber and rowed upstream

to Rome, where Gaius was like a man awakened by his friends for exercise – surely you've had this experience, eh? A friend sleeps late, you arrive for your morning run, and he pretends he's ready? You know what I'm talking about. Gaius's ship was still on stocks and his oarsmen had spent the winter making babies and propping his new vineyards. So we set a rendezvous and went back to sea.

North of the straits, we picked up a Carthaginian merchantman. He surrendered at once, but swore he was part of a convoy for Sardinia. We had six days until our rendezvous, so we rowed east along the north shore of Sicily looking for the convoy.

We swept for eight days and found nothing.

We left our Carthaginian prisoners on their own coast of Sicily. I watched Demetrios's homeport go by under my lee, and considered dropping down for a chat. He had to be there.

But sometimes, it is best to leave a man alone.

So we rowed north, to Ostia.

Two days there – see, I have the logs. Two days there, and our crews were sick. The place is deeply unhealthy, and the spring mosquitoes were brutal, and men were fevered. And no sign of Gaius. Dionysus grew angry, and threatened to leave us. We were drinking in a waterfront taverna so filthy that I had my pais wipe our table down with his chlamys, which he then threw onto a heap of filth rather than wear. One of the porne who served the wine picked it up and put it on.

When Achilles said it was better to be the slave of a bad master than King of the Dead, he hadn't seen porne in Ostia.

It was an oppressive place.

I sent Doola upstream in a small boat while I kept the squadron together by force of will. A dozen of my own carefully trained oarsmen deserted – or wandered off – or simply got sick.

Two days later, Doola returned – alone.

'He'll join us later in the summer,' Doola said. He scowled, which was unlike him. 'He's a great man now,' Doola said.

Dionysus snorted, and later that night gave full vent to his feelings – wasted time, lost oarsmen, disease, suffering, the missed chance of a great capture.

But the gods meant us to be there.

That night, a dancer came to our taverna. We were surly drunks, but she was a fine-looking woman – not young, but in high training, with muscled legs and arms. She danced beautifully, some foreign dance that was just enough like our women's dances at home to make me weep wine-soaked tears. We showered her with money, and she smirked, and the taverna's porne cursed her and glared.

The taverna's owner, a surprisingly young and innocent-looking villain, caught the woman unawares and tried to take her earnings. He didn't even bother to threaten her; he just grabbed the front of her chiton.

She threw him over her hip and slammed his head on the dirt floor.

My lads cheered and threw more money.

She bowed and smiled. She was missing some teeth, and was none too clean, but in Ostia she looked like a fine courtesan. She bowed and did a little skip on her feet. Seckla hooted – Seckla, let me say again.

Doola grinned at me. Megakles stood up and yelled, 'Show us your tits!' Sorry, ladies. But that was his speed, and he was a sailor.

Our dancer smiled and pulled her chiton over her head, as easily as a snake wriggling out of its skin, and stood naked, one hand on her hip. She had a matching pair of bruises inside her thighs and a nasty cut at the top of her right thigh, but otherwise, she was the best-looking woman any sailor needed to see, in Ostia or anywhere else.

We roared, and more coins were tossed.

She reached out and grabbed Seckla and kissed him – and hooked his chlamys off his shoulder and wrapped herself in it. She was grinning.

The innkeeper started to get off the floor. She flicked one nicely arched foot at him and it caught him on the temple, and he was out.

Quite a performance.

She collected her coins, showing a great deal of herself, doing little acrobatics like walking on her hands – naked – to pick up coins, and doing the splits and backwards handsprings and such stuff. She put the coins into a bag around her waist that seemed to be her only permanent possession. This process went on a long time, because men threw more money and she had to come up with ever more inventive methods of picking it up.

Finally, she pulled Seckla's cloak around her and suddenly, with a spring, she was sitting on the bench across from me, where I sat beside Dionysus.

'You two are the captains, yes?' she asked.

Dionysus shrugged. 'Yes,' he said.

I pointed at Neoptolymos, who was very carefully not looking.

'He's a captain. So's young Achilles, there.' Achilles was Dionysus' hard-bitten second.

Achilles, whose real name was Teukes, gave me a mock glare. He was older than any of us, and calling him 'young Achilles' was, well, teasing, of a sort. Hah, hah.

At any rate, she leaned across the table, and I couldn't really keep my eyes on her face, if you take my meaning. I was old, but not so very old.

'I have something to sell,' she said, with a wink.

'I'm sure any man in this room will buy,' I said.

She shook her head. 'Not that. I don't sell that – what do you think I am? A whore? I'm a dancer. Listen, trierarchs. I have something to sell. The value of it won't last.' She shrugged, a lovely motion.

Dionysus was quicker witted than I. 'Information?' he asked.

She smiled at him. 'Perhaps,' she said, reaching up to put her hair back up.

It takes a superior courage to be a woman, alone in a room full of pirates, wearing nothing but a borrowed cloak and dickering over the price of information. I couldn't do it.

'Are you a slave?' I asked.

She raised her eyebrows. 'On and off,' she said. She shrugged. 'Just now, I own myself.'

'Tell me your information and I'll tell you what it's worth,' I suggested.

She smiled. 'You have a special herb and I won't ever get pregnant?' she shot back. 'You'll pay tomorrow? Your rich aunt just died and you haven't got the bequest yet?'

'How did you know?' I asked.

She leered. 'Don't *be* like this. I have something amazing to relate, and you are my only customers. By Aphrodite, gentlemen!'

'How much do you want, then?' Dionysus asked.

'A talent. In gold.' She looked back and forth, evaluating our reactions.

'Ten silver drachma would seem to be more your price,' Dionysus said.

'Ten silver mina,' she said.

'Wait!' I said. 'Is this shipping information?' I asked.

She grew demure. 'Perhaps.'

'On this coast?' I asked.

She looked down. 'No. But by Aphrodite, gentlemen, it's an opportunity for wealth, beyond—' She shook her head.

'How'd you get it, then?' I asked.

'A gentleman friend told me some things,' she said, smiling.

'Navarchs don't actually whisper secrets to porne,' Dionysus said, his voice hard. 'Go and ply your trade with the others, woman.'

She looked at me. 'Why? You two are heroes. I *want* to tell you. Death to Carthage. Eh? We all hate the bastards. Why can't I make a killing with you?'

Dionysus caught her, pinned her hand to the table and put a knife against her wrist.

'Hey!' she said, and then the confidence went out of her.

'I wager this is a trap,' Dionysus said. 'You are far too expensive and far too out of place to be here. Who told you to come here?'

She wriggled. 'Damn you! Every porne on the waterfront knows who you are and how much cash you have! I know something worth knowing! I won't give it for free!'

Dionysus rolled his dagger blade over her wrist, and she whimpered. He was a cruel bastard. In fact, he liked inflicting pain – it wasn't just that he was a strong leader. He *liked* watching his men suffer when he trained them.

'I can maim your hand,' he said. 'Or your face. Or have every oarsman on my ships fuck you till you die. Now talk, whore.'

I can be a hard man. I've killed a lot of men, and some women. But this sort of thing sickened me.

On the other hand, I was fairly sure Dionysus was right.

Seckla, on the other hand, was watching, and he wasn't having any of it. 'Let her go,' he said, lurching up to our table in drunken arête.

Dionysus pushed the blade down harder.

She moaned. 'I'm not—'

Seckla pulled at her hand. I'm sure he didn't mean to cause her more pain, but he rotated her body and she screamed: 'Fuck you, you bastards! I'm not lying!'

Dionysus leaned back and let her go.

She snatched her hand away and nursed it against her breast. She seemed smaller and dirtier. She began to cry.

'Why?' she asked, looking at me. 'Why did he have to do that?'

'I'll slit your nose, next,' Dionysus said. He leaned back and motioned a porne for wine. He looked at me. 'You can't believe any of this.'

I rubbed my beard.

Dionysus rolled his eyes, even as Seckla tired to comfort the dancer and she kept away from him. 'Listen, if you want this woman, lean her against the wall and take her from behind so you don't have to listen to the shit that spews from her mouth,' he laughed. 'It's a door that opens and closes a great deal.'

I shook my head. 'She has a fair amount of courage,' I said. 'I want to hear her information.'

She turned and threw herself at my knees. 'Please!' she said. 'I will—'

I raised a hand. 'Listen to my terms. You want to offer us a target, yes?'

She nodded emphatically. 'A rich target.'

'So,' I said. 'You come along, as our guest. I will make you some guarantees – swear oaths with you. You will receive a share of our take – when we make the capture. Not before.'

She shrank away. 'Never. Go to sea – on a pirate ship? You must think I'm simple.' She laughed. It was a terrible laugh. 'That's not the way I want to die – raped to death by criminals.' Her eyes flickered to Dionysus. 'I thought you were different – the heroes of Lades and Marathon.' She spat.

Dionysus shrugged. 'I think Arimnestos is too kind,' he said.

She spat on the floor. 'My curse on all your kind,' she said, and ran out of the taverna.

Seckla glowered at me.

I nodded. 'Go and chase her down and make her a better offer,' I suggested.

He stumbled after the dancer. Now, I don't think Seckla had shown interest in five women in his entire life up until then, so you may find my choice odd, but women can be sensitive to these things, and Seckla was *not* a hard man. Seckla suffered every time he had to fight – every wound he inflicted sat on him. He was only with us because of his love for me – and for Neoptolymos and Doola and Daud.

He followed her into the edge of darkness.

I remember telling Dionysus that he was a right bastard. I remember him telling me I was a fool.

★

In the morning, Seckla was sleeping with the woman wrapped in his arms on a palliasse of straw under the upturned hull of the *Lydia*. She was as pretty in the morning, rising from her blankets, as she was in the night – and as naked. She ran into the water and bathed, and wrapped herself in Seckla's chlamys and planted herself in front of me.

'I'll come. I lift my curse, trierarch. I offer my apologies, but your friend hurt my wrist something cruel. Seckla and I have made a deal.'

Seckla said, 'I gave her my word. She gets the same share that I get.'

I was staggered. 'Seckla – listen, lady. Without meaning to dicker, he can't offer you the same share he has. Not without seven men voting to agree.' I glared at him.

'She can have my share, then,' Seckla said.

'We'll split it,' she said. Her eyes were interesting. She could be cold as – well, as cold as a warrior. Or quite the passionate thing. She'd settled her claws into Seckla, and I couldn't decide if she was a porne or not. In her heart, I mean. In fact, she was.

Dionysus came up.

She slipped behind Seckla.

'Good morning, young lady,' he said. He looked at me. 'Slit her throat and let's be on our way.'

She stepped back.

He grinned. Seckla stepped up to him, fists clenched. Dionysus, however, was twenty years his senior and had a dignity not usually found in pirates – although, come to think of it—

'Let her alone,' Seckla said.

'It's a trap,' Dionysus said. 'One of the Carthaginians you've robbed is setting you up. Or that fellow – what's his name? Who enslaved the lot of you.'

'Dagon,' I said. While I loathed Dagon and wanted him under the edge of my sword, I didn't really think of him all that often, and I didn't see him as – well, as intelligent enough to plan something like this. He was sly – crafty – evil. But not capable of setting a trap with, of all unlikely allies, a woman.

I looked at the dancer. 'What's your name?' I asked.

'Men call me Despoina,' she said. When I made a face, she shrugged. 'I was born to Geaeta.'

'Where?' I asked.

'Athens,' she said.

I shrugged. 'Beware,' I said. 'I know Athens fairly well.'

'Really?' she said. 'I'd have said you were a Boeotian bumpkin who had visited once or twice.'

'Not bad,' I allowed. 'Tell me where the bronze-smiths gather.'

'The Temple of Hephaestos, on the hill below the Areopagus,' she said.

'What's the rostra?' I asked.

She rolled her eyes. 'Anyone knows that. The speaker's stone in the Pnyx.'

'How did Miltiades die?' I asked.

'His wound festered while Cimon tried to raise the money for his debts,' she said.

I looked at the ground. 'Damn,' I said. My emotion must have showed.

Her eyes softened. 'Don't tell me you really are the great Plataean?' She laughed. 'Come on. Arimnestos of Plataea is dead. Everyone says so.' She looked at me. 'I wish I could ask you about Plataea.'

'How is it with Aristides?' I asked.

She shrugged. 'We're not exactly bosom friends,' she allowed.

'What are you doing in Magna Greca?' I asked.

She looked around. Men were watching from a distance.

'I was sold,' she said. She raised her face defiantly. 'I was a free woman, but I was sold. As a porne. I ran, and got caught. They sold me to a Carthaginian.' She shrugged. 'I lived. They did n't know I could swim. I jumped over the side at Rhegium. I'm better-trained than any kid on this coast. Better-looking, too.' She shrugged. 'And I won't be a slave again, and I don't open and shut for free, either.' She looked at Dionysus.

'A pretty story,' he said.

'Fuck you, pirate,' she said.

His fist smashed into her cheek and she fell. 'Speak respectfully, whore,' he said. 'I am not your equal.'

'Women who sell their bodies are so much lower than men who kill for money,' she spat from the sand.

He looked at me while Seckla fumed. Don't imagine Seckla was too much the coward to fight for his woman. It was more complex than that. Dionysus was a superior officer and also an old friend of mine. And Seckla didn't trust his sleeping companion yet.

Anyway, Dionysus looked at me. 'I'm inclined to try her,' he said.

'If it's a trap, we'll fight our way out,' I said. I remember grinning.

He shrugged. 'The best way to get out of a trap is never to enter it.'

'We need Gaius,' I said. I looked at the woman, who was rubbing her cheek. Dionysus liked to hit women. I'd figured that out. 'Despoina, how much time do we have?'

She considered rebellion. I saw it on her face. She considered telling us all to fuck ourselves. She had a lot of pride and a lot of ... arrogance for a woman who'd been so ill used.

But good sense won out.

'If you believe me, you need to catch them at the new moon,' she said.

That gave us two weeks.

'Where?' I asked softly. I held her eyes.

'Do we have a deal? I split Seckla's share?' she breathed.

'If you tell the truth, and we get a prize, you will have a sizeable share,' I said. 'Not less in value than one half of Seckla's share. Is that agreeable? And I guarantee your body, your person and your freedom on my oath to Zeus, the God of Kings and Free Men, and I offer you bread and wine, hospitality and guest friendship from my house to yours until my heirs and yours are all shades in Elysium.' I held out my hand. 'Unless you betray me or mine, in which case, by the same oath, I will hunt you like the Furies and cut your throat.'

Seckla nodded at her and gave her a small smile. 'He means it.'

She smiled back, and took my hand. 'Deal,' she said.

Dionysus snorted in disgust.

'New Carthage,' she said. 'The tin fleet.'

19

Carthage got her tin from Iberia, as I've mentioned. Four times a year, when the Iberians had filled the Carthaginian warehouses, they sent a fleet to pick up the tin and sail it home – half a dozen round ships guarded closely by a squadron of galleys.

This was, well, I won't call it common knowledge. It was *uncommon* knowledge. Shippers, tin miners, bronze-smiths and pirates knew it.

I'd say that the Carthaginians kept the movement of the tin fleets secret, but that wouldn't do justice to how secret they kept it. They didn't want the Greeks to know where the tin came from, or how much there was. Most merchants – even tin traders – thought that the tin came from Etrusca, or Illyria. Or some hazy point outside the Gates of Heracles.

Geaeta had quite a story – an adventure of her own, with knife-fights, lovemaking and clever escapades worthy of Odysseus. I even believed a few of the stories. She had courage and strong muscles, and I can witness that those two things alone can win you free of slavery.

Her story – the parts that made sense and I believed – was complex. She had started the spring sailing season in a slave pen in Carthago, and gone west in a consignment to New Carthage, a colony on the Inner Sea coast of Iberia facing the Balearic Islands. She said that she was sold off to a brothel there, and two weeks later, the first ships of the spring tin convoy had arrived, all badly storm-damaged by a freak spring storm in the strait.

'They were all afraid, and angry,' she said. 'All the owners. All the rich men.' She shrugged. 'Your friend says navarchs don't talk to porne. Maybe; maybe not *his* kind,' she spat. 'But most men talk. And good friends – a pair of them will hire a pair of girls – you know, together.' She shrugged. 'And the men will chat while—' She shrugged again.

'I got the captain of one of the round ships,' she said. 'He had had quite a scare. That's when men talk the most. He almost lost his ship – and his life. He went to the temple four times while he was staying in my room.' She shrugged, smiled. 'He wanted me.' She made a face – pride and revulsion together. 'He wanted me every hour of the day and night – besotted, he was. So he paid a bribe to the brothel owner so that I could come with him to Carthage and back – he was being sent for replacement oarsmen and all sorts of chandlery that New Carthage didn't have.' She met my eyes. 'The day we left, news came that the other survivors of the tin fleet had returned to Gades. And that we could expect them in fifteen days, at the new moon.' She looked around. It was the evening of our second day at sea. She'd told the story enough times that it had a polished ring to it that made her sound like a liar. The problem was that she was a damned good storyteller, and that didn't actually help her veracity.

Gaius – now a surly, somewhat domineering Roman magnate who clearly didn't want to go to sea that summer – shook his head. 'Dionysus is right,' he said. 'You can't believe a word she says.'

Seckla spat. 'I believe her,' he said.

Gaius made an obscene suggestion as to exactly why he believed her, and Daud laughed and laughed. It was good to hear the Keltoi man laugh; he had been silent for so long. His second brush with slavery had all but ruined his cheerful disposition, leaving him dour.

'How'd you come to be in Ostia?' Daud asked, when he was done laughing.

'I jumped ship at Rhegium,' she said.

'Why, exactly?' I asked. 'I mean, why would a Carthaginian ship bound for Carthage ever come anywhere near Rhegium?'

She shrugged. 'How would I know?' she said. 'I'm not a great sailor. When we were at sea, he'd, um, make use of me when he pleased, and otherwise the boat went up and down, men ran about and the oarsmen all watched me like cats watch rats. I swore I'd never go to sea again.'

Gaius pursed his lips and scrated his red hair. 'I'm leaving my farms at a touchy time – to be killed by the Carthaginians,' he said. 'Perhaps if I'm lucky, I'll only be a slave.'

Geaeta looked pointedly at his waistline. 'At least you know you won't be sold to a brothel,' she said.

Gaius wasn't used to being talked to that way, much less by a mere woman. He stomped off.

That night, Dionysus said to me, 'She's either real, or she's the most gifted actress I've ever seen.'

I agreed. I believed her. Most of the time.

Of course, it was possible. It was all plausible. Ships go off course. But an unarmed merchant ship headed for Carthage should have avoided the north coast of Sicily – the Greek coast – like a plague. He should have run south and coasted Africa.

On the other hand, she was just the kind of girl who got the trierarchs in a brothel – not a broken spirit in a vaguely fleshy body, but a passionate woman with good looks and a mouth. If I owned a brothel, I'd buy a dozen of her.

Hah! Sorry, ladies. A man can dream.

We coasted northern Sicily. Secretly, every night when I landed, I asked the men of the towns whether they'd ever seen Geaeta before, or a ship bearing her. None had. She said she'd never landed in any of them. Of course, a round ship is more at the mercy of the winds and Poseidon's whims, and never has to land. It can carry food and water for weeks.

All of her story was plausible.

We landed next on the south coast of Sardinia – close enough to home to think about chucking the whole thing. But we didn't. The prospect of riches can be as intoxicating as wine.

South of Sardinia, we picked up a pair of Carthaginian traders, half a day apart. I caught one, and Dionysus caught the other. Neither skipper knew anything about a tin convoy, but both admitted there had been a ferocious storm in the Straits of Heracles a month before.

Their cargoes were valuable – grain in one, and olive oil and hides in the other. We concentrated the cargoes into one of them and put a dozen men aboard under Giannis and sent her north to Massalia. And went west with the second capture filled to the gunwales with water and dried fish, a crew of fishermen under Vasileos sailing her. With our consort to provide food for a thousand rowers, we managed to make the five-day crossing to the Balearics in three days – with seven hundred and fifty mythemnoi of food and as much water. No fleet could have done it, but a handful of pirates—

Listen, I've made Dionysus sound like a monster in the matter of the girl. He wasn't a nice man. He had fine ethics but didn't apply them to women – at all. But he was an excellent sailor, a fine navigator and he planned. I learned on that trip how to calculate food expenditure. Off Alba, we had a round ship in consort, but we hadn't used her for food. Dionysus' method allowed a squadron of triremes to keep on the sea virtually for ever – as long as the owners were rich enough to buy stores. A thousand men eat a lot.

Nine days out of Ostia, and we were on a beach on the south coast of the Balearics. I'd landed there before, and I liked the beach. And then we were away south. We cruised warily off Ebusus and landed on a tiny islet, and then we slipped off the beach in the first light of a new-minted summer day and crossed to the Iberian coast, and worked our way along with a favourable wind for two more days.

The second evening, a pair of local boats saw us from seaward as we were landing. Dionysus was off the beach in a flash, and he took them both – no fishing boat can outrun a warship, as I had reason to remember. We ate their fish as the crews sat, disconsolate.

Dionysus and I questioned the two fishing captains. They knew New Carthage, and feared it, it was clear. Nether knew anything about the tin fleet. Both expected to die.

Neither knew anything about a big squadron of Carthaginian triremes setting a trap for pirates, either, to be frank.

Dionysus was planning to kill them all, but I insisted we leave them there on the beach, alive. Well, not all of them. Four men 'volunteered' to row with my ship. I took them.

We were off into an overcast morning of light rain. We crept down the coast: the wind was wrong, so we rowed into a light headwind, our five-ship squadron spread across thirty stades of sea so that we would sweep up any ship we might want to catch.

It was mid-afternoon when Neoptolymos – he had a Carthaginian ship so he was the most landward of the sweep – signalled that he could see New Carthage. An hour later, the town was visible in the haze, her red tile roofs glinting against the rising red-brown of the hills behind the town.

The harbour was empty. So were the seas.

After fifteen days of frenetic rowing and planning and training and sailing, our disappointment was palpable.

I had to admit that we hadn't planned for the situation that confronted us. We planned either to fight our way out of an ambush, or swoop down on our prey. In fact, we found a fortified town with a heavily walled inner harbour – empty. Nor was there a powerful naval squadron waiting for us.

In the fading, ruddy light, I rowed up alongside Dionysus and hailed him.

'Have you cut her throat yet?' he asked.

I laughed. 'No. She says we're late.'

'Or early,' he said. 'I don't like it; the whole town's empty.'

'Now what?' I asked.

'Now we take the next ship in,' he said.

That didn't take as long as I feared. We stayed at sea all night, ate cold rations from our merchantman and the dawn showed us a Phoenician ship under oars coming up from the darkness to the south and east, from the coast of Africa. Neoptolymos dropped down and took her with only a cursory fight.

I winced to watch Neoptolymos, a decent man, slam his fist repeatedly into the captured Phoenician trierarch. Torturing prisoners is cowardly, to me. I didn't like what I was seeing.

Heh.

Then he was brought aboard my ship.

It was Hasdrubal.

He had a bad cut under one eye and another on a corner of his mouth, which was ripped open by repeated blows. Even as he landed on my deck, Neoptolymos, who followed him over the side, hit him again.

The Illyrian laughed mirthlessly. 'I can't stop hitting him,' he said.

'Make him stop!' pleaded the Carthaginian.

He didn't recognize me.

I'd like to say that I stopped Neoptolymos from tormenting the man, who was already broken.

Listen, there's limits. I try to be the man that Heraclitus taught, and not the thug I might have been. But sometimes—

An hour passed. Dionysus dropped onto my deck. He looked down at the wreckage of a human body on my ship.

He laughed.

'I thought you were too soft for this life,' he said. 'Ares! Kill him.' He looked at me, a little sickened, I could tell.

'He enslaved us,' I said. 'He killed Neoptolymos's sister.'

Dionysus nodded. Looked away. 'Have you vengeful Furies even asked him about the tin fleet?' he asked.

Neoptolymos nodded. 'He passed it two days ago, headed east. Under full sail.'

The same wind that we'd rowed into.

Dionysus nodded. 'Let's chase them,' he said gently. 'This is a waste of time.' He picked up Hasdrubal and threw him over the rail into the sea without asking us.

Neoptolymos growled.

I seemed to awaken.

Sometimes, when I fancy myself a better man then other men, I think of two things from the ten years between Plataea and Artemisium. I think of how I treated Lydia. I think of what I did to Hasdrubal.

He didn't even scream when he hit the water. He sank, unable even to swim.

Choked and drowned.

Slowly, I hope.

All of his marines had been killed, and, of course, Dagon wasn't aboard. His ship was a small merchant galley of fifty oars, with the usual collection of broken men as oarsmen – men he'd played his own role in breaking, no doubt. As soon as Neoptolymos's marines came down the gangway, the oarsmen had ripped the rest of the crew asunder.

It is odd that there are so many bad captains, as the payback is so ruthless.

We took the ship and the oarsmen. It was ballasted in wine for the western stations. So we gave our oarsmen good African wine every night as we ate salt fish and rowed and sailed east.

We tried every trick. We wet our sails to take the breeze when it was coming over our sterns, and we sailed on a quarter-reach with both boatsail and mainsail drawing together – a rare point of sailing even in our rig, and very fast, so that for a whole day we made perhaps thirty stades an hour.

We had advantages and disadvantages. We knew where our quarry was going, and elected to cut the corner – they would have crossed directly to Africa, while we went on a long hypotenuse, slanting away east, south-east. We were neither lucky nor unlucky in our winds, and of course, our quarry had the same winds. Best of all, we knew about them and they, we hoped, knew nothing of us.

Dionysus knew the waters better than I, and he was making for Hippo, on the north shore of Africa, about six hundred stades from Carthage.

This was more blue-water sailing than most of our oarsmen

had ever seen. We were lucky to have so many veterans from our adventures in the Outer Sea. Sailors like nothing better than to tell a shipmate *This ain't nothing, brother*, and I stood between the oars on the third night, the taste of salt anchovies barely drowned in wine on my tongue, listening to my oarsmen.

'You ain't seen nothing, mate,' said Xenos, a fisherman's son from Massalia. 'We were nine days at sea off Iberia – the Outer Sea coast of Iberia, mate – in a storm so bad men cut their wrists rather than face another day. As Poseidon is my witness.'

'And when we tried to run from Gaul to Alba,' says another voice in the darkness, 'Poseidon blew us over the edge of the world.'

'And then what happened?' asked a sceptic.

'A Titan blew us back,' said the storyteller. 'I'm here, ain't I?'

Five days at sea.

Even with the prospect of boundless riches, sailors will eventually tire of bad food and back-breaking labour. Even sailors.

Five days of rowing – for the most part. We were low on water and out of food. Men spoke poems in praise of bread. No lie: bread is the thing you miss most at sea.

Well, many men were missing something else. Geaeta was not inhibited by the presence of two hundred crewmen, and Seckla's continuing education at her hands – and more – was noisy, demonstrative and sometimes annoyingly emotive. I have said before that a woman – especially a desirable but unavailable woman – aboard a ship is a fine thing for morale, but to be sure, a desirable and sexually active woman aboard a ship with two hundred men just makes the one hundred and ninety-nine more difficult.

Myself, I took to pulling my cloak around my head, despite the heat.

I won't say the crew was near mutiny – merely that I thought it possible that Seckla would be murdered. I confined him to the sailor's deck amidships, and read Geaeta my best speech on being a shipmate. She laughed, but obeyed. She knew that she was still on sufferance. Most men believed her story, now – I did. But she understood.

Another day. We finished the water.

We sighted land. We'd sighted it for days, but that evening, Dionysus laid alongside and told me that we were hundreds of stades short of our landfall and that we had to land anyway.

I knew that.

In the last light of a summer evening, we rowed into a river mouth. We rowed until the water was fresh and drank it straight from the stream, reaching through the oar-ports to drink out of wooden cups. The water was brackish – not even fresh. But men were badly dehydrated, and most of them drank and pissed it away immediately – pardon my frankness – but we were close to the edge.

We landed in the darkness, put a guard over the wine and slept. In the morning, the marines caught a shepherd boy who said we were west of Kissia.

Dionysus shook his head. 'Poseidon hates us. We're hopelessly behind.'

Morale plummeted. Things might have gone ill, but we made a landfall, got water and sent the shepherd for his father and paid silver for the whole flock and ate it, too.

Next morning, full of mutton, we rowed east. We stood well out as we passed Kissia, which had a pair of triremes on her open beach. I proposed we burn them on the beach, but Gaius wanted to go home and Dionysus wanted to try for the tin fleet for two more days – right up to the walls of Carthage.

We landed that night with the twinkling lights of Hippo in the distance and the smell of their fires in our nostrils.

In the morning, when the sun rose, we saw that her harbour was full of ships.

Full of ships.

Dionysus turned and hugged his helmsman. Most of the men on our ship hugged Geaeta.

Sixteen ships, though. We'd chased a gazelle, and caught a lion.

20

The Bay of Hippo stretches a good sixty stades from promontory to promontory, forming a superb natural harbour with shelving beaches running into the fertile lands above. The 'city' is really three or four communities all the way around the half-moon curve: there's a fishing village, a sailor's village with wine shops and an entrepreneurial agora, there's a fine town with walls and homes for the rich, and there's a slave town that stretches along the downwind side of the beach. If I keep telling this story, I'll eventually tell you how I came to know Hippo and Carthage so well, but for the moment, just take my word for it.

Top up my wine, lad. Ah! Lesbian wine. When it crosses my lips, I feel young again.

Where was I? Ah.

We sighted the Carthaginian tin fleet.

Dionysus was a ship's-length ahead of me. We were under oars, the wind heading us as it had for ten days. There was a commotion aboard my ship, and Doola came aft to tell me that Dionysus was standing on his stern platform and asking for me.

I ran forward along the gangway. I ordered the marines into their armour as I went. My heart beat fast, and my old – well, let's call it what it is, eh? – my old greed for glory was suddenly *there*.

So much for maturity.

I ran onto the bow platform. Dionysus hailed me from his stern and bellowed, 'Let's take them!'

Even as he called, he was turning his ship.

Megakles was following him, and the oars were in perfect order, with Doola sounding the time as Seckla put him in his thorax.

I stood on tiptoe on the bow rail for a long breath.

The enemy ships were not in supporting range. Why would they be? They were a day out from home in a Carthaginian port, not in the face of the enemy. And who had ten warships to come after their fleet?

We had five.

Their warships were mostly clustered at the western end of the crescent. The seven big tin freighters were three stades farther east, opposite the agora. It was early morning, well before the hour when a gentleman puts on his chlamys and wanders down to the agora. Only slaves are awake at such an hour.

And pirates.

I scratched my beard, took another breath and raised my fist.

'Let's take them!' I roared back.

Behind me, on my own deck, the rowers grunted in unison and there was a rumbling – of approval, I hoped.

I'm not usually one for speaking when going into action, but I ran amidships and stood by the mainmast.

'Listen, philoi! The whole treasure of Carthage lies under our rams, and all we have to do is take it. Some of you have your own quarrel with Carthage. Some of you would like to be rich. There's five hundred ingots of tin over there, maybe more. Enough for every man here to buy a farm and twenty slaves to work it for him.'

My maths may have been weak. But they cheered.

'But they aren't weak, the men of Carthage. So listen carefully for orders, and when we board, I want every man coming with a roar. Right? Here we go.'

It was something like that. They roared, and on the ships behind, Gaius and Neoptolymos probably said something similar.

We rowed. I was not willing to use my rower's energy yet, and Dionysus must have been of a similar mind, so we rowed at a walking pace in line ahead. Dionysus was first, and I was second; Neoptolymos third, Teukes fourth. Vasileos had our round ship, and Daud, who had seen plenty of sea time, had asked to be placed in command of Hasdrubal's pentekonter. He had a difficult job. We put two-dozen good oarsmen into his ship and took the hardest cases out, but the pentekonter was always sagging behind – a slow, old ship. That's how Hasdrubal had ended up, and well deserved, too.

At any rate, we pulled into the east wind, and as we closed with the westernmost part of the convoy – the tin ships – we saw men waking up, running down the beach, pointing at us, and so on.

I had all the time in the world to put on my gleaming, magnificent new panoply. I walked along my catwalk, feeling rather like Ares come to life. Men reached out to touch me. That's praise.

The enemy warships were coming awake.

Men were pouring down the sand, working like Titans to get those ships off. The round merchantmen were anchored out, with their round stone anchors holding them near the beach.

I watched them all. As usual with a fight, everything seemed to be moving very slowly – right up until the moment when everything would suddenly go very fast. Our surprise was slipping away, and I began to wonder if we'd have been better to come in at ramming speed and try to crush the enemy triremes where they lay. But it was too late for that, now.

Doola came up next to me, bow in hand. He looked under his hand at the merchantmen.

'I want you and Seckla and ten men of your choosing to go into that one,' I said, choosing the third ship out from the beach. 'Put her sails up and get into the offing. And then run for Massalia.'

He looked at the warships. 'You might need every man,' he said.

'I might. But I'm not aiming for a heroic last stand,' I grinned. 'Just take it and run. Pick up Vasileos and Daud as you go.'

He nodded. 'You think it is a trap?'

'Nope,' I said. I could feel the strength in my sword arm. 'I think we've bitten off more than we could possibly chew.'

We didn't bother to ram the merchants – we wanted them intact. My *Lydia* shaved alongside my chosen victim, my starboard side oars in and across in perfect order, and my archers watched their rigging while my marines went up a ladder and across from our standing mainmast to theirs. Boarding from the mast was one of Dionysus' tricks. It had a number of advantages, and in this case, where we really had reason to fear a trap, even a handful of men well above the enemy deck allowed us some security. A merchant's sides are much higher than a trireme's, which makes boarding difficult and dangerous. A merchantman packed with soldiers would make a tough target and a perfect trap.

But not that day.

Our men stormed aboard as cleanly as they might have in a drill – better, because their blood was up. The ship's keeper – the only man aboard – jumped over the side and swam for shore.

Doola crossed over with his chosen volunteers. Too late, I realized that Seckla was taking Geaeta. I saw her run up the boarding plank, long shins flashing in the early summer sun.

Well, she was or she wasn't a spy. I doubted she could kill Doola.

I got my marines back as the first of the Carthaginian triremes came off the beach, six stades away.

These things have a life of their own. You might ask why we didn't make a plan, and I'll say that had we hung off the coast to make a plan, we'd have found them in a defensive circle, or their triremes coming out after us. Dionysus was confident, and so were all the rest of us.

That said, my plan depended on the others following me. Because I took my marines aboard, got them into the bow and headed due east into the oncoming enemy. I hoped that my consorts were coming with me.

Leukas, my Alban, had the deck with the sailors. He was acting as oar-master in Doola's absence. I gave him the nod to go to ramming speed. He gave me a thumb's-up.

Anchises and Darius led the marines, and I joined them. They were big men, and all my marines were now bigger men than I – I'd had a year to pick and choose the best, and arm them like heroes, too.

I pointed to the lead enemy ship off the beach. 'We're going to go aboard her and take her,' I said. 'Anchises, kill your way aft and take command. The rowers ought to obey you. If they don't, Darius, you kill a few. Until they obey. Understand?'

Both men grunted.

'Row clear and run north. Look for Doola. Got it?'

Both men nodded. The other marines nodded.

Across the narrowing strip of water that separated us, the Carthaginian trierarch had just realized that I meant business and that his friends were coming to help him. He had the best ship and the best crew, and like such men, he thought he could do everything himself. Of course he did. I was another such man. But now he was coming to ramming speed, and he realized that win or lose, he was alone.

The next best Carthaginian was *just* getting his hull in the water.

I looked aft at Megakles. He waved.

Both ships went for an oar-rake, and both ships got their oars in. They were fine sailors with superb helmsmen, for the most part. We raced down their starboard side, and the grapnels flew in both directions. We were going so fast that some of the grapnels ripped free, and I saw a rope snap as the whole weight of two racing ships came to bear on it. The flying end of the rope struck my pais and ripped his face off the skull beneath, and the poor boy screamed and screamed. It was one of the most horrific wounds I've ever witnessed.

I had to put him down. That felt bad.

I'd planned to free him. He'd served me so well.

Pah. It still tastes bad.

And then we were slowing. Both ships were turning – fast – heeled over from the weight of the other ship. I got my spear free of the dead weight of my former slave, and I needed action. I was about to weep. I really felt bad about the boy.

I was up on the rail before the ships stopped moving.

A Carthaginian marine threw his javelin at me. It missed by a hand's breadth, and I leaped down into the rowers – one foot on the cross-beam, and one flailing wildly for a moment until I got it down – and one of the rowers grabbed my foot. My spear went straight down into his open mouth – I still remember that kill. Poor bastard. Rowers should never try to fight marines unless they get off their benches first. Remember that they are in three tiers, and that they can't really stand – or support each other. If they have weapons, they stow them under their benches – hard to get at, hard to use.

I pushed up towards the catwalk. This was an undecked trireme, like an Athenian – in fact, it might have been a captured Athenian ship. Rowers in three tiers open to the sky, and a catwalk all the way down the centre line. Most of the enemy marines were on the catwalk, using pikes over the heads of the rowers.

I took a pikehead on my aspis. My attacker was trying to push me down into the rowers. I batted the pikehead aside and made my jump. I landed badly, lost my balance and my armour saved my life as a spear cut some unintended engraving between my shoulder blades. The mark is still there – see? Look, right there. That's death, honeybee. But not for me.

I had to put a foot back, and by luck – nothing better than luck – my foot landed on the cross-beam and I didn't fall. I stabbed with my spear, and my two opponents – one with a pike fifteen feet long and one with a short spear – stabbed at me, pushing me down.

The man with the short spear tried to parry my spear with his own, but he had his spear too near the haft and I had the leverage, and I pressed his aside and ran mine home. He had armour – leather and bronze. But my needle-sharp spearhead pricked him – not a killing blow, but by the feel in my hand I knew I'd punched the point into him and he flinched and gave a cry, and I rifled my spear forward again, at his helmet, and he stepped back.

The pikehead slammed into my helmet, and I saw stars. But I kept my footing and pushed forward into the space of the wounded Carthaginian, and now I had both feet on the catwalk.

I had both feet under me. But now I had enemies ahead of me and behind me on the catwalk.

I slammed my aspis as hard as I could into the man behind me, using the bronze-clad edge as a giant axe. I caved in the face of his rawhide and wicker shield and broke his arm. Then I turned, pivoting my hips, and thrust backhanded with my spear – thumb up, spearhead down, like a dagger blow. It is the most powerful spear blow, but of course, when you deliver it, you are wide open to your opponent, as your shield is behind you. It is like the famed Harmodius blow.

None of you cares about the technicalities of good fighting. A pox on you, then! My spear-point went in over the pikeman's arms, right through his helmet and into his brain, and down he went, dead before he hit the deck. But his weight snapped my spearhead – the beautiful needle point must have been a little too hard, and it snapped short.

Of course, I didn't notice right away. I sprang forward into the next man – another shielded, armoured man with a heavy, short spear and a javelin which he threw at me as soon as he had a clear throw, but I sank beneath his throw like a dancer – oh, I was the killer of men, and Ares' hand was on my shoulder. I passed under his throw and rammed my spear under his shield and into his shin – but the tip of my spear was gone and the spear-point wouldn't bite.

I hurt his shin, though. He tried to back up, but there were other men on the deck, now.

In his confusion, I whirled, changed feet and rushed aft. I got two paces, and threw my spear into the next enemy marine. It glanced off his shield and vanished into the oarsmen, and I drew my new, long xiphos from under my arm. A lovely weapon – almost like a spear with a long, slender blade, slightly wider at the tip. I rotated my right wrist, reached over his big rawhide shield and stabbed down – my weapon caught armour, grated and went straight home through his throat, while his spear flailed over my shoulder.

I pushed past his corpse and the next man slammed his aspis into me and pushed me back, and I cut low with my xiphos and realized that my opponent was Anchises. As my blade rang off his greave, he roared, and we were screaming at each other to stop – comic, in its way.

We'd carried the ship. The trierarch was trying to surrender in the stern, the helmsman was on his knees and Darius killed them both with two blows. Foolish, and clean against the laws of war. On the other hand, we were badly outnumbered, and it was the very heat of the action.

Neither of them was Dagon, either.

I hoped, every time I faced a Carthaginian ship.

'Swords up!' I yelled. 'Swords up! Stop!'

Anchises joined his calls to mine. It took a long minute to stop the killing.

The ship was ours. I turned Anchises to face me. 'Get under way – north!'

He nodded. I ran down a cross-beam – the same one I'd boarded on, I suspect, and leaped back aboard *Lydia*. Ran aft to Megakles.

The next three or four Carthaginians were off the beach, or nearly so. To the west, Dionysus was clear of his merchant ship—

And turning out to sea.

'Bastard,' I said. Dionysus was going to cut and run.

Doola's ship had her sails down and some way on her.

I was broadside on to the approaching Carthaginians because that's how the impetus of the grappling action had ended. We wasted valuable time poling off our new capture.

Neoptolymos cleared his merchantman and came on.

My decks looked curiously empty, because Doola had most of the deck crew and Anchises had my marines. We inched forward. The lead pair of Carthaginians was already at ramming speed.

'Have your outboard oarsmen row!' I shouted at Anchises.

Twice.

Time passed slowly.

He got it.

The former Carthaginian rowers had no reason to love us. Men who have never been in a ship fight always imagine that when a ship is taken, the rowers – if they are slaves or have been mistreated – should rise for their new masters. It does happen that way, but only if the old captain was abusive and foolish. Otherwise, they tend to be more afraid of their new captors than they were of the old. Hard to explain, but I've seen Greek slaves, newly 'freed' all but refuse to row for Greek marines – at Artemisium.

Ah. Artemisium. Your turn is coming.

Our two ships, the grapnels gradually coming off, rowed pitifully. We must have looked like an insect on its back. But we rotated back, so that I was bow on to the enemy and Anchises was stern on. And then we got the last grapnels off and poled off, so that he rowed away headed west, and I rowed away headed east.

It wasn't a battle-winning manoeuvre, but it saved us.

What happened next was from the gods.

I had little choice but to pass between my opponents. They were side by side, at ramming speed, coming down my throat. If Megakles could manage it, we'd pass between them and rake their oars.

But my opponents hadn't been born yesterday. The helmsman on the northernmost of the pair flicked his steering oars to close up with his consort.

By the whim of the gods, the southernmost ship chose to do the same thing.

The two ships didn't slam together. Instead, they brushed one another with a sickening tangle of oars, to the sound of screams as oarsmen died or were broken on their tools.

It seemed to happen very slowly. The ships didn't quite collide, but slipped together like two pieces of fabric sewn up by a matron.

If I'd have any friend close by, or any marines, I'd have tried to sink them.

But instead I passed inshore of the two ships and my archers shot into them, and then we were past. In the bow, Leukas had readied a dozen jars of oil. He knew what I intended.

We were at ramming speed, and by our luck – and fast manoeuvring – we'd passed inshore of the two locked vessels and isolated the next three ships to launch all to the north and east, on the other side of the accident. All three began to turn, their oars working both sides, portside oars reversed.

We ran down on the four triremes still fully on the beach, and as we passed, the pair of us heaved oil jars into the bows of each with a long rag aflame. Two of the four went out. The third caught, spectacularly. Our six archers poured arrows into the stricken ship and then we were turning out to sea.

We'd run through their whole squadron. The three ships that had turned, end for end, now had to pick up speed.

The two ships that had collided were picking themselves apart. Even three stades away, I could hear their officers screaming at each other. I watched the fourth ship on the beach get off. A brave man threw my fire jar over the side, burning himself badly in the process.

But my immediate opponents had troubles of their own. They had all turned to follow me, and Neoptolymos was coming at them from the opposite angle. And behind him, Gaius was up to full speed, his oars chewing the sea to froth.

Eight to three. If Dionysus had turned back, we'd have been eight to five, and with our superior marines—

He kept rowing.

Teukes, his second captain, turned out to sea.

It was one of those times when it is senseless to curse. The gods had been kind enough. Without the two overeager helmsmen, we'd already have been dead men.

'Leukas! Ready about ship!' I called.

Leukas looked at me as if I'd lost my mind. Megakles' expression was a fair match.

It was a snap decision. Like my earlier one, to attack the Carthaginian squadron before it formed up. And perhaps both were incorrect. If I'd taken one ship and run, Doola and I might have made it. But I swear we'd have lost the others. And at this point, the only advantage our three ships had was that we caught them between two angles, and forced them to make decisions. If I ran for the open sea, to my mind that left Gaius to die.

Our port-side oars reversed their benches and pulled, and our ship turned end for end. Five enemy ships came at us. Neoptolymos and Gaius were coming up on *them* from behind and gaining at every stroke, because our oarsmen were better – and because they were free men pulling for the chance of riches.

And I'd forgotten Anchises. I left him pulling away to the west with an unwilling crew.

Most of the Carthaginians didn't realize that his ship had been taken, and they swept past.

Anchises stood amidships and offered his oarsmen a share of everything that was taken.

And turned his bow back east, towards the enemy.

A second Carthaginian ship caught fire on the beach. Sparks from the first? The hand of the gods?

Who knows.

We had turned to fight, and now the odds were seven to four, with two of the enemy ships damaged and somewhat unwilling, and one still barely off the beach.

Lydia was almost to ramming speed. I ran aft and joined Megakles in the steering oars, and we aimed to go beak to beak with the lead enemy ship – they were an echelonned line, not of intent, I think, but because the better, faster ship pulled away from its allies.

'As soon as we touch, reverse your benches and back water!' I roared. We couldn't fight a boarding action. Not a chance. I might hold their rush for a hundred heartbeats, but I couldn't stop twenty men from boarding me – not on my big sailing decks. Nonetheless, when my orders were given, I sprinted forward, taking a spear off the stand by the mainmast.

I got to the marine box over the bow and stood there, in all my armour, and savoured the moment. The finest sailors in the world, and we were holding them.

I raised my sword and roared, 'Heracles!' at the onrushing enemy ship.

I was still shaking my sword when her bow moved a few degrees.

He declined the engagement and turned north, out to sea.

He could do that. We weren't in a thick fight, like Lades. We were in an open bay, with stades between ships. He turned north, and we passed under his stern.

The other two raced past to the south. Even as they passed, I saw them raising their mainmasts.

The fourth ship passed close enough that their archers lobbed some shafts at us. My archers returned fire. They had their boatsail mast up and the sail on and drawing. The mainmast was slow going up. One of my archers – a skinny kid I'd purchased in Ostia who swore he could shoot, and damn, he could – put a shaft into a sailor pulling a rope, and the whole mainmast swayed and fell over the side.

The ship yawed. It didn't quite capsize, but it shipped water, rocked and Neoptolymos slammed into it, his ram catching the stricken ship broadside on at ramming speed as we shot past.

That was perhaps the most devastating single arrow I've ever seen shot.

I thumped the boy on the shoulder and gave him his freedom on the spot.

The two damaged ships were creeping away to the south, along the coast. Four of the merchantmen had gone ashore in a mass. They were beached, and lost to us. Two were under full sail, headed out to sea.

For a moment, I thought we might snatch the two damaged triremes. But instead of running out to sea, they beached, side by side, under the walls of the town. The city militia were pouring out of the gates, now, a hundred cavalrymen and then a thick column of Numidian archers.

A really great trierarch might have had the lot. Had we had time to plan—

But it was a great day, and the gods were kind. Equally, *we* might all have been dead, or taken. It was close.

Gaius's marines swept the enemy's deck and Neoptolymos backed his ram out and the wreck sank.

And we turned north.

Dionysus rejoined us in late afternoon, and while I was tempted to berate him, I had seen enough sea fights to know that all I had was a gut feeling. He leaped aboard, alone.

'Well fought,' he said. He embraced me. It's hard to be really angry with a man who is calling you a hero and a demigod. 'You fought like Heracles.' He shrugged. 'Perhaps I should have lingered. But—' He met my eye. 'I assumed we were going to grab what we could and run.'

I nodded.

'I was afraid that if I didn't attack them, they'd close around us,' I said.

He shrugged. 'You might be right,' he said. And grinned. 'Still friends?'

I'd been cursing his perfidy all afternoon, so naturally I shrugged and said, 'Of course.'

He laughed. 'We did it,' he said. 'I propose we head for Syracusa. You wanted to raid Illyria this summer: if we head north to Massalia, that's the summer over.' He smiled. 'And besides, we can't sell all that tin in Massalia.'

We landed on Malta's little island – Gozo, where the witch enticed Odysseus. It has nice harbours and good food and sweet water and no Carthaginians, despite the proximity. We drank deep, slapped each other on the back and inspected our captures.

We had tin. But only one ship was laden with tin – about sixty ingots, each as heavy as a man could carry, deeply stamped with the Carthaginian inspection mark. It was also full of hides – big, heavy bull's hides, some of the finest I'd seen.

But the ship Doola had taken didn't have a single ingot of tin on board. The central hold was full of Iberian grain, and the bilges, which we missed at first, were full of small ingots of silver. Almost a thousand small ingots of silver.

Of course, tin-mining yields silver. Any smith knows as much.

But I suppose we'd never really thought about it.

It was past the summer feast when we landed in Syracusa. We entered the port in a squadron: three warships in the lead, three merchantmen in the centre and three more warships astern. Syracusa had seen much larger fleets, of course, but not many with Carthaginian captures so blatantly displayed.

Within an hour of landing, both Anarchos and Gelon had sent me messages requesting that I attend them.

While Doola sat in his warehouse and sold our new fortune in tin, I walked up the steep streets in my best cloak and entered Anarchos's house. His slaves were as well mannered as ever.

I sat opposite him on a couch, and drank excellent wine. He had just been for exercise and was covered in oil, which made him look younger.

'Still the hero, I see,' he said, after a pause.

I remember grinning. The fight at Hippo had restored something to me. Something I'm not sure I ever knew was missing. But the word 'hero' was not, I think, misplaced. I had tried to be a man. I hankered for the warmth of human contact – for a wife and a shop to work bronze.

But what paltry things they were – love, friendship – next to the feeling in the moment when the lead enemy warship turned away from me. Any of you understand?

'Lydia is ready to leave,' he said. 'Gelon is about to discard her.' He shrugged. 'She is not a natural courtesan. Do you ever know regret, hero?'

I writhed at his tone. 'Yes,' I said.

He nodded heavily. 'Me too.' He sat up on his couch. 'Let us try and give her another life, eh?'

'The crime lord and the pirate?' I asked.

362

He laughed bitterly.

'You love her,' I said.

'Oh, yes,' he said.

Men are complex, are they not? But this is my tale, not his.

I walked up the town, a little drunk and very maudlin. I walked into the street of armourers, and stopped at Anaxsikles' shop.

He was standing in the back, staring at a helmet, shaking his head. He showed it to me.

'Beautiful, as usual,' I said.

He shook his head. 'Look more closely,' he said.

It was true. Under careful inspection, the left eyehole was slightly lower than the right.

'Apprentice?' I asked.

He shook his head. And sat. 'I think my eyes are going,' he confessed. And burst into tears.

It was that kind of day.

'Would you marry Lydia, if she was available?' I said.

He looked up. 'What?' he asked.

'Lydia. If she was available – if I could carry the two of you to another city, where you could be a citizen – a full citizen, with voting rights. Would you go, and marry her?'

He looked at me. 'Why?' he asked.

I shrugged. 'I helped ruin her. So did ... another man. We are willing to make good our error.'

He looked around. 'Leaving home ... my mother, my father.' He looked at me. 'But, yes. I'd walk across my lit forge to have her.'

Just for a moment, I had a flare of pure, brutal jealousy.

'Let me try to make this happen,' I said. 'If it will work, I will send you word. We will leave very suddenly – I don't think that Gelon will be happy to lose you. Or me, for that matter.' I smiled. 'Or even Lydia. It might be tomorrow. It might be the end of summer.'

He nodded. 'You've made my day.'

That made me happier.

'How was the armour?' he asked.

'Like Hephaestos himself made it,' I said.

He made a gesture of aversion. 'Don't say that!' he groaned. 'That's the kind of talk that makes the gods angry.'

★

Gelon wanted to hear about our fight. And demanded a tenth of the profits. In many ways, Gelon and Anarchos resembled one another. In the end, I got him to settle for a lump sum in silver – forty silver talents. A fortune.

I went back to Anarchos and informed him. Of everything – the payment to Gelon, the bronze-smith's wedding plans.

Anarchos sat sullenly and drank. 'I am old,' he said bitterly. 'I would marry her and take her to another city. But she would never have me – who would?'

What could I say?

I left him to his bitterness.

The next day, we paid off our debts in the city and filled our merchant ships with food and mercenaries – almost a hundred men hired off the docks. I picked up a dozen Nubian archers being sold as labourers – fool of a slave-master. I got them at labour prices. I bought back their weapons from another dealer and put them in armour. Their leader was Ka, and he was taller than some houses, as thin as a sword blade and he could draw a Scythian bow to his mouth as if it were a child's bow. Ka's lads were very pleased to be bought, in that I promised them their freedom and wages in the immediate future.

Doola had turned our tin into gold. But if we paid off our oarsmen, they'd never be seen again. So we made a single payment that night, about one-twentieth what every man had coming. Doola gave them a fine speech – more than a thousand men standing by torchlight on the beach between the quays on the Syracusan waterfront – and he told them how much money they had coming at the end of the Illyrian expedition, and exactly why we weren't paying in full until that trip was over.

I suppose they might have rioted. But money – lots of money – has a magical quality. It is often better in the offing than in reality, and no one knows that as well as a sailor.

Gaius and Neoptolymos, Daud and Sittonax, Vasileos and Megakles and Doola and Seckla and I all lay on couches that night, with twenty more men – Anchises, red-faced and too loud, and Ka, shining black and deeply versed, it appeared, in Aegyptian lore, debating with Doola.

Gaius rolled over to me, probably to avoid having to watch Geaeta and Seckla on the next couch. But he met my eye and we laughed like boys. He held out a silver wine cup and tapped it against mine.

'I guess this is the last time,' he said. 'It is time I grew up and became a rich fuck on a farm.'

I shrugged. 'You were doing well enough this spring when we found you,' I said.

Gaius rolled his eyes. 'That is what worries me. Rome is such a backwater. When we put Neoptolymos on his throne, you'll go back to Athens.'

'Plataea,' I corrected, automatically.

'And we'll never see you again,' he said.

'Oh, the sea's not that wide,' I joked.

He nodded. 'Well,' he said, 'here's to the last of youth.'

I drank to that, because I shared the sentiment. I was thirty-one years old. Not bad, you think. But that's quite old for a warrior.

Hah! Little did I know what the gods had in store.

We were pretty drunk when the pais came. He was ten or eleven – pretty enough, if that sort of thing is to your taste. He bowed deeply and held out a scroll tube to me.

Lydia is at my house. She awaits her transport. It should not be you. She expressed the deepest gratitude to me that I had found her a husband.

I regret that I will not be here to attend you. I will not see you again, I fear, so I offer you this boy as a token of my regard – you mentioned yours had died.

Through the fumes of wine, I had to read the note three times.

Then I sent the boy to fetch Anaxsikles. I was half sober by the time he came, and sent him to fetch his bride from Anarchos.

I begged Doola to carry them to Croton for me. He accepted gravely, and embraced me.

I confess that I stood in a doorway near the ship, and watched Anaxsikles bring her down to the shore. The only skiff was loading the archers. He picked her up, and she snuggled her head into his shoulder. He carried her out into the water and handed her up to the sailors on the deck, and then leaped up into the round ship's waist, and she put her arms around his neck.

Bah. Why do I tell this?

More wine.

Doola sailed long before dawn. I suspected that Gelon would be none too happy when he found out that his smith and his mistress were gone, so I ordered my drunken, orgiastic crews rounded up. We were a surly, vicious pack of scoundrels in the first light of dawn.

My new boy wanted me to come with him to Anarchos's house to fetch his belongings. He also insisted that he was free, not a slave, and that I should ask Anarchos.

The crime lord lived close enough to the water that it was the matter of a few minutes to go there. And I wanted to tell him that she was away.

I suppose I hadn't read his letter closely enough.

The pais found him. He wasn't in his andron – that's where Lydia had waited for Anaxsikles. The andron smelled of her. I slammed my fist into a wall. If you don't understand why, well, good for you.

But in the back, near the courtyard, he lay on top of his sword, which he'd wedged between two paving stones. He was quite dead.

Men are complex. To my lights, he died well, and was a man I could, if not admire, at least – call a friend. Here's to his shade.

We got to sea before the sun was high. My new pais cried and cried. I am fairly certain he believed that Anarchos was his father.

And perhaps he was.

His name was Hector.

Ah, you smile! Yes, Hector. Finally, he comes into our story.

Doola was gone over the horizon, and I confess I had a million fears that day, that the Carthaginians would snatch up his ship. Only in the cold, clear light of day did I realize that his ship held Lydia, Anaxsikles and all our treasure, and I had sent it off unguarded.

Men are fools.

But the gods watch over drunkards and fools.

We lay that night on a beach north of Katania, and the next night we evaded the whirlpool and crossed over to Rhegium. Doola was a day ahead of us, which suited me. We made the beautiful beaches of Rhegium in mid-afternoon, and when the setting sun gilded Mount Aetna over on the Sicilian side that night, we were already in the waterfront tavernas. I sat with Gaius. I was poor company.

A single trireme came in, with a small merchant ship trailing astern, making tacks to get in under wind power. The ship was well handled, and the longer I watched it, the more convinced I was that it was Giannis.

The trireme was Athenian. I could see that by its light construction, the way it moved – how low it was to the water. A warship. A shark.

The warship landed first. A crew really shows itself in landing: a well-conducted ship spins end for end a stade offshore and backs into the beach. It's not a tricky manoeuvre, for a veteran crew, but it always shows a crew's skills.

This ship was beautifully handled. Not just the helmsman, but the oarsmen. Mine were good. These were better.

A pleasure to watch them.

'I'm going to go and praise that man,' I said, pointing at the new arrival.

Gaius nodded. 'Beautiful,' he admitted. 'Does this mean we have to do more drill?'

'You'll miss Dionysus, when you are watching your slaves plough your fields,' I laughed. It was my first laugh in eight hours.

We wandered down to watch the new arrival. His oarsmen were already buying food from the farmers who hastened down to the beach – sacks of charcoal were being bargained for, and the braziers were already coming out of the bilges.

The man with his back to me, dickering with the local farmers, looked familiar.

He turned just as I came up, and we saw each other.

Cimon.

We threw our arms around each other and hugged, slapped each other's backs and hugged again. This went on for a long, long time.

In fact, I cried.

Look, thugater. I'm crying now.

'You bastard! You said to meet you in Massalia!' Paramanos hugged me, too, there on the beach at Croton. I tried not to look at the town. We were on the beach for the night, and Dano sent her greetings and a gift of wine. There were two more black ships on that beach – Paramanos's, *Black Raven*, and Harpagos's *Storm Cutter*.

Friends ... friends are men who, when they think that you are dead, will come halfway around the world because you ask them, and because they want so much to believe that you are alive. I hadn't seen these men since – well, since the beach of Marathon, almost eight years before. There were a dozen Athenians I knew – there, for example, was Aeschylus, who fought in the front rank at Marathon and at Lades; there was Phrynicus' young nephew, Aristides. Harpagos, my former right hand, was still a lisping islander, as strong as an ox, with the beginnings of grey in his beard. Mauros, my helmsman. Come to think of it, Paramanos got his start as a helmsman, too. Start with us, that is. He was Cyrenian, and had fought for the Phoenicians before I took him in the sea fight off Cyprus back in the Ionian War.

'That's a new ship,' I said, pointing at *Storm Cutter*. My old *Storm Cutter* was a heavy Phoenician capture. Heh! I took her and Paramanos in the same sweep of my spear.

'The original is firewood,' he said. 'Athens has a fleet, now – not a dozen vessels from rich men, either. We have more than a hundred hulls. Aegina—' He laughed aloud. 'Aegina isn't a naval power any more.'

Young Aristides nodded vehemently. 'Athens is a better place for the common man,' he said, with all the arrogant pomposity of the young.

Had I ever been that young?

'Anyone been to Plataea?' I asked.

There was some shuffling of feet.

I introduced my friends of the last six years to my friends from Athens. Seckla was abashed, for a while – Gaius, on the other hand, kept looking at Cimon, chuckling, and saying, 'So you really are Miltiades' son?'

I suppose they might not have got on – Cimon was the son of a hundred generations of Eupatridae, and Seckla was a Numidian former slave; Daud was worse, an out-and-out barbarian, and Sittonax didn't even like to speak Greek.

However, piracy is its own brotherhood. I listened with half an ear as Harpagos poured out the tale of Athens' war with Aegina, and Themistocles' daring political manoeuvre, by which he took the profits of the new silver mine and bought Athens a public fleet. Next to the reforms of Cleisthenes, it was the greatest political revolution in Athenian history. If Cleisthenes gave all the middle-men – the hundred-mythemnoi men – a noble ancestor and the right to think themselves aristocrats and fight in the phalanx, so Themistocles bought Athens a fleet, and gave all the little men – free citizens, but without franchise – a weapon as mighty as the spear. He gave them the oar.

Nowadays, we take it for granted that every Athenian *thetis* is a rower. Athens rules the waves, from here to the delta of Alexandria and across the seas to Syracusa, too. But in those years between

Marathon and the next stage in the Long War, Athens was just feeling her way as a power.

I watched as Gaius began to talk to Cimon about raising horses, and Doola found common cause with Harpagos on the subject of trade. Seckla stood nervously with his attractive courtesan – a woman who couldn't resist male attention and suddenly had a beach full of it. But in time, Mauros – my former oar-master, and fellow hero of Lade – started to talk, first to Doola, and then to Seckla, and then they were all talking to Paramanos – four Africans on a beach full of Greeks.

Aristides the Younger was amazed to meet an actual Keltoi barbarian, and managed not to sound as condescending as he might have. The fires roared, the wine was excellent and as darkness fell, and I was apologizing to Cimon for the fiftieth time that I wasn't with his father at the end, Dano herself came down the beach with a dozen of her friends.

'It is like having the battle of Marathon brought to my town,' she said. 'So many famous men. Ari – in truth, my friend, when first you told me you were Arimnestos of Plataea, I thought you one of those men who lie habitually.'

Cimon was deeply pleased to meet the daughter of the great Pythagoras. He bowed – Greeks seldom bow – and was allowed to kiss her cheek, very Italian and not very Greek, and he actually blushed. So did Giannis, who had come with Cimon from Massalia.

Aeschylus just stood there, drinking it all in.

'How is Aristides?' I asked, when chance threw us together.

'You mean, the real one?' he asked, raising an annoyed eyebrow at Phrynicus' graceless nephew.

I smiled.

'He's a great man, now. He and Themistocles are rivals – enemies, really. I'm not sure if they don't hate each other worse than either one hates the Persians. Aristides has inherited the Eupatridae – he leads the oligarchs.' Aeschylus shrugged.

'What? Aristides the Just?' I shook my head.

'Politics in Athens is different, my friend. Themistocles has raised up the thetis, and he'll end up giving them the right to serve on juries – mark my words – and that will be the end of us.' Aeschylus was an old-fashioned man, despite his relative youth.

Of course, looking at them, I realized that my friends were ageing as fast as I was myself.

That was a shock.

Aeschylus had grey in his beard. Harpagos had a white mark – the scar of a Persian arrow from Lade – in his beard, but his hair was getting grey, too. And to see Dionysus talk to Cimon – Dionysus had been our trierarch at Lade; Cimon and I had been mere ship's commanders. Now we commanded squadrons, and Dionysus, I could see, was quite old. Perhaps fifty. A decade younger than I am right now.

I'd watched him put a Carthaginian marine down, just recently. He wasn't that old.

But we weren't any younger, and I couldn't help but notice that the annoying Aristides the Younger was the age I'd been at Sardis.

Seventeen.

Zeus. I'm lucky I was allowed to live. So cocky. So *sure*.

For the first time that night, I watched older men – proven men, men of unquestioned worth. I wondered, when the young men competed on the beach – on Chios, or again at Lade – I wondered how many older men watched me, and thought I was an arrogant pup and too young to know any better?

Age. Your turn will come, my young friends.

But enough. It was a great night – so many friends. Such laughter, such wine; and we were not so very old, either.

Finally, the sun peeped over the horizon. We were lying on straw, above the high-water mark, and we'd seen the night through, and slaves were picking up the amphorae and the broken cups. Dano lay by Cimon on a kline of straw – lucky Cimon – flirting with Paramanos, who appeared to know more of Pythagorean philosophy than any of the rest of us – but he'd been raised at Cyrene.

They were talking about mathematics, and Cimon laughed, and then raised himself on his elbows to speak over his companions. 'So, Ari, why have you called us all here?'

Some men laughed, and others hooted.

But they all fell silent.

'I was hoping we could all spend the summer raiding Carthage,' I said, to the rising sun. 'But the summer has slipped away like youth. I have a friend here who is a prince of Illyria. We were slaves together. I thought that if I could raise my friends, we'd have enough of a fleet to sail north of Corcyra and restore him to his hill fort, kill all his enemies and perhaps pick up a few bars of silver into the bargain.'

Paramanos grinned. 'There's not a one of us who couldn't use a few bars of silver.'

'I heard there was a tin fleet,' Cimon said.

Dionysus was drunk. 'Too damned late, Athenian!' he shouted. 'We took it all!'

I shook my head. 'We took a third of it. That's a story for another night, friends. We have ten ships. With ten ships, we could probably conquer any island in the Aegean. With these men? But if you will follow my lead, we will restore Neoptolymos, and perhaps take a few Carthaginians on the way.'

Cimon nodded. 'I'm not likely to turn back now: there's nothing else going on this summer, although you had best pay well, you old rascal – I've rowed from Athens to Massalia and back to Croton to find you.'

I laughed. 'I have a few coins,' I admitted.

'I don't want to linger,' he said. 'The Phoenicians are everywhere in the east – there's no getting a cargo into Aegypt. Men say that the King of Kings and his Phoenicians have made a pact with Carthage. And there is war in Aegypt.'

I shook my head. 'I keep hearing that,' I said. 'But I see no proof. The Phoenicians are no real friends of the Great King's.'

'Supposedly there are embassies going both ways, even now,' said Paramanos. 'In Cyrene, I heard that your – how should I say it, your friend? Hipponax's son Archilogos? – is taking a squadron to Carthage. Or perhaps took one, last season.'

Cimon shook his head. 'That, at least, is not true. He was in Mytilene a month ago.' Cimon smiled in the rising sun. 'I spoke to him. We're not at war. I'd just heard the message that Ari was alive. I told Archilogos. That was a pleasure.'

I coughed. 'But you'll all come north against Illyria?'

Paramanos looked around at the Greeks. 'Why do you think we came here? For a rest?' He laughed.

Cimon scrambled to his feet, apologizing to Pythagoras's daughter. My pais refilled his cup. He poured a long libation of priceless Sybarite wine to the immortal gods, and then raised his cup to the rising sun.

'Phobos, Lord of the Chariot of Fire, and Poseidon, Lord of Horses and swift ships and the Sea, with a thousand beautiful daughters; Athena, matchless in guile, who loves men best when they are most daring; Aphrodite of the high-arched feet, and all the other immortals! Hear us! We thank you for this night of mirth and friendship. And we ask your blessing!'

371

We all cheered.

Great days. And after that night, I had a hangover of Homeric proportions.

Worth it.

We spent another day provisioning our round ships and making our plans. By then, local rulers were sending embassies to the 'men of Marathon'. A rumour went out that Dano had hired us to avenge her father on the Sybarites.

We sharpened our weapons, and drilled.

We had a farewell feast with the Pythagoreans. Vegetables, it turns out, are perfectly palatable.

I saw Lydia, at a distance. It is odd how you know a person by their shape and movement, when you couldn't possibly see their face. I knew her, and I knew the man with his arm around her.

There is no happiness of mortal men that cannot be marred in an instant.

Part IV
Illyria

παραμειψάμενοι δὲ Θρινακίαν νῆσον Ἡλίου βοῦς ἔχουσαν εἰς τὴν Φαιάκων νῆσον Κέρκυραν ἧκον, ἧς βασιλεὺς ἦν Ἀλκίνοος. τῶν δὲ Κόλχων τὴν ναῦν εὑρεῖν μὴ δυναμένων οἱ μὲν τοῖς Κεραυνίοις ὄρεσι παρῴκησαν, οἱ δὲ εἰς τὴν Ἰλλυρίδα κομισθέντες ἔκτισαν Ἀψυρτίδας νήσους: ἔνιοι δὲ πρὸς Φαίακας ἐλθόντες τὴν Ἀργὼ κατέλαβον καὶ τὴν Μήδειαν ἀπῄτουν παρ᾽ Ἀλκινόου. ὁ δὲ εἶπεν, εἰ μὲν ἤδη συνελήλυθεν Ἰάσονι, δώσειν αὐτὴν ἐκείνῳ, εἰ δ᾽ ἔτι παρθένος ἐστί, τῷ πατρὶ ἀποπέμψειν. Ἀρήτη δὲ ἡ Ἀλκινόου γυνὴ φθάσασα Μήδειαν Ἰάσονι συνέζευξεν: ὅθεν οἱ μὲν Κόλχοι μετὰ Φαιάκων κατῴκησαν, οἱ δὲ Ἀργοναῦται μετὰ τῆς Μηδείας ἀνήχθησαν.

Having passed by the Island of Thrinacia, where are the kine of the Sun, they came to Corcyra, the island of the Phaeacians, of which Alcinous was king. But when the Colchians could not find the ship, some of them settled at the Ceraunian mountains, and some journeyed to Illyria and colonized the Apsyrtides Islands. But some came to the Phaeacians, and finding the Argo there, they demanded of Alcinous that he should give up Medea. He answered, that if she already knew Jason, he would give her to him, but that if she were still a maid he would send her away to her father. However, Arete, wife of Alcinous, anticipated matters by marrying Medea to Jason; hence the Colchians settled down among the Phaeacians and the Argonauts put to sea with Medea.

Apollodorus, *Library* I.9

21

And then we sailed for Illyria.

I won't say that nothing happened as we cruised up the west coast of Magna Greca. I'll just say that, bar one incident, I don't remember anything. There was a lot of fog – I remember that! And I remember that on our second morning, as we rowed north through the fog, Dionysus' ship fell afoul of Cimon's, with much cursing and shouting. Since they were reckoned two of the finest trierarchs on the seas, the rest of us revelled in their distress. Like men do.

The only incident I remember well arose out of the fog. I'm going to guess it was the third or fourth day, and again, we launched off a small and rocky cove, just big enough for our ships, with bellies full of lobster and our ships laden only with fresh water. But the fog was everywhere – some trick of the gods – and every morning, to a depth I hadn't ever seen before. It took all morning to burn off, and for long hours the sun was a golden orb in the haze.

At any rate, that morning, as we rowed north – again, rowing because there was no wind at all – we were trying to practise signalling. Dionysus was making himself increasingly unpopular with the other captains by insisting on drill and signalling when we knew we were after no prey loftier then some Illyrian pirates in pentekonters. No one likes to work that hard. Had we been rowing north to fight the Persians at Lade, we might have felt differently – although, come to think of it, when we rowed to Lade, we all hated Dionysus then, too.

The sun climbed above us in the haze, just visible – one of the few times in your life you can look directly at him in all his glory. And as with the other days, just past midday the fog suddenly burned off, as fast as a bird crossing the sky, so that in one moment it was all we could do to see the ships ahead and behind us in line, and then we could see three ships ahead, and then I could see Dionysus up at the head of the line, and then—

And then we could see the merchant trireme, six stades away, and just as surprised to see us as we were to see him.

Every ship, even Dionysus, turned out of the line as fast as their oarsmen could respond to volleys of orders, and went from a slow cruise to ramming speed. The triemiolas raised sail, as the fresh wind was suddenly coming off the land.

We could all see it was a Phoenician. Or perhaps a Carthaginian.

And he could see us, too.

His oarsmen beat the water into a froth, like a good Athenian matron making soup the evening before a feast day, and he struggled to get his mainsail up.

It was a race, of sorts. But a horribly unequal one, between ten ships in high training with full crews and marines and sailors and clean hulls, against a lone merchant with fifty oarsmen and old sails.

He could sail much closer to the wind then we could, of course. So as soon as he had his mainmast rigged, he lay over and ran north, and we all lost the wind and had to row.

Lydia was fast, but Paramanos's new *Black Raven* was like a racing shell with a ram, and Cimon's *Ajax* was as fast as Paramanos. Dionysus' *Agamemnon* was as fast as either.

Oh, how we exhausted ourselves! We raced along, our oars all but touching the nearest ship. A missed stroke might have been disaster.

But we were heroes, of course. We didn't miss any strokes.

We caught the merchant at mid-afternoon, about the hour a gentleman rises from his nap and goes to the agora – not in Plataea, ladies. Men work all day in Plataea. But in Athens.

We caught him, and he surrendered without a fight. Who would even try to fight, with ten sharks all around him?

Cimon's hull was the first to come aboard his, and Dionysus was second. We carried the captured ship to the next beach and pulled her up the sand and gravel. The oarsmen were cleared off and the deck crew, the miserable owner and the trierarch all cowered together.

She had a cargo of cheap Carthaginian pottery, some Greek wine with Ionian labels that must, itself, have come off a capture and copper with the Cypriote mark. The copper was valuable. The wine we broached on the spot for our oarsmen.

Cimon and Dionysus began to argue over the spoils. Paramanos wandered over to where I stood, seeing to it that *Lydia* was carried well up the beach and rolled over to dry her hull. He nodded to me.

'I thought this was your little expedition,' he said.

I shrugged.

'Cimon and Dionysus are going to gut each other over a handful of copper,' he said. 'Not because it's valuable, but because they are important men and each has to be first.'

I sighed. The party was over.

Sharing spoils: always the moment when arête goes by the board and life among pirates becomes difficult.

I walked across the sand, cursing how it burned the sides of my feet. It was deep and soft. Try walking with determined gravity and manly elegance across deep sand.

They weren't quite spitting like Lesbian fishwives. Not quite. But close.

'Friends,' I said. 'This is unseemly.'

That may not seem like a very telling remark to a pair of bloody-handed pirates, but the two of them immediately pivoted on their heels to face me. 'Unseemly?' Dionysus said. 'I don't remember asking your opinion.'

'As long as you are in my squadron, you can listen to any opinion I choose to deliver,' I said.

Dionysus' mouth opened and closed.

Cimon laughed, slapped my shoulder and nodded. 'You're right, Ari! My apologies. You divide the spoils.'

I snapped my fingers and there was my pais with a stool.

As I sat, Dionysus stood, arms akimbo. He glared at me for a long fifty heartbeats or so.

'I'm not in your squadron, pup,' he growled. 'You are in mine.'

I shrugged and sat. 'No, my friend. I invited you to sail with me. You joined me.'

'I have drilled and drilled this squadron—'

'I appreciate that. But that's not command. Please; you understand command. You commanded at Lade. I asked all my friends on this expedition. It is – pardon me – mine. If anyone could dispute this, it would be Neoptolymos.'

The Illyrian had come up, with all the other captains and a number of other leaders: the commander of the mercenaries from Syracusa, a Spartan called Brasidas; Doola and Sittonax, Vasileos and his nephew; Aeschylus. They gathered around my stool like any Greek assembly – all talking, all with an opinion to offer.

Neoptolymos shook his head.

Paramanos, who had never thought very highly of Dionysus, nodded. 'You are in command, Arimnestos. Not this wine bag.'

I shook my head. 'No insults. Dionysus, I will divide the spoils between the ships that performed the capture.'

I think, just for a moment, that he was so angry he considered leaving us. This is a thing I have seen men do. Two hours before, if asked, I think he would quite happily have allowed that I was the trierarch, in as much as anyone was. But having once got his back up—

Or perhaps it had been an error to allow him to drill the squadron. But he was, quite possibly, the greatest trierarch of our time – the finest innovator, the best tactician. It was from him that I learned how to perform the *diekplous* and the wheel, perhaps two of our most important tactics.

At any rate, he took a breath – I think to denounce me. And Geaeta did a handstand – something you have to see to believe, done in a chiton – and came to rest by me. She smiled at Dionysus. 'You are eldest,' she said. 'And men talk of you as one of the noblest men of your generation.' She smiled at him, as if the two of them were the only two on the beach.

Sometimes a woman can say something that would be a matter for swords between men.

His face was almost purple, but she went on. 'Please, let us not mar this day and this week.' She put a hand on his arm – she, who he had called a whore a dozen times.

He bent slightly at the waist, looked at the sand for a moment, cocked his head at me and smiled ruefully.

'It is hard to take orders from a younger man,' he said.

I nodded.

'When you are my age, see how you like it.' He looked as if he was going to say more, but he swallowed it. 'Never mind. Cimon, my apologies.'

'And mine to you, sir. I spoke in heat.' The two clasped arms like men in the gymnasium.

I looked at the stack of copper ingots. It was worth a small fortune – to one man. It was, to be frank, worthless to two hundred oarsmen and marines.

I looked at the two of them. 'Gentlemen,' I said, 'this is a small amount of booty. I propose that, rather than dividing it, we have a foot race, and the fastest man takes all the copper. And we dedicate the game to Olympian Zeus, pour the wine down our throats and offer some of the sheep I see on that hill as sacrifices.'

Cimon laughed.

Dionysus laughed.

A seventeen-year-old oarsman from Etrusca won the foot race. We crowned him in olive and his mates helped him carry his copper onto Gaius's ship. Gaius put his olive wreath on his mast for luck.

That's the incident that I remember.

Oh, I ran. Of course I ran. I lost in the first heat – Aristides the Younger flew past me from the start. I was placed fifth among eight men.

I felt old. But men said I had made a fine decision, as wise as Odysseus.

As the sun set on our sacrifices, and their smoke climbed to heaven – Cimon was a priest of Zeus, of course, like all the men of his clan – Dionysus put his arm around me. 'Let's sacrifice the prisoners,' he said.

Men began to call for it. Men who surprised me. Young Aristides, for example, and many of the other unblooded young. Paramanos smiled and looked away. Doola shook his head vehemently. Sittonax sidled closer to me.

'I had no idea,' he said. 'I've never seen a Greek sacrifice a man.'

'And you won't here,' I said. 'By Zeus, are we as bad as barbarians?'

I seldom swear by Zeus. But some things—

I walked across the sand, as drunk as a sailor, and stumbled to the prisoners with a hundred oarsmen and officers behind me. Most of them knelt in the sand. The Carthaginian helmsman grabbed Paramanos's knees and began to beg for his life in Phoenician.

The trierarch eyed me steadily. He didn't kneel.

'You are a free man,' I said. 'Go – walk away.'

He didn't say a word. He caught the eyes of his mates and picked up a bundle at his feet. Paramanos, somewhat surreptitiously, handed the helmsman a sword.

The Carthaginians were off up the beach before most of my audience knew I'd let them go.

'You really are too soft for this,' Dionysus said, wine-soaked breath in my face.

I shrugged. 'Perhaps,' I said.

★

Like I said, that's the only incident that sticks in my head.

Word must have been out that there was a squadron at sea: the Adriatic was as empty as a mud puddle after rain. The morning after we released the Carthaginians, the wind came up – a favourable wind – and we sailed across the Adriatic. Our swords were sharp, and we were as ready as men can be.

We landed south of Dyrachos an hour before nightfall on a late summer evening: the sun took his time going down to the west, over the mountains, and we were ashore and camped before the night was dark. Insects chirped and it *sounded* like Greece. It *smelled* like Greece.

We built no fires, but rolled in our cloaks and slept on the sand, and in the morning we were up long before the sun.

'Now I need a horse,' Neoptolymos said. He and the Spartan, Brasidas, stood together, both in full armour.

'Because you don't want to walk?' I asked.

'I intend to ride around and raise my friends and relatives,' he said. 'Dyrachos is sixty stades – that way.'

I had slightly different notions of how to proceed, based on years of experience with Miltiades. I sent all my archers inland under Ka, and before I was done with my stale bread and sour wine, Ka was back, all but bouncing on the balls of his feet like an eager hound with a fine bay led by the halter.

He had four prisoners and a dozen horses. Ka was from the far south of Aegypt – Nubia, and not Numidia, South even of the Kingdom of Adula, of which, if you stay with me long enough, you'll hear more. To be honest it was years before I truly understood the difference. But both peoples love horses, ride superbly and view horse-thieving as a natural part of life.

We started our march for Dyrachos before the sun cleared the distant coast of Italy, and Ka and his men were all mounted, with Seckla laughing along with them. Seen together, Numidians and Nubians are as different as Keltoi and Hellenes, and yet they rode like Scythians, knees high, hips moving with the gait of the animal, and with their dark skin they looked like centaurs on their stolen bays.

I kept Neoptolymos from riding inland. I feared that he would be taken or killed, and that he would give himself away. He accepted my 'guidance' with an ill grace, and the command party was a surly group as we trudged inland over the first low ridge. The khora was incredibly prosperous – fields of oats and barley stretching away in a beautiful patchwork. Harvest wasn't far off.

Once we were clear of the coastal scrub, we had excellent sight lines – which, of course, meant we could be easily observed. I sent Ka and his scouts well ahead, blessing the gods I had made such a provident purchase. The Nubians knew their business: they rode south and east to the horizon, collecting every horse on that flat plain and terrifying the inhabitants.

I have to say a word about Illyria. The Illyrians are like Hellenes – indeed, many of their aristocrats claim Hellenic descent, and they share our gods and heroes, although they have some cruel monsters of their own. They are far more warlike than Hellenes – the whole of Illyria is in a perpetual state of war, and every man's hand is against everyone else, or rather, perhaps I should say that every aristocrat's hand is against every other aristocrat. They have no 'hoplite class' of farmers. There are only the rich, and slaves. The only real way for slaves to win their freedom is by fighting: they arm their slaves for war, and the bravest are promoted to the aristocracy. On the other hand, the least effective warriors are captured and made slaves, or killed.

You might think that this vicious system would create superb warriors. Perhaps it does, but I never met them. Mostly it creates brutal, ignorant aristocrats and a society of semi-slave land-tillers with nothing but contempt for their 'lords', who can't seem to grow food or protect them. Neoptolymos was a fine man and a pretty fair spearman – but I taught him that. And slavery mellowed him.

By the time the sun was high in the sky, we'd marched twenty stades or more and we had a dozen prisoners – local men, all 'unfree' but more like overseers than like slaves. Neoptolymos insisted we take them, because he said they would report to his uncle if they could.

In fact, Neoptolymos, after seven years with me, had reverted to being an Illyrian. He wanted to kill them all.

From the eldest of them, we heard the story of the last few years. Epidavros had seized power after arranging for Neoptolymos's murder, but after that, things had gone wrong. He had seized power with the support of the Carthaginians, but he failed to deliver the tin he had promised, and so the Carthaginians had abandoned him. His own cousins had begun to raid his borders, and take his land and his slaves, and he had spent the last two years in a constant state of war.

Last summer – while we were bringing our tin over the mountains – he had gone to sea with a dozen pentekonters and taken a pair of Phoenician merchantmen, and Carthage had sent a reprisal raid which had burned the shipping in his harbour, including a pair of Greek merchantmen who he had seen as his most promising new allies.

I'd like to moralize and say that Epidavros got what he had coming to him, but that's Illyria.

However, because of the Carthaginian raid, his petty kingdom was as alarmed as the house of a man who has been robbed. The overseers all agreed that by now, Epidavros had been fully informed of our force – he had coastal towers every few stades, or so they claimed.

Neoptolymos wanted to start burning things.

We camped that night at the edge of a stand of ancient oak trees in the foothills, having marched farther east than we needed. I wanted to hug the edge of the hills and avoid detection – and obvious moves like taking the direct route. We sat down in messes: a hundred mercenaries, another hundred marines and a dozen aristocrats, plus Ka and his Nubians. An odd collection, but, I think, as deadly a raiding force as I ever commanded.

I was warming to the Spartan, Brasidas. He was quite the gentleman, with fine manners and a ready smile. He almost never spoke – just met your eyes and grinned. If he agreed, he'd nod and if he disagreed, he'd raise his eyebrows.

'What are you doing here, Brasidas?' I asked. 'Spartans never leave home. They're afraid of water!'

He grinned and rolled his eyes. Meaning, 'So you say, Plataean.'

'You are allowed to speak, you know,' I said.

He nodded gravely. And smiled. Meaning, 'When I have something to say, perhaps I will.'

'A Theban cut your tongue out?' I asked.

He smiled and took a drink of wine. 'No,' he said.

'I wish you Spartans would learn to say what you mean in a few words!' I laughed. He was very likeable.

He smiled, and raised his cup to me.

He was built like a wrestler, with long limbs and lots of muscle. He was a handsome man, but most Spartans are. His equipment was very plain.

Cimon was sitting with me. He said, 'Why'd you leave the land where Helen bore sons to Menelaus, Brasidas?'

Brasidas shrugged. 'Bored,' he said, and smiled. He made a face, and held out his cup to my pais. 'Poor,' he admitted.

Cimon nodded. 'My father had many Spartan guest friends. Their mess fees are high – a man needs two or three estates to pay.'

Brasidas nodded.

'If anything goes wrong – if crops fail, or helots revolt – a man can find himself without his mess fee.' Cimon watched the Spartan carefully. It was an odd form of social interrogation. Cimon would make guesses, and we'd watch his body language for confirmation.

Brasidas was a patient man. He had the kind of strength that is beyond mere temper, or the need to prove itself. But he got up, swallowed the last of his wine, nodded and walked off.

Meaning, 'None of your business.'

Cimon rose to follow him, but I held him back. 'It's his business,' I said. 'Let him go.'

Cimon nodded.

Neoptolymos joined us, his face thunderous in the firelight. 'Why won't you let me burn these farms!' he demanded. It was odd – a sign of how I was growing, between Heraclitus and Dano, but I couldn't help but be amused at the complete contrast between the taciturn Spartan and the emotional Illyrian.

I put a hand on his shoulder. 'By the end of the week, they'll be your farms,' I said. 'Why burn them?'

'He'll raise his cousins and his war band and we'll – accomplish nothing.' He all but pouted. He didn't seem like a man in his mid-twenties, but like a very young, very angry man.

I put my arm around him. He fought me for a moment, and then he grunted, and I saw he was crying.

'Don't worry,' I said. 'We'll get him.'

That's what leaders do. We sound positive.

The Nubians were away in the wolf's tail of dawn. We moved along the road between the fields – a dry, sun-baked track. There was a storm brewing away to the south, and thunder sounded in the distance like the grumbling of the gods.

Around mid-morning, Ka brought back another dozen horses, and Daud and Sittonax took two of them and rode off with another dozen men who could ride, doubling our scout force.

A ridge rises from the plain, about forty stades inland, and we had marched around to the east of it, and now we passed along it, keeping the ridge between us and the sea. We joined the 'main road' – I use the term very loosely – south of a fortified settlement called Pista.

If all was going well, our ships should be off Dyrachos by now, snapping up any fishing boats in the offing and making trouble. And being very visible. In late afternoon, after marching maybe seventy stadia, we crossed the Ardaxanos River – in late summer, it was scarcely deserving of the name. We moved right up until dark, and we camped at the top of a low hill twenty-five stadia from the town of Dyrachos. We hadn't seen any opposition, and with twenty horsemen covering a broad arc before us, I didn't really expect ambush. At nightfall, Daud took all the mounted men on a sweep to make sure we weren't going to be surprised in the morning.

My intention was that we storm the town at daybreak, but the truth on the ground was very different from Neoptolymos's description. He remembered the ridge as running right down to the town, but it wasn't that simple, and there was open ground all the way to the coast from where we were camped. I stood on the hilltop in the last light, looking at the sea in the distance and worrying. We'd eaten our rations, and even plundering the farms we passed wasn't feeding us. Really efficient plundering takes time, and slows a march to a crawl, and we had moved fast. Moving a force fast requires discipline and supplies.

In the morning, we would be out of food. Further, our rendezvous with our ships was for noon the next day, and if we missed it ... Well, things were about to grow very complicated indeed.

I didn't sleep well. I dreamed of the Keltoi girl throwing herself over the side. And Miltiades, the night after Marathon, saying he was with the gods. And Lydia ... not speaking, but just looking at me with a face full of hate.

I rose in the dark and prayed. I'm not much of a prayer, but that morning, I felt close to death. When I rose, my joints hurt, my hands ached and the old wound in my leg burned. And away to the south was a line of dark clouds that boded ill for a sailor.

There was a sheep that had strayed onto our hill, and I walked down, trapped it against a cliff and grabbed it. I built a small fire and sacrificed the sheep to Zeus and burned its thigh bones.

And took the meat up the hill for my mess, of course.

We got a late start. Our sentries weren't as alert as they ought to have been: we'd awakened slowly and the sun was rising by the time we cooked my sheep. Nor could I feed mutton to two hundred men from one animal. Sittonax took a dozen horsemen out, and they were back before they left, riding hard.

Brasidas spotted them returning and ordered his men to arm.

I was still greasy from mutton as I saw the dust cloud. My pais helped me into my thorax. I put on the whole panoply: it was obvious we were going to fight.

So much for my careful strategy.

Sittonax rode in about the time that I had my arm-harness on. He rode up, controlling his horse effortlessly, and dropped off.

'Six hundred men. No kind of order, not much armour, a dozen horsemen. Headed this way.' He shrugged. 'I think they've marched all night.'

Six hundred?

I scratched my jaw. 'Officers!' I bellowed.

Neoptolymos looked at me. He was in his magnificent armour, and he made a brilliant show. He looked like Achilles' son. 'He has raised all his people,' he said simply. 'He has his retainers, the local lords, and his best slaves. If you had let me raise my relatives, we'd match him spear for spear.' He shrugged.

Well, hubris is always with us. All I'd done by marching around the mountain was to give him time to raise his troops. Of course, I had given my own troops time to shake off their sea legs and eat a few hot meals.

'Right,' I said, looking around. 'We have half the heroes of Marathon. We have armour, discipline and a good night's sleep.'

Cimon raised an eyebrow. His father used to say that all that mattered in a land fight was how many men you had.

But Cimon was good enough not to say so.

'We'll move right at them,' I said. 'Right down the road. When we're close – really close – we form up and go right in. No mucking about and no shouting insults. They'll try and get formed and go around our flanks. All we need to do is get Epidavros and kill him – right?'

Neoptolymos nodded.

Brasidas nodded, too. 'I get it,' he said.

'Form a good phalanx,' I said. 'Daud – you and Ka and Sittonax stay mounted and harass them. Pick off any man on the edge of their formation – get behind them and shoot arrows. Best of all, don't let their right flank form.'

Ka wrinkled his brow.

Daud shrugged.

'Get in close, and crowd them, and when they come at you, ride away. Then go back. Don't let them form their line.' I'd watched the Saka and the Persians do it. I knew what a handful of horsemen could do to infantry.

I put a stick down on the ground. 'This is their column, marching,' I said. 'At some point, when we are close enough, they pick a field and start to form. Right? And you get in on their right, and make trouble – right in their faces – while they want to be shouting orders and getting the laggards to stand in a shield wall.'

Cimon laughed. 'Cavalry tactics from a sea-wolf.'

We ate the last of our stale bread with the last of our olive oil, and drank the last drops of our wine. To Neoptolymos, I said, 'We're lucky.'

He glared at me.

'Your uncle could have cowered in his town. We'd have had to go to the ships.' I was watching the storm to the south. It might not be today, but it was coming.

'You think we can win?' he asked me.

I shrugged. 'Of course!' I said.

When your wife asks if you think she is beautiful, what do you say?

Cimon came up to me as we prepared to march. The sun was already hot. My hands were shaking. He looked at the sky. 'I was made for better things than dying here,' he said.

I nodded. I remember that moment. I slapped his shoulderpiece. 'Good,' I said. 'Don't die.'

He laughed, and that laugh spread over the column, because every man could hear me.

'Let's go!' I shouted, and we were off.

We came down off our hill – some of you maidens may wonder why I didn't hold the hilltop, and the answer is water. At any rate, we raced along the road, as fast as men in armour can move. We were fit, strong men and we could go quite fast.

Two stadia past the foot of the hill, we crossed a little stream. I made everyone drink, and fill their canteens. Then I stood and shook. I swear that the minutes it took those men to fill my canteens were as long as any minutes in my life. Command has a level of fear that is absent in mere service. In command, it is just you and the gods.

Two more stadia, and Daud came back to report that the enemy were just *there* and moving slowly, over the next low ridge. There were sheep on the ridge, and I turned to the mercenaries and Brasidas.

'We're going to run up that little hill,' I said.

Brasidas nodded and checked the laces on his sandals.

Word spread down the column. Men took a slug from their canteens. And then we ran. It wasn't a sprint, or a *hoplitodromos*. And almost immediately, men fell out – greaves have to fit.

A column of men in armour makes a remarkable noise, running. It raises the heart, that noise – the feet pounding together, the slap of leather and bronze. It is the sound of Ares – one of his many sounds.

Men jogging towards the enemy may tire, but they don't have time to feel fear. Because it all hurts.

We ran up the hill. We lost about twenty men, but we reached the crest of the low ridge on the road well ahead of our enemies.

I turned to my pais. 'Catch me a sheep,' I said.

He nodded. Ran off.

The top of the ridge had a definite crest, and it was open – short, cropped grass rolled away down the far side. The Illyrians were coming up the hill in no particular order, and by Ares, they were close. We weren't a stade apart. Our field was bounded by scrubby woods, that had once been an olive grove, to the north – they ran most of the way down the hill – and a low stone wall on the south of our hill that I had to hope would anchor my line. I assumed it wouldn't have to hold anyone long, because my cavalry would slow their right flank, where, if they were like Greeks, all their best men would be.

'Form your front,' I called.

Men were breathing hard, but they got it done – well. Brasidas ran effortlessly along the front of his forming line, slapping, cajoling – suddenly his mouth was full of words. I noted he never swore or defamed a man. He said things like, 'Well run, Philios!' and, 'You're looking like Ares come to earth, Draco!'

Cimon had his handful of Athenians on the far right. Our front rank was brilliantly armoured, and in the centre, Neoptolymos stood out from the line. He raised his spear, and screamed a long war cry.

In the enemy line, men stopped and stared.

Of course, until that moment, Epidavros and his men thought we were a raiding party.

Neoptolymos took off his helmet, and his blond hair shone in the sun. He shouted again. I've heard him tell the story, so I know he was challenging his uncle to single combat.

Illyrians do that sort of thing.

But Epidavros didn't get a chance to play the hero, or the coward, because there was a rumble, like the thunder of the day before, and suddenly all of our mounted men burst from the end of the old olive grove and rode for the flank of the column.

Battles – especially small battles – can be very complicated animals indeed. And the notion that men can really plan what happens in them is sheer hubris. Daud was on the wrong flank. He had confused – as many amateurs do – *our* right flank for the *enemy's* right flank.

Balanced against that, his surprise as he appeared was total. The whole enemy force flinched. And he and Sittonax and Ka, Doola, Seckla and their men didn't look like twenty-four horsemen. They looked like a thousand. Their hooves made the earth shake.

They didn't charge home. They rode right past the tail of the column on the road, throwing javelins and shooting bows, and they circled around in short reins and came back, riding along the flank of the column. Seckla took a wound where a brave Illyrian slave stepped out of the column and stabbed at him – they were that close. But the javelins and bows put a dozen men in the dust.

'Forward,' I shouted.

Our line went forward.

Sometimes, it works.

Our line was formed, and theirs was not. Our cavalry had scared them, and Neoptolymos was palpably alive. To my mind, everything that was going to go our way was going our way, and it wasn't going to get any better if we stood there at the top of the hill.

We moved at a fast walk, and our phalanx spread out. We'd only practised together a few times, on beaches and the like, so our order wasn't perfect – gaps showed immediately.

But we were the Pyrrhiche dance team of Plataea compared to our opponents, who hadn't yet pulled their helmets down over their faces.

Daud's men turned like a snake for a third pass at the enemy. Seckla and another man reined in their horses and slipped off at the top of the hill. The Illyrians started to form their line.

The back end of the enemy column was slow to get the word, or perhaps hesitant. A gap opened between the centre of the enemy line and what should have been their left.

Daud put his heels to his horse and raced for the gap with all my horsemen on his tail. The Illyrians at the back of the column, who by all rights should have panicked and run, decided instead to *charge* – uphill, by Ares – into my horsemen.

Except for fifty or so of them, who started killing the others from behind.

Of course, Epidavros had placed his least trustworthy men on his left. Neoptolymos's cousins.

I slowed our advance. I needed cohesion, not impact. 'Dress the line!' I roared. 'On me!'

The phalanx, such as it was, closed up. Men lapped their shields over their neighbour's to the left, and our advance slowed as men turned half sideways, and began the crab-walk that hoplites use when they are at the synaspis – the closer order.

The best-armoured man on the other side – I assumed he was Epidavros – called something to his men, and they roared and charged us.

An Illyrian charge is a fearful thing, and not very Greek. Or rather, perhaps it is exactly what we looked like at Marathon, when we ran at the Persians. But there were a lot of them, and they came at us screaming, and their front rank men had armour and big spears – they were big men, too.

Exactly opposite me was a towering figure, like a giant. A head taller than me, with shoulders like an ox and a giant aspis the size of a table in a taverna.

I hate fighting big men.

But my daimon was there, too. And as they roared and ran at us, I was Arimnestos of Plataea and no man's slave or chattel. And this *was* my fight.

When he was three paces away, I threw my heavy spear. He was running. Try to run with your aspis covering you.

He took it in the chest. He had a bronze thorax, and his last thought was the shock that my spear went through it.

Second to last thought, I guess. He stood and looked at it for long enough that I stabbed him in the throat with my second spear, ripped it clear and stepped up onto his back to kill my second man, a roaring madman all teeth and rage. He seemed to be trying to embrace my shield. I gave him my spear tip, instead, and my spear broke, and while I drew my sword, my line gave a great roar and pushed forward. We had the hill. We were four deep, a forest of skilled spearmen, and a great many Illyrians died in the first seconds of that meeting. The line gave a push, and suddenly we were ten paces down the hill, and men were stumbling back.

Epidavros roared for his men to stand. He was a few feet from me, faced half away, and Neoptolymos shoved Brasidas aside, took his uncle's thrust on his shield and thrust back, but the well-armoured man fell back a step and made a good shield parry.

Fair fights are for fair men.

I reached out with the tip of my sword and slapped his *sauroter* so that his spear turned in his hand. He half turned – the panic obvious in his open-faced helmet – as Neoptolymos's second thrust took him in the cheek, carving through his teeth and jaw and into the back of his throat.

I knew, in some trained portion of my mind, that I had left the enemy to my left for too long, and I turned my head and thrust with my shield just in time to catch a thrust coming from that direction, but Gaius, bless him, was there, and he powered forward, shield-cut the man, forcing him to raise his aspis, and then cut beneath it into the man's leg—

And we had won.

War is chaos, and a battlefield is so much a piece of the outer night that no man can really tell you exactly what happened in any one place, but from what I saw, it appeared that Neoptolymos's Illyrian cousins cut into the back of the attempted charge at Daud's cavalry, panicking the enemy left, which then became a mob of frightened men and not part of an army. Daud's charge – foolish under other circumstances – passed into the gap, killing few enemies but sewing despair. And Neoptolymos killed his uncle, our front broke their front and they ran.

I doubt the fighting lasted as long as it takes a man in armour to run the hoplitodromos. We didn't win because of my brilliant plan; or discipline, or armour, or the hill behind us, or our cavalry. All contributed a little, but the will of the gods and a healthy draught of luck won us the day.

And the furies, their wings and claws beating at Epidavros. May he rot.

22

I'd like to say that Neoptolymos forgave his uncle's relatives and retainers, but he didn't, and there was a lot of blood in the next few hours. His cousins gathered around him, shouting out each indignity that they had endured at Epidavros's hands, and they mutilated the man's corpse. Then they started to execute the prisoners – slave and free, noble and peasant.

I could have stopped it.

But I didn't.

I suppose that I had secretly wanted Dagon to be in the harbour. He wasn't. But there were three Carthaginian ships, all small coasters, and we took them from the land while Dionysus closed the harbour mouth, and as the storm came up at sunset, our triremes came onto the harbour beach, safe from the storm, which raged for three days with Adriatic ferocity while the streets of the stronghold ran with blood.

I know philosophers who praise the Illyrians and the other barbarians for the purity of their way of life – the honesty of a world where a man's strength is in his hands and his weapons. As a warrior, I realize that this may sound hopelessly pious, but as the rain-thinned blood ran down the cobbled streets of Dyrachos, and Epidavros's relatives, retainers and womenfolk were hunted, raped and executed, I could only think of them all as barbarians. It can happen in Greece. It *has* happened in Greece. But by the gods, we do what we can to avoid it.

Dionysus took Epidavros's daughters as slaves to sell in Syracusa. In brothels.

Neoptolymos sat on an ivory chair in the citadel. He had blood under his nails.

I have blood on my hands, too. I embraced him and wished him well, but I wanted no more of Illyria. He loaded me with gifts: gold cups, an Aegyptian ostrich egg, a silk cloak from Cyprus – he was open-handed with his uncle's riches. Which was as well, as all of us had oarsmen to pay.

On the first fine day, I piled all of our loot, our plunder and our gifts on blankets on the beach, with silver ingots and bronze kettles, helmets, swords, spearheads—

We began the division of the spoils. I sat on my stool to adjudicate arguments. Will that girl clean up well when she stops crying? Can she weave? Compare her value to the value of that silver inlaid helmet – what's between her legs is softer, but a moment of fever and she's a stinking corpse, and the helmet will protect your head.

Ah, thugater, you hide your head. What do you think those scenes in the *Iliad* are about, when men divide the spoils?

It took two days.

There were the Carthaginian prisoners. By then, we had learned from them that Dagon had escaped us by less than two weeks. But at sea, two weeks is an eternity, and his ship had been clear of the Adriatic before our sails nicked the horizon. At any rate, I took the prisoners, as I was determined to send the bastard a message.

Men made their marks on everything. And there was some rearranging of crews. Most of my oarsmen wanted to go home to Massalia. Not Leukas the Alban, or some of the others. And Daud and Sittonax were done: we'd sworn oaths, and now they were satisfied. They would be going home. Doola and Seckla would return to our little town under the mountains.

I was going back to Plataea.

We loaded the spoils on different ships, and we exchanged oarsmen.

We drank together, one last time. It is odd, I think, and speaks directly to the power of the gods and of our oath, that of the seven who swore one day on a beach in Etrusca, we all lived to go to Alba, and six of us gathered on a beach in Illyria to say goodbye, despite slavery, war, betrayal and murder. We sacrificed an ox, sent his thigh bones to Zeus and asked the King of the Gods to witness that we had fulfilled our oaths to each other. Gaius and I made all of them swear to be guest friends, and each of us swore to visit the others again.

Giannis took the pentekonter for the oarsmen who were bound for Massalia. Megakles just shrugged. 'I'll go where you go,' he said simply. 'As long as I never have to serve under that fuckhead again.' By whom he meant Dionysus.

Doola and I had a long conversation the last night at Dyrachos. Perhaps someday I'll tell you what we said. He felt I was making a terrible mistake in going home.

'Violence burns you like fire,' he said.

'You sound like Dano,' I said.

He shrugged. 'I no longer eat meat. And now that I have fulfilled my oath, I will go back to Croton and become an initiate,' he said. 'You should, too.'

I am a man of war. Sometimes, when one man wrongs another, only violence will settle the matter. We argued.

But we embraced.

And the next day, I sailed for Athens, with Cimon, Harpagos and Paramanos under my stern. And Sekla on my deck. He embraced Doola, but he came with me.

'You get wounded in every fight,' Doola said. 'In the end, you'll be killed.'

Sekla grinned. 'Everyone dies,' he said. 'I want to see Athens. And then perhaps I'll go home.'

The full irony of the next part can't come home to you, children, unless you understand that I thought that was the end of adventure. I was at Sardis, Lade and Marathon. I went to Alba.

I was thirty-one years old, and it was time to grow up and go home. Face the burned-out forge. Kiss my sister. Grow a crop. Perhaps arrange for another wife; children.

Certainly that's what Cimon and Harpagos and Paramanos and Sekla and I discussed the next two nights, as we worked our way down the coast of Illyria, past Leucas and landed at last at Ithaca. I felt like Odysseus returning, and we made some jokes. The truth is, too much blood had been spilled at Dyrachos for too little, and we were not ourselves. I have found that men of blood can go into black moods for little reason. That was one of those times, for me. Indeed, as we rowed south towards the Peloponnese, the same darkness began to come over me that had driven me off the cliff at Alkyonis when I tried to kill myself. I was savage to Megakles, who bore it with amused resignation, and to Ka, who glowed with his own rage, and to Sekla, who grinned and paid me no further attention.

That night, though, I saw a satyr near Pheia. Men say they are myth; other men say they live only in the Chersonese, or only in Scythia, or only around Olympia. I know what I saw, and the wonder of seeing it transfigured me. I had walked off the beach to have a piss, and I came back all but glowing. Cimon believed me – told me he had seen one himself in the south of the Peloponnese – while Brasidas ridiculed me and told me to grow up.

Brasidas had come with us as a passenger – he had the money to pay his mess bill – or the term of his exile was over. Either way, it might have been the longest speech I'd heard from him up until that date.

'You sound more like Thales than like a Spartan,' I said.

'All Spartans are philosophers,' he said.

'They have to talk about something in between fighting,' Cimon said.

I had decided to sail all the way to Athens to sell my loot, before going across the mountains to Boeotia. In truth, I think I was delaying my return home. Now that I'd decided on it, it scared me. Or rather, confronting my sister scared me, and the thought that she might have died in the meantime.

I thought a great deal about Odysseus, to tell you the truth.

The next day, the sky was red at dawn and we debated spending the day on the beach, but the rain, when it came, was gentle, and we put to sea.

But the visibility got worse and worse, and by midday, I couldn't see any of the other ships. The wind was rising, and I turned the bow for shore.

And the wind changed.

We had had the wind alongside all day, and now it swung from west to east and came up with a howl, almost as fast as I can tell the story. An hour later it was as dark as night, the wind howled in the rigging and the rowers were exhausted, and I knew I couldn't land the ship in this.

I had sailed the Western Ocean and I had been captain of my own ship for fifteen years, at that point. But I would have liked to have Paramanos, Harpagos or Demetrios or Doola at my side – or Miltiades or Cimon, for that matter. All of them, better yet.

I was with Megakles at the steering oars.

'We have to turn and run before the wind,' I shouted.

Wearily, he nodded.

Well, I hoped he agreed.

I ran down the sail deck to Leukas and Sekla. Held their arms while I shouted in their ears – that's how bad the wind was. Leukas looked at the sea for a moment, as if he hoped that something would save us – a friendly sea monster, perhaps.

Then we began to run along among the oar benches, crawling when we had to. We told every oarsman what we were going to do. Every one.

Because turning a galley across big waves in a high wind is suicide. We had no choice. Only excellent luck and fine rowing and the favour of Poseidon would win us through.

I ordered Sekla to get the boat-sail up. I needed Leukas to get the oarsmen around, and I was going to be at the steering oars with Megakles. But the boatsail required timing and boatsail courage – and Sekla had plenty of both. He took Ka and the archers.

Even from the bow I could see nothing to the east, but I thought I could hear breakers under the wind.

There was no time to think.

I got on the starboard steering oar. I caught Megakles' eye, and he nodded.

The wind roared. We rose on a wave.

'About *ship!*' I called, with every force I had.

The port-side rowers reversed their benches as the bow fell off from the wind. The wind wanted us broadside. We were still climbing a great breaker.

And then the port-side oars bit.

The starboard oars pivoted through another stroke.

There was a *crack* forward, where Ka had cut the boltrope of the boatsail, and it filled. Filled, cracked, slapped ... and tore in half.

But in those heartbeats while it was intact, it swung the ship a third of the way around, and the oars now had purchase, and the bow was a little west of south.

We hit the top of the wave, and we weren't broadside on, and started down.

The two oar-banks gave a great heave, like hoplites pushing at the climax of battle.

Our bow came around another point while the wind screamed, and then—

We were around. Even the ruins of the boatsail were enough to keep the bow pointed west, and now we were running free, and the rising sea was under the stern. Megakles used to swear we were close enough to Prote that he could have thrown a rock and hit the shore. I don't know.

I never looked back.

We spent the night at sea, running before the wind and rain. The turn was terrifying, but it was, in many ways, less fearsome than that soaking, endless maw of darkness and freak waves that rolled across our seas against the wind, making my life and Megakles' an endless torment of crisis.

But we did it. On and on, and finally the sky was a paler grey.

The mainmast went about morning. The pole was bare, of course, but the force of the wind had borne upon it all night, sometimes lashing it back and forth, and never had I thought so ill of the ship's rig. And finally, there was a thump from below, a scream as an oarsman was pulped by the swinging stump of the mast, and then it was gone over the side.

Will of the gods. It might just as easily have gone through the shell of the ship and broken us in half, but it didn't. It killed one man. It only had two heavy ropes supporting it, and we cut them away with swords as fast as we could – took a wave that soaked every man aboard and nigh filled us with water, and then the rags of the boatsail took the windboatsail and we were back on course, bailing like mad.

That was the last gust of the storm; we were all but sunk. The wave that struck us filled the bilges, and a trireme is a difficult ship to empty of water. Our rowers were already exhausted, and now they were trying to pull the weight of five thousand mythemnoi of water through the waves. The boatsail kept us alive, but we were wallowing, and had the storm risen again to its former ferocity, we would have foundered right there.

We bailed and bailed, and rigged our wooden pumps, and used helmets and buckets and clay pots and anything we had to get water over the side. We tossed the dead man's corpse to Poseidon.

Little by little, we won our ship back from the sea.

I can't tell you how long we bailed. I only know that every man not rowing was standing in the icy water between the thranites' legs, passing buckets up or taking empty ones down and dumping them as fast as we could. And then, when Megakles reported that we were steering and the wind had died away, I went up to the sail deck – curiously naked without a mainmast – to a calm grey day with a hint of a breeze and every chance of sun later.

The sea.

I ordered Leukas to belay bailing long enough to rig the second boatsail.

In no time, we were moving smartly, and all the oarsmen were bailing, and men began to complain about the lack of water to drink. That's when I knew we were going to live.

I knew we were well south of the Peloponnese, in the great blue deep between Carthage, Sicily, Athens and Cyrene. I watched the water for a while, and let the wind take us south and west. The rowers were exhausted. I needed land, water and food.

Men slept fitfully, and I told them all we would be another night at sea. I served out half the water we had, and all the grain and stale bread. And a dozen flasks of wine.

It was, thanks to Poseidon, an easy night.

As the sun touched the eastern rim of the aspis of the world with her rosy fingers, we saw a trireme lying under our lee – low in the water, and unmoving, without even a boatsail rigged.

We didn't even have to run down on her – our ship was pointed at her. I thought for a little bit she might be Cimon's, or Paramanos's, but as we got closer I thought she was Harpagos's *Storm Cutter* until I remembered that the old Phoenician ship was gone, replaced by a sleek Athenian hull. This was no Athenian. This was a heavy Phoenician warship, the kind that fills the centre of their line in battle.

As we manned the oars and Brasidas armed the marines, we saw them doing the same. The damaged ship began to crawl away from us and her archers lofted a dozen shafts, and one of Ka's men was killed outright.

They were rowing directly away from us, which was insane. We had the wind. They couldn't outrun the wind. It was shockingly poor seamanship – not that they were going to escape. Fewer than half their oars were being worked.

I motioned to Leukas, and he took in our boatsail when we were two stadia apart and we rowed – not that my lads were rowing better than theirs, but I had a great many *more* exhausted, desperate men. I'd like to think my first intention had been rescue, before the arrow killed Ka's man.

Now, as we closed, the arrows came thick and fast. Ka's Nubians returned them, shaft for shaft. I went forward with Brasidas. We were going to ram the Phoenician's stern, and board.

I made it to the foredeck with only two arrows in my aspis. On

Lydia we had a screen built in front of the marine's boarding station – long experience had shown me how dangerous this post was, in a ship fight. My screen was riddled with arrows.

We were ten horse-lengths apart. I could now see why my opponent was running straight downwind.

He had no steering oars.

Damned fool! He started the fight by lofting arrows at us. A fight he couldn't win.

From the Phoenician ship, there was a roar of rage and a sound of many women screaming.

Another arrow struck my aspis. It struck hard enough to rock my body back, and the head of the arrow drove through three layers of good willow and one of bronze, and the light bronze head protruded a good three fingers above my naked arm in the porpax.

Ka's lieutenant, Artax, took an arrow that went through the wooden screen and hit his bow, shattering the wood and horn. Artax stood there, with the lower arm of the bow in his hand, staring at it.

I reached out, threw a hand around his neck and pulled him to the deck. Before he got killed.

The truth was, my Nubians were losing the fight. They'd put a great many arrows in the air, and they had the wind behind them.

But they were exchanging arrows with Persians – Persian noblemen, I was guessing by the length of the shafts and their thickness. Warriors trained from youth to draw the bow and shoot well. Bows that I had to struggle to draw – arrows as thick as a lady's finger and as long as my arm.

My aspis fielded another one. Look, thugater – it is the third aspis there, with the raven in bronze. See the holes? All from that day. Count them! Eleven holes. Each time an arrow shot by a Persian nobleman hits you, your body staggers as if you've taken a blow, and when two hit together, you rock back a step.

Ka had an arrow through his bicep. The blood was red, and his skin didn't appear so dark. He slumped to the deck, his back against the lower part of the screen.

'Sorry, lord,' he said.

I shook my head. He and his Nubians had done pretty well, considering.

Brasidas was crouched behind me. The Spartan was brilliantly trained, but he wasn't stupid. And my marines were crouched in rows, ready to go over the bow.

I wished for Doola and his heavy bow.

'Keep your aspis up. When you jump from our ship to theirs, go fast, and keep your aspis towards the archers. Understand me?' I shouted the words.

Men nodded. The man behind Brasidas – Darius – licked his lips.

'I never thought I'd be fighting Persians again,' he said.

'Ah,' said Brasidas. He brightened. 'These are Persians?'

I nodded. 'At least half a dozen of their noble archers,' I said. 'Someone on that ship is important.'

We were very close. I wasn't going to raise my head to find out just how close, but the archery had stopped and I could hear the sound of swords, screams from men who were wounded and the shrill keening of women. Quite a few women.

I raised my head above the screen.

We were passing down the enemy side. You can't board over a well-built trireme's stern, of course – the stern timbers rise like a swan's neck over the helmsman's station, and there is no purchase for any but the most desperate boarder.

Megakles was running up the enemy's side. He – or Leukas – had coaxed a burst from our oarsmen, and now we shot along, our oars came in and we crushed the few oars the Phoenician had over the side. Our bow struck their side just forward of the rower's station and we spun the enemy ship a little in the water, and had we been at full speed, we'd have rolled her over and sunk her right there – it was a brilliant piece of helmsmanship. As it was, we tipped the heavier ship, our ram biting on his keel or some projection below the water-line and our bow catching his gunwale, so that he took on water.

'*At them!*' I shouted.

I don't remember much of the boarding action because of what came next, but this is what I do remember.

I pulled the rope that held the screen and it fell forward, and I jumped up onto it, ran a few steps and leaped for the enemy ship. I got one foot on the gunwale, and had one heartbeat to see the whole ghastly drama.

Right in the stern, around the helmsman's station, stood four Persians – helmets, scale shirts, long linen robes and fine boots. One was still shooting, and the other three were armed with short spears and swords. Behind them, packed into the swan's neck, were a dozen women – some screaming, and some clutching daggers. In and among the women were two corpses – one of a Persian with gold bracelets and gold on his sword, his head in the lap of a woman in a long Persian coat with sleeves and a shawl. Even as I watched, she laid his head to the side and took his sword from his hand.

Forward of them was a horde of desperate men with various weapons: boarding pikes, spears, broken oars, swords and fists. The pile of dead in front of the Persians told its own story.

I leaped down onto the afterdeck. Phoenicians are often decked directly above the rowing compartment. This one was decked over the after-rowing area, like *Lydia*.

Brasidas landed on the deck behind me.

'Clear the riff-raff away from the Persians,' I ordered.

The desperate, dehydrated, unfed oarsmen should have been easy meat. But they were not. There were an awful lot of them, and their desperation was total.

Let me tell you how fighting is. While I was killing them, I never thought of how I had been in the very same position, once. Of how understandable was their desperation. I called them riff-raff – hah! I have been riff-raff.

But they were beyond fear. It was like fighting Thracians – they came at me, first in ones and twos as their rear ranks discovered us, and then the mass of them, trying to crush us or throw us over the sides before we got all of our marines on their deck and formed up.

I was hit repeatedly in the first moments. And never have I had such cause to bless an armourer as I did Anaxsikles. I took a heavy blow on top of my outstretched right foot – and the bronze turned it. A boarding pike went past my aspis on my naked right side and scored my bronze-armoured thigh, and the blow slipped away, turning like rain from a good roof. A thrown javelin left a deep dent in my right greave, and then the shaft rotated and slapped hard into my left ankle, and there was bronze there, too.

Their screams and roars were those of a hundred-headed monster, and that monster had two hundred arms and unlimited stores of strength. The press of men struck my aspis and I staggered back a step, and behind me was empty air and water.

Listen, then. This is who I was.

As they came to contact, my spear flew like the raven on my shield. I had a trick I'd practised for a year – rifling the spear from my shoulder on a leather lanyard, so that, in fact, I threw it about the width of a man's palm. But the leather never left my hand and armoured wrist, so that I could tear it out of a corpse. When done just right, the spear would either take a life, or bounce off a shield or armour and return to my hand like a magical thing.

Ah, the man from Halicarnassus doubts me. Hand me that spear – the heavy one. I'm not so old that my hand cannot hold a spear. Watch, my children.

Three times into the old beam – in as many heartbeats. No man can block all three, unless the gods give him strength.

Ah, you interrupted me with your doubts, young man.

Listen, then.

My first blow went into the bridge of a man's nose, and before he fell to the deck, my second blow went deep into his mate to the right, and the man fell to the deck clutching my spear. I stepped forward into the moment of time created by the kills and twisted my spear in his guts, ripped it clear and killed a third man with my sauroter as the spike rotated up.

Just like that.

By the will of Heracles, my spear didn't break, and I threw it forward again on my wrist thong and missed, and my bronze spike slammed into an unarmoured man.

My right side was naked, and every heartbeat I waited for the spear in the ribs that would end my fight. I had boarded confident that we would break the Persians in a moment, and now I was fighting for my life.

But nothing came into my right side. A man threw his arms around my aspis, seeking to break my arm. I thrust forward with both legs into the press and he tripped, and my sauroter went into his mouth and out again. His limbs loosened and he fell. Brasidas tapped his aspis against me on my right to tell me that he was there.

I whirled my spear over my head, changing the sauroter for the spear point. Roared my war cry: 'HERACLES!'

They all came at us at once, and there was a long time there that I remember nothing, except that I killed men, and no man killed me. They were soft and unarmoured, and I was covered in bronze. They were not warriors, and I was trained from boyhood.

And yet they almost had me, again and again.

Desperation makes all men equal. A small man in a Phrygian cap caught my spear arm and tore my spear away – broke my balance, dragged me forward and a dozen blows fell on my armour and helmet. One – a spear – punched that small hole in the backplate of my thorax. See?

I got the sword out from under my arm. My fancy long-bladed xiphos was too damned long – hard to draw in a press. I couldn't get it clear of the scabbard and I almost died trying.

Two men were trying to press me to the deck. Brasidas killed one – I saw his spearhead – but he had his own dozen opponents.

I went to one knee. Something cold was in my right side, and something hot was trickling down the middle of my back.

A woman screamed. I thought I knew that woman, and that scream.

I got my foot under me and pushed. My right hand gave up on the xiphos and went instead to the stout dagger I always wore at my right hip. Like a beautiful thought, it rose from its scabbard and my hand buried it in my immediate grappling adversary's arm. He had to let go. I must have stabbed twenty times, punching with a dagger, over and over, as I cleared the space around me. I was blind – sweaty, and my helmet twisted just a fraction on my head – but it didn't matter, and any man I could touch, I cut, or stabbed.

I felt an aspis press into my back.

I heard Darius shout, 'I'm here, lord!'

I rotated my hips, and let him step forward. Only then did I discover that the little rat with the cap had dislocated my left shoulder, and my shield hung at my side like a dead thing. It's odd what your body can do, when it is life or death.

We had ten marines aboard by then, doing what they did best – they had to fight to get into a formation, and we lost one, but when Brasidas and nine hoplites were formed in a rough line, five wide and two deep, they were unstoppable on a ship.

I got my helmet off. Only then did I see that my right hand was pouring with blood. Apparently at some point I grabbed a blade.

I dropped the aspis off my left arm.

Leukas came onto our deck. He had good armour and a Gaulish helmet, and carried a long sword. He led a dozen of our deck crewmen, who were better armoured than many poorer hoplites.

His sword whirled – I'd never seen him fight. He was full of fury, and I remember thinking that he should be trained. An odd thought to have in a fight.

But his no-holds-barred approach was ideal for facing down a crowd of badly armed men, and when the deck crew crossed behind him, the fight began to be a massacre.

I stood and breathed. And bled, of course.

And then I turned and walked over the pile of corpses towards the Persians.

I had no aspis, and one of them – the youngest by ten years, I'd guess – had an arrow on his string.

I *knew* one of these Persians.

'Greetings, brother,' I said to Cyrus. I reached up my bleeding hand and tipped my helmet back.

Cyrus was the centre Persian. He was a superb swordsman, and a fine archer. I've mentioned him before, and his brother Darius, and their friend Arynam. The world is truly very small, at least among fighting men.

Cyrus laughed, and his teeth showed white in his old-wood face. 'Ari!' he shouted. In Persian, he said, 'Brothers, we are saved. This one is my friend – my sword brother.'

We embraced, and I bled on his armour and apologized.

'Tell your women they don't have to stab themselves,' I said. I slapped Cyrus on the shoulder. I felt alive.

Behind me, the desperate oarsmen threw down their weapons and begged for mercy. The Persian woman by Cyrus dropped her weapon and threw back her shawl. And stepped forward into my arms.

Sometimes, I think that we are mere playthings of the gods. And sometimes, that they mean us to be happy.

Men were dying at my back.

There was blood running over my sandals.

A friend of my youth stood at my shoulder.

I saw none of them, because the woman in my arms was Briseis.

Epilogue

My voice is gone, and I've talked enough – the Halicarnassan's stylus hand must hurt like fire, or be cramped like an oarsman's after a long row. And my thugater must be tired of hearing her old man brag – eh?

I'll wager you'll come back tomorrow. Because tomorrow, I'll tell of how we went to Aegypt; how we explored the Erytherean Sea. How we found Dagon.

But what you'll come back for is the fight with the Persians. At Artemesium, where the Greeks showed Persia we could fight at sea. And at Thermopylae. Where the Spartans showed us all how much like gods we could be.

I was thirty-one, and I thought the adventure was over. It was just beginning.

Historical Afterword

As closely as possible, this novel follows the road of history. But history – especially Archaic Greek history – can be more like a track in the forest than a road with a kerb. I have attempted to make sense of Herodotus and his curiously modern tale of nation states, betrayal, terrorism and heroism. I have read most of the secondary sources, and I have found most of them wanting.

Early in the planning of this series, it became obvious that something would have to happen between Marathon – in 490 BCE, and Thermopylae/Artemesium, in 480 BCE. There was a commercial temptation to move from military campaign to military campaign. I resisted it. While war was a major force in Greek culture, there were other forces—

About the time that I started this series, I got a copy of Robin Lane Fox's *Travelling Heroes*. Then I saw a copy of the *Periplus of Hano* and the Hakluyt Society's *Periplus of the Erytherean Sea*, two ancient sources on routes to Sub-Saharan Africa. Then I read a dozen articles on the ancient tin trade. Somewhere around page 50 of Tim Severin's *Jason Voyage* I knew what my hero would do during the ten years that separated the two military events that most of my readers expected.

Could a Greek have travelled from Athens to Britain in 485 BCE? Euthymenes of Massalia may well have reached Britain in 525 BCE or so, and Pytheas (also of Massalia) certainly reached Britain by 330 BCE or roughly the time of Alexander. Recent archaeology has found several apparently 'Greek' graves in the valleys of the Seine and Rhone, and current scholarship on ships and boats supports the notion of a regular trade from the tin mines of the north down to Massalia. In fact, it seems increasingly likely that the Mediterranean world never lost touch with the north and Britain after early Mycenaean contacts, and the increasing crisis over tin (a crisis which some have likened to the oil crisis in our modern world) may in fact have brought Britain a certain notoriety early on.

I pride myself on research and, for want of a better phrase, 'keeping it real.' I spend an inordinate amount of time wearing various historical kits in all weathers – not just armoured like a taxiarch, but sometimes working like a slave. So I wish to hasten to say that I have rowed a heavy boat (sixteen oars) in all weathers; I have sailed, but not as much or as widely as I would like; I have been in all the waters I discuss, but often on the deck of a US Navy warship and not, I fear, in a pentekonter or a trireme. Because of this, I have relied – sometimes heavily – on the words of ancient sailors and their excellent modern reenactors, like Captain Severin. I am deeply indebted to him, to a dozen sailors I'm lucky enough to count as friends, and to the Hakluyt Society, of which I'm now a member. All errors are mine, and any feeling of realism of accuracy in my nautical 'bits' belongs to their efforts.

I also have to note that just before I began work on this book, I helped to create the reenactment of the 2500th anniversary of the Battle of Marathon. We had about one hundred and twenty reenactors from all over the world. You can find the pictures on our website at http://www.amphictyonia.org/ and you really should. It was a deeply moving experience for me, and what I learned there – because every reenactor brings a new dose of expertise and amazing kit – has affected this book and will affect the rest of the series. I have now worn Greek armour for three solid days. Fought in a phalanx that looked like a phalanx. You'll spot the changes in the text. I wish to offer my deep thanks to every reenactor who attended, and all the groups in the Amphictyonia. I literally couldn't write these books without you.

And, of course, if, as you read this, you burn to pick up a xiphos and an aspis – or a bow and a sparabara! Go to the website, find your local group, and join. Or find me on my website or on facebook. We're always recruiting.

Finally – neither the Phoenicians nor the Persians were 'bad'. The Greeks were not 'good'. But Arimnestos is a product of his own world, and he would sound – curious – if he didn't suffer from some of the prejudices and envies we see in his contemporaries.

At the risk of repeating what I said in the afterword to *Marathon* – the complex webs of human politics that ruled the tin trade and Carthage's attempts to monopolize it – the fledgling efforts of Persia (perhaps?) to win allies in the far west to allow them to defeat the Greeks on multiple fronts – these are modern notions, and yet, to the helmsmen and ship owners of Athens and Tyre and Carthage and Syracuse, these ideas of strategy must have been as obvious as they are to armchair strategists today. The competition for tin was every day. Trade and piracy were very, very closely allied. If my novels have a particular *point* it is that the past wasn't simple. In Tyre and Athens, at least, the leading pirates were also the leading political decision makers.

In the last two books, I've said that '*it is all in the Iliad.*' Well – in this book, it is all in the *Odyssey*, and I've gone back to that source again and again. I have enormous respect for the modern works of many historians, classical and modern. But they weren't there. Homer and his associates – they were there.

I have seen war at sea – never the way of the oar and ram, but war. And when I read the *Iliad* and the *Odyssey*, they cross the millennia and feel *true*. Not, perhaps, true about Troy. Or Harpies. But true about *war*. Homer did not love war. Achilles is not the best man in the *Iliad*. War is ugly.

Arimnestos of Plataea was a real man. I hope that I've done him justice.

For more action from

Christian Cameron

Read *Tom Swan and the Head of St George – Part O[...]*

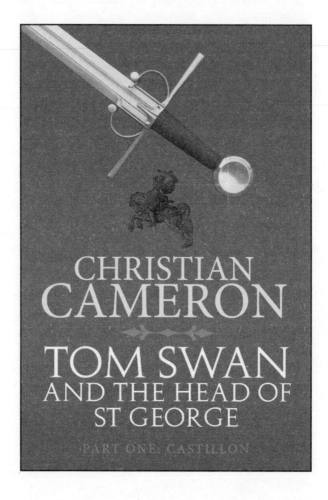

The start of a fast-paced serial – a swashbuckling
adventure full of intrigue, action and conspiracy

An e-book exclusive.

Buy now from your preferred e-tailer